CLASSICS Illustrated®

Charles Dickens
DAVID COPPERFIELD

essay by
Emily Woudenberg
The Dickens Project
University of California at Santa Cruz

ACCLAIM BOOKS
STUDY GUIDE

David Copperfield

art by Henry Kiefer
adaption by George Lipscomb
cover by Gene Ha

For Classics Illustrated Study Guides
computer recoloring by Colorgraphix
editor: Madeleine Robins
assistant editor: Gregg Sanderson
design: Scott Friedlander

Classics Illustrated: David Copperfield © Twin Circle Publishing Co.,
a division of Frawley Enterprises; licensed to First Classics, Inc.
All new material and compilation © 1997 by Acclaim Books, Inc.

Dale-Chall R.L.: 6.2

ISBN 1-57840-039-2

Acclaim Books, New York, NY
Printed in the United States

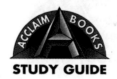

STUDY GUIDE

BACK HOME, I WAS SURPRISED THAT MY MOTHER WASN'T THERE TO GREET US . . .

WHY, PEGGOTTY, ISN'T SHE COME HOME?

YES, YES . . . WAIT A BIT, MASTER DAVY, I'LL - - I'LL TELL YOU SOMETHING!

YOU'VE GOT A PA!

I DON'T WANT TO SEE HIM!

HOWEVER, I WENT INTO THE PARLOR AND MET MR. MURDSTONE, A HARD CRUEL MAN . . .

DAVY!

NOW, CLARA, MY DEAR. CONTROL YOURSELF, ALWAYS CONTROL YOURSELF! DAVY BOY, HOW DO YOU DO?

LATER, MR. MURDSTONE'S SISTER CAME TO LIVE WITH US . . .

SHE SOON TOOK OVER THE MANAGEMENT OF THE HOUSE. MY MOTHER HAD NO MORE TO DO WITH IT THAN I DID . . .

SLOWLY THE MURDSTONES DOMINATED OUR HOME . . .

OH, DAVY, DAVY!

NOW, CLARA, BE FIRM WITH THE BOY. DON'T SAY, "OH, DAVY, DAVY!" HE KNOWS HIS LESSON OR HE DOES NOT KNOW IT.

HE DOES NOT KNOW IT!

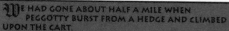

REMEMBERING THE SIGN UPON MY BACK, CREAKLE CAME TO WHERE I SAT...

HOW IS THIS FOR A TOOTH, HEY? IS IT A DOUBLE TOOTH, HEY?

I DON'T KNOW, SIR. WHATEVER YOU SAY, SIR.

DOES IT BITE, HEY?

IF YOU PLEASE! YES, SIR!

TAKE CARE OF HIM HE BITES.

FROM NOW ON, YOU NEEDN'T WEAR THAT SIGN. IT'S IN MY WAY WHEN I WANT TO CANE YOU.

YES, SIR!

TAKE CARE OF HIM HE BITES.

MR. MELL WAS KIND AND I LIKED HIM.

DAVID, YOU'RE A GENTLE BOY AND YOU LEARN YOUR LESSON WELL.

OH, THANK YOU, SIR!

POOR TRADDLES WAS CANED MORE OFTEN THAN I.

WILL YOU DRAW SKELETONS ON YOUR SLATE AGAIN, HEY?

NO, SIR! WOW! WOW!

I COULDN'T UNDERSTAND TRADDLES: HE FORGOT PAIN SO SOON.

I ADMIRED STEERFORTH. HE SEEMED SO FAR ABOVE THE REST OF US.

STEERFORTH, WHY DO YOU NEVER GET A CANING?

I GO WITH CREAKLE'S DAUGHTER. SHE'S QUITE FOND OF ME. ANYWAY, IF CREAKLE DARED TOUCH ME, I'D KNOCK HIM DOWN!

THEN, ONE DAY, STEERFORTH DID SOMETHING THAT MADE ME FEEL VERY SORRY FOR MR. MELL.

SIT DOWN, MR. STEER-FORTH.

SIT DOWN YOURSELF AND MIND YOUR OWN BUSINESS!

WHEN YOU MAKE USE OF YOUR POSITION OF FAVORITISM HERE, SIR, TO INSULT A GENTLEMAN WHO HAPPENS TO BE LESS FORTUNATE THAN YOURSELF...

YOU ARE AN IMPUDENT BEGGAR!

WHAT DID YOU MEAN BY SPEAKING OF FAVORITES?

I MEANT THAT NO PUPIL HAD THE RIGHT TO AVAIL HIMSELF OF HIS POSITION TO DEGRADE ME.

I CALLED HIM A BEGGAR. IF HE IS NOT, HIS NEAR RELATIONS ARE. LET HIM DENY IT.

MR. MELL, WE'LL PART, IF YOU PLEASE!

I TAKE MY LEAVE. JAMES STEERFORTH, I HOPE YOU LIVE TO BE ASHAMED OF WHAT YOU HAVE DONE THIS DAY!

OUR THANKS TO MR. STEERFORTH FOR PRESERVING THE INDEPENDENCE AND RESPECTABILITY OF SALEM HOUSE.

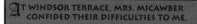

THAT ENVENING...

MR. MICAWBER IS KNOWN TO MR. MURDSTONE. HE WILL RECEIVE YOU AS A LODGER.

MY ADDRESS IS WINDSOR TERRACE, CITY ROAD. I -- IN SHORT -- LIVE THERE!

AT WINDSOR TERRACE, MRS. MICAWBER CONFIDED THEIR DIFFICULTIES TO ME.

MASTER COPPERFIELD, I MAKE NO STRANGER OF YOU ... WHAT I MEAN TO EXPRESS IS, THAT THERE IS NOTHING TO EAT IN THE HOUSE.

DEAR ME! I HAVE THREE SHILLINGS IN MY POCKET. TAKE THAT.

NO, MY DEAR, I STILL HAVE A LITTLE SILVER LEFT. WILL YOU TAKE THIS TO THE PAWN BROKER.

YES, MA'AM.

THE MICAWBERS' DIFFICULTIES INCREASED, AND THEY WERE PUT IN JAIL FOR DEBT.

MASTER COPPERFIELD, HEREIN I HAVE PETITIONED HIS MAJESTY IN BEHALF OF HIS UNFORTUNATE SUBJECTS, WHO ARE THROWN IN PRISON FOR DEBT.

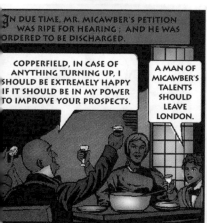

IN DUE TIME, MR. MICAWBER'S PETITION WAS RIPE FOR HEARING; AND HE WAS ORDERED TO BE DISCHARGED.

COPPERFIELD, IN CASE OF ANYTHING TURNING UP, I SHOULD BE EXTREMELY HAPPY IF IT SHOULD BE IN MY POWER TO IMPROVE YOUR PROSPECTS.

A MAN OF MICAWBER'S TALENTS SHOULD LEAVE LONDON.

GOODBYE, MASTER COPPERFIELD.

I'M GOING TO LEAVE LONDON TOO. I'LL WRITE TO PEGGOTTY FOR MONEY AND TRY TO FIND MY AUNT IN DOVER.

BUT, WHEN I WAS READY TO LEAVE LONDON, A FELLOW RAN AWAY WITH MY BOX AND MY MONEY.

IF YOU FOLLOW ME, I'LL LEAD YOU TO THE POLICE. I KNOW YOU'RE RUNNING OFF.

HE'S GONE WITH THE MONEY PEGGOTTY SENT ME.

HAVING PAWNED MY JACKET AND MY WAISTCOAT, SO THAT I COULD EAT, I STARTED WALKING ON THE ROAD TO DOVER.

SLEEP CAME UPON ME AS IT CAME UPON MANY OTHER OUTCASTS . . .

AT LAST, I REACHED DOVER AND FOUND MY AUNT.

IF YOU PLEASE, AUNT. AM YOUR NEPHEW. AM DAVID COPPERFIEL

OH, LORD

SHE GOT UP IN A HURRY AND COLLARED ME.

MERCY ON US !

JANET, GO UPSTAIRS, GIVE MY COMPLIMENTS TO MR. DICK, A SAY I WISH TO SPEAK TO HIM.

I LIKED MR. DICK AND WAS CONCERNED ABOUT HIM . . .

AUNT BETSEY, IS MR. DICK ANYWAYS OUT OF HIS MIND?

OF COURCE NOT! HE'S A MAN OF MOST REMARKABLE JUDGMENT, THOUGH HIS BROTHER TRIED TO PUT HIM AWAY. I WOULD NOT ALLOW IT AND TOOK HIM IN.

LATER, I WAS SENT TO CANTERBURY TO BE PUT TO SCHOOL.

MR. DICK, I SHALL EXPECT YOUR VISITS.

AT CANTERBURY, WE WENT INTO THE HOUSE OF MR. WICKFIELD, AN ATTORNEY.

MY GRAND - NEPHEW -- I HAVE ADOPTED HIM, AND HAVE BROUGHT HIM HERE TO PUT HIM TO A SCHOOL WHERE HE MAY BE THOROUGHLY WELL TAUGHT AND TREATED. WHICH SCHOOL DO YOU RECOMMEND?

BEFORE I CAN ADVISE YOU PROPERLY, WHAT'S YOUR MOTIVE IN THIS?

FIDDLESTICKS! YOU CLAIM TO HAVE ONE MOTIVE IN ALL YOU DO. YOU DON'T SUPPOSE THAT YOU ARE THE ONLY PLAIN DEALER IN THE WORLD?

AY, BUT I HAVE ONLY ONE MOTIVE IN LIFE, MISS TROTWOOD.

I SOON LEARNED THAT MR. WICKFIELD'S ONE MOTIVE WAS TO PROVIDE FOR HIS DAUGHTER, AGNES.

SINCE MY WIFE DIED, MY DAUGHTER, AGNES, HAS BEEN MY LITTLE HOUSEKEEPER.

SHE LOOKS JUST LIKE HER MOTHER. AGNES, THIS IS TROTWOOD COPPERFIELD, MY ADOPTED NEPHEW.

LEAVE YOUR NEPHEW HERE. HE'S A QUIET FELLOW AND WON'T DISTURB ME. IT'S A CAPITOL HOUSE FOR STUDY.

TROT, BE A CREDIT TO YOURSELF, TO ME, AND TO MR. DICK, AND HEAVEN BE WITH YOU.

I WILL DO MY BEST.

I WENT, ACCOMPANIED BY MR. WICKFIELD, TO THE SCENE OF MY FUTURE STUDIES . . .

DOCTOR STRONG, I'VE BROUGHT YOU A NEW SCHOLAR, MASTER TROTWOOD COPPERFIELD.

I SAY, LIKELY LOOKING CHAP. DON'T YOU THINK SO, ANNIE?

A VERY BRIGHT LOOKING BOY, DOCTOR STRONG.

I LATER LEARNED THAT ANNIE WAS DR. STRONG'S WIFE, AND THAT HER COUSIN WAS A CHAP NAMED JACK MALDON, A WORTHLESS LOAFER, IN LOVE WITH ANNIE . . .

WICKFIELD, HAVE YOU FOUND A SUITABLE PROVISION FOR MY WIFE'S COUSIN YET?

NOT YET.

THAT EVENING, MR. WICKFIELD HAD MALDON CALL ON HIM . . .

DOCTOR STRONG HAS MADE PROVISIONS TO SEND YOU OUT TO INDIA. HAVE YOU DINED?

THANKEE. I AM GOING TO DINE WITH MY COUSIN ANNIE. GOODBYE.

I MET MR. WICKFIELD'S CLERK, URIAH HEEP, AND I DID NOT LIKE HIM.

PERHAPS YOU'LL BE A PARTNER OF MR. WICKFIELD'S BUSINESS ONE OF THESE DAYS.

OH, NO, MASTER COPPERFIELD, I AM MUCH TOO 'UMBLE!

SOME NIGHTS LATER, THERE WAS A PARTY AT THE DOCTOR'S, HONORING JACK MALDON'S DEPARTURE.

FAREWELL, MR. JACK. A PROSPEROUS VOYAGE, A THRIVING CAREER ABROAD, AND A HAPPY RETURN HOME.

ONE DAY, WITH MR. WICKFIELD'S PERMISSION, I ACCEPTED AN INVITATION TO VISIT WITH URIAH HEEP AND HIS MOTHER...

MY URIAH HAS LOOKED FORWARD TO THIS, SIR. 'E 'AD 'IS FEARS THAT OUR 'UMBLENESS STOOD IN THE WAY...

I AM SURE YOU HAVE NO REASON TO BE SO, MA'AM.

I HAD BEGUN TO WISH MYSELF WELL OUT OF THE VISIT, WHEN A FIGURE WALKED IN...

MY DEAR COPPERFIELD, THIS IS A MOST EXTRAORDINARY MEETING. WALKING DOWN THE STREET, REFLECTING UPON THE PROBABILITY OF SOMETHING TURNING UP...COPPERFIELD, HOW DO YOU DO?

MR. MICAWBER!

A FRIEND OF MY FRIEND COPPERFIELD HAS A CLAIM UPON MYSELF.

WE ARE TOO 'UMBLE, SIR, TO BE THE FRIENDS OF MASTER COPPERFIELD. 'E 'AS BEEN SO GOOD AS TO TAKE 'IS TEA WITH US, AND WE ARE THANKFUL TO 'IM; ALSO TO YOU, SIR, FOR YOUR NOTICE.

SHALL WE GO AND SEE MRS. MICAWBER, SIR?

IF YOU WILL DO HER THAT HONOUR, COPPERFIELD.

TAKING LEAVE OF THE HEEPS, WE WENT TO A LITTLE INN, WHERE THE MICAWBERS HAD A ROOM...

MY DEAR, ALLOW ME TO INTRODUCE YOU TO A PUPIL OF DOCTOR STRONG.

WHY, I'M AMAZED!

MY DEAR, IF YOU WILL MENTION TO COPPERFIELD WHAT OUR PRESENT POSITION IS, I WILL GO AND LOOK AT THE PAPER THE WHILE.

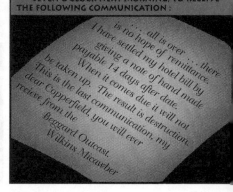

I MADE FOR THE INN, BUT ON THE WAY, I SAW THE MICAWBERS RIDING OFF IN A COACH. THEY DIDN'T SEE ME AND I SUPPOSE THAT WAS BEST.

BEFORE I KNEW IT, MY SCHOOL DAYS WERE OVER AND I WAS ON MY WAY HOME WITH MR. DICK . . .

MASTER COPPERFIELD, YOU WERE MY BEST SCHOLAR. YOU WILL MAKE YOUR WAY IN THE WORLD.

TROTWOOD, COME BACK AND SEE US.

WELL, TROT. I'M RIGHT PROUD OF YOU. I'M GOING TO LET YOU LOOK AROUND A BIT BEFORE CHOOSING A PROFESSION.

I SHOULD LIKE TO GO TO YARMOUTH TO SEE MY OLD NURSE, PEGGOTTY.

IN LONDON, I MET MY OLD FRIEND, STEERFORTH.

I CAME HERE TODAY. I HAVE BEEN ADOPTED BY MY AUNT AND HAVE JUST FINISHED MY EDUCATION. HOW DO YOU COME TO BE HERE, STEERFORTH?

I'M AN OXFORD MAN AND AM ON MY WAY TO MY MOTHER'S. WHY NOT COME ALONG?

MOTHER, THIS IS DAVID COPPERFIELD, MY OLD SCHOOL CHUM.

YOU ARE WELCOME HERE AT HIGHGATE, MR. COPPERFIELD.

AND, DAVID, THIS IS MISS DARTLE -- FOR YEARS A COMPANION TO MY MOTHER.

MY COMPLIMENTS, MISS DARTLE.

WHAT IS THE REASON FOR THAT SCAR ON MISS DARTLE'S UPPER LIP?

WE DON'T GET ALONG. I HIT HER WITH A HAMMER WHEN I WAS A CHILD.

I'M GOING DOWN TO YARMOUTH TO SEE MY OLD NURSE, PEGGOTTY. HER BROTHER AND NEPHEW HAM, YOU REMEMBER, VISITED ME AT SALEM HOUSE.

THAT BLUFF FELLOW WHO LIVES IN A BOAT? IT WOULD BE WORTH A JOURNEY TO MAKE ONE WITH 'EM.

THAT EVENING STEERFORTH AND I VISITED WITH MR. PEGGOTTY AT THE HOUSE - BOAT. WE LEARNED THAT HAM AND EMILY HAD BECOME ENGAGED TO BE MARRIED...

I'M AN OLD SEA PORCUPINE, MYSELF, AND I COULDN'T SEE LITTLE EMILY ENGAGED TO A BETTER MAN THAN HAM.

I GIVE YOU JOY, MY BOY, MY HAND UPON THAT, TOO.

AFTER SEVERAL PLEASANT HOURS WE TOOK OUR LEAVE...

BE CAREFUL NOT TO STUMBLE UPON THE ROCKS.

GOODNIGHT. I'M GOING TO SEE PEGGOTTY TOMORROW.

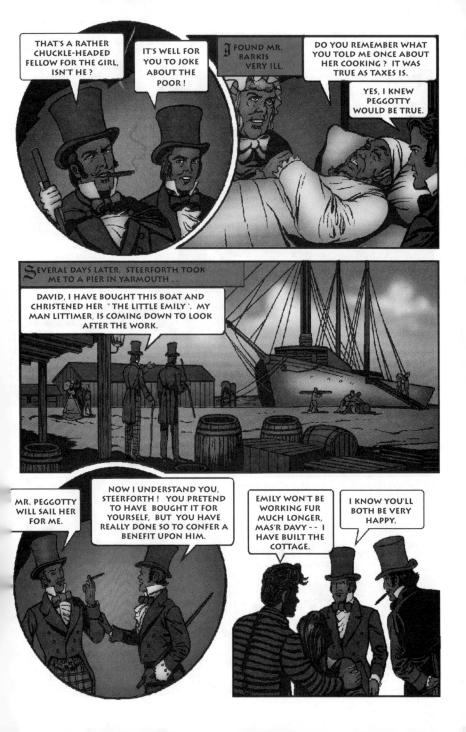

THAT'S A YOUNG WOMAN, MAS'R DAVY, THAT EM'LY KNOWED ONCE, BUT DON'T OUGHT TO KNOW NO MORE.

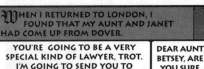

WHEN I RETURNED TO LONDON, I FOUND THAT MY AUNT AND JANET HAD COME UP FROM DOVER.

YOU'RE GOING TO BE A VERY SPECIAL KIND OF LAWYER, TROT. I'M GOING TO SEND YOU TO DOCTORS' COMMONS.

DEAR AUNT BETSEY, ARE YOU SURE YOU OUGHT TO SPEND THE MONEY?

I HAVE NO OTHER CLAIM AGAINST MY MEANS, AND YOU ARE MY ADOPTED SON.

THE FOLLOWING MORNING, WE WERE ACCOSTED BY AN OLD BEGGAR . . .

I'LL SOON GET RID OF THIS FELLOW.

NO, NO, CHILD! YOU DON'T KNOW WHO HE IS. GET ME A COACH, MY DEAR, AND WAIT FOR ME IN ST. PAUL'S CHURCHYARD. I MUST GO WITH HIM.

DRIVE STRAIGHT ON!

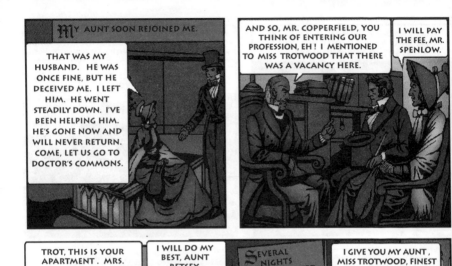

NEXT DAY, A MESSAGE CAME FROM AGNES, INVITING ME TO VISIT HER. I WAS SO ASHAMED THAT I DID NOT KNOW HOW TO ANSWER.

THE LADY DESIRES AN ANSWER, SIR.

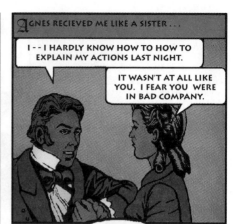

AGNES RECIEVED ME LIKE A SISTER...

I -- I HARDLY KNOW HOW TO HOW TO EXPLAIN MY ACTIONS LAST NIGHT.

IT WASN'T AT ALL LIKE YOU. I FEAR YOU WERE IN BAD COMPANY.

STEERFORTH NOT GOOD COMPANY? AGNES, HE'S THE FINEST FELLOW EVER, AND MY BEST FRIEND.

NO, TROTWOOD, I WOULDNT' SAY THIS WERE I NOT SURE.

I SHALL BE HERE A FEW DAYS MORE, TROTWOOD. MY FATHER, WHO IS NOT DOING WELL AT ALL, HAS HAD TO COME TO LONDON. HE HAS HAD TO TAKE URIAH HEEP INTO HIS BUSINESS.

WHAT! THAT SCOUNDREL, HEEP!

I TRIED TO BE CONSIDERATE OF HEEP BECAUSE OF HIS POWER OVER THE WICKFIELDS.

AND, MISTER COPPERFIELD -- THOUGH I AM STILL 'UMBLE, I AM RISING IN THE WORLD; AND SOME DAY, I HOPE TO MARRY AGNES.

WHAT!

WHY, YOU DIRTY ...

I WAS INVITED TO SPEND A WEEK AT MR. SPENLOW'S IN THE COUNTRY. THERE I MET AND IMMEDIATELY FELL IN LOVE WITH HIS DAUGHTER, DORA, WHOSE GOVERNESS WAS ... MISS MURDSTONE ...

MY DAUGHTER, DORA, JUST RETURNED FROM SCHOOL IN FRANCE, AND HER GOVERNESS, MISS MURDSTONE.

OF ALL CREATURES!

NEXT DAY ...

NOW, JIP, YOU MUSTN'T BARK AT SUCH A PLEASANT PERSON AS MR. COPPERFIELD.

OH, TO BE IN JIP'S PLACE AND HAVE MY NOSE PETTED BY THAT HAND.

YOU LIKE MILK, DON'T YOU? WELL, IF YOUR FATHER DON'T PAY HIS BILL, YOU GET NO MILK TOMORROW!

BUT, PLEASE, SIR -- WE'RE EXPECTING TO HAVE SOME MONEY IN A FEW DAYS.

SEVERAL WEEKS LATER, I WENT TO SEE TRADDLES ...

COPPERFIELD, I'M GLAD TO SEE YOU!

TRADDLES!

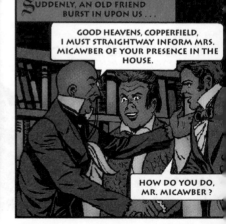

COPPERFIELD, I AM ENGAGED TO THE DEAREST GIRL IN ALL THIS WORLD, AS WE CAN'T SEE HOW WE CAN AFFORD TO BE MARRIED YET, OURS WILL BE A LONG ENGAGEMENT. BUT WE HAVE MADE A BEGINNING TOWARDS HOUSEKEEPING.

SUDDENLY, AN OLD FRIEND BURST IN UPON US ...

GOOD HEAVENS, COPPERFIELD, I MUST STRAIGHTWAY INFORM MRS. MICAWBER OF YOUR PRESENCE IN THE HOUSE.

HOW DO YOU DO, MR. MICAWBER?

I AM AT PRESENT, COPPERFIELD, ENGAGED IN THE SALE OF CORN UPON COMMISSION. IT DOES NOT PAY. I AM, HOWEVER, DELIGHTED TO ADD THAT I HAVE NOW AN IMMEDIATE PROSPECT OF SOMETHING TURNING UP...

I HAD INVITED THE MICAWBERS AND TRADDLES TO DINNER, BUT MRS. CRUPP HAD NOT DONE A COMPLETE JOB ON THE MUTTON ROAST

IN TRUTH, COPPERFIELD, THE MUTTON IS NOT WELL DONE. BUT THAT NEED NOT MAR OUR DINNER. I HAVE MYSELF OFTIMES...

SUDDENLY, STEERFORTH'S PERSONAL VALET APPEARED AS IF FROM NOWHERE AND GAVE PERFECT SERVICE...

WHERE DID YOU COME FROM, LITTIMER, AND WHERE IS MY FRIEND, STEERFORTH?

FROM YARMOUTH SIR, AND I EXPECTED TO FIND MR. STEER FORTH HERE AT YOUR HOUSE, SIR.

NOW, I WILL DRINK TO THE DAYS WHEN MY FRIEND COPPERFIELD AND MYSELF WERE YOUNGER, AND FOUGHT OUR WAY INTO THE WORLD SIDE BY SIDE.

IN SHORT I MUST GIVE ANOTHER NOTE OF HAND TO FINANCE MY ENTERPRISES. I SHALL NEED A SIGNATURE TO THE NOTE.

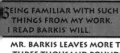

BEING FAMILIAR WITH SUCH THINGS FROM MY WORK, I READ BARKIS' WILL.

MR. BARKIS LEAVES MORE THAN THREE THOUSAND POUNDS. OF THESE, HE BEQUEATHS THE INTEREST ON ONE THOUSAND TO MR. PEGGOTTY. AT MR. PEGGOTTY'S DEATH, THE PRINCIPAL IS TO BE DIVIDED EQUALLY BETWEEN PEGGOTTY, LITTLE EMILY AND ME. ALL THE REST, HE LEAVES TO PEGGOTTY.

NEWS WAS WAITING AT MR. PEGGOTTY'S...

MY LOVE, MAS'R DAVY, HER THAT I'D HAVE DIED FOR, IS GONE!

EMILY GONE!

YOU'RE A SCHOLAR AND KNOW WHAT'S RIGHT AND BEST. WHAT AM I TO SAY INDOORS? HOW AM I EVER TO BREAK THE NEWS TO HIM, MAS'R DAVY?

LET MR. PEGGOTTY READ HER LETTER.

EMILY RUN AWAY? SHE LEFT THIS LETTER? I WANT TO KNOW THE MAN. WHAT'S HIS NAME?

FOR SOME TIME, THERE'S BEEN A GEN'LEM'N AND HIS SERVANT ABOUT HERE.

STEERFORTH!

I'M GOING TO SEEK MY NIECE THROUGH THE WURELD, AND BRING HER BACK.

NO, NO, DAN'L NOT AS YOU ARE NOW. SEEK HER IN A LITTLE WHILE.

WHEN I RETURNED TO MY ROOMS, I FOUND MY AUNT AND MR. DICK WAITING FOR ME WITH THE NEWS THAT MY AUNT HAD LOST ALL HER MONEY, AND THAT I WOULD HAVE TO SEEK WORK. I HURRIED TO TELL DORA...

DORA, DARLING, COULD YOU MARRY A POOR BEGGAR?

JIP, HOW CAN HE SAY SUCH MEAN THINGS TO ME!

DORA, I TELL YOU, I AM POOR, MY AUNT HAS LOST HER FORTUNE, AND I MUST GO TO WORK.

I WILL GIVE YOU ALL MY MONEY!

MR. DICK WAS A VERY MONUMENT OF MISERY.

TROTWOOD, IS MISS BETSE GOING TO STARVE? WHAT C DO TO HELP?

SHE'LL NOT STARVE, M DICK, I'M GOING TO G SOME WORK TO DO AF HOURS AT DOCTOR COMMONS.

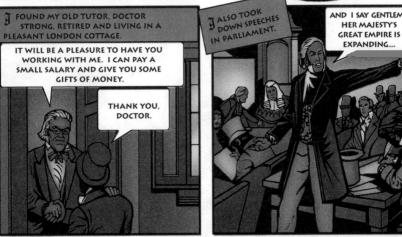

I FOUND MY OLD TUTOR, DOCTOR STRONG, RETIRED AND LIVING IN A PLEASANT LONDON COTTAGE.

IT WILL BE A PLEASURE TO HAVE YOU WORKING WITH ME. I CAN PAY A SMALL SALARY AND GIVE YOU SOME GIFTS OF MONEY.

THANK YOU, DOCTOR.

I ALSO TOOK DOWN SPEECHES IN PARLIAMENT.

AND I SAY GENTLEMEN HER MAJESTY'S GREAT EMPIRE IS EXPANDING....

AND I BEGAN TO MAKE MONEY WRITING FOR MAGAZINES.

YOU'RE DOING QUITE WELL TROT. I'M VERY PROUD OF YOU.

YES, AUNT BETSEY, AND I'M BUYING TWO COTTAGES, SIDE BY SIDE IN HIGHGATE.

THEN, ONE MORNING, AS I ENTERED DOCTORS' COMMONS...

MR. SPENLOW, IS DEAD!

MY DORA! WHAT WILL BECOME OF HER?

SPENLOW'S DEATH LEFT ME FREE TO VISIT DORA, WHO HAD GONE TO LIVE WITH HER TWO AUNTS.

I WISH TO ASK FOR DORA'S HAND IN MARRIAGE.

MR. COPPERFIELD, YOU SEEM TO BE GETTING QUITE FAMOUS WITH YOUR WRITING. WE WILL CONSIDER YOUR REQUEST AND GIVE YOU YOUR ANSWER IN DUE TIME.

AND, MEANWHILE, HEEP CAME UP TO LONDON...

MR. WICKFIELD AND MYSELF HAVE KNOWN IT FOR A LONG TIME - MRS. STRONG IS UNTRUE. THAT'S WHY JACK MALDON RETURNED FROM INDIA.

IF IT IS TRUE, GENTLEMEN, I FORGIVE HER. I DID GREAT WRONG IN IMPOSING MY AGE UPON HER YOUTH.

THEN MR. DICK DID SOMETHING THAT NO ONE ELSE COULD HAVE DONE.

MRS. STRONG, GO TO YOUR HUSBAND, TELL HIM THE TRUTH, AND RESTORE HIS CONFIDENCE.

JACK MALDON AND I WERE CHILDHOOD SWEETHEARTS. BUT, EVEN THEN I ADMIRED YOU. AND SINCE I HAVE BEEN MARRIED TO YOU, I HAVE LOVED YOU AND I ALWAYS WILL,

I HAVE NEVER BELIEVED ANYTHING BUT GOOD OF YOU.

AND WE LEFT THEM HAPPILY EMBRACED.

THE TWO COTTAGES IN HIGHGATE.

ONE IS FOR YOU, DEAR AUNT. THE OTHER - WELL, I'M GOING TO MARRY DORA.

BLIND, BLIND, BLIND! TROTWOOD, YOU ARE BLIND!

I PRONOUNCE YOU MAN AND WIFE.

AY, MAS'R DAVY, SHE SAILS WITHIN A FORTNIGHT. EMILY AND ME'D BE PROUD TO HAVE FRIENDS OF YOURN ON THE VOYAGE, AND WE CAN BE HELPFUL TO EACH OTHER IN AUSTRALIA.

AND, ON MY WAY BACK TO WICKFIELD'S OFFICE, I RELEASED MICAWBER FROM THE SHERIFF'S OFFICER.

MY DEAR COPPERFIELD! JUST IN TIME!

MR. MICAWBER, I'LL ADVANCE THE MONEY FOR THE VOYAGE AND FOR GETTING YOU SETTLED IN AUSTRALIA.

MADAM, IF YOU WILL ADVANCE ME SEVERAL HUNDRED POUNDS, I'LL DRAW UP A NOTE OF HAND, WHICH I WILL SIGN IN THE BEST OF FAITH. SOMETHING HAS, AT LAST, TURNED UP.

SEVERAL DAYS LATER, I RECEIVED SAD NEWS...

DORA'S VERY SICK. MY AUNT AND I ARE LEAVING FOR LONDON. WILL YOU GO WITH US? DORA WANTS TO SEE YOU.

YES, TROTWOOD.

WE FOUND DORA DYING.

IT IS BETTER THIS WAY. I WAS A POOR WIFE. AGNES, LOOK AFTER HIM.

OH, DORA! DORA!

SOON AFTER DORA'S DEATH, MR. PEGGOTTY, EMILY, MARTHA AND THE MICAWBERS, WERE READY TO SET SAIL FOR THEIR NEW HOME IN AUSTRALIA.

FAREWELL, MY FRIENDS, FAREWELL! BUT YOU SHALL HEAR FROM ME!

THAT NIGHT, I DECIDED TO VISIT ABROAD TO CLEAR MY THOUGHTS.

AH, HOW MANY DEAR REMEMBRANCES, MANY ERRORS, MANY UNAVAILING SORROWS AND REGRETS FILL MY MIND TONIGHT. I MUST LEAVE ENGLAND FOR A WHILE.

AND, AS I DESCENDED INTO A PLEASANT ITALIAN VALLEY A PACKET OF LETTERS REACHED ME.

LETTERS FROM ENGLAND, SIGNOR.

THE LETTERS WERE FROM AGNES, AND I WROTE TO HER THAT NIGHT BEFORE I SLEPT.

WHILE IN ITALY, I DREW UPON THE HAPPENINGS OF MY LIFE, AND WROTE.

I LANDED BACK IN LONDON ON A WINTRY AUTUMN EVENING.

THAT'S DAVID COPPERFIELD, THE FAMOUS AUTHOR.

I HAD RISEN IN THE WORLD AND SO HAD MR. CREAKLE.

MR. COPPERFIELD, I INVIT YOU HERE BECAUSE, SIN YOU ARE A FAMOUS AUTHOR NOW, YOU MIG WANT TO WRITE ABOUT MODEL PRISONER.

SHOW ME THE PRISON, MR. CREAM PERHAPS I SHALL SEE SOME THINGS THAT I SHOULD LIKE TO INCLUDE BOOK THAT I'M WRITING CALLED DAVID COPPERFI

TWENTY-SEVEN. WE'RE VERY PROUD OF HIM. HE'S OUR MODEL PRISONER.

I'M NOW COMPLETELY 'UMBLE, AND FEEL MUCH BETTER THAN I EVER FELT OUTSIDE.

DAVID COPPERFIELD
CHARLES DICKENS

It was 1849, and Charles Dickens was one of the most successful authors writing in English. By the age of thirty-seven, he had seven famous novels to his name. His *Christmas Books* had practically invented our modern idea of Christmas (think of Ebenezer Scrooge, Bob Cratchit, and Tiny Tim from *A Christmas Carol.*) As energetic as he was creative, Dickens had also founded and edited magazines and newspapers, organized and acted in plays, and provided financial support and advice in running a nineteenth-century battered women's shelter.

Dickens was also ready to change the way he wrote his novels. His beloved sister Fanny, ill with tuberculosis, had died that summer at the age of thirty-eight. While sitting by her bedside he had found his thoughts returning to their childhood together. Some of these memories were happy, and many, especially those dating from his father's imprisonment for debt, were very painful.

Yet he could not stop thinking about those times. He tried writing an autobiography, but said that was "too distressing to continue." A friend, John Forster, suggested that he do something different—write a novel in the first-person. Dickens had just finished his last novel, *Dombey and Son*, in April 1848, and he was ready to begin a new one. That novel was to be *The Personal History, Adventures, Experience & Observation of David Copperfield, the Younger of Blunderstone Rookery*. We call it simply *David Copperfield*.

What was the experience of childhood and young manhood that Charles Dickens drew upon for his new novel? He was born in Portsmouth, England, on February 7, 1812, the second of eight children. His father worked as a clerk in the British Navy, and the family's means were always stretched to the limit to support the children in precarious middle-class comfort.

Unfortunately, Dickens's father, John, could not live within his income—the figure of the spendthrift Mr. Micawber in *David Copperfield* is drawn from Dickens's memories of his father—and the Dickens family was always on the verge of bankruptcy. Finally, in 1823, the threat of financial disaster caused the family to relocate to London. Dickens was taken out of school (he had had only four years of education) and was sent to work at a job he hated, in a "blacking warehouse" where young boys were employed to label and wrap bottles of shoe polish and varnish. He was only eleven years old. A few days after he began work, his father was imprisoned in the Marshalsea Prison for debt. The Dickens family moved into the prison to be near him, but Charles was left living in a rented room so he could continue working up to twelve hours a day to earn money for the family.

John Dickens was released from prison after three months, but it was not until weeks later that he withdrew Charles from work and sent him to the Wellington House Academy, where he attended school for the next two-and-a-half years. The school was not well-run, and like the fictitious Mr. Creakle in *David Copperfield*, Dickens's headmaster at Wellington House frequently used the cane on his pupils. At the age of fifteen Dickens's formal education came to an end, and he went to work as an office boy for a firm of London lawyers. He taught himself shorthand and worked first as a clerk in Doctors' Commons (a collection of London law courts) and eventually as a reporter in the British Parliament in London. Industrious, determined, and very observant, Dickens also began writing newspaper articles about some of his own experiences in London.

Meanwhile, he was falling in love. For three years he was obsessed with the pretty and flirtatious Maria Beadnell, the daughter of a prosperous banker. They had what was then called "an understanding"—an informal engagement to marry—but her parents didn't approve of the nineteen-year-old who was barely earning his living as a reporter. Worse, his father had been imprisoned for debt! Maria was packed off to Paris to study (and to get her away from Charles); when she returned, she had changed her mind about marrying him.

Dickens began publishing magazine sketches about London life and manners. These were collected into his first book, *Sketches by Boz*. His first real literary success came the following year with *The Pickwick Papers* (1837), which established Dickens as a major novelist at the age of twenty-five. Dickens's readers loved the characters, the humor, and the sheer vitality of his writing. Serial publication also helped in its success. Since the novel came out in cheap separate parts, it was very affordable. Besides, the suspense of waiting to read the next monthly numbers made people eager to buy the latest installment. Altogether, he published fourteen serialized novels during his career; *David Copperfield* (1849-50) was his eighth. As well as writing immensely popular novels, Dickens founded and edited magazines, toured England and America giving dramatic readings from his works, produced and acted in plays, and supported many charities. Charles Dickens died of a stroke in 1870, leaving his last novel, *The Mystery of Edwin Drood*, unfinished.

Characters

David is the protagonist, who narrates the story of his life from his birth in the village of Blunderstone (in Suffolk, England) up to his second marriage and success as a novelist. The book is his autobiography. Since the story is told entirely from David's point of view, his opinions and preoccupations shape the story for us. This gives the novel immediacy and power and also makes David into a complex and realistic literary character. His story is presented from two perspectives—that of David the adult narrator, who tells the story and whose viewpoint remains relatively constant, and that of David the character, who goes through many changes from childhood to adulthood. To separate his adult narrator from the developing child, Dickens uses various techniques to point up the difference between the child's and the adult's world. Much of the first part of the story is told from the child's perspective. In the novel's opening chapters (not developed in the Classics Illustrated version) David describes in detail his infant impressions of learning to recognize people. As a toddler beginning to walk, for instance, he describes how the finger of his childhood nurse maid, Peggotty, felt just like a nutmeg-grater.

Clara Copperfield. Clara was a governess before she married, and she's widowed even before her son David is born. With her beautiful long hair, she is "unusually youthful in appearance even for her years." Childish in many ways, she can be "pettish and willful." Clara is delicate in health, naturally dependent, and very attracted to the virile Mr. Murdstone. Once married to him, Clara does not resist when he and his ill-tempered sister, Miss Murdstone, proceed to take over the household. She gives in to Mr. Murdstone's harsh discipline of her own child, David, even when he's imprisoned for days in his room and fed "on bread and milk" as punishment. In the novel Clara is portrayed as a loving but incompetent mother who abandons her son to harsh reality. She "betrays" David again when she bears a replacement for him—a new son. However, she and the child are too frail to live long, and David becomes a true orphan at nine.

Peggotty. Plump, homely, and huggable, Peggotty (whose first name is also Clara) functions as second mother to the child David. As his nurse, she spends much more time with him than his own mother does. To Peggotty, he is "Master Davy," a term of intimacy but also of respect (she's still a servant). It is Peggotty who breaks the news to David that his mother has remarried. Peggotty herself is unmarried (a fact very important to the young David, who is extremely jealous of any other masculine presence in his little world.) Although strong and capable, she is helpless against the economic power of the Murdstones and is "cast off" (fired) from her job as a children's nurse after the deaths of David's mother and her baby. Fortunately, the cart-driver **Barkis** (another villager) has been more than "willin'" to marry her for years, and she can now establish her own home. The loss of Peggotty makes David even more of an orphan in the world.

Mr. Peggotty. When Peggotty takes him to visit her brother, Mr. Peggotty, in Yarmouth, David falls in love with his charming, "ship-looking" house, and he idealizes the Peggottys as his second family. Though a "bachelordore, Mr. Peggotty ("as good as gold and as true as steel") serves as a father-surrogate for David and for his orphaned nephew and niece, Ham and Little Em'ly." The differences in dialect between David and the Peggottys mark the class difference between them that will become more important later in the novel.

Ham Peggotty. Ham, the son of Mr. Peggotty's drowned brother, Joe, is Little Em'ly's cousin and Peggotty's nephew. A minor but important character, Ham is a straightforward, faithful, and perhaps overly-trusting fisherman who becomes the devoted admirer of Little Em'ly.

Little Em'ly. Little Em'ly first appears in the story as a child of David's age. Shy and admiring, she's also an orphan (a fact which much attracts David). Her ambition in life is to become a lady. She begins as David's childhood sweetheart, is later engaged to Ham, but elopes with Steerforth.

Mrs. Gummidge. The last member of the Peggotty "family" (none is actually related as parent and child) is the "lone lorn creeture" Mrs. Gummidge, widow of a friend of Mr. Peggotty's. "Her troubles make her contrairy," and Mrs. Gummidge feels things more than others and sighs mournfully for her lost husband. The use of the catchphrase "lone lorn creeture" identifies her instantly and is one of Dickens's methods of creating character by using humorous verbal tags. Though she fulfills many of the functions of a mother—she cooks, cleans, and knits—Mrs. Gummidge does not seem particularly maternal to the young David, perhaps because she doesn't fit his picture of a cheerful, warm, nurturing mother. As her name suggests, however, she provides the adhesive that holds this "family" together.

Barkis. Peggotty's husband Barkis, who drives the cart that transports David to and from Yarmouth, is another instantly recognizable Dickens character who is identified by the tag-phrase, "Barkis is willin'." Ever-faithful, he finally wins Peggotty in marriage, and they live happily until his death, at which point Dickens gives us one of those sentimental death scenes much loved by Victorian audiences (see *Death-bed Scenes*).

David the Child. Like all children, David is sensitive, egocentric, literal-minded, and impressionable. One of his childhood tasks is to learn to de-code adult language and figure out what is expected of him. He has the impulsive temper of a child, and bites his stepfather's hand fiercely when punished. He is vulnerable and completely at the mercy of elders, and the adult David uses the child's perspective to dramatize the unfair power of adults. At the tender age of eight David must go off to the boarding school chosen for him.

Mr. Murdstone. When he marries Clara and lives with them, Mr. Murdstone appears to David as a "hard, cruel man," intent on disciplining and educating David. Mr. Murdstone introduces a masculine element in opposition to Clara's femininity, and David resents his domination. This was not always so. In a scene not included in the CI adaptation, Murdstone and David go on an outing together. The young David is initially attracted to Mr. Murdstone's masculine energy and handsome thick, black whiskers. It is only after the marriage that he comes to dislike Mr. Murdstone, who turns into a cruel tyrant.

Miss Jane Murdstone. Miss Murdstone, a "gloomy-looking" woman with very heavy eyebrows that meet over her nose, is the most "metallic lady" that David has ever seen. Miss Murdstone doesn't like boys, and she takes over the management of the household in a manner almost as firm as that of her brother. She and her brother adhere to the stern religious doctrine of "spare the rod and spoil the child," and Clara and Peggotty are no match for this grim rigidity. Later it is revealed that she and Clara Copperfield shared the same profession of governessing.

SHE SOON TOOK OVER THE MANAGEMENT OF THE HOUSE. MY MOTHER HAD NO MORE TO DO WITH IT THAN I DID . . .

Aunt Betsey Trotwood. Aunt Betsey, another older woman who doesn't particularly like boys, is the aunt of David's father. A "tall hard-featured lady, but by no means ill-favored," with "a very quick, bright eye," she paid off her husband because they didn't get along, and is opposed to the idea of marriage. When David runs away from his job at the Murdstone and Grinby's Wine Shop, he seeks refuge with Aunt Betsey. She gives him shelter, a name (Trotwood Copperfield) and protection from the dreaded Murdstones, whom she vanquishes in a fantastic scene involving donkeys.

T LAST, I REACHED VER AND ND MY AUNT.

IF YOU PLEASE, AUNT. I AM YOUR NEPHEW. I AM DAVID COPPERFIELD.

OH, LORD!

Mr. Dick. Mr. Dick (whose true name is Mr. Richard Babley, though no one ever uses it) is one of those Dickensian comic characters, like

Barkis, who have a ruling passion: Mr. Dick is writing a "Memorial to the Lord Chancellor" (a kind of history), but can't keep the name of King Charles the First from getting into it. (Mr. Dick's futile labor to finish his masterpiece allows Dickens to poke fun at professional writers.) Mr. Dick's vacant manner, his submission to Aunt Betsey, and his childish delight when she praises him make David suspect that he's a little mad. Perhaps he is more a wise-fool, for Mr. Dick has a way of stating the obvious that cuts through problems of communication. His aunt's goodness to Mr. Dick seems to reassure David that she's really kind-hearted and indeed, might be a mother-figure for him.

James Steerforth. At Salem House School, David meets the aristocratic James Steerforth, an older, more fearless student who takes David under his wing and gives him the nickname "Daisy." David is immediately attracted to the handsome Steerforth, as well as to the arrogance and mystery that are part of Steerforth's nature. Steerforth has his faults: he

MR. DICK, YOU'RE A MAN OF RARE JUDGMENT. THIS IS DAVID COPPERFIELD. WHAT SHALL I DO WITH HIM?

WHY—I SHOULD WASH HIM.

publicly insults the schoolmaster Mr. Mell (who is dismissed as a result) and gets away with it because Headmaster Creakle is in awe of his upper-class manners. Later, David and Steerforth get reacquainted in London. David (now seventeen) is hungry for the affectionate friendship that he believes Steerforth feels for him. Soon Steerforth is invited by David to meet the "Yarmouth family" (the Peggottys), and this initiates the crisis of Little Em'ly and Steerforth.

Miss Mowcher. With her very large head, extremely little arms, and bright gray eyes, Miss Mowcher is a "little morsel of a woman." She supports herself by coming to the homes of her clients to cut and curl their hair (and use a little dye if necessary). She knows just how to flatter clients like James Steerforth so they tell her everything. In the novel she's responsible also for helping Steerforth to lure away Little Em'ly. Miss Mowcher appears only once in the CI adaptation, but she's one of those minor characters who steal the scene and live on forever. Characters like her are called "grotesques" because they're so bizarre, comic, and energetic that they don't fit into the usual categories of realistic fiction.

Mr. Micawber. When David is pulled out of school at ten years of age and sent away to work in the Murdstone and Grinby Wine Factory, he meets one of the great comic characters in Dickens. Wilkins Micawber's whole life can be summed up by the famous advice he gives David: "Annual income twenty pounds, annual expenditure nineteen, nineteen and six, result happiness. Annual income twenty pounds, annual expenditure twenty pounds ought and six, result misery." Always just sixpence away from financial disaster, Mr. Micawber dresses with flair and speaks in comic flourishes. Courtly, talkative, and "in short," a spendthrift, Mr. Micawber is another possible father-figure for David. In

Pounds, Shillings, Pence

English money in Victorian times was based on a system of pounds, shillings, and pence. In David's time a pound (worth about $25 in today's money) was made up of 20 shillings, and a shilling was worth 12 pence. A sixpence would be half a shilling, or about 75 cents.

their apartment in London, the Micawbers create a home for their lodger, David. But it is an insecure home, and, like John Dickens, Mr. Micawber is soon in prison for debt. When released he must leave London to escape his creditors, a situation that will repeat itself in Canterbury when David meets him again. With his undisciplined extravagance and irresponsibility, Mr. Micawber signals to the growing David the importance of hard work and thrift as the best route to middle-class security. Mr. Micawber appears throughout the novel and changes from clown to savior by the end.

Mr. Wickfield. It is in Mr. Wickfield's refined and elegant house that David boards while he attends Dr. Strong's school in the English town of Canterbury. Mr. Wickfield is a lawyer who looks after the estates of rich men.

Handsome, with luxuriant white hair and "a certain richness in his complexion" (probably from drinking port wine), Mr. Wickfield is the model of a prosperous, respectable lawyer. He prides himself on being calculating and analytical; his identifying catch-phrase is "what's your motive in this?" His own motive in life is to provide for his daughter, Agnes. Unfortunately, he is not as wise as he thinks he is, and his pride leads him into trouble.

Agnes Wickfield. Agnes first meets David when they're both about eleven years old. Her mother is dead, and Agnes runs the household. Called "my little housekeeper" by her father, she's already "womanly" (the favored Victorian term for femininity and domesticity) on a small scale. With her bright yet modest face, and her placid, sweet expression, she reminds David of a portrait in a stained

The Angel in the House

The Victorian doctrine of "separate spheres" was reinforced in law, literature, medicine and religion. Woman's personal lives were supposed to revolve around home, husband, and children, while men's lives focused outwards on the more public and competitive world of work and politics. As the distance between the two worlds increased in the 19th-century, women became "specialists" in emotional and spiritual management for their families, responsible for providing a stable refuge for husband and children in a rapidly-changing world. This ideal domestic woman was called "The Angel in the House" (after a popular poem), and David several times refers to Agnes as "my good angel." Women were in charge of moral education and religion, because their purity and innocence about the outside, corrupting world made them perfect for it. (This meant that they had to stay pure and separate.) Of course, most women weren't selfless, dependent saints, and (especially in working- class or poor homes) it was hard to remain innocent of the outside world. But for the middle class, where the model predominated, it was a powerful social ideal.

A Satirical Aside

What is this prison scene doing in the story? David's sudden visit to Mr. Creakle and his "model prison" seems very improbable in terms of the plot. Victorian readers would have instantly recognized an ongoing debate about the correct treatment of prisoners, and Dickens was taking advantage of popular interest in this problem. What one side saw as "coddling," the other side viewed as humane treatment of the inmates. Criticizing social problems was part of his reason for writing, and Dickens himself was on the side of those who felt that it was "spoiling" prisoners by isolating them in their own cells and feeding them good meals. He couldn't resist making fun of the Model Prison by presenting Creakle—who cruelly beat his students at the Salem House School—as its head and Uriah Heep, that master of hypocrisy, as its model prisoner.

---

glass window, and this connection with saintliness and virtue will remain with David. Agnes acts as a kind of moral "barometer"—she senses that David's so-called friends in London are leading him into bad habits, and she tells him so. For many years, he thinks of her as a sister, though he's possessively jealous when Uriah Heep indicates his *own* plans for Agnes.

Uriah Heep. Mr. Wickfield's clerk, Uriah Heep is about fifteen years old when he meets David, but to David there is something ageless about him. Red-haired, red-eyed, and without eyebrows or eyelashes, Uriah reminds David of a skeleton, but with repulsively clammy hands. David dislikes him from the beginning, and Agnes is also suspicious of his influence on her father. Though professing himself as "very umble" (his accent marks him as of a lower class than the students of Dr. Strong's school), Uriah Heep knows how to manipulate people. "If a person is to get on in life," says Uriah, "he must get on umbly." Uriah manages to humble himself into a position of influence over Mr. Wickfield. He also has a

strange power over David. David is as obsessed with Uriah (especially as competition for Agnes) as Uriah is with him. At one point in the novel, David's primitive anger comes out in a dream where he repeatedly drives a red-hot poker through Uriah! Heep is also the

The Fallen Woman

The opposite of The Angel in the House in Victorian novels was the Fallen Woman, who had slid right off her pedestal. "Fallen" refers to the story of Adam and Eve in the Garden of Eden. By the 19th-century, Eve's sin meant sexual experience before or outside of marriage. In literature, the Fallen Woman usually tumbled into the lower-class, if she wasn't already in it. In Victorian literature women were also presented as always vulnerable to "slipping," always potentially "fallen." Recall that the character of Little Em'ly is remembered by the adult narrator as both an angel *and* a wild, rash child. In the 19th-century, the term Fallen Woman was also a synonym for a prostitute.

unwitting means of making Mr. Micawber into a savior who figures it all out: "Who stole Miss Betsey's fortune and ruined Mr. Wickfield? It was Heep! I have got to the bottom of this crooked mess and there I found no one but Heep!" Finally, Uriah Heep is one of those Dickensian characters that can never be completely contained by the plot. His final appearance in the Model Prison is strange, to say the least: "I'm now completely umble," says Uriah, "and feel much better than I ever felt outside."

Mr. Spenlow. Mr. Spenlow works in Doctors' Commons, the law court where David is sent to work to learn the profession. In his black gown with white fur, with his "undeniable boots" and the stiffest of shirt-collars, Mr. Spenlow represents the prosperous professional class that David wishes to enter. Mr. Spenlow conveniently has a daughter, Dora.

Dora Spenlow. Dora Spenlow is another motherless child. She's a child-woman like Clara Copperfield, and David describes her in the exact terms he used for his mother: "pettish and willful." To David, the flirtatious and pretty Dora has all the feminine virtues: she can play the guitar, sing, and speak French. He falls instantly in love with his "captivating, girlish, bright-eyed, lovely Dora." The adult David makes fun of the adolescent David, who is so smitten that he wishes he were Dora's little dog, Jip. In the character of Dora, David's two main motivations—romantic love and finding success in the law—come together, but it is an unstable combination. Aunt Betsey Trotwood foresees that they are too young to marry and that Dora is incapable of being the kind of capable, clever, and above all, domestic wife that David needs. But the two young lovers can't see it. The story of their married life is the unfolding of his aunt's warning, and Dora's pathetic death-bed words show that she realizes it: "It is better this way. I was a poor wife." (See next page).

Martha. A young and pretty worker in the same dressmaking

WE FOUND DORA DYING

IT IS BETTER THIS WAY. I WAS A POOR WIFE. AGNES, LOOK AFTER HIM.

OH, DORA! DORA!

cation.) Told from David's perspective, the novel is the story of maturation, of finding the right profession, of discovering a suitable wife and founding a family.

But from another perspective, one outside David's, his story looks different—more like the history of someone who is determined to consolidate his own class position, yet unaware of his own motives. David was originally born into the minor gentry (the bottom rung of the aristocratic upper class), but lost his upper-class status when father and mother died. Even if Mr. Murdstone had been a sympathetic figure, he would only have been able to confer middle-class status on his step-son.

Looking at David's admiration for Steerforth from another angle, it seems motivated less by simple friendship and more by the desire to win a patron who can help him achieve upper-class status. Notice that David never defends Mr. Mell against Steerforth's rudeness, even though he disapproves of it. And David is strangely unaware of his motives when he brings Steerforth down to Yarmouth to meet the grown-up Little Em'ly even though he has had many hints that Steerforth is flirtatious and sensual. David's desire to marry Dora Spenlow, the daughter of a prosperous member of the professional class (the top rung of the

establishment as Little Em'ly, Martha is the first official "fallen woman" in *David Copperfield*. She has been "disgraced" (seduced by a man without marriage), and everyone in town knows about it. "Take me out of the streets," she implores Em'ly and Ham when she comes to them for money to leave Yarmouth, but it is to the streets of London that she is headed. While there, she eventually helps to rescue Little Em'ly, also seduced and abandoned.

EMILY, HAVE A HEART AND HELP ME LEAVE THIS TOWN WHERE I AM DISGRACED!

The Plot

It's a tribute to Dickens's greatness as a story-teller that he can tie up all the strands in his elaborate and multi-layered plots into a final conclusion! In *David Copperfield* the thread that ties all the various sub-plots is the story of David and his development into a successful adult member of his society. (Critics call this kind of fictional story by the German term "Bildungsroman," or novel of edu-

Death-bed Pathos

Dickens brought death-bed scenes to new heights of emotional release, as he played on his readers' sympathy for the death of the innocent and the faithful in a world that was seen as too harsh and corrupt for them to survive. In *David Copperfield* there are two such scenes, when Barkis "goes out with the tide" and when Dora dies lingeringly. Shedding tears over such scenes allowed his audience to feel a sense of community in having a good cry together for a good cause (which can still happen in movie theaters). Dickens was writing in a time when most readers were sentimental about dying children (note that both Barkis and Dora are childlike, if not exactly children). Such death-bed scenes were dramatic "crowd-pleasers," and besides, anticipating Dora's lingering death kept people buying those magazines!

---

middle class), looks less like true love and more like another effort to rise to the station he feels he deserves. It is only after he loses Steerforth's friendship and Aunt Betsey's financial support that he shifts his goals towards success in middle-class terms. Finally, from an outside perspective we see how similar the grown-up David is to his childhood enemy, Mr. Murdstone. Both are middle-class, ambitious men who marry child-wives and ultimately make them unhappy.

There are also at least three other related plots, all linked together by the presence of David. The first plot, extending throughout the entire book, is that of the child-wife and the search for a true (read "suitable") mate. (And search it is: David is constantly on the move between Blunderstone, Yarmouth, Canterbury, London, Dover, and back again.) Clara Copperfield, Dora Spenlow, and Annie Strong are all literary examples of the

attractions and the difficulties of marrying a child-wife. Despite their feminine charms, Clara can't mother David as he needs and desires, and Dora isn't able to be the sort of wife he wants. Annie Strong represents another version of the child-wife, though she doesn't actually die in the end—just continues in a lifeless marriage.

The second plot is the Em'ly-Steerforth story, with its melodramatic narrative of the fallen woman, Mr. Peggotty's determined quest to search for her "through the wureld," and Em'ly's eventual re-establishment as a strong and womanly emigrant in Australia. In this plot two alternate versions of the fallen woman appear: Rosa Dartle, who was also seduced by Steerforth in her youth, and Martha, who becomes a streetwalker until her emigration to Australia allows her to start over. The sexy and attractive James Steerforth has been able to manipulate others, as well. His own mother is incapable of seeing his faults, and spoils him. Miss Mowcher is persuaded by James to take his letter to Little Em'ly, therefore helping in that seduction. And finally, David himself is fascinated by Steerforth's easy strength, upper-class manners, and physical attractive-

I TRIED TO BE CONSIDERATE OF HEEP BECAUSE OF HIS POWER OVER THE WICKFIELDS.

AND, MISTER COPPERFIELD -- THOUGH I AM STILL 'UMBLE, I AM RISING IN THE WORLD; AND SOME DAY, I HOPE TO MARRY AGNES.

WHAT!

ness. Much of this plot is concerned with David's disillusionment with Steerforth and his recovery from his infatuation with him. This infatuation ends only when the author kills off Steerforth, who drowns in a dramatic sea-storm scene not in the Classics Illustrated adaptation.

A third plot revolves around the actions and manipulations of Uriah Heep, who dominates and defrauds Mr. Wickfield, steals Aunt Betsey Trotwood's fortune (which is in Mr. Wickfield's keeping), and even dares to aim for Agnes as a wife. Again, from one angle Heep is a figure of evil who deserves to be cast out. But from another perspective, David's dislike of Heep seems startlingly excessive (remember David's dream of the red-hot poker with which he attacks Heep?) It is as if the adult David can't admit to himself how similar they really are. Both want to "rise" by studying law and marrying the right woman. Viewed in this light, the striving, determined Uriah is only an exaggeration of David's

qualities, which David never seems to realize.

There are also sub-plots of the sub-plots: Aunt Betsey Trotwood's mysterious aversion to men and marriage, and the Old Beggar who accosts her and turns out to be her long-lost husband; and, near the end of the story, the union of the Peggottys and the Micawbers for the purpose of emigrating, and their eventual success in far-off Australia.

Remembering and Autobiography

David Copperfield called his project of arranging and writing his life story "my written memory," and the power of remembering—particularly of childhood—is one of the major themes of the novel. On one level the narrative presents the author's use of his own memories. This is a novel where the many similarities of life experience between Dickens and his protagonist, David Copperfield, are always luring the reader into considering them as one and the same. Dickens heightens this temptation by making David into an autobiographer himself, writing his own story of a sensitive and talented writer. David even refers to himself as author of the novel *David Copperfield*. (See next page).

A second level of remembering involves the double-perspective of the two Davids, with the childhood memories of David filtered through the adult's retelling of them, sometimes simultaneously. For instance, we readers perceive the world through the young child's perspective, even as the adult narrator chooses which memories to relate. When David tries to translate the Peggottys' phrases into his own language (like "drowndead" into "drowned"), the adult narrator's ironic memory of "drown-dead" is present too. As David grows up, the gap between the adult and the child narrator gradually narrows.

The Vulnerable Child

Charles Dickens was the first novelist to make childhood a major literary theme, with a child as the emotional center of a novel. Before this, there were few children in literature. With his strong social conscience, Dickens felt himself to be part of a crusade to abolish the abuses he saw inflicted on Victorian children. Part of this concern arose from his own feelings of abandonment as a child, but part was because of the genuine mistreatment of children that he saw around him. Mainstream Victorian religion viewed children as potentially wicked and in constant need of discipline: the whippings depicted in Mr. Creakle's school were allowed by law. The children of poverty were even more vulnerable. They were sometimes exploited as beggars or thieves (as in *Oliver Twist*) or might be expected to work twelve hours a day in factories, where the laws about worker-safety were very lax. Many times they lived on the street, like the homeless Jo in *Bleak House*. Of course, not all nineteenth-century children were oppressed or physically abused, but Dickens's sensitivity to children made him intolerant of even isolated instances.

Most vulnerable of all is the child with no parents. In nearly every one of his books orphans or "half-orphans" (missing one parent) are prominent characters. *David Copperfield* contains an unusually large number of these unfortunate children: David, Ham, Little Em'ly, Traddles, Clara Copperfield, Martha, Rosa Dartle, and Dora Spenlow (technically not a child when she becomes orphaned, but very immature) have all lost both parents, while Annie Strong, Steerforth, and Uriah Heep have lost their fathers. Agnes Wickfield has been motherless since she was a baby. Of all his books, *David Copperfield* persuades us the most that Dickens identified himself with children left parentless, and victimized by an unfeeling society.

The Quest for Home

In his identification with orphans, Dickens wrote about the desperate need to find a substitute parent and a nurturing home. *David Copperfield* is filled with this quest. Since Clara is not a strong mother-figure, Peggotty becomes David's substitute-parent, but she's dismissed by the Murdstones after Clara's death, and David's home itself is threatened. Mr. Murdstone (the name suggests his hardness) is a possible father-figure, but in fact his cruel discipline is just the opposite of what a child needs to thrive.

At first, Aunt Betsey Trotwood is a hard, almost masculine presence in David's life. During the course of the novel she becomes a maternal figure who plays a significant part in shaping David's childhood. At the end of the novel, David says "my poor mother could not have loved me better, or studied more to make me happy." For all her bluster, she's kind and tender when she takes David into her home, and she swaddles him and bathes and dresses him. After all the shocks of his mother's death, his work at Murdstone and Grinby's, and his difficulties in school, he's now, in a way, reborn. Aunt Betsey also shapes David's character by introducing him to a possible profession. When he plans to marry Dora, his aunt tells him her opinion of the marriage (he's "blind, blind, blind"), but like a wise par-

ent, she does not interfere further, and she nurses Dora devotedly when she is ill. However, the Trotwood household does not fit the usual family pattern: Aunt Betsey lives apart from her real husband, and the asexual Mr. Dick is the only male presence.

In the course of the novel David investigates other surrogate-families. The Steerforths' home includes a blindly-doting mother, a hostile companion in the person of Rosa Dartle, and a son who has no morals. The Wickfield father and daughter are divided by Mr. Wickfield's obsession with his daughter Agnes's happiness, which keeps him from confiding in her about his financial worries. The Heep family of mother and son is presented as a grotesque parody of "like mother, like son."

The Micawbers are one of the few families in the novel that comes complete with father, mother, and children. The Micawbers act as surrogate parents while David lives with them. Their financial crises and frequent moves create anything but a secure refuge for an orphaned boy, and, though kindly and loving to David, the family is ultimately too unstable to nurture him.

The one family that does exhibit devotion to its children, the Peggottys, is actually not made up of parents and children. Though a "bacheledore," Mr. Peggotty is a hard-working surrogate-father who shares his house with an adopted family of a

Knowing your Place in Victorian England

It's tough for us, Americans at the end of the 20th-century, to keep track of, let alone fully accept the importance of, rank in Victorian society. We can more-or-less keep straight royalty versus peerage versus commoners, but each of these classes was divided into more subclasses. The way you addressed another person, or were addressed, or the order in which people went in to the dining room at a dinner party, could have major consequences. Here's a primer of rank in English society—a short list, since a long one could run for pages!

royalty	The Sovereign (King or reigning Queen) Prince of Wales, children of the Sovereign (in birth order) Relatives of the Sovereign
peerage	Dukes/Duchesses Marquesses/Marchionesses Earls/Countesses Viscounts/Viscountesses Barons/Baronesses
titled non-peers	Baronets/Lady (ie., Baronet's wives—no term for this rank) Knights/Ladies (ie., Baronet's wives—no term for this rank)
untitled commoners	Gentlemen and their wives Military Men Tradespeople Farmers Laborers, Farm Hands Paupers

All of this doesn't take into account

things like membership in the Clergy (the Archbishop of Canterbury, as the head of the Church of England, precedes the peerage, as do the Sovereign's Officers—the Lord Chancellor and folk like that). Even when you get down to the level of untitled commoners, distinctions of rank were calculated very carefully. Marriage was one factor: if everyone at a party was untitled, the oldest *married* woman was led in to dinner by the host of the party, and every married woman there would outrank the *un*married women. *But*, if the unmarried Lady Jane Ffish, daughter of the Duke of Thrupenny, was there, she would outrank all the other woman. Incidentally, Lady Jane would carry her "courtesy title" with her regardless of whom she married. If she married Mr. Foxxe, she would become Lady Jane Foxxe; Mr. Foxxe might marry into her fortune, but would not become Lord Foxxe!

Dickens's characters are, for the most-part, commoners—but that category takes in a lot of territory, from the wealthy and privileged to the lowliest beggars and thieves. It's unlikely that the Peggotty family would have known the proper way to address a Duke (it's "Your Grace"), but they were certainly aware of who was their inferior and superior. What marks Victorian society is how (relatively) easy it could be for someone as "'umble" as Uriah Heep to aspire to move up the ladder to a higher station.

widow and two orphans. Tender and protective, especially to little Em'ly, his devotion to his family is unquestioned. His fierce paternal love drives him to search the world over for Em'ly's seducer, Steerforth, and welcome her home when he finds her. To David, this working-class family seems to prove that good parenting transcends class.

Charles Dickens viewed nineteenth-century society as basically disorganized and unhealthy, and he was convinced that bad parenting and violated children were the result. To him, family relationships were rarely harmonious. Even his idealized families, like the Peggottys, had their problems. From an outside viewpoint, Mr. Peggotty's obsession with Em'ly might be dominating and unhealthy. From Em'ly's point of view, running off with Steerforth might be the only way to avoid marrying her cousin Ham and remaining at home for the rest of her life.

Debt: Go Directly to Jail

Like Mr. Micawber, Charles Dickens's own father spent time in prison for debt, and like Micawber, he was eventually released. To us, the idea of throwing someone in jail for owing money may seem odd, even counterproductive: if you're in jail, how can you possibly earn the money to repay your debts? In those pre-credit card days, you couldn't use plastic for your purchases—but you could buy on credit, and tradespeople were often very generous about how much credit they'd extend, and how long they'd wait for payment. But when generosity and patience ran out, a tradesman might take you to court. If it was found you hadn't enough money to pay off your debts, you were declared a Bankrupt, your name was published in the

London Gazette (the better to warn off future generous tradesfolk!), and your possessions—house, furnishings, clothes, down to the last tea-spoon, were sold off to raise money for your creditors.

If you were arrested as a Debtor, however, you went to jail—at least until your court appearance. There you could be found not to be a debtor, or you could pay off the debt...or (if you *refused* to pay off the debt) you could go right back to jail again. After three months in jail (sometimes, as with Dickens's family, the whole gang went to prison with the debtor) you could be released, if you signed over your property to your creditors. This system was in place until 1869, the year before Dickens's death.

It's the Law

David Copperfield is peppered with lawyers and law clerks; David himself is "articled"—apprenticed—as a law clerk to Mr. Spenlow, in Doctor's Commons.

As with almost everything else in Victorian England, different lawyers had different status. Lawyers who argued in court had a higher status than those who prepared cases and handled legal paperwork (although this second sort of lawyer did most of the direct "client management" and was the one who hired the trial lawyer). Court lawyers were divided into Barristers (who pled in Chancery—a sort of combination property and appeals court); Serjeants (who pled in the common-law courts: King's Bench, Common Pleas, and the Exchequer); and Advocates (who pled in the admiralty and church courts). The lawyers who hired them were (respectively) Attorneys, Solicitors, and Proctors. And because, under law, the client's fee to the barrister was not a fee but a *gift*, if you stiffed your barrister, he had no recourse—couldn't even sue to get his money!

The Doctor's Commons mentioned in *David Copperfield* was, like the Inner Temple, the Middle Temple, Lincoln's Inn and Gray's Inn, was one of the inns, a center for Advocates and Proctors who practiced in the church and admiralty courts. While David would have needed a doctorate in civil laws from either Oxford or Cambridge to appear in court, there was no such requirement to become a proctor.

The whole system became a lot simpler in the late 1800s, when the court systems were reorganized, leaving only two classes of lawyers: barristers and solicitors.

Study Questions

• While you read this novel look for similarities between David Copperfield and Charles Dickens. (Notice the reversal of their initials, for instance.) What incidents from Dickens's life reappear in David Copperfield's story? How is the author Dickens "rewriting his own past?" Do you feel that knowing the details of Dickens's life adds anything to the experience of reading *David Copperfield*? If so, how and why? Are there any dangers in identifying David with Dickens too completely?

• The famous opening line of the novel is very suggestive: "Whether I shall turn out to be the hero of my own life, or whether that station must be held by anybody else, these pages must show." Consider the significance of this opening sentence. What is a "hero?" What qualities make someone heroic? If not David, who else in the novel might be the hero?

• In general, there were three social classes in nineteenth-century England: the upper classes (including the aristocracy), the middle class, and the working class. What different classes are represented in this novel? Identify the different characters' class-standing, and think about the way their class-standing influences how David relates to them. Why do you think he has so much trouble with working-class people (waiters and transport-drivers)? What class is Steerforth? Uriah Heep? The Peggottys? The women in the novel? Finally, what class (or classes) does David belong to in the novel?

•The relationship between David and Steerforth is very ambiguous. How critical is the adult narrator David of Steerforth? What are the signs of the alternating attraction and repulsion that he feels for his friend? Why do you think he invites Steerforth down to Yarmouth,

home of the beautiful grown-up Emily? How much is David responsible for the future troubles in the family?

•Think of all the women in *David Copperfield*, and how they measure up to the ideal of The Angel in the House. What characteristics do the "Angels" share, and what distinguishes "the others"— those non-angelic women like Rosa Dartle, Little Em'ly, and Martha? Which of these women seem more "real" as characters? Finally, what does David's attitude towards women reveal about him. How about the author of the book himself?

•Uriah Heep has been called the novel's "scapegoat"—the figure generally believed to be responsible for all the other characters' problems, who must be cast out of society in order to bring back happiness and security. What other roles might Uriah play in the story? What would the story be without Uriah? What would the story be like if told from Uriah's viewpoint? If you check out the source of David's and Uriah's names in the *Bible* (II Samuel, 11.14-26), you'll see that in this passage, King David manipulates King Uriah and steals his wife from him. Why do you think Dickens chose these particular names for his novel?

•Dickens often introduces characters who seem to be doubles of each other—Little Em'ly and Martha, or Clara Copperfield and Dora Spenlow, or David and Uriah. Identify and list other doubles and pairings like this that you find in *David Copperfield*. Why does Dickens use doubles and pairings in his book? How are they useful to the reader?

About the Essayist:

Emily Woudenberg is a doctoral candidate and a member of The Dickens Project, a consortium of universities and colleges with headquarters at the University of California at Santa Cruz.

Laura Gallier's book *The Delusion* is a very entertaining and thought-provoking read. It's full of relevant content no matter your faith perspective. I am excited to see its impact on bookshelves as well as on the big screen.

MAURICE EVANS, former NBA player

The Delusion is a great book that allows both teenagers and adults to dive in and get captivated by Owen's life. I couldn't put the book down as I found myself visualizing the details and looking forward to what happened next. The truths behind this fictional book are outstanding.

RODNEY BLAKE COLEMAN, M. ED., Assistant Principal,
Anthony Middle School

The Delusion is a page turner that I couldn't put down, and neither could my husband and teenage son. Laura Gallier has a firm grasp on the challenges that our students face today, and her novel reveals challenging, eye-opening truths.

KELLY MARTENS, president and founder, Lighthouse for Students

As a film producer, I'm constantly looking for great stories. With *The Delusion*, Laura Gallier has delivered on all levels.

CHAD GUNDERSON, Out of Order Productions

I appreciate Laura Gallier taking the time to help us remember where the real battle is. *The Delusion* was a priceless reminder that we must be constantly exchanging the lies of the enemy, and our culture, with the truth of God's Word. The book is a fresh perspective on where our true power comes from: PRAYER. That's where the real victory is gained.

WADE HOPKINS, former NFL player and Regional Vice President,
Fellowship of Christian Athletes

Laura effectively depicts the day-to-day battle between good and evil through powerful story and imagery. As a father, it is a wake-up call to the responsibility I have as the spiritual leader in the home, to recognize the battle that is raging and to stand firm for the sake of the next generation. *The Delusion* is a must-read for every father.

RICK WERTZ, founder and president, Faithful Fathering, faithfulfathering.org

LAURA GALLIER

THE DELUSION

WE ALL HAVE OUR DEMONS

Tyndale House Publishers, Inc.
Carol Stream, Illinois

Visit Tyndale online at www.tyndale.com.

Visit Laura Gallier online at www.lauragallier.com/delusion.

TYNDALE and Tyndale's quill logo are registered trademarks of Tyndale House Publishers, Inc.

The Delusion: We All Have Our Demons

Designed by Jacqueline L. Nuñez

Edited by Sarah Rubio

Published in association with the literary agency of D.C. Jacobson & Associates LLC, an Author Management Company. www.dcjacobson.com

The Delusion is a work of fiction. Where real people, events, establishments, organizations, or locales appear, they are used fictitiously. All other elements of the novel are drawn from the author's imagination.

For information about special discounts for bulk purchases, please contact Tyndale House Publishers at csresponse@tyndale.com, or call 1-800-323-9400.

ISBN 978-1-4964-2236-1 (hc)
ISBN 978-1-4964-2237-8 (sc)

Printed in the United States of America

23	22	21	20	19	18	17
7	6	5	4	3	2	1

For my mother, who has put up with plenty of my storytelling!
Thank you for believing in this book and in me.

It doesn't matter whether you want to be in a spiritual battle—you are in one. The battle is between good and evil, and you are the prize.

DR. CHARLES F. STANLEY

PROLOGUE

It was bad enough I had to up and move in the middle of my senior year, but to be the new guy at a high school where eight students had committed suicide since September?

I felt cursed.

By spring break, three more students were gone. Eleven total. Dead.

But that wasn't the worst of it.

Even though the students died by their own hands, their deaths were provoked—and I'm the only one who could see what tormented them. Believe me, I tried to warn people. I begged them to listen, but they wouldn't. Not even the people closest to me.

Chances are, you won't take me seriously either.

My stories are twisted and bizarre—and so terrifying that I'm sometimes told to shut up a few minutes into them—but I can't.

And who knows? Maybe you're one of the rare ones—one of a small minority willing to venture beyond your five senses to believe in what is rarely seen. What intentionally stays hidden.

What I wished I'd never seen.

It all began on a typical Monday morning.

Well, typical for me.

ONE

A DEEP, GUTTURAL GROWL jarred my eyes open. It was so dark I couldn't see a thing, but I knew where the sound was coming from. Exactly where she was, crouched low to the floor.

My psychotic dog was at it again.

I didn't move. Maybe she'd give up and lie down. For once, let it go—whatever *it* was.

But she kept on, this time with a snarl. I had no choice but to throw my sheets back and peer over the foot of my bed. "Stop it, girl. It's okay."

Labrador retrievers are known for their protective instincts, but my dog's senses were way off. More nights than not, she'd fixate on my closed bedroom door and growl like an ax murderer was stomping down the hallway.

I tapped the mattress. "Daisy. Get up here."

She didn't budge.

"Come on, girl. Nothing's there."

This time, I was wrong.

My door flung open and collided with the wall, sending Daisy scurrying under the bed and me scrambling to my feet. A silhouette stood

1

in the doorway, framed by the hall light. This was no ax murderer. Still, I wasn't entirely relieved.

Mom.

What does she want now?

She steadied herself against the door frame, her hair still wrapped in a towel from last night's bath. Her pasty-white bird legs looked even thinner than usual.

"Owen?"

Don't step in here. Don't come in my room . . .

She usually ended up knocking something over. And somehow she'd always make it my fault.

I grabbed my cell off my nightstand—6:03 a.m.

She managed to slur a few words, but I interrupted. "Go lie down, Mom. I'll make breakfast in a minute."

A half hour later, I had gotten dressed, fed my dog, pressed start on the coffee maker, and was sorting through the mail left in a heap by the microwave. My stomach leaped into my throat when I came across a slim letter stamped with a cardinal-red logo. Finally, the letter I'd been waiting for—working my guts out for—since my freshman year.

I exhaled, trying to rid my body of nervous tension. I didn't get anxious very often, but this was Stanford. My dream university. I tore into the envelope. In less than sixty seconds, I'd know if I'd succeeded or bombed.

I read at warp speed. "Admissions Committee carefully reviewed . . . much consideration . . . regret to inform you that your application . . ."

And just like that, my number one goal was facedown in the water.

I wanted to protest, to somehow convince the letter to change its mind and rewrite itself. But reality began to seep in like the damp cold of the drizzling rain outside.

It occurred to me that maybe my mother was right, that I was too ambitious. Maybe the world had enough doctors already.

I crumpled the letter with the rest of the junk mail and hurled the wad clear across the kitchen. It felt good seeing it slam into the recycle bin.

Maybe if there hadn't been a sink full of dishes, I would have sat and sulked.

I rinsed my mom's sticky wineglasses, battling the sting of disappointment. *It's not the end of the world,* I reminded myself. I'd already been accepted to my hometown university, Boston College. Hardly a bad plan B.

And it fulfilled my second biggest goal: to get out of Masonville, Texas. For good. I'd been here three months and still couldn't get used to seeing cattle graze next to busy streets.

I stared at the wet streaks on the kitchen window and shook my head. Another dreary day. It was like a gang of storm clouds stalked this Hill Country town, bringing downpours and gloom and charcoal-colored sunsets.

But the press loved the weather. The ominous drizzle was the perfect backdrop for their never-ending news coverage about the Masonville High suicides. Sure enough, on the TV mounted to the kitchen wall, a reporter was going on and on about the deaths. She was interviewing some psychiatrist whose big words failed to offer any solutions.

What would cause a whole string of people to murder themselves? As much as I prided myself on having logical answers for everything in life, this was beyond me.

I wiped dishes dry while footage played from the last town hall meeting. Same as all the others: sobbing mothers, finger-pointing fathers, school administrators pleading with the crowd to stay calm.

Then it was back to the know-it-all reporter. She was one of the worst. With every suicide at my school, she was among the first to flock to our campus in a race to broadcast the latest tragedy. It was like having ravenous vultures perched over you every day. Watching you. Licking their beaks.

Thanks to the media, the nation was now captivated by the so-called Masonville Suicide Saga. It was reporters like this one who made our brand-new school out to be the eighth wonder of the world, the ultimate reality freak show. I'd go to class today knowing that people all over the world were on the edge of their seats, wondering who would off themselves next. And how.

This was *not* how I'd envisioned my senior year.

I texted my kind-of-girlfriend, Jess: **About to leave.** We'd been spending time together for two months now but had yet to make it official. I wasn't big on commitment, and I guess she picked up on that.

I carried some buttered toast and a cup of coffee into the living room for my mom, who was sprawled on the sofa. Why was she lounging around while *I* made breakfast? This was my life. Most days I was pretty good at dealing with it.

Today? Not so much.

But it wasn't all bad. With the exception of her constantly correcting my grammar and making me learn a new Latin word every week or so, she pretty much left me to myself.

I set the food on the coffee table, along with a bill she needed to pay today. Two weeks ago, actually. Then I grabbed my backpack and headed out the door to see my baby—my 1986 Ducati Scrambler motorcycle. Iconic yellow panels.

My mom may have been a near failure as a parent, but she managed to do a few things right—like get me this Italian bike two years ago for my sixteenth birthday. It needed some work, but I couldn't complain. It was a classic.

Thankfully, today it started right up.

Ten minutes later, I pulled into Jess's circular driveway and stared at her mammoth house, a stark contrast to my place. It's not that my mom couldn't afford better; we were living in her childhood home because it had been willed to me by her parents. To *me*, even though my mom hadn't spoken to them in decades and I seriously had no idea they even knew I existed. The plan was to fix up the place and sell it for a decent profit. And the key to the house showed up just in time, when we needed to get out of Boston fast.

I never did understand how my mom managed to bank a six-figure income while working a few hours here and there as an online tutor—and I didn't really care to ask—but with Jess's dad, there was no mystery. He was a real-estate genius.

I sent Jess a text, then ran up the slippery steps to her front porch, holding the new pink helmet I'd gotten her. When she didn't come out, I grabbed the thick knocker on her front door and hit it against the mahogany.

And there I stood.

And stood.

By now, the drizzle had picked up. I texted Jess again, then looked toward the three-car garage. The door was open. Weird.

As usual, Mr. Thompson's Tesla was gone, but so was Mrs. Thompson's SUV. Jess's convertible was the only vehicle there. I knocked again, with my fist this time, and rang the doorbell. It chimed like a pipe organ.

Nothing.

I called Jess's cell. Straight to voice mail.

Stay calm.

I texted: **Where are you? You okay?**

I sucked in a damp, deep breath and ran into the garage. It wasn't my place to go barging in, but the door to the house was locked anyway. I tried knocking again. Still no answer.

I hurried to my bike, glancing back at the front door through the rain, then put my helmet on and sat with the engine off. I didn't care that I was getting soaked. My pulse pounded against my watch. I forced myself to breathe deep, squeezing my handlebar grips.

Most people in my shoes wouldn't be so alarmed, but most people weren't burying classmates every few weeks. Truth is, I'd been worried about Jess. She'd seemed down lately. She'd get quiet all of a sudden, and not even our inside jokes would get a laugh out of her. When I'd ask what was wrong, she'd just shrug.

I hated that.

Still no word from her, so I started my bike and pulled back onto the street. I noticed an old man in a white, vintage-looking pickup truck parked across the street. More like he noticed me—he stared a hole through me, then tipped his cowboy hat.

I gave somewhat of a nod, then took off, hardly touching the brake all the way to school. Maybe Jess's mom had driven her, but wouldn't Jess have told me? She'd been riding to school with me every day for a month now. Our bonding time, she called it.

Unwelcome images paraded through my mind, vivid and colorful. Jess on her bedroom floor, not breathing. An empty pill bottle a few inches from her open palm.

Maybe her mother is rushing her to the hospital right now.

That would explain the garage door left open, the missing SUV, Jess's parked car.

I exhaled, slow and steady. Jess would never hurt herself . . . would she?

I played my music through my earphones, but that didn't stop the mental footage. A school-wide announcement. A funeral procession. Me in my new black suit I'd worn way too many times already.

I turned my music up. *Jess is fine. I'll see her in a few minutes at school. Nothing to worry about.*

I wiped blobs of rain off my helmet visor, and by the time I neared the intersection two blocks from my school, I could see better. Unfortunately.

Religious fanatics surrounded our campus. They shouted and held up signs, protesting as if our suicidal student body were defiling their holy planet. Their posters said all kinds of cruel, idiotic things. My personal favorite: "Satan lives at Masonville High."

I shook my head. Just yesterday I'd vented to Jess that if Satan *did* exist, he'd be outside waving a sign with them.

From day one, the protesters had creeped Jess out.

"Why do they hate us so much?" she'd say.

I'd just sigh. "Who cares?"

But I had to admit the hostile scene was becoming unnerving. Especially today. My stomach hurt, sloshing with nervous adrenaline, and these people were not helping me fight the urge to puke.

A lanky guy with stringy red hair shook a fist. "It's the end of the world! Repent or perish!"

Wouldn't you know it—traffic stopped, putting me next to him for a good two minutes. Let's just say that if looks really could kill, I would have flatlined.

The light changed, and the freak ran alongside me, shouting nonsense. I made a hand gesture to let him know what I thought of his hate speech.

Eyes back on the road, I instantly squeezed hard on the brake, unable to breathe.

Television network vans lined the curb outside my school. That obnoxious reporter was scurrying to get in front of a camera.

Please . . .

Not Jess.

TWO

A DOZEN NEWS CREWS stood in the rain. Drivers honked. Protesters glared. Catatonic students huddled under umbrellas, gawking at the chaos.

It was a familiar scene I could never get used to.

Teachers motioned for students to get inside the building, but most didn't budge. What could the administrators do about it?

All I cared about was asking around until I found a name for suicide number twelve.

I parked crooked and jumped off my bike, desperately scanning the parking lot. Jess always stood out. But today . . .

Where can she be?

More tormenting mental images.

I spotted one of Jess's friends, Ashlyn, on the front steps of the school. "Hey, have you seen—"

The red-haired nut shoved between Ashlyn and me, planting himself in front of me like he was executing a man-to-man defensive move. "Repent! God is punishing you!"

I could see now through the slimy strands of hair stuck to his face that one of his eye sockets was missing an eyeball—an observation I could have lived without.

"Move!" I pushed past him, nearly knocking him over.

"Child of Satan! Judgment is coming!"

I wanted to unleash my own judgment, but an out-of-breath police officer got ahold of the kook, gripping his arm and knocking his pathetic sign to the ground. "Time to go," the cop said. "You're not allowed on school property."

The man flailed his arms and yelled something about the First Amendment, but the officer yanked harder, forcing him away. Finally, some justice.

I lost sight of Ashlyn but caught up with Stella Murphy and some guy as I sloshed through puddles, drenching the bottom half of my jeans. "Who was it?"

"Don't know yet." The guy sipped some Coke through a curvy straw. "But I heard it was a girl. Alcohol and sleeping pills."

I strained to breathe.

"Either of you guys seen Jess?" My voiced cracked.

Stella painted on lip gloss. "No."

Coke Sipper shook his head.

I took off toward the school. I had no idea where to look for her, but I wasn't just going to stand around. I was nearing the entrance doors when I felt a hand on my shoulder. I turned, and my world was bearable again. Jess.

I hugged her as tight as I could, almost suffocating us both. "Where were you?" I was panting like I'd just run a marathon. She clung so hard to my shoulders that her feet came off the ground. Finally we let go.

"I told you I had tutorials this morning, remember?"

She hadn't told me, but I had no desire to try and prove her wrong. "I saw your car in the garage and I thought . . ."

"I had my mom drive me." She pulled me close again. "That way I can ride home with you."

"That's what I thought. I just . . . Never mind."

I rested my chin on top of her head, holding her umbrella over us as the morbid images I'd had of her surrendered to peace of mind.

Stella caught up with us and wedged herself under our umbrella. "It was Emma Lancaster."

"Emma is number twelve?" Jess's lips quivered. "She—she's in my third-period class."

Stella's eyes narrowed and she leaned even closer. "She *was* in your third-period class."

Jess's chin dropped and her shoulders slumped. I felt like I was watching her sink into an emotional pit—the same hole I'd been trying to pull her out of for about a week.

So much for peace of mind.

Suddenly some man was there, holding out a microphone, motioning to us from the curb. The light on the TV camera made us all squint.

Great. The last thing we needed was a nosy reporter butting into our lives.

"Tell me, any of you know Emma? Did you know she was having suicidal thoughts?"

"Um, I knew her," Jess said, "but—I mean—I didn't . . ."

"I knew her super well." Stella grinned like a pageant girl. "She seemed, like, a little down the last few weeks, but we're all kind of down, ya know?"

There was no disguising her excitement at appearing on TV. "How's my hair?" she whispered to Jess.

"Disgusting."

"Really?" Stella fluffed her long hair with both hands.

"I was talking about you. Your hair looks fine."

Typical Jess. No filter whatsoever.

"Uh, we should go." I grabbed Jess's hand, and we turned our backs on Stella and headed toward the school. I knew already not to press too hard trying to cheer Jess up. Still, I held out hope that we could get through another depressing school day, then put the stress and sadness behind us. I would've really liked to put the whole school year behind us, but with graduation more than two months away, the only option was to tough it out.

I knew I had what it took. But Jess?

We were almost inside when she dropped my hand and stopped walking.

I turned to her. "You okay?"

She stared up at me, exhaustion weighing on her flawless face. "I don't think I can take this anymore, Owen."

A voice came from behind us: "What do you mean by that, Jess Thompson?"

Uh-oh. Principal Harding had appeared out of nowhere, looking pitiful—swollen eyes, soggy hair, splattered rain boots. "I'm arranging for you to meet with a counselor today."

"But I don't need to—"

"It's not up for debate, Miss Thompson." Harding pulled a pink slip and a pen from her raincoat.

Jess huffed. "Uh, you can take that paper and—"

"Of course she'll go, Ms. Harding." I made wide eyes at Jess. She rolled hers, but a second later, she flashed a small grin at me. I smiled back. And winked.

"Teacher's pet," she whispered in my ear, before taking the slip from Ms. Harding like an obedient child. She gave me a bigger grin. Maybe I actually *had* managed to cheer her up.

I'd at least managed to keep her from getting detention.

The walk to Jess's first-period class was gloomy. Most students were moving like zombies. A few hugged. Others zoned out, blocking everything with earphones.

My favorite teacher at Masonville High, Ms. Barnett, stood in the hallway smiling at everyone. Guess it was her attempt at spreading some joy.

We needed it. Seriously.

It's hard to say whose fault it was, but as we neared Jess's classroom, she and a blonde girl majorly collided. Jess managed to hold on to her purse and backpack, but the other girl's stuff flew everywhere.

"Really?" Jess tiptoed over the mess.

"I—I didn't see you." The soft-spoken girl looked up but for less than a second. She dropped to the floor and started grabbing things.

"It's fine," Jess said, without even looking at the girl. "Let's go." She pulled me toward her classroom.

"Wait." I bent down and grabbed a notebook and a few markers. "Here."

"Thanks."

I couldn't tell if the girl's cheeks were always that pink or if she was embarrassed. And I couldn't remember her name—she'd been assigned to show me around the school on my first day, but I'd hardly seen her since.

"Sorry." I handed her another marker off the floor and nodded toward Jess. "She's been stressed lately."

"Um, yeah." The girl zipped her pencil bag. "She's been stressed since kindergarten."

I grinned and snorted—I couldn't help it.

"What did you say?" Jess stepped toward the girl.

She opened her mouth, but then turned and walked off.

Jess huffed. "That's what I thought."

"Easy, babe." I put my arm around her. "Save some attitude for the counselor."

"That's not funny."

I kind of thought it was, but I said sorry anyway. We hugged, then she went to class.

On the way to my classroom, I noticed two stern-looking men wearing rubber gloves rummaging through a locker down the row from mine. It had belonged to Emma Lancaster. Number twelve.

I hadn't been friends with her—couldn't even picture her face—but it still made me queasy to think that we must have walked past each other almost every day.

What could have been so bad about her life that she saw death as the only way out? I mean, my home life had to be as bad as anyone's, if not seriously worse, and I managed to keep it together.

I made it to first period before the bell, but I doubt my teacher would have marked me tardy anyway—not when news of another suicide had just hit. My friend Lance came up next to me, his girlfriend glued to his side. "Number twelve, dude." He ran his hands through his wavy blond hair, then shook his head.

"I know. This school year can't end fast enough."

I'd met Lance my first week at Masonville. He liked motorcycles as much as I did, but when I found out he was a Red Sox fan, I knew we'd be good friends.

I sat at my desk and stared at the Smart Board but didn't read it—just thought about how another student was dead. Gone forever.

And ever.

At least I didn't know her, so I didn't have to go to her funeral.

Two rows away from me was a vacant seat that, just a month ago, had belonged to Brady Hopkins—a popular guy who'd put his father's gun to his temple and pulled the trigger. I closed my eyes, but that only made it worse, the image of his empty chair cemented in my mind.

I hated that chair. Why didn't someone just sit in it? Instead it sat there, cold and lifeless, like Brady—a constant reminder that few things in life are as permanent as death.

As usual, Principal Harding made an announcement encouraging students suffering grief over today's loss to go to the office and meet with a counselor. Also as usual, the guy next to me talked over the announcement, bragging about everything from what size buck he'd shot over the weekend to how fast he'd driven his dad's Ferrari last night down a two-lane highway.

Who hands their kid the keys to their Ferrari?

I pretty much got along with everyone, except this guy—Dan. He was Jess's ex-boyfriend, but he couldn't seem to get the *ex* part through his head. He wanted her back bad, so of course, he hated me.

"Hey, Owen." Dan talked loud enough for everyone to hear. "Your dad ever take you hunting?"

He knew it was just my mom and me. I clenched my jaw and narrowed my eyes at him, ready to fire back, but our teacher stood front and center and told us to get our laptops out. She was looking right at me.

That was the last complete sentence she said all period.

The suicides were hard on us students, but even more draining on the teachers. I was told the first death back in September, when the school first opened, had been considered an isolated incident, but now? Suicide had become more like a plague. Or like some sadistic lottery—any minute another student's number would be up.

My third-period teacher had us move our desks into a circle, then take turns sharing our opinions about why the suicides were happening. As usual, it was hard to get anyone to talk, and the ones who did had lame theories.

One guy actually suggested it might have something to do with global warming. I sighed really loud.

Lance and I were the first ones to make it to our lunch table. I intentionally sat with my back to the window. Outside was the morbid "Rest in Peace" fence, a makeshift memorial to the suicide victims. The chain links were covered top to bottom with balloons, stuffed animals, notes—whatever people could make stick. And there were photos of each suicide victim hung in chronological order according to their last day on earth. Jess always sat next to me, and I didn't want her having to stare at that.

Lance looked at me with a sneaky grin. "You ask Jess to prom yet?"

Talking about stuff like that helped our school day feel normal.

"Yeah."

"Dang!" He pounded his fist on the table. "You beat me to it."

Yeah, right. Lance wasn't the type to move in on his friend's girl. And anyway, he and Meagan had been together for two years. I liked Meagan, but it got a little old the way they spent every second together. Lance and I had hardly been able to hang out, just the two of us.

"Can I ask you something?" I leaned across the table. "How's Meagan doing, you know, with the suicides?"

"Fine." He sipped his Dr Pepper. "She's good. Why?"

"Jess is getting—I don't know. Down, I guess."

"Yeah, Meagan's been worried about her."

"Really?" So it wasn't just me.

After school, I sat on my motorcycle and waited for Jess. Most of the protesters were gone by then, but a few lingered in a nearby intersection. An Asian man rang a tarnished bell. He wore a sign that said, "Do you hear death?"

Um, no.

A guy who looked like he'd quit his job with a traveling carnival stood across the street selling T-shirts that said, "I survived a semester at Masonville High." Even I knew that was tasteless.

I looked out at the untouched land that surrounded the school—tall grass framed by dense woods. It belonged to me, over a thousand acres—part of the inheritance from my grandparents. The plan was to sell it along with the house, but my mom had yet to take initiative to call a real estate agent. Or to make any improvements on the house.

As Jess walked up, I noticed how gorgeous she looked, even in a plain T-shirt—her sun-glossed skin practically begging me to touch it. The holes in her high-dollar jeans were a major dress code violation, but I guess the teachers had given up on getting her to comply.

I got my keys out. "So, how'd it go with the counselor?"

She sighed. "Awesome."

Ah. The one-word answer thing. I didn't like it, but I kept trying. "You feeling better?"

She climbed on my bike and wrapped her arms around me. It felt good. Really good.

"I know what you're thinking, Owen."

"The counselor taught you to read minds?" My stab at comic relief fell flat.

"You think I'm gonna get depressed and go off and—"

"Shut up, Jess!"

She leaned to the side and glared at me.

I didn't mean to yell at her, but I didn't feel like apologizing, either. She'd never once apologized to me. But more than that, I meant what I'd said. I was sick of talking about death. Sick of dreary moods and sulky conversations. And I didn't want to hear the word *suicide* one more time.

I started my bike, and an idea came to me.

Once we got past the parking lot traffic, I sped down the side street beside the school, but instead of heading toward Jess's neighborhood, I veered off the road onto the uncut grass. I made a sharp turn down a dirt trail and drove fast, snaking through forty-foot pine trees. Technically my trees, on my property.

The rumble of my motorcycle sent birds into flight. Jess squeezed tighter. I couldn't see her smiling, but I knew she was.

Surrounded entirely by woods now, I slid to a stop. I'd barely parked my bike when Jess jumped down and took off running like a track star, giggling, darting down a slippery hillside. I laughed and chased after her.

Mud flung from her ankle boots and hit me in the chest. I resisted the urge to pass her, and let her lead the way to what was becoming our spot in the woods—a patch of rocks peeking out from the brush under a tight cluster of towering trees. This is where we came on days like today, when the world was closing in and suffocating us.

I love that feeling of being out of breath but unable to wipe the grin off my face. We collapsed on the rocks, knowing any second the moisture would seep through our clothes. Jess crossed her arms over her bent knees and sucked in air. I did the same.

Other than an occasional bird chirp, the only sound was our heavy breathing. Slowly, I caught my breath. The stampede in my heart became a mild thump, and my arms and legs started to relax.

"You hear from any universities?" Jess gripped my hand.

"Stanford is a no."

"Really?" She sounded more relieved than concerned. "Boston College?"

I stared at the dirt. "Nah, not yet." I was sure that, had I told her the truth, it would have just made her sad.

"Your grades are awesome, Owen. I know you'll get in." She gazed above my head. "I have no clue what I'm gonna do. But I have to get out of my house—out of this jacked-up town."

Jess was smart, but she pretty much blew off school, so there weren't many options for her now.

She dropped her chin. "My dad is really disappointed. All my cousins are at Ivy League schools."

I reached over and ran my fingers through her silky, chocolate-brown hair, then rubbed my hand across her shoulders. I made my way to the back of her neck, thinking maybe I could massage away some of her stress.

"Things will work out," I said.

Honestly, I wasn't sure where she'd end up, and I was even less sure what would become of us. As much as we liked each other, our future was as clear as the mud caked on our shoes.

Jess looked me in the face. "Owen, do you ever feel, like, depressed sometimes?"

Ugh. I'd brought her here to get away from depression, not talk about it. But there was no way I was going to tell her to shut up twice in one day. I'm not that stupid.

She turned to face me. "There's this heavy feeling that weighs down on me sometimes, almost like it's pressing on my chest or something. Like this—" She swallowed hard. "Like this misery that creeps up all of a sudden. Do you know what I mean?"

Yet another drastic mood change. I felt like I was swinging at a curveball I never saw coming. "Is it like—a sad feeling?"

She picked up a rock and threw it, visibly disappointed that I couldn't relate. "It's more than feeling down. It's like this awful emptiness drops over me for no reason at all. It happens during random times at school or when I'm alone in my room. Do you ever feel that?"

"Feelings are overrated, Jess. I live by what I know. The facts."

"It's like this eerie unhappiness that follows me around." Clearly, she'd given no thought to what I'd just said. "And even though I try super hard to ignore it, it finds me. Especially when I lie down to sleep. It's like turning the light off signals this miserable feeling to seek me out. And I wonder if that's what happened to Brady Hopkins and Emma Lancaster and the others. Were they so smothered by this feeling that they decided to end it all?"

I was at a loss. And more worried than ever about Jess.

She scooted closer to me. "This girl today was talking about how Emma said she heard voices. And now she's number twelve. Crazy, huh?"

"They make meds for stuff like that, Jess." I cupped her face and lifted her eyes to meet mine. "Promise me that no matter what you're feeling—no matter what's going through your head—you won't do something stupid. Something permanent. 'Cause if you did, I—"

"Shh!" She slapped her palm over my mouth. It hurt, but I didn't let her know it.

"You hear that?" Her eyes darted in one direction, then another, while the rest of her body stayed frozen. "There's something here."

THREE

"YOU DON'T HEAR THAT?" She stared deep into the woods, not blinking.

"Uh, nope." Okay, so I was picking up on something, but it was faint, and I was hoping she'd drop it. I wanted to get beyond talking and on to other things. "Let's not worry about—"

"I think it's underneath us. What *is* that?"

Once Jess made up her mind, that was it. I gave up on getting my way and made somewhat of an effort to listen. "It's probably a drainage ditch or something. It's been raining for days." It sounded like rapids, liquid tumbling and sloshing.

"Seriously, Owen? It's way bigger than a drainpipe. Listen."

I couldn't have cared less, but out of respect for her, I closed my eyes and silenced my breathing. Sure enough, I not only heard it, I felt it. Something stirring below ground.

"Maybe there's an underground spring." I leaned back against a rock, straightened my legs, and folded my hands behind my head. My work was done.

"So—you're just gonna sit there?"

Should've known.

"All right, Jess. I'll see what I can find."

It didn't take long to notice that the deeper I went into the woods, Jess on my heels, the louder the odd sound got. We walked for what had to be at least half a mile, stepping over unearthed tree roots and piles of leaves reduced to wet globs of brown.

I arrived at a thick wall of brush and branches and looked back at her. "You really want me to get through all this?"

Of course she did.

I kicked some of the limbs, breaking them in half, then pulled at the entangled clutter. Jess helped too. When a few holes opened up, we stopped and peeked through.

Jess gasped. "What's this?"

I scanned the scene—a large enclosed clearing in the woods, so dark that it already looked like dusk in there.

I kicked harder now, eventually making a gap we were both able to squeeze through. We stepped into the dirt-covered area—a thick line of trees framing a nearly perfect circle of empty space. About thirty feet across, if I had to guess.

Jess clutched my hand, and we walked to the center, then stood back-to-back, looking up. Sprawling oak trees formed a ceiling high above our heads, the branches interlocked like bony fingers so that minimal sunlight broke through. It made sense that it was much dryer and cooler inside here—the tree cover was like an immovable dark umbrella.

In a way, it was scenic. But way too dingy to be pretty.

Jess spun around slowly, taking it in. "This is your property, right?"

"Yeah." It was weird to think I owned this.

Given the sound and feel of movement beneath our feet, it seemed if we reached down, we'd touch turbulent water. But there was nothing but dry dirt and crunchy leaves.

Jess wandered to the edge of the tree line. "Check this out."

A web of vines concealed a redbrick water well, weathered and cracked. A rope hung from an old but sturdy wooden crankshaft mounted to the well. I leaned forward and gave the rope a tug. "This thing has to be a hundred years old."

Jess put her cell in flashlight mode, then shined it down. It's hard to say how far down the bottom really was, but it was deep enough that I felt kind of queasy leaning over the side. Nothing but a worn wooden bucket on the ground down there, still attached to the rope. The earth was so dry the mud was cracked.

Jess and I walked around the clearing some more, but we never did locate any water.

Suddenly something made an eerie, high-pitched howl. I would have sworn it was an owl, but Jess got spooked. We'd walked nearly all the way back to my motorcycle when she stopped and yelled my name. I thought she'd spotted a venomous snake or something.

"I left my cell phone in that dungeon."

I didn't waste time getting frustrated—just did the manly thing and started back while she sat on my bike and played music on my phone.

It wasn't hard to spot her neon pink phone case on the ledge of the well. I grabbed it and turned to go.

But this time, *I* got spooked.

Something was rustling in the trees. Not like a creature scurrying along the ground or birds fluttering leaves but something big. Heavy footed. Headed toward the clearing.

All I had time to do was duck behind the well.

I held my breath and waited. Then . . .

It took me a minute to make sense of what I was seeing. An old man in overalls and a cowboy hat, clutching a large pair of limb cutters. He started whistling an upbeat song as he headed straight for the well.

I didn't want to startle him, but I saw no point in hiding anymore. I rose slowly. He saw me but didn't flinch, just smiled and kept coming toward me.

I recognized him now. This was the man I'd seen outside Jess's house this morning. The one who'd stared at me from inside his white pickup.

"You here to help?" He smiled wide.

"Help?"

He didn't pause, just started cutting vines away from the well. He worked like he had the strength of a young man. The whole scenario was super weird.

He nodded toward Masonville High. "You go to that new school over there."

Seemed like it should have been a question. I went ahead and said, "Yeah."

"Tragedy ever since those doors opened." He shook his head. "Untold loss."

I nodded, then peered into the distance, anxious to get back to Jess. Of course I had questions I'd have liked to ask this guy—like, where had he come from, and why bother with this useless well? But I couldn't stand here all day.

I was about to say, "See ya," and go, when he stopped snipping, leaned the cutters against the side of the well, and looked at me. I mean *looked* at me, like he had that morning, like he was staring through my skin.

I swallowed hard. Fidgeted. But couldn't shake the awkward feeling— like I was standing there naked.

His brown eyes were as dark as his skin yet had a golden tint I'd never seen before. They struck me as kind but intense. I felt the need to look away.

"How 'bout you and I have a drink?" He turned to the well and began to crank the handle.

"Um, that's okay. I need to get back. There's a girl waiting on me."

"You worried about her?"

I didn't know if he meant right now or in general, but I said yes. Either way, it was true.

"This town could use a young man like you. One who looks out for others." He'd nearly hoisted the bucket to the top by now.

"Just so you know," I told him, "that well's dry."

"No, it's not."

"Uh, yeah, it is." I tried not to sound rude. "We just shined a light down there."

"No. It isn't."

One more turn of the handle and the bucket was up, sloshing over with water.

"That's . . . I saw it, and it was definitely dry."

The man let out a hearty laugh, then pulled two paper cups from his pocket. He blew in them and used his finger to wipe particles out. Gross.

He scooped water into both cups, then handed me one. It was torn along the rim—used, for all I knew. He lifted his cup as if to say cheers, then downed the water.

"Um . . ." No way I was drinking that water, especially after I looked in the cup. "There's stuff floating in here."

He grinned. "City boys. Think a piece of dirt's gonna kill 'em."

I hadn't told him I'd moved here from the city, but I figured my accent tipped him off.

I tried to hand the cup back, but he wouldn't take it.

"Go on." He had a gentle smile.

"I'll pass." I reminded him that someone was waiting on me, then felt the need to add, "My guess is this water is loaded with bacteria." I dumped it out, then crushed the cup. He took it from me this time.

I thought for sure he'd back off now, but as I turned to go, he piped up. "Brave enough to save his mama's life but scared of a little sip of water."

I froze. Then spun around. "What'd you say?"

I hadn't told anyone what had happened the night my mom and I left Boston for Texas—and I was sure she hadn't either. I had no intention of *ever* telling that story. But it was true. What the man had just said.

"How did you know that?"

He smiled bigger and raised his cup. "Let's have a drink."

That was it. All the strangeness I could take. "I've gotta go." I took off again, faster this time. As I was about to squeeze out of there, I mumbled to myself, "This town's messed up."

"Sure is," he said, somehow hearing me from all the way across the clearing. "Been messed up for a long time."

And with that, he went back to trimming, apparently content for me to go. But I just stood there. There was something this man wasn't telling me.

FOUR

I DIDN'T STAND THERE long before the man asked me another question, still working to tame the chaos of vines around the well. "You have ideas about what's causing the suicides?"

From across the clearing, I made my best attempt at a logical theory. "Seems to me some people are strong, and others—not so much. The weak ones can't handle life's pressures. They give up and end it all, then the stress of the suicides causes other weak people to give in to it themselves. It's a vicious cycle."

"I see," he said. He didn't seem impressed by my answer.

"What about you?" He'd put me on the spot—it seemed fair to do the same to him. "You have a theory?"

The old man turned to face me. "Sabotage."

"Huh?" What was he talking about? I walked fast to the center of the clearing. "You're saying someone's plotting the suicides?"

He nodded, his cowboy hat bobbing up and down.

"How's that possible? Suicide is self-inflicted."

The man rubbed his hands together, wiping away dirt. "Suicide is provoked. Every time." His voice echoed off the trees.

I furrowed my brow. "What do you mean?"

He swept our surroundings with a glance but said nothing.

"Provoked by who?" I probed again.

He just went back to trimming.

That's when it clicked. This man was a conspiracy theorist. Irrational. Deranged, for all I knew. Maybe even a protester along with the other psychos that flocked to my school.

I was out of there.

I drove Jess home, we said our good-byes, and I watched her step inside her marble-floored house. I'd decided to put the weird man in overalls out of my mind, but on my way home, our conversation gnawed at me. How'd he know about my mom? And that well . . .

It was dry. I was sure of it. But the bucket came up full.

I was still some distance away when I spotted a truck parked in my driveway—a blue Chevy I'd never seen before. I pulled up next to it, killed my bike's engine, and sat there, knowing full well what would happen next. I'd open the front door and find some man on the sofa next to my mom. She'd jump up and introduce me to the guy like there was nothing disgusting about the situation.

No, thank you.

I took off. Minutes later, I was blazing down the dirt trail behind Masonville High, then charging through the woods on foot, headed back to the murky clearing.

It was sunset by the time I got there and nearly pitch black inside the tree-shaded circle. I used my cell to light my steps, determined to take a closer look at the well. There was no way I'd get my brain to stop turning long enough to fall asleep tonight if I didn't figure this out.

Yeah, it was eerie here at night, but I wasn't about to chicken out. I pressed my waist against the brick ledge and leaned over the well, careful not to drop my cell. Just like I thought, there was no water down there.

Not a drop.

I was about to turn the handle, but the instant I reached for it, something pressed down hard on my shoulder. My heart nearly leaped out of my chest.

I spun around, out of breath, working hard to steady my light. "What are you doing here?" I'm sure I sounded angry.

The old man stood a foot away, smiling at me from the blanket of black that engulfed the clearing. "Had a feeling you'd be back."

"So . . . you were waiting for me?"

I found that odd. *Really* odd.

He walked past me and sat on the brick ledge. "You have an interest in my water well?"

"Actually, ah . . ." I cleared my throat. "It's my well. I own all this."

His eyebrows shot straight up. "So this is *your* property." I picked up on some sarcasm, like he was a step ahead of me. "Well then, want a drink from *your* well?"

"No, sir. I want an explanation. How'd you know about my life?" I pointed to the well. "And how'd you draw water from a dry source?"

He gave a long exhale. "I imagine you're like most people. Have to see to believe." He crossed his arms. "Problem is, some things you have to believe, or you never will see."

"What are you *talking* about?"

He began to turn the handle. "What do you plan to do with your life, young man?"

"Get back to Boston. Become a doctor."

"You wanna save lives?"

"Yes, sir. I do."

He paused his hoisting of the rope. "Young people are dying, son— right here, at your school. An entire town in upheaval, demanding to know why. Guessing at what to do."

"And?" I took a step toward him, still shining my cell light. "What can *I* do?"

A few more cranks, and the bucket dangled over the well, water spilling over. It made no more sense than it had the first time. "How's that happening?" I demanded.

The old man reached into the pocket of his denim overalls and, like before, pulled out two paper cups. He extended one to me. "Some things only make sense in hindsight."

I was getting irritated now, but I did my best to keep being polite.

"Look, I want you to tell me who you are and what's going on." I shined my light on the overflowing bucket, then back on his face. "Please. I came here for answers."

He grinned, then scooped water into the cups. Held one out to me yet again.

I sighed, my irritation out in the open now. I took the cup and stared at it. "Wait . . ." The rim was ripped in the exact same place as before. "I crushed this cup, but it's not creased."

The man shrugged.

I used my finger to pull out a floating speck. "What's the point of this?"

"Some things only—"

"Make sense in hindsight. Got it." I shook my head. Huffed. Eyed the water. "I drink this, you talk?"

"Get all the answers you want." He lifted his cup to chin level. "And then some."

I raised the cup to my lips, gave a reluctant sigh. "*Utquomque.*" Latin for *whatever.*

And with that, I leaned my head back and swigged it down.

The water tasted normal.

The old man drained his cup, then just stood there. Staring at me.

"So?" I crushed the cup. Again.

"So . . ." He stood. "Now I go."

He walked into the shadows.

"Wait!" I kept my light aimed at him. "Where are you going?"

He lifted an eyebrow like it was obvious. "Home."

"But you said you'd talk to me."

"I said you'd get answers." He pulled the brim of his cowboy hat lower on his forehead, winked, then walked away whistling, apparently fine with walking in the dark.

"Thanks a lot." My tone was loaded with resentment. But what could I do? Wrestle him down and force him to explain? I could still hear him whistling long after he faded out of sight, that same song from earlier.

I stumbled a few times but finally made it back through the woods to my motorcycle, with no more answers than the last time I'd been here. I was shoving my helmet on when it hit me.

Pain.

I mean *pain.* It hijacked my gut. Worst stomachache ever. It felt like that well water had turned to ice daggers in my belly. I'd never felt anything like it before. And my head was throbbing.

Big surprise—the water was obviously unsanitary. What had I been thinking?

I drove home with two goals in mind: don't wreck, and don't barf in the helmet. I almost pulled over several times but pushed through, desperate to get to my toilet bowl and flannel sheets.

I clung tightly to the handlebars with every turn, considering possible diagnoses. The most probable: I'd just ingested a ravenous parasite that was feasting on the lining of my stomach. And giving birth to ice-cold larvae. At an astounding rate.

Don't panic.

I nearly clipped the mailbox as I careened into our driveway. At least the blue truck was gone.

It was all I could do to pull my keys out of the ignition. *Am I really that weak?*

I slid off my bike and accidentally dropped my keys on the damp pavement. By the time I grabbed them, I had a full-blown migraine, the shakes, and what felt like frozen claws trying to slice through my abdomen.

I tried to throw up in the bushes, but nothing came out.

I reached the front door, anxiety gripping me. The porch was spinning. How was I supposed to get my key into the lock? Finally something went my way. I gave the knob a twist, and the door opened.

I normally wouldn't ask my mom for help, but the feeling that death was breathing down my neck compelled me. I needed to know where she put the bottle of ibuprofen and that pink stomach-relief stuff.

"Mom?" My keys crashed onto the wood floor. I stumbled toward the sofa. *"Mom!"*

I buckled and toppled onto my side, my head connecting painfully with the floor.

"Are you here?" For all my effort, I couldn't project my voice beyond a whisper. I rubbed my forehead with one hand and covered my mouth with the other.

The only light on was in the hallway. Wonderful. The one time I didn't want to be home alone.

I heard the patter of Daisy's nails tapping the floor, but I was too disoriented to see where she was. "Help me, girl," I whispered. She panted in my ear.

I lay there in the fetal position and dug my fingers into my sides. My face radiated heat, but my gut remained chilled.

I would have called someone, but I had no clue where my cell was.

I surrendered to the pain and let my eyes drift shut. I considered the real possibility that the water was contaminated and I might not survive drinking it. Had the old man intended to kill me?

I had a sudden, disturbing realization: if I died, it might look like a suicide.

Fear gave way to exhaustion and a final crushing thought.

I don't want to be number thirteen.

FIVE

A BLINDING WHITE LIGHT penetrated my closed eyelids.

Maybe there is an afterlife.

Then a tongue slurped the side of my face, drenching me with drool and reality.

Daisy. "Back off, girl."

I squinted and shielded my eyes from the sunlight. I was still on the living room floor.

So . . . I had cheated death and would live to see another day.

I could only be so grateful—the pain in my stomach was still there, throbbing so bad I wanted to cut my gut open so I could rip it out. It was like a glacier was burrowed in my midsection. At least my headache was gone, but my back was killing me. I missed my mattress.

I sat up like an arthritic grandfather. My mouth was a desert.

From the looks of things, my mom still wasn't home. Typical.

I bent my knees and tried to get a feel for whether I could stand. I leaned on the sofa, then put my feet under me. That worked.

The wall clock read 7:43 a.m. So much for first period.

"Oh no. Jess." I looked around for my phone and spotted it by the front door. I scrolled through a flood of text messages from her, then replied: **Sorry I didn't come get you today. Be at school soon.**

I tossed my phone on the kitchen counter. At least I could fix whatever *I* wanted for breakfast today. I was famished and dying of thirst. Maybe if I ate something hot, like oatmeal, it would melt the freeze in my belly. I microwaved some oatmeal and consumed it, but the ice remained.

I thought maybe a steamy shower would do the trick.

It didn't.

I grabbed some clothes from my closet, then paused. My room was darker than it had been a half hour ago. The sunlight was fading as more storm clouds rolled in. Guess I should have seen that coming. I considered staying home. I had a stomachache, after all. But I needed to keep up my attendance if I wanted to exempt out of finals.

I was dressed and out the door by 8:30 a.m. The sun had officially checked out, and the wind blew harder than usual. I had taken only a few steps down my driveway when I heard a terrible noise—like nails on a chalkboard. No, more like an army of razor blades attacking a jagged rock. I looked in the direction of the racket. Nothing there.

I started to mount my bike, but then I realized that the revolting sound was behind me, closing in. I whirled around.

A jogger entered my line of sight. But she didn't look right.

At all.

What. Is. That?

My body went numb as I tried to make sense of the ghastly scene. A slender, attractive brunette out for a morning jog . . . with what looked like eight-foot chains dragging behind her. The four bulky metal tails grated against the cement, drowning out the rhythm of her tennis shoes pounding the street. The chain links snaked, staggered, and slapped the pavement.

The woman tilted her head from side to side, seemingly on beat with the song in her headphones.

Is this some sort of joke?

She ran past me, and I traced the chains with my eyes, up her legs and back, all the way to a chunky, tarnished shackle fastened snugly around her neck. The metal links were bound to the collar at the top of her spine, just under her ponytail.

As if that wasn't freaky enough, four or five black cords about as thick as my thumb spewed from the back of her head. They jutted straight out several inches, then hung down to the small of her back, swaying from side to side, smacking the chains.

"That's jacked up."

Did I say that out loud? I wasn't sure. But what I was seeing was more than bizarre.

It was somehow *evil*.

The jogger finally paced out of sight. It occurred to me to run to the edge of my driveway and look some more. But no way. I wanted her and her freakish metal trappings to get lost. The skin-crawling sound lingered, making my already soured belly churn even more.

I needed a second to get my head on straight, so I went back inside. I normally wouldn't leave my backpack on the driveway—my laptop was in there—but I was so creeped out, I walked off without it.

I went to the kitchen, splashed warm water on my face, then sank back into the sofa. The ticking of the wall clock was grating. I kept mentally replaying the soundtrack of those grotesque chains.

My mind worked through possible explanations for Freddy Krueger's girlfriend jogging by my house.

She's training for a triathlon, and the weight of the chains and cords are helping her bulk up.

No. She works as a clown—not a happy one who goes to birthday parties but a horrifying one. A clown who leads haunted hotel tours. And she's about to go to work.

Maybe she was on lockdown in a prison and somehow broke free.

While wearing athletic gear.

And headphones.

None of my theories added up, so I turned on the TV. It took a while, but I finally felt myself relax.

I glanced at my cell. 9:06 a.m. I'd just overreacted to the icy feeling in my abdomen, that's all. No need to keep a death grip on the throw pillow. Time to move on with my day.

I locked the door and walked to my motorcycle, that threatened feeling pretty much gone. But seeing my jostled backpack plopped right where I'd left it made me uneasy all over again.

I couldn't get the image of the jogger out of my mind.

What was so scary about her? It had to be the way she looked . . . enslaved—as if, without her knowing it, something had shackled and claimed her as its own. Something powerful. And cruel.

I normally was out of my driveway in three seconds flat, but not this time. My hand hovered over the brake. Maybe the Bloody Mary jogger was circling back.

I glanced around and saw that someone—some kids, probably—had spray painted the word rage in large lowercase letters on the fence across the street.

Losers.

I made it to the stoplight at the end of my neighborhood without seeing any joggers. Should I tell Jess—or anyone—what I'd witnessed this morning?

The light changed, and I pulled forward, glancing at the grocery store parking lot on my right.

"What the . . . ?"

My eyes locked on a well-dressed man at the gas pump. Were those chains draping behind him? Cords coming from his head?

Please, no.

My attention jumped to the girl two pumps down. She had them too.

I drifted into the curb on the grassy center median, and someone laid on his horn. I came to a stop, but my mind was reeling.

"Get out of the road!" a guy yelled. The woman in the passenger seat beside him opened her door and mouthed something at me.

They each had a fat shackle around their neck.

My bike was sideways in the middle of the lane, but I sat there, unwilling to move, terrified of taking my eyes off the metal monsters around me. A mechanic stared from outside the auto repair shop across the street, then waved his arms at me. When I didn't respond, he turned back toward the shop, pulling his chains along. The sound of metal scraping cement invaded my ears.

This is not happening!

It occurred to me to call 911, but the man who had honked at me had gotten out of his car and was now approaching. I managed to grip my bike's handlebars, fully convinced that if I didn't drive away, he'd kill me.

I pulled back hard on the gas and took off. If I happened to plow over the mutated guy, oh well. I made an illegal U-turn and sped back in the direction of my house. I don't know if the light was green or not, but I blazed through the intersection into my neighborhood.

It felt like a bad case of déjà vu. On steroids.

I flung my bike into park and sprinted toward my house like I was being hunted. Was I?

As I reached the porch, I happened to glance at the garage door. Whatever blood remained in my face drained out. The word *suffer* was painted on there, just like the graffiti on my neighbor's fence. How had I overlooked it?

I raced upstairs and locked myself in the bathroom, collapsing to the floor, clutching the sides of the toilet. I tried to barf again and again, but I couldn't. I was panting like a dying dog, drooling on the toilet seat.

What just happened? How did those shackles . . .

Wait—do I have one?

I hadn't noticed anything unusual about my appearance when I'd showered this morning, but everything had changed since then. Humanity was now under attack. Or I was officially psychotic.

I stood slowly, bracing myself against the wall. My legs were Jell-O; my skin, cold and tingly. Fear breathed down my neck.

But I had to know.

I swallowed hard, then inched my way around, eyes shut. I told myself I'd open them when I was facing the mirror above my sink. A few more steps, then . . .

SIX

I FORCED MY EYELIDS OPEN and studied my reflection. No demon dog collar. I exhaled, then turned and checked the back of my head. No freaky dreadlock cords either.

Relief.

I was still bothered by the sight of myself, though. It was like a stranger was looking back at me. I rushed to my room and crammed my face in my pillow. I was beyond delusional. I needed to be locked up—or at the very least, sedated.

Did someone follow me?

I peered out the blinds, then yanked them shut, in full paranoia mode.

The front door! Did I lock it?

I shot downstairs, checked the lock, then ran back up to my room and shoved my desk in front of my door. I burrowed under the covers and hid there. For hours. I drifted in and out of sleep, wrestling over what I had or hadn't seen.

The more I thought about it, the more convinced I became that it was all in my mind, some sort of psychosomatic episode that only felt real.

It's not easy to accept that you're crazy—that your formerly sound mind is now overrun with hallucinations just because you did something rash the night before. I was almost certain the well water had poisoned me. Toxified my brain.

My phone was outside, in a holster on my bike, and it would stay there forever as far as I was concerned. Leaving the house was no longer an option.

My mom still hadn't come home.

Eventually I pulled the covers off and looked for the clock that sat on my bedside table. I'd knocked it to the floor.

2:08 p.m.

I sat up and took a panoramic glance around my room. My stuff was the same, but I felt far removed—homesick even though I was home. I tried convincing myself I'd been sleeping all day, and this morning's horrifying events were merely lingering images from a fever-induced nightmare. But I knew better. My desk was in front of my door. Irrefutable proof.

It hit me that I was missing track practice. Then it occurred to me that I might have a life-sucking brain tumor. What if, instead of sitting barricaded in my room, I should have been rushing to the nearest emergency room? Getting prepped for surgery?

But I trembled at the thought of going *anywhere*.

I was desperate to talk to someone—Jess, Lance, my mom—anyone who knew me before I became delusional. I needed my phone, but could I grab it and get back inside without being mauled by steel-trapped zombies?

I lifted one slat of my wooden blinds up half an inch. No one.

I grabbed a sweatshirt and pulled the hood over my head, then dug in my junk drawer until I found sunglasses. My Louisville Slugger baseball bat in hand, I drew a deep breath. Time to make my move.

I took slow, calculated steps down the stairs. Daisy sat by the front door, wagging her straggly tail.

"No walk today, girl. No way."

I clutched my bat in one hand and slowly turned the lock with my other. Visions of this morning's jogger overwhelmed me. I imagined her leading a charge against me, kicking the door down the instant I cracked it open, followed by the disgruntled guy who'd honked at me and a horde of other chained and corded monsters.

I peered through the sheer curtain panel. The coast was clear.

My hand hung motionless on the doorknob. I could hear my stampeding pulse. My stomach was subzero. But I had to act.

I swung the door open and sprinted to my bike, avoiding looking at the malicious word painted on my garage door. In seconds, I had my phone and was back inside. I slammed and locked the door, then pressed my weight against it, fighting to catch my breath.

Jess had texted me: **Where are you???!!!!**

I swiped my phone, anxious to call her, then stopped. How do you tell your prom date you're seeing chains and cords everywhere? Hanging off people?

I hadn't talked to my best bro back in Boston in a month, and he was too far to help me. I called Lance, pacing in circles in my living room while his cell rang. I got his voice mail.

"Hey, Lance. You know I don't usually leave messages, but—I—I just really need you to call me. Like, the minute you get in the locker room. Something really, um, terrible happened to me today. I mean, I'm okay, I think, but—no, I'm not okay. Just call me."

I hung up and texted him.

I wasn't sure about calling my mom. I couldn't remember the last time I'd gone to her for comfort. I only recalled babying her a million times. Bringing her boxes of Kleenex after bad breakups and putting damp washcloths on her forehead on hungover mornings.

I collapsed back onto the sofa and called her anyway.

"Hey, Owen."

She sounded sober and upbeat. I instantly felt a little better.

"Hey, Mom, where are you?"

"I stayed at Teresa's house last night. I brought my laptop with me. Been editing papers all day. You remember Teresa, don't you?"

Yeah, right. She was at some guy's house. I didn't know whose, and I didn't care.

"I'm sorry. I should have let you know I wasn't coming home."

As usual, our roles were reversed.

"I've had a really, really bad day, Mom."

"You have?" I cherished the sound of concern in her voice. "What happened?"

"I don't feel good. I'm kind of—seeing things or something. Scary things."

"Oh." There was a long pause. "What do you mean?"

"People don't look right." I turned sideways on the sofa and dug my feet under a cushion. "It's hard to explain. When are you coming home?"

"In about a half hour. Why don't I pick up some chicken?"

"No! Please. Just come straight home."

"Oh . . . um, okay. I can do that."

My mom was so different when she wasn't drinking. She actually kind of felt like a mom.

I counted down the minutes until she came home, but I wasn't sure what to tell her. If I spilled my guts, she'd be no help—she'd just head straight for her liquor stash. If *I* couldn't handle something, *she* sure couldn't. And drinking was her go-to crutch. That and pathetic men.

I clung to the sofa and took comfort in the normal humans on TV, even on the Shopping Channel. Why didn't the people outside my house look normal? It just didn't add up.

I sat there drowning in my own cognitive typhoon until finally I heard the garage door open. I turned and faced the kitchen, knowing she'd enter from there any second. I was desperate to see a familiar face.

"I'm in the living room, Mom."

I heard her fumbling through the mail. Seriously? She went traipsing down to the mailbox at the end of the driveway instead of coming straight in to check on me?

"You got a letter from Boston U."

"Great, Mom—can you please come here?"

Finally, I heard junk mail hit the recycle bin. But then . . .

No.

I tried to deny the echo in my ears—metal skimming the tile floor, then the hardwood. I couldn't bring myself to look. I stared into my lap, hardly blinking.

"How are you feeling?" I could see her silhouette in my peripheral vision, but I didn't dare lift my head.

My phone dinged. It was Jess: **You okay? I'm worried. Call me!**

My mother lowered herself into the lounge chair across from me. A nauseating quiver crept up my back.

"What happened to you today?" She opened an envelope.

"I told you. I've been seeing really horrible things."

I felt her staring at me, silently looking me over. "Are you on something?"

I balled my fists and glared at her, no longer slumped over. How dare she? Good news, though—there was nothing weird about her appearance. I was still incensed but more relaxed than I'd felt all day. "Mom, why would you even ask me that?"

"Well, you sounded strange on the phone. And you wouldn't be the first teenager to get high."

I popped my knuckles—mostly because it drove her nuts—then crossed my arms. "Getting plastered isn't *my* thing."

She averted her eyes, guilty as charged. But she was never one to admit to her vices.

She got preoccupied again, digging through that stupid envelope, but that was fine with me. I was just relieved to see her looking normal. I studied her—she wore a flowing skirt with a loose-fitting silky blouse. A scarf encircled her neck.

Why had I thought I'd heard chains scraping across the floor? Maybe it had come from outside. Or maybe I was a basket case.

My mom shifted her weight, removed her shoes, and tucked her legs up on top of the chair cushion.

Clank. My adrenaline kicked in again.

"So are you sick?" She reached across her chest up to her shoulder and unwound her scarf, a layer at a time.

"I just don't feel like—"

It was like my lungs just quit working. My mother's scarf cascaded to the rug, and now I could see it. A shackle. Hulking, rusty, squeezing Mom's throat. I must have looked like I was about to pass out.

"What, Owen? You don't feel like what?" She paused, then leaned away from me. "You're scaring me."

Irony at its worst.

I felt myself inhale. "I just—don't know—what else to tell you."

She sighed, then put one foot on the floor and bent forward in her chair, extending a hand. I shuddered back into the couch cushions. She pressed her eyebrows together.

"Hand me the remote, Owen!"

I should have known she wouldn't push me for more information. She was an expert at changing the subject. I guessed she just didn't care enough.

I didn't have the remote. It was at the end of the coffee table, beyond our reach. "I'll get it," I said.

Too late. She was on her feet. My jaw dropped as a wall of chains draped over the back of her chair, forming a metallic canopy. There were too many to count. She bent over, and a dozen gnarled cords slid and dangled down her left shoulder. She stepped to grab the remote, and the chains jerked from behind the chair, slamming to the floor. It was like a crate loaded with pots and pans was hurled down from the second story of our house, shattering at her feet.

I sprang up and covered my ears, stumbling backward, afraid to be in the same room with her. She didn't notice—the noise or my reaction.

"Owen, bring me a Diet Coke out of the fridge. And take some Aleve. That'll make your headache go away."

In the midst of my catastrophic mental breakdown, I had two oddly practical thoughts. One, I never said I had a headache. Two, as far as I knew, we were out of Diet Cokes.

I took a few steps in the direction of the kitchen without turning my back on her. "Mom?"

"What?" She flipped through the channels, totally unaware I was dying inside.

Frustrated as I was with her, I hated the sight of that shackle encasing her throat. Where had it come from? Was it really there?

Either I needed serious help, or she did.

"What, Owen? Out with it."

"Never mind." I should have known better than to look to my mother for sympathy. She didn't have it in her.

I opened the fridge, refusing to cry. Sure enough, no Diet Cokes. I slammed the door shut.

Why is this happening to me?

I grabbed a stack of bills by the microwave and launched them at the wall, then collapsed into a chair at the breakfast table and stared out the window, rocking back and forth like a lunatic. As if on cue, Jess's Mustang convertible pulled up.

I darted out the door at the back of the kitchen and sprinted through the garage toward the driveway. I didn't care if some scary figure lurched at me. If I could just get to Jess, my world would flip right side up. At least for a moment.

The door on the driver's side opened, and I ran faster. She reached out to me. I could smell her perfume.

But then my legs jarred to a halt. Refused to go any farther.

I couldn't hug her. Couldn't touch her.

No way.

I couldn't get near anyone with a shackle.

SEVEN

It was impossible to sleep. Or eat. Or concentrate.

All of mankind, including the people closest to me, had morphed into metal-clad aliens overnight. I didn't know if they were out to harm me or not, but I was terrified of them either way.

It was eleven o'clock at night, eight hours since I'd seriously offended my girlfriend, and she was still texting me every couple of minutes. Jess had never been shy about dropping four-letter words, but this was getting ridiculous.

Don't get me wrong—I understood why she was upset. Right when I should have thrown my arms around her, I stared at her in horror, then ran like she was infected. But for all I knew, she was.

I was still too frightened to try and reconcile with her.

Lance had called, but I had ignored him, too, in case he was shackled and chained like the rest of them.

Why wasn't I?

I sat next to Daisy in the squeaky bed I'd inherited with the house and tapped my head against the wall. For the first time ever, I let the thought tiptoe in . . .

Maybe I should escape. For good. Just . . . end it all. My mom had more than enough sleeping pills.

No. That's wrong. I can't.

I tried to focus on something else, like piecing together some answers. But the dark ideas kept coming.

I could sit in my car in the closed garage with the engine on.

Maybe I could borrow Lance's hunting rifle.

I shook my head. What was *wrong* with me?

And then I started to smell something. It was nasty. Like rotten meat. And getting stronger.

Daisy sat up and sniffed the air.

"What is that, girl?"

I checked my trash can—just a few scraps of paper and an empty Nutella jar. I poked around in the closet and under my bed, but I didn't see anything. Oh well. It stank bad, but I had much bigger problems. I had to *think*: come up with a reasonable explanation for my circumstances, and more important, a way out—one that didn't involve a coffin.

The weird thing was, I felt doomed, but it was everyone else who *looked* doomed.

I powered up my laptop and searched for "people wearing chains." All that came up was stuff about fashion trends, jewelry, and some blog about a supposedly hilarious picture someone took of a Walmart shopper.

I didn't believe in extraterrestrial beings, but just in case, I clicked through a bunch of websites about alien invasions. None described anything like what I was seeing.

I decided to search for "seeing things that aren't there." That didn't help my anxiety one bit. From what I read, I was most likely suffering from schizoid personality disorder—a diagnosis that scared me so bad I slammed my laptop shut and buried every inch of my body under my covers.

It's a strange thing to hope that you have a brain tumor, but I'd take that over some incurable mental disorder. At least brain tumors are operable.

Sometimes.

I made up my unstable mind. When the sun came up, I'd check myself into the hospital, even if it meant having shock treatments or my skull sawed open. Sure, I could end up banished to some godforsaken insane asylum, but that was better than suffering in ignorance and denial. Probably.

By four thirty in the morning, though I didn't feel like eating, my frozen stomach was shrieking for food. I left the protection of my room, went to the kitchen, and forced down a peanut butter and jelly sandwich and a sip of milk. The silence while I sat at the table drove me nuts—or more nuts. I was miserable. This degree of loneliness was foreign to me. It was like I was stranded alone in the middle of the ocean, yet my worst fear was that someone would find me.

I thought stuff like this only happened in nightmares or movies. But here I was, trapped in a demented universe—a real-life zombie apocalypse undetected by everyone but me.

I didn't know if it was real or imagined, and I couldn't decide which was worse.

Slouched over in my chair, I clung to hope the best I could. Surely I'd find a solution. I was, after all, in the top 5 percent of my class, the go-to guy to score a clutch basket when the stakes couldn't get higher. I never claimed to be a Boy Scout, but if anybody could find his way out of a wilderness, I could.

I pulled my shoulders back and sat up straight. *I trust in logic. Reason always prevails. I'll figure this out.*

Despite my confident resolution, I was desperate to get back under my bedsheets. It was the only safe place on the planet, as far as I was concerned.

I tiptoed up the stairs and down the hall, paranoid that I'd wake my mother, even though I usually couldn't wake her when I tried. Once I passed her bedroom, I let out a deep breath I hadn't even realized I'd been holding. I was relieved to be that much closer to my room, even if it did smell like something had died in there.

But wait. My mom's door was open.

I knew what I needed to do, but it took me a second to find the courage.

I went back.

Her night-light cast dim golden hues, just enough for me to see her sprawled across her mattress in a drunken coma. I took a careful step forward, then another. As much as I hoped there'd be nothing, from a few feet away I could see chains flung in every direction. And the nauseating shackle.

Time to face my fear.

I stood at the foot of her bed and watched her sleep. She was on her back but angled onto her right side, breathing through her open mouth. Her petite body was framed by the eerie metal mass. Cords were coiled like snakes through her disheveled hair. I leaned in. From this close, they appeared to be braided strands of a dark, leatherlike material studded with tiny, sharp-looking specks—chips of glass and ivory or bone, if I had to guess. The cords got thinner on the ends, like rat tails, and seemed as pliable as cable wires. Not that I was willing to touch one.

I moved closer, bracing myself against the mattress, and zeroed in on a chain dangling a foot away from me. Freezing air assaulted my face. The links were more massive than I'd realized—at least five inches long and as thick as my thumb. I exhaled, and a cloud formed around my chin.

It was an out-of-body experience, watching my hand glide in slow motion toward the metal. Surely it wouldn't kill me to touch it.

Right?

Finally, the tip of my finger made contact. The metal was frigid. I jerked away, but then pressed in again, trying to clutch the chain with my palm. I couldn't. My fingers didn't wrap all the way around, and I couldn't hold on anyway. Too icy.

I blew warmth on my trembling hand, making more fog, then gathered the corner of a plush blanket and wrapped both hands in it. I reached a third time, then hesitated. The colliding metal might wake my mother . . .

No. Only I would hear it.

I grabbed the chain and pulled as hard as I could, but it was impossible to lift it even an inch. I let go and traced the winding links with my eyes, focusing harder when I spotted a bizarre apparatus attached to the bottom link, hanging off the side of the bed—a half cylinder with a hinge in the middle. Some sort of open cuff.

It had dents and dings like it had been dragged all over creation behind my mother, and it appeared scorched inside, stained with black soot. Cold as it was, I ran my finger over the cuff, venturing to feel inside, then touching the outside.

I felt something rough under my numb finger. I reached for Mom's cell on the nightstand and shined the light on the cuff.

Couldn't be.

I blinked and blinked, but they wouldn't go away. Words, chiseled into the cuff in crooked, sloppy letters like a small child had scribbled them on there.

charles allen mabry

Who?

My delusions were getting more far fetched. This had to be coming from inside my head, even though I had no idea how I could have dreamed up anything like this.

I counted fifteen chains in all, each with a cuff suspended on the end. I stepped to the side to examine another but was drawn instead to two straggly cords intertwined among the chaos spewing from the back of my mother's head.

Just when I thought I'd studied them enough, I saw something toward the end of a cord—a grayish tattoo-looking mark etched into the black pigment:

angry

All lowercase.

There was no question now. I'd totally lost it.

I collapsed to the floor. I was in a fight against despair—and losing. Then . . .

No. Freaking. Way.

I shined my mom's cell at the ceiling.

victim.

Lowercase letters. Black graffiti.

The phone slipped to the floor, and my mother tossed in her bed. That sent me scrambling out of her room, and I didn't stop until I was in my bed, hugging a pillow so tight I thought it might rip open. Just like my world.

I needed help—competent, extensive help from a mental health expert, with strong meds. And maybe a straitjacket.

I stayed curled in a ball for hours.

"You gonna make breakfast?" Mom. At least some things hadn't changed.

I wasn't sure if it was the depression, the chill in my stomach, my ailing mind, or my body physically shutting down that pinned me to my mattress, but I could barely move. I heard my mother's chains clanking down the hallway, getting closer.

I was much better at creating cover stories than coming clean, but it was time to tell the uncensored truth. My mom wouldn't take it well, but at least I might be able to talk her into driving me to the ER—although the thought of leaving the house terrified me, not to mention being confined in a car with a shackled driver.

She burst into my room and looked at me without a hint of motherly affection. "Get out of bed, Son."

I propped myself up on my elbows and cleared my throat. That took a lot of effort. At least the rancid smell in my room was gone.

"Mom, who is—"

"Owen . . ." She narrowed her eyes. "You're so pale. Are you okay?"

"No."

"What's the matter?" She stepped forward, dragging her metal.

"I told you. I'm seeing things. Awful things that I shouldn't be seeing."

"Like . . . ?"

"Chains." I pushed the sheets back and put both feet on the floor. "Words. A name. All kinds of irrational things."

"I don't under—"

"I don't understand either, Mom! But it's happening!" I was on my feet now, pacing.

"You need to calm down."

"You need to *help* me!" I dug my fingers into my scalp. Thoughts swarmed in my head like agitated wasps. "Who's Charles Allen Mabry?"

She flinched.

"Wait, Mom, do you—you actually know him?" I moved toward her. "Is that a real person?"

My whole life, I'd known that my mom kept secrets from me. I could only hope she'd be honest now.

She faced the window, then snapped her head around toward me. "What are you trying to do? Dig up my past? Throw it in my face?"

"What? I—no. I just—"

"I've done the best I can, Owen. Mind your own business!"

She started to storm off, but I grabbed her arm and made her face me. Her chains gathered at my ankles.

"So you *do* know him?"

She did nothing but breathe hard.

"Mom, tell me. I have to know!"

Her chin sank into her chest.

"Mom!"

"It was a long time ago," she said. More like mumbled.

"So Charles Mabry is real?"

She pulled her arm away and looked up, her lips pressed together tight. "You were what, four years old? Gimme a break!"

She ran out of the room.

I fell back onto my bed. I didn't think it was possible to become more confused.

Eyes closed, I thought back, panning through memories as fast as I could. *Charles Mabry.* Then it hit me. Charlie—the shaggy-haired guy who reeked of cigarettes and beer. He'd hung around the house for a while, a few months maybe, when I was little. I remember he got mad and smashed some holes in the wall with my T-ball bat, but that's about all I could recall.

I tried to come up with a reason—some sort of formula—that would explain how I saw that man's name etched on a cuff dangling from one of my mother's chains. I got nowhere.

I'd been convinced I was hallucinating . . . but what now?

The front door slammed, and I watched through the blinds as my mother jerked her SUV into reverse. So much for having her drive me to the hospital. Oh well, I needed to rethink my plan anyway—go back to when everything started and work my way forward.

It didn't take long. It was obvious. All hell had broken out after I made the asinine decision to drink that well water offered by the bizarre man in the woods.

I needed to know what was in that water.

I had a new plan now. But I dreaded going through with it.

EIGHT

I THREW ON A SHIRT and jeans and my American Eagle baseball cap and grabbed my mom's spray bottle of Mace from her nightstand, just in case.

Time to hop on my bike and drive to the woods behind Masonville High—easier said than done. My new agoraphobia threw a major kink in my plan.

I stood at the front door squeezing my keys, waiting for the fear to subside. It didn't. I leaned and stretched from side to side and rolled my neck in circles, trying to loosen up and get a grip. Then my cell phone rang, and I jumped, hurling my keys in the air.

Calm down!

I looked at my phone. Jess. I couldn't ignore her forever.

"Hello?" I already wondered if answering was a mistake.

"Wanna tell me what's going on?" That's the clean version.

"I, uh, don't feel good."

"Well, I'd like to be there for you, Owen, but you won't let me. Why did you run away from me yesterday? And why aren't you returning my texts?"

"I'm dealing with something. I drank some water in the woods, and everything's been messed up since."

"What?" She sounded even more annoyed now.

I took a deep breath. *Here goes nothing.* "Jess, I've been seeing things. I thought it was all in my head, but then something happened this morning, with my mom, and now I'm not sure. Does that make sense?"

"Um . . . no. Have you gone to the doctor?"

"Yeah." So I lied. Like I was going to admit I'd done nothing but hide under my covers.

"You sure this isn't about prom?"

"What?"

"I've heard from, like, all these people that you'd rather go with Cindy Rosenberg. Is that it? You're ignoring me 'cause you're too scared to tell me?"

Seriously? Jess was still in high school world. I wanted to tell her how ridiculous she was being, but all I could come up with was, "I barely know Cindy."

"Well, Stella said she heard you say you'd much rather go with her. Prom is in a month, Owen. I can't believe you'd pull this."

Nothing about the prom scene was even remotely appealing at this point, but I promised over and over that I wanted to go with her, not Cindy. It didn't matter, though.

Finally I got tired of it. "You know what, Jess, you're right. This is all a big scheme to dump you."

"It is?"

"No!" I pounded my fist against the door. Daisy tucked tail and ran. "I'm not doing well, Jess. Can you please try to understand?"

"Oh, I understand fine." She hung up on me.

Wonderful. Was I wrong to expect a little compassion? Maybe the cords in her head were preventing her.

I slid my phone into my pocket and refocused on finding the nerve to leave my house. I counted to three, then forced myself to walk—more like sprint—to my motorcycle.

I actually liked that it was drizzling. Surely that would discourage metal-bound joggers from taking to the streets.

I drove fast, refusing to look at drivers, but I couldn't shut out every-thing. My icy gut churned when I saw spiteful, black-letter graffiti stains on several houses and on the side of a fast-food building.

I passed Jess's neighborhood, which sank me further into loneliness. I missed her—the old her, with her pretty, unshackled neck and nothing but soft hair hanging from her head.

I made it down the dirt path and parked in the same wooded spot as before, then checked an incoming text. Jess again.

I thought you cared. Have you lost your mind?

There was no right way to answer that.

I charged through the woods, feeling creeped out, but I made it to the clearing unharmed. The sound of the rampaging waters was just as noticeable as two days ago, only now it caused the hairs on the back of my neck to stiffen.

I peered into the well. It was totally dry, the bucket sideways in the dirt.

I wondered what would happen when I drew the bucket up—if it would inexplicably hold water like it had for the old man.

Where was he? I looked around, nervous he'd sneak up behind me again. But I'd welcome the chance to ask him some questions. I had a long list of them.

As I turned the handle, I battled the feeling that I was being watched—spied on by something predatory lurking in the woods. Maybe this was the strange sense Jess had been talking about. Or maybe my schizoid paranoia was flaring up.

It wasn't easy to shine my cell light into the well and turn the handle at the same time, but I managed it. And there, before my disbelieving eyes, the bucket steadily filled with water. Out of nowhere. Water level rising with every turn of the crank.

I didn't stand around and marvel. I just scooped water into the plas-tic bottle I'd brought. I let go of the crank, and by the time the bucket hit the dry well bottom, I was already hurrying across the clearing.

The walk back to my bike was uneventful, apart from the unsettling compulsion to look over my shoulder every two seconds.

I was nearing my neighborhood when I noticed two small boys

running up a driveway, having a blast in their swim trunks in the afternoon drizzle. I stared at their bare backs. There was nothing—no chains, no cords. I slammed the brake. Had the poison finally passed through my system?

A lady—I assume their mother—stepped onto the front porch, holding beach towels.

"Ugh!" I rammed a fist into my open palm. She was shackled.

Confusion squeezed my brain like a tight-fitting helmet. The kids had no metal. Why? And how come that lady had two chains while my mother had more than a dozen? And what was up with those big cuffs at the ends?

My aggravation level was near boiling. When I pulled up to a stop sign that had *die* painted on it, my frustration spiked. I drove way too fast the rest of the way home.

Having a dad would have come in handy my whole life, but never as much as now. I wished I had a father to run to. Not a coach. Not a friend's dad. My own dad. But he'd walked away when he found out my mom was pregnant. Slammed the door and never looked back.

My mom felt the need to throw that in my face whenever I'd ask about him. It would shut me up. Like she wanted.

What kind of man marries a woman but makes her swear not to get pregnant?

I flung myself on the sofa in front of the TV. Daisy flopped down at my feet. Everything in TV land looked fine.

Whatever.

I was determined to get that water sample to Ms. Barnett, my advisory teacher who taught chemistry. If I came up with a good enough excuse, I was sure she'd help me. The thought of going to school gave me chest pains and shortness of breath, but I wasn't going to let that stop me.

Only sissy boys get scared. One of my mom's ex-boyfriends had taught me that. Come to think of it, I'm almost positive it was Charlie Mabry.

There was a knock at the door. No need to ask who was there. No matter who it was, I didn't know them anymore.

"Owen, it's me."

Lance.

It felt good to hear my friend's voice. I turned the lock and begged the universe to let me see him without anything around his neck.

No such luck. He and his girlfriend, Meagan, stood on my porch, both shackled and chained.

"Hey, dude, we've been worried about you. Are you all right?"

I gave him a blank stare. He returned the favor. Meagan squeezed Lance's hand, looking like she'd rather be . . . well, anyplace else.

"You gonna let us in?"

I was afraid he'd ask me that.

I opened the door and stepped away. Then came the stomach-churning sound of chains scraping the floor.

Lance didn't hesitate to take charge. "Meagan, why don't you hang out here while we go upstairs and talk a minute?"

I didn't allow shackled people in my room, but okay.

Meagan gave him a sweet smile, then took a seat on the sofa. She really was cute, apart from her metal trappings, of course.

Lance followed me up the stairs. It was all I could do not to cover my ears. I sifted through the events of the last two days at hyperspeed, trying to settle on how I'd break the news. I sat stiffly on the corner of my bed. Lance relaxed on the floor.

"You skipped practice to come see me?" I said.

"Coach said it was fine." Lance reached up and grabbed a sports magazine off my desk and thumbed through it. "I mean, he wasn't happy yesterday when you missed practice, but when you were absent again today and no one had heard from you, I think he was more worried than mad. Are you gonna be okay for the meet tomorrow?"

About that. How do you run a race while dodging chains and swatting people's cords out of your face? "I don't know. I'm really . . ."

He closed the magazine. "Are you down or something?" He was probably worried I'd be number thirteen. His instincts weren't far off.

"Yeah, I'm down, but it's not what you think. It's worse."

"What do you mean?" He scooted closer. "Did your mom do something?" Since moving to Texas, I'd only told Jess about my mom's drinking. But Lance had sort of picked up on it after being at my house a few times.

"No. I did something. Something really stupid."

"Okay . . ."

I rubbed up and down on my face a second, then started spilling my guts. I told him every deranged detail, starting with how I'd drunk water from a well that had made me so sick I'd thought I might die. He asked me if I was feeling better now, so that's when—after I warned him not to freak out—I told him about the chains and the cords and the graffiti everywhere.

Confessing made me feel lighter, like I was pulling myself out of quicksand. What a relief to have a friend like Lance.

Too bad things tanked from there.

Lance searched my face, a half smile on his. "Chains. Right."

His disbelief hit me like a cannonball in the chest. "I know it's ridiculous, Lance, but please try to understand."

He stood and crossed his arms while I fidgeted with my sheets.

"You're not making any sense, Owen."

"I know, but I need you to believe me anyway."

"Help me get this. Who do you see wearing these chains and stuff?"

"Everyone." I left off the part about not seeing it on the little kids. That was too much to explain right now.

"So, what about me?" He licked his lips and grinned. "You see something?"

The longer I said nothing, the less he grinned.

"Do you?"

I sensed this would be a defining moment.

"Yes. On you. Meagan. Jess. My mom. People I don't know, too."

He sighed and rubbed his forehead, hard. "Owen, you need to go to the hospital. You got ahold of some bad crap, and it's seriously twisting your mind."

"I know—I thought that too. But then something happened this morning, with my mom." I knew my story was growing even less believable, but I had to keep trying.

He shifted his weight and sighed. "And?"

I explained about seeing the chain cuff with the guy's name on it and my mom's reaction when I asked her about him. I hoped Lance was about to help me put together some clues, throw out some possible explanations. Instead, he threw his hands up. "So you see chains on me? Right now?"

I wanted to knock the smirk off his face, but at the same time, I understood it. He was barely wading in the madness I'd been drowning in for two days.

"Yes. You have a shackle around your neck and three chains attached in the back."

"And I've got spooky tentacles coming out of my head?"

"More like cords. But I can't see how many. You'd have to turn around."

That did it. He gripped my shoulders. "Owen, this is insane!" I don't think he meant to squeeze me that hard.

"Did you hear what I said?" I stood and pleaded my case. "I see it! Clear as day! And I hear it too. And the name on my mom's chain cuff—"

"There's nothing there! Nothing's hanging from my neck or poking out of anyone's head." He pointed to his reflection in the closet door mirror. "See?"

"I understand that you can't—"

He called me a name I don't feel like repeating. I sat back on my bed and slouched over. Buried my face in my hands.

Lance moved to the doorway and stared back at me. "Look, man, I'm sorry, okay? Just . . . get some help. I'll tell Coach you have a migraine or something. Let someone figure out what's wrong with you, all right?"

I couldn't hear his footsteps going down the stairs, just the grating racket of his chains. I watched out my window as he and Meagan got in his Jeep and left.

I leaned against the wall and slid to the floor, my fists balled so hard my nails left marks in my skin.

The closest guy friend I had in this worthless town didn't believe me.

It was depressing, but it only hardened my resolve. I had to get to school in the morning and have that water tested. But how would I survive a crowd?

What else would I see?

NINE

My MOTHER STAYED IN her room all morning. I put some toast on a plate in the microwave for her. I wasn't trying to be thoughtful; I just missed my old routine.

If I left in five minutes, I'd have enough time to give my sample to Ms. Barnett, then get back on my bike and off campus before the first-period bell rang. I honestly didn't care anymore about class attendance or schoolwork or track meets.

No need to factor in time for picking up Jess. I figured she'd be at Emma Lancaster's funeral this morning, anyway. Hopefully lots of people would. I wasn't happy the girl was dead, but I did like the idea of the hallways being less crowded.

I promised myself I'd do what I had to this morning without over-thinking it, without letting fear get the better of me.

I'd just sat down on my motorcycle when a familiar, sickening sound sent quivers swimming through my body. The female jogger I blamed for triggering this whole psychotic upheaval was jogging past my house again. I was sure it was her. Like I'd ever forget that woman.

I took heart. She still struck me as evil personified, but she didn't send me into a panicky whirlwind this time. I needed that boost of confidence.

As soon as I turned onto the side street by my school, I could see protesters swarming, only this time there were chains and cords all over the place. My palms started to sweat. It felt like my throat was swelling shut. I pulled off the road and inhaled, long and slow.

The weight of uncertainty sat like a boulder on my chest. But I couldn't turn back, not until I had some answers. A logical, reliable explanation. And hopefully a cure.

I eased my way back onto the street, giving a thank-you wave to a driver who was nice enough to let me into the flow of traffic. Never mind that she had hardware gripping her neck.

I tried to calm myself. *They look like monsters, but they don't seem out to kill you.* My body wasn't buying my pep talk. I was getting more light headed by the second.

I managed to pull into a parking spot. That felt like a real accomplishment. So did peeling my fingers off the handlebars, one by one. I clutched my backpack straps—my specimen bottle inside—then made up a mantra: "Act like you don't see a thing. Get to Ms. Barnett. You can do this."

Somebody slapped the back of my shoulder and about sent me into cardiac arrest. I pulled it together as fast as an unstable person can. It was one of my track buddies. "Hey, Walt." I slipped my helmet off, mumbling my mantra.

"You're running in the meet today, right?"

"Um, probably not." Okay, so I *could* carry on a conversation while surrounded by metal-clad humanity. Good to know.

"Dude, Coach is gonna kill you."

That was a very real concern of mine.

"I'll talk to him," I said, even though I knew I'd be long gone before seventh period.

I kept my eyes pasted to the pavement as Walt and I walked up the steps and into Horrorville—the foyer by the front office. The clashing of hundreds of chains dragging every which way overloaded my senses. And it was freezing.

Walt eyed me. "Hey, you okay?"

"I don't feel good. But I'll be fine." I tried to pull off a grin, but my cheeks were too cold.

Why did my school feel like Antarctica? Walt didn't seem to notice. No one else did either. But I started to shiver.

Walt gave me a jab on the arm and walked away, but not before I saw three chains attached to the shackle around his neck and four cords hanging from the back of his head.

I dodged through the crowd with my face angled toward the floor, stepping over countless chain links and cuffs before arriving at Ms. Barnett's classroom. She was talking with a student. I didn't like seeing my favorite teacher trapped in metal.

I tried to be patient but couldn't keep from fidgeting.

"Hey, Owen!" Ms. Barnett walked over to me even though the student at her desk was midsentence. She looked me up and down, concern showing in her eyes. "Are you okay? You don't look good."

Restlessness, a belly shiver, and ghastly sightings have a way of taking a toll on a person.

"I'm all right," I lied, wiping my icy nose. "I have a favor to ask. Could you examine this for me?" I handed her the demon water.

"Where'd you get it?"

"A bucket. In my backyard."

It's embarrassing to admit, but I had a lifelong habit of lying to keep myself from looking stupid. No premeditation; just a knee-jerk reaction. I mean, what moron drinks from an old, unfiltered, not to mention *dry* well? The backyard bucket seemed like a better explanation. At the time.

"My dog drank some, and now she's sick. Acting . . . off. I'm wondering if the water's contaminated. I figured since you're a chemistry teacher—"

"Naturally I'd be able to do that cool stuff like on *CSI*, right?"

"Well, I was hoping you could run some lab tests and tell me if there's anything in it—toxins or something?"

She stared at the bottle, turning it back and forth. I counted three cords spiraling down through her curly brown hair. "I'll see what I can do, but I'm really swamped right now."

"So how long do you think it will take?"

"I'm pretty sure I could have some results for you by Monday."

Four days? For all I knew, I'd be dead by then.

"Could you do it sooner?"

She gave me a tight-lipped, exasperated smile. "Take your dog to the vet, Owen, and I'll let you know what I find. On Monday."

I tried to look normal as I backed out of the classroom, but probably failed. The bell was about to ring, so the halls were almost empty—a welcome reprieve. I was nearly to an exit door when Principal Harding stopped me.

"Owen Edmonds, isn't your first-period class that way?" She pointed to the classrooms on the other side of the hall. Only two cords in her head.

I knew better than to challenge her. I nodded, then walked that direction. My plan was to turn and get out of there as soon as she left me, but the problem was, she never did. She opened my classroom door as the bell was ringing and winked at my teacher. Then she gave me a pat on the back, like she'd done me a favor.

I was really irritated, but I gave in and sat at my desk. I'd leave right after class.

I stared out the window so I could avoid making eye contact with Lance.

The same three oak trees I saw every day remained anchored in the grass, leaves fluttering in the overcast drizzle. Gusts of wind shoved a smashed McDonald's sack aimlessly along the ground, and I actually felt sorry for it. I could relate.

I craved a normal life more than food and oxygen combined.

Jess's ex, Dan, started in on one of his dumb rants. Went on and on about how he'd shot the biggest hog in Texas and gutted it himself. Whatever.

Out of habit, I looked over at Lance, but he turned away. I wanted things between him and me to go back to the way they had been, but I didn't know how to make it right. I couldn't apologize for what was happening to me.

It took great restraint to keep from jumping out of my skin when the tall girl seated in front of me, Jess's friend Ashlyn, kept leaning back, waving her blonde-streaked hair and both of her sharp-tipped cords under my nose. I didn't have to look hard to see a word etched into one of them:

anxious

Then the other:

vain

Unbelievable. I was seeing things jutting out of people's heads that were labeled with . . . what? Troubled attitudes or something.

Ashlyn was complaining to another girl that a guy named Spenser had used her. From the sound of it, she'd given him the one thing he wanted, and he'd given her the one thing she didn't want: a breakup text.

Ashlyn had only one chain, and it was coiled on the floor less than an inch from my left shoe. I thought about dropping something on purpose as an excuse to take a closer look at the open cuff, but no one was paying attention to me. So I just leaned and stared.

There it was, clear as day, inscribed on the outside:

spenser robert colson

This had to be psychological—my brain projecting a first name I'd just heard and using subconscious creativity to add a middle and last name. Maybe the name I'd seen on my mom's chain was some cosmic coincidence. My disturbed mind had drawn on repressed memories and pulled up a name.

Hard to believe, but what other possibilities were there?

The teacher was giving instructions for an upcoming book report. I typed *Spenser Robert Colson* in a notes app on my cell. Just then a putrid smell wafted in my direction. It reminded me of the stink that had invaded my room the night before last. I looked around, but no one else was reacting. The nauseating stench got stronger. I put my hand over my nose. The guy next to me gave me a "What's up?" look.

That second, my eyes darted to the closed door. I must have moaned or something, because several heads snapped in my direction. Believe me when I say this was beyond anything I could ever make up, toxified brain or not.

Its feet were stained dark with filth and sludge, and its rotten toenails projected several inches past its three bony toes. Asymmetrical scraps of black, tattered fabric shrouded its form and raveled just above its scrawny ankles. What looked like hip bones protruded beneath its slovenly garments, and its shoulder width seemed twice as wide as it should be. The thing was beyond emaciated but somehow still clinging to life.

And nearly as tall as the ceiling.

After the hideous being passed through the closed door, it stepped—yet also glided through the air as if riding on some hellacious conveyor belt.

I clutched the sides of my desk and leaned back as far as I could, shoving my chair into the desk behind me. The thing jerked its mutilated bald head around and glared at me. It slithered closer and closer, seeming bent on murdering my soul.

It was obvious that this vile being could not possibly have been born from a mother's womb. Its skin was thin and gray like cinder block, eroding in spots. The smell of decay was unbearable.

The creature began moving down the aisle on my left. It had to be at least nine feet tall. I closed my eyes and tucked my chin in my chest, bracing myself for the assault.

Seconds passed. Nothing happened. I heard unintelligible whispers and hesitantly raised my head. The thing had stopped just short of me. It was mumbling but not breathing. It seemed to have no need for air.

I heard my teacher's voice. "Let's review the steps for constructing an A+ book report. You guys do know what an A+ is, don't you?" My classmates chuckled. How? The most heinous creature of all time hovered in our midst, projecting fear into the atmosphere like ice-cold chemical pollution. How could they not feel it?

The creature stood motionless, peering down at Ashlyn. I forced myself to look up at its face, trying to make sense of its masculine jawline and feminine cheekbones. All of its features were disproportionate and out of whack. Its face was slashed all over—festering slices covering every square inch—and its parched lips were drawn back like a panting beast about to strike. Sweat dripped from its dirty chin.

It didn't blink. Not once. Its clothing looked soiled and damp and reeked of vomit and burnt flesh.

I was desperate to escape but didn't dare move.

Suddenly the thing dropped to the floor. I watched as it extended its left arm, placing its disjointed wrist into the open cuff at the end of Ashlyn's chain. Like the rest of the creature, its hand was scarred and grossly malformed. I held my breath as the cuff slammed closed. I shuddered at the ringing reverberation of metal on metal.

I wanted to warn Ashlyn, but how?

The creature stood upright again, hoisting the two-ton chain off the ground like it didn't weigh anything. It glared with absolute hatred at Ashlyn, as if it despised the mere sight of her.

Its movements suddenly became spastic and rushed. It leaned in over Ashlyn's head. With its cuffed arm raised, it used its other hand to draw her cords to its gnarled face. Like worms roused to life, the cords began squirming while the creature scanned them as if only a certain one would do.

The monster finally chose a cord and extended its elongated fingers, beckoning. Then the cord slithered its way into the center of the creature's palm. Like a bloodsucking worm, the cord began to burrow into the bottom of the intruder's hand. The foul being rapidly pulsed its fingers, as if coaxing the cord to penetrate deeper into its wrist. I covered my mouth, repulsed by the slurping sound.

Ashlyn's attacker raised its eyes and surveyed the room like a paranoid assassin. I felt like a coward, sitting there doing nothing, but how was I supposed to intervene?

In the midst of the horror, my teacher had the nerve to call on me.

"Owen, what's another composition mistake we want to avoid?"

I dropped my hands from my mouth, but my jaw stayed wide open. I couldn't comprehend her question, much less answer it. All eyes were on me. I searched for any indication that anyone else could see the beast by my desk.

My mind crashed—a cognitive Ctrl-Alt-Delete. Nothing was firing. None of my classmates looked familiar.

"Owen?"

"Just—say—anything." I heard myself speak, the words bypassing my brain and slurring off my tongue.

"Well, that's true. We don't want to use random statements in our report that just take up space but carry no relevant purpose or description." How she miraculously assigned meaning to my mindless muttering, I'll never know.

The corrupted figure raised both hands and began winding the chain and cord around its wrists, taking up the slack. It then jerked its arms into its hollow chest, and something dusty and shadowy jarred inside of Ashlyn. I could only see it for a second.

The being continued mouthing something at her—an echoing whisper and a hissing mumble that sent an electric chill down my spine. I couldn't understand its words, but I knew without a doubt that they were malicious.

Ashlyn raised her hand and responded to a question, still totally unaware that she was being assaulted.

Finally, a somewhat lucid thought: *Take a picture.* With the creature's back now to me, I grabbed my phone and pointed it at Ashlyn. But the creature didn't show up on my screen. Neither did Ashlyn's chain or cords. Through the lens of my cell camera, the world looked safe and innocent.

Surely this was proof of my insanity. I was trapped in a mind trick, a torturous mirage.

The bell rang, and my heart skipped a beat. I fumbled with my phone, and it crashed to the floor behind the giant's grimy heels. I let it lie there.

Ashlyn stood and chatted with the girl across the aisle for a few moments, then made her way to the door. The living dead was still connected to her—one with her—making every move in sync with its prey.

I wanted to tell her, but how could I make her believe me? *I* didn't believe me.

They moved out of sight.

There was no easy way to get up and walk away after witnessing that kind of horror. I felt nailed to my chair.

I'd never believed in God, devils, angels, ghosts, goblins, or haunted houses—surely there was a reasonable, scientific explanation for what I'd just seen. Something was in that water, something hallucinogenic. That had to be it. Ms. Barnett would discover what it was, and then I'd be prescribed some sort of antidote and get my old life back.

In the meantime, I had to get up. Second-period students were pouring in. So were their chains. I grabbed my phone, then concentrated on putting one numb foot in front of the other. I entered the hallway with my head down. Someone called my name. Walt again.

"Owen, wanna go shoot hoops this weekend? Heard you were a star player at your old school."

I nodded, giving zero thought to his question.

"Awesome. See you later, man."

Where had Ashlyn and the huge creepy thing gone? I crossed the main hallway that cut through the center of the school, about to head for an exit, when I made the bold decision to look up.

Bad idea.

I froze in my tracks. Someone slammed into me from behind, but I didn't budge. There were a dozen of them, rag-clad giants moving among the flow of students.

I couldn't take it.

I sprinted out the door and through the rain to my motorcycle. Someone called my name, but I didn't look back. I paid no attention to speed limits, red lights, or stop signs. Once home and barricaded in my room, I gave myself permission to break down.

I yelled.

I punched my pillow and threw things.

I clawed at my face and neck and pounded the ice in my stomach.

I have no idea how long that went on. I only know that what little sunlight there had been was gone when I began regaining some sense of control. I heard my mom say something about going out to eat, but I ignored her.

I sat pressed into the back corner of my room, plucking strands of carpet and pushing them into a pile.

After all of my analyzing, I'd arrived at one distressing question: *I'm probably seeing evil that isn't there, but what if it is . . . and everyone else is blind to it?*

It was improbable, irrational, and, quite honestly, scary beyond comprehension. So I tried to dismiss it and cling instead to the hope that my condition would soon be explained—and remedied—through medical science.

My life depended on Ms. Barnett's results.

Monday could not come fast enough.

TEN

THE WEEKEND WAS a blur of nerve-exploding nightmares and conflicting discoveries. A quick social media search confirmed that Spenser Colson was a real person, a junior at my school, and he was definitely the guy Ashlyn had been talking about. Her status said she was in a relationship with him. His said, "Single."

For the life of me, I couldn't figure out how or why I was seeing names on cuffs, but now that I'd witnessed the chains used as monstrous torture tools, I was even more obsessed with making sense of it.

Coach came to my house on Friday, along with a school counselor. I thought they'd never quit knocking.

Lance sent me a text on Saturday afternoon: **Heard Jess is going to prom with Dan. What's up?** Maybe it was Lance's way of trying to smooth things over. Fine by me, but if I couldn't get him to believe me, our truce wouldn't last long.

I was relieved to know I was off the hook for prom. But Dan? Why would she go back to her egotistical ex? *Nice choice, Jess.*

It was Sunday night, and I was hanging my entire future on Ms. Barnett's explanation tomorrow of what parasite or poison was in that water. Around midnight, I left my bunker/bedroom and headed to the kitchen to fix a bowl of Apple Jacks. I did a double take when I saw the word 𝑔𝑢𝑖𝑙𝑡𝑦 scribbled above the living room window. It hadn't been there the day before. The blizzard churned in my gut.

On Monday morning the sky was radiant blue, the first beautiful day in a long time. *Maybe the scary things don't come out on sunny days.*

I'd obviously watched too many vampire movies. I drove by a convenience store, and right there in broad daylight was another one of the ghastly beings, linked to a guy, just like I'd seen with Ashlyn. So they weren't confined to my school. Another bitter disappointment.

I pulled over and stared at it.

What are you?

I couldn't explain its existence, much less identify its species, and I still didn't know for sure if it was real or a delusion. But I had to call it something. It didn't take long for me to decide on a name. *Creeper.*

I pulled back onto the road and sighed. Did naming them mean I'd sunk to a deeper level of psychosis?

I finally made it to Ms. Barnett's classroom. Without hyperventilating, too.

"Hi, Owen. I've got some results for you." She headed toward me, hands in the pockets of her starched white lab coat.

"Great." It was the most enthusiasm I'd felt in a week. "What did you find? Something toxic? Parasitic?"

"Nope. The lab results indicate that this water is pure."

It felt like my energy was draining out through my fingertips, taking my hope with it. Ms. Barnett said something about an excellent Ph level and an abundance of minerals.

"Are you sure, Ms. Barnett? Did you check for rare contaminants?"

"Well, I'm not the FBI, but I gave it a decent look."

"So the water is pure enough to drink?"

"Appears so." She kept smiling.

"You're sure?" I couldn't get past the denial.

I've heard it said that right before you die, your whole life flashes before you. In that instant, that happened to me, only it was my future. I would never go to med school or be a doctor. Never travel to another continent, watch a game at Wrigley Field, or get married. Without a diagnosis and remedy, a normal life was out of the question.

"How is she, by the way?" Ms. Barnett asked.

"Who?"

"Your dog." She crossed her arms, stepping close. "What's going on, Owen?"

I knew better than to spill the facts—that had gotten me nowhere—but I did crave some guidance. "Nothing in my life is adding up anymore. Everything is—petrifying."

She leaned toward me. "I'd quit adding and start subtracting or multiplying. Find a new life formula, Owen. A shift in perspective. It's usually a good thing, a step on the path to maturity."

She gave me a motherly hug, the kind that includes pats on the shoulder blade, but I left my arms at my sides. It was the most contact I'd had with a shackled person. "I'm writing you a pass to go speak with a counselor. You can—"

"No. I'll be fine."

A second later, she handed me a pink counselor slip and the printout of the lab results, then walked beside me as I shuffled out of her classroom. I didn't thank her.

What now?

I had no plan B. No sensible next step or strategy. My feet walked without any directive from my brain, carrying me to my first-period desk. I hadn't intended to go to class, but I had no idea where else to go. I stared at a random spot on the wall, unflinching. Until Dan opened his big mouth.

"I'm gonna party all night with Jess after prom."

I snapped out of my stupor and took a long look at him—past his sun-glossed brown hair and pretty-boy face to the bolted shackle around his neck. He had eight cords jutting out of his head, skimming the back of his Abercrombie shirt, and ten or so chains lay spiraled next to his expensive shoes. If I could have lifted one of those freezing suckers, I'd have strangled him with it.

I let his comment go. For now.

Ashlyn took her seat in front of me. She was alone, as in not escorting a Creeper. She seemed fine, like nothing had happened.

Our teacher passed around a sheet of paper and asked us to write the name of the book we'd selected for the upcoming book report. I wrote down the title someone else four names before me had picked. That's all I recall of that class.

The bell rang, and I wandered into the hallway. I noticed more words written on walls and a few lockers. Oppressive words like despair and anger. And there were droves of Creepers among us. I could smell their nauseating odor even when they were out of sight.

My freakish observations mixed with the mundane. Teachers piled a ton of makeup work on me. It was nearly impossible to concentrate, but I found it sort of comforting to make an effort to do schoolwork. A connection to my old life.

Lunchtime came, and I was actually glad to see my friends. I was adjusting to the fact that, as monstrous as they looked, people weren't trying to hurt me. I finally understood . . .

They were prey, not predators.

I grabbed a few things from the vending machines, then sat in my usual spot next to Walt and some other jocks, including Lance. He and I were polite but hardly talked.

Jess sat at my table, between Meagan and Ashlyn, ignoring me.

I still wasn't sure what to do now that my toxic-water theory had been debunked, but I forced myself to stay calm, pulling open my bag of Cheez-Its along the seam instead of ripping it into a thousand pieces like I wanted to.

I tried to go along with the table talk, but people hardly looked my way. Had Lance blabbed about me?

I was down to my last cracker when I glanced across the cafeteria and saw a Creeper closing in on a girl, swooping down like a vulture on a carcass. I watched it shrink to the floor, then hoist up again with a chain fastened to its wrist. Between spastic glances in every direction, it fumbled through her cords, then picked one.

I could just sit there and do nothing, but that was getting old. I figured the worst that could happen is the Creeper would kill me, and that would almost be a gift. My friends already thought I was crazy, so nothing to lose there.

I took one last sip of my Powerade, then made the trek across the cafeteria, enduring the increasing drop in temperature as I got close to the assailant. I walked up to the girl, ignoring the Creeper behind her back and her giggling, whispering friends.

Freshmen.

"Hey." I fought the instinct to run.

She looked around, finally pointing to herself.

I nodded, then reached out. She eased her hand toward mine, then held my hand about five seconds longer than normal.

"I'm Owen."

"I know," she said. A girl held up her phone and snapped our picture. More giggles.

"I'm—Riley." She didn't sound certain of her name.

The grotesque ritual was in progress. The Creeper fluttered its fingers, enticing a cord stretching from Riley's head to burrow beneath its skin, sinking into its palm. Its garbled whisper sounded like an ensemble of anguished cries mixed with hissing. It gave me goose bumps.

"I need to talk to you, Riley."

She cast a wide-eyed glance at her equally wide-eyed friends. A girl prompted the others to get up and give us some privacy. Perfect.

I lowered into the chair across from her. "Do you feel okay?" My tone was more fatherly than friendly.

"Um. Sure. Yeah. I'm fine." She grinned, showing a mouthful of braces.

"You sure? Nothing tingling or aching?"

She shook her head, narrowing her eyes in confusion.

"I know we don't know each other, and this is gonna sound crazy, but . . ." How could I explain? "I'm wondering if you feel different than usual. Maybe sort of an . . . eerie sense?"

"Uh. No."

My gaze drifted above Riley to the Creeper's jacked-up face, and I zeroed in on the festering wound stretched across its forehead. I couldn't peel my eyes away.

Riley squirmed in her seat. "What are you—?"

"Don't move!" I tilted my head.

What I had assumed were random gashes and scars on its face began taking shape in my mind, forming a word out of battered flesh:

hopeless

It looked like a brand, a deep burn on the Creeper's decomposing forehead.

Riley glanced over her shoulder.

"Hey." I leaned in, both fists on the table. "Are you . . . ? Have you been . . . ?" I swallowed hard. "Are you feeling *hopeless* right now?"

As the word shot off my tongue, the Creeper's head jerked in my direction, its threatening eyes targeting my face. I ducked down, almost wetting my pants.

She shrugged her shoulders. "I'm all right."

I leaned close enough to whisper. "Are you sure?" I knew I was making her uncomfortable, but under the circumstances, I didn't care.

She slumped over and bit the side of her lip. "I'm okay. I guess." Even less convincing.

"Riley, I know this sounds weird, but if you happen to start feeling hopeless today—" The Creeper growled at me like a ravenous bear. "—please don't listen to those feelings. They're not coming from you and they're not real. There's always hope."

I needed to listen to the advice I was giving. "Promise me you won't give in to . . ."

Did I dare say it a third time?

". . . sadness." No reaction from the Creeper. "Promise?"

"I'll try." She sounded like she was defeated already, her smile now a drooping frown. She stood and crumpled her lunch sack, then stared at me, eyebrows raised. But I'd just given her all the advice I had.

"See ya." I didn't know what else to say. I walked off, leaving her standing there, tethered to a hellion.

But something inside me had changed.

Without intending to, I'd taken Ms. Barnett's advice. I'd found a new formula. I still wanted help for myself, but at the same time, I wanted to *give* help—to people like Riley. Time to quit obsessing over my sanity and switch gears, especially since I was more convinced than ever that what I was seeing was somehow real. Maybe another dimension intruding on ours?

I was trapped in an evil mystery that had to be solved—for my sake, yes, but for everyone else, too. I wasn't carrying torture tools like they were. Surely that meant there was hope for them. I wouldn't stop until I found a way to intervene, to free them.

But first, I had to get through seventh period.

My coach called me into his office and gave me what can only be described as a bipolar lecture. First he'd shout, launching white balls of spit at my face, then he'd ask if I was all right. This up-and-down interrogation went on for most of the class period. I finally convinced him I'd been sick, which was basically true, and that I couldn't run in this week's track meet. It was our last one of the season, and we weren't going to win whether I ran or not, so he let me off the hook without too much grief.

I'd always considered my coach one of the strongest men I knew, but his half-dozen chains ruined that.

As I was leaving school, I saw Jess across the hall, at her locker. She took a step toward me, but then stopped when Dan moved deliberately between us. Jess wrapped her arms around his neck, and he pulled her body to his.

I turned and made my way toward the main exit doors, stomping my heels into the floor, squeezing my keys. Jess wasn't just dating Dan. She was flaunting it.

I couldn't stand her flirting with him. More than jealous, I was worried about her. She'd told me stories about how he'd lost his temper with her. Grabbed her so hard during an argument that he'd left a bruise on her arm. And now she was back with him?

On top of that, right or wrong, I was beginning to measure people—okay, *judge* people—by the number of chains and cords they had. People like Dan and my mom had tons. People like Riley and Ms. Barnett had just a few. Jess was basically in the middle.

I was out the door and almost to the parking lot when I did a double take, skidding to a halt.

How is that even possible?

ELEVEN

A GIRL WITH NO SHACKLE. Or chains. Or cords.

And get this—she had a brilliant golden glow emanating from her feet onto the cement around her. It was mesmerizing, like nothing I'd ever seen before, but I guess that goes without saying.

I followed as she moved toward the gym, her long blonde ponytail swishing back and forth. She looked to the side, and I recognized her—the girl who'd slammed into Jess last week. The same girl assigned to take me on a school tour my first day. I could almost remember her name. She lived in the neighborhood next to mine; I recalled her telling me that.

I studied her as she bounced up to a friend and started talking her ear off, then disappeared with her behind the girls' locker room doors. I waited outside until a female coach ran me off.

It came to me—*Ray Anne*.

I had to talk to her. Uncover the secret behind her freedom.

She was now my official plan B.

The harder I tried not to look at the accusation above my living room window, the more it consumed my attention:

guilty

I diverted my eyes to my cell phone, watching the minutes click by, anxious for evening to come so I could get on with my mission. It felt good—invigorating, really—to have a next step in mind.

On social media, I found a picture of Ray Anne Greiner standing outside her house, and I planned to drive around her neighborhood until I located it. Ideally I'd knock on her door around seven o'clock, before sunset but after normal families ate dinner. For now, I sat on the sofa eating pizza rolls and watching mindless television, rubbing circles over my stomach. Nothing stopped the chill.

The next thing I knew, my dog was growling, and it was dark outside. I opened my groggy eyes. 8:33 p.m. Later than I'd planned to head out, but not too late. I stretched.

"Quiet, girl."

Daisy was on all fours making that inquisitive doggy face, nose aimed at the stairs. I stroked her head, but she didn't budge, just flared her gums.

"Maybe if the vet hadn't cleaned your teeth, you'd be a little more intimidating." I smiled for the first time in I didn't know how long.

I tried to pet her again, but she dodged my hand and started barking. Loudly. The strip of fur along her back stood on edge.

"Hush, Daisy." I wasn't smiling anymore. She did this sometimes, but tonight it was freaking me out. "Stop it."

I heard chains banging around upstairs. "Mom's getting up, that's all." As if I could reason with a dog.

My mother's bedroom door collided with the wall, and Daisy ducked her head and ran to the side of the sofa. A blast of cold hit me, carrying a familiar, rancid stench. I rolled over the back of the sofa and crouched down without taking my eyes off the staircase.

It was normal for our stairs to creak now and then. It was *not* normal for the wood to sound like it was buckling under the weight of my petite mother. Daisy scurried behind the sofa too, pressing against me, a low-pitched growl rumbling in her throat. Neither of us blinked.

I saw my mom's bare feet coming down the stairs. Then her silky robe. Then her thin shoulders. Then . . .

"Mom!"

It was the worst possible scenario. A Creeper towered behind her back, advancing in stride with her. She looked like a dwarf shadowed by a dragon, entering the living room bound to it through a chain and cord.

"Behind you!" I stood and pointed like a maniac.

She looked over her shoulder the best she could, tipsy as usual, then glared at me. "What's the matter?"

Daisy barked her head off.

"It's got you!"

"Quit it, Owen," my mom slurred. She stumbled toward me, rubbing the sides of her head. "Tell that dog to shut up."

I backed away, nearly tripping over Daisy. "Mom, there's a giant . . . It's a massive . . ."

"What's gotten into you?" She finally quit coming at me and leaned on the sofa, catching her balance before stretching to grab a wineglass off the coffee table. She peered into it. "Clean enough." She headed for the kitchen.

I had to try again. "You're in trouble!"

She spun around, one eye narrower than the other. "Excuse me?"

Her attacker was only a few feet away from me. I dropped my head back. All the way back.

"Are you the one who does this to my mother? Makes her cry all the time?"

It didn't take any notice of me. It just kept gazing down at my mother's head like a witch tending her brew.

"Accuser!"

I didn't think, just read what I saw on its mutilated forehead. And when I did, the Creeper squinted at me and opened its mouth so that its menacing rows of teeth jutted out. Then it lowered its big head and hissed in my face like a two-ton cobra.

I covered my head with both arms and—I admit it—screamed like a girl.

"What's *wrong* with you?" My mom stared.

I backed away—more like fell backward—cupping my nose, then talked so fast I couldn't catch my breath. "I told you, I've been seeing things, Mom! Things people aren't supposed to see. Or can't see. I don't know, but it's horrible. It's evil! And I'm not trying to scare you—I'm really not—but Mom, there's a huge, awful, Creeper-thing attacking you. Right now! It's attached to you, and it hates you. Hates all of us!"

"Stop it, Owen!"

I followed her across the kitchen, talking louder as she rummaged through her liquor cabinet.

"I know it sounds like a lie or something made up, but please, Mom, I'm begging you. Please believe me. I wouldn't lie about this. I wouldn't even know how to make this stuff up!"

She poured herself a glass of wine like we were chatting about the weather, then wandered back into the living room, shaking her head.

"Stop!" I stepped in front of her and pointed. "Do you see that? What it says above the window?"

"I don't see anything. Owen, I need you to—"

"Okay, fine, you can't see it, but someone—something—wrote on our wall. *Guilty*. It's right there. I need you to believe me!" My cheeks were blazing hot.

"I know what this is, Son."

"You do?" The thought that she might have some answers for me was like a tourniquet for my hemorrhaging soul, even if it was coming from a Creeper-bound person.

"I'm not an idiot." She took a sip of her drink, nearly spilling it. "You're on something."

Not this again. I walked an aimless circle around the coffee table, raking my fingers through my hair. "I'm completely sober, Mom. I need your help!"

She sighed. "Like the priest used to say, I can't help until you confess."

What a load of garbage.

About the only thing I knew about my mom's childhood was that she hated being forced to go to Mass. That, and she ran away at sixteen to escape from her abusive parents. My mom didn't respect the priesthood any more than I respected . . . well, her.

But she was all I had.

"I'm telling the truth, Mom."

She took another sip. "Sure you are."

That was it. I gave up and charged up the stairs, unwilling to be near Accuser another second. But halfway there, I stopped and faced my mom, the words welling up inside me like lava. "You're a lousy drunk, you know that?"

She winced and covered her mouth.

The Creeper nodded, twisting its lips into a sinister, satisfied grin.

TWELVE

I DIDN'T LIKE THAT I'd insulted my mother, and I really didn't like that it seemed to make that Creeper happy, but I could only feel so bad about it.

She'd had it coming.

I'd missed my chance last night to go see Ray Anne, but there was no way I'd let that happen today. There had to be a way to liberate people, and I was betting Ray Anne held the key. As furious as I was with my mother, I'd free her if I could. And Jess, and Lance, and, if I knew how, all of humanity.

Okay, maybe not Dan.

The protesters didn't intimidate me today. Sure, it was irritating to be surrounded by a loudmouthed mob of crazies, but compared to the Creepers, they were houseflies. Even the deranged redhead—pesky but harmless.

I was sick of walking through the school with my head down, like a puppy with its tail tucked between its legs. I kept my chin up today, dealing with the waves of anxiety as they came, all the while searching for Ray Anne.

The presence of Creepers outside and inside the school not only gagged me but kept me so cold I trembled all day. They were everywhere, drifting among us. Some crouched in dark corners. Others hovered in midair. Some actually crept up the walls and along the ceiling, like gigantic spiders, twisting their long, skinny necks to stare down on us while their torsos and legs stayed facing upward.

I noticed they would gather around trash cans and inside stinky bathrooms—at home in filth, I supposed.

People gave me a hard time for dressing like it was winter. Stella Murphy wouldn't shut up about it, so I flat out told her, "I'd wear shorts too, if there weren't icy, evil creatures everywhere."

She laughed. I didn't.

Between classes, I ran up and down the halls, looking for Ray Anne, asking people if they'd seen her. Most didn't even know who she was. I tried getting Walt to sneak a copy of her schedule to me during his office aid period, but he was afraid of getting busted. Wish that was my biggest fear of the day.

I now noticed more shackle-free students—a much-needed boost of encouragement for me. I didn't know any of them, but I caught up with one guy before fourth period. "Hey, I have to ask you something. You know you glow?"

Yeah, that didn't go well.

As for me, I didn't know what to make of my condition. No shackle, but no shine either.

After school, I kept an eye on the girls' locker room doors but never saw Ray Anne. I was back to my original plan. I'd go to her house.

Dan's fully loaded Ford F-150 was parked down the row from my bike, and there was Jess, hugging all over him. I couldn't get used to it. And today . . .

Dan had a Creeper attached to him. This particular one made me break out in a cold sweat.

Ever seen a goat's eyes? That's what this Creeper's pupils looked like—solid black horizontal lines immersed in dark red. And its eyeballs were bulging out of their sockets. Its slimy, blackened tongue hung out past its chin and came to a sickening point, curling and contorting like it had a mind of its own. The four letters singed into its forehead were clear even from a distance:

lust

How fitting.

"Jess, get away from him." I reached a hand out to her.

As usual, Dan had an arrogant smirk. He pulled Jess's chin to keep her attention, and she actually let him.

"You had your turn," he said. He didn't have the guts to look at me. My *turn*?

Jess meant about as much to him as a Coke can. He'd use her up, then crush her and toss her in the trash heap—with the help of that obscene Creeper, no doubt.

But what could I do to convince her of that?

I took the long way home to clear my head. It didn't work. I thought about getting into my mom's liquor cabinet, but no. Surely the only thing worse than seeing Creepers was being drunk and seeing Creepers. And honestly, just the *smell* of liquor had always nauseated me.

Around five o'clock, I got a text from Jess: **Come outside.**

She was at the end of my driveway, in a skirt so short even I was surprised. I walked up to her, and she grabbed my hands, giving me a spunky smile—her way of trying to mend things, it seemed.

"Take me to the bridge."

I didn't know what bridge she was talking about, but I agreed to drive her. She slid onto my motorcycle and wrapped her arms around me. Like old times.

Man, I want my old life back.

We parked in front of a railroad bridge on a hilly back road that stretched over a river some fifty feet below.

"This is where I go," she said, taking my hand and leading me onto the bridge. "When I need to get away. And think."

We reached the center, and she stood back, away from the railing.

"What?" I leaned on the metal rail and looked back at her. "Afraid of heights?"

She cut her eyes like she was embarrassed. "You know . . ."

Then I remembered. Jess couldn't swim. She'd had her first asthma attack while taking lessons as a child and refused to go near water ever since.

I reached my hand out. "I'd never let you drown." I finally talked her into inching her way to me. Then we both stood there, taking in the awesome view—the kind of scene you'd expect to see on a puzzle box.

I kept quiet—not to be stubborn, but because I couldn't possibly explain the latest events of my life. Or what I knew was attached to her boyfriend.

She broke the silence. "I guess you heard I'm going to prom with Dan."

"Impressive choice."

"Well, what was I supposed to do? You don't want anything to do with me, and he's been begging me to get back with him."

I tried not to get so frustrated that I offended her before I'd made my point. "Have you forgotten, Jess? How mean he was to you?"

"He's on meds now. He's doing a lot better." She pulled a ponytail holder off her wrist and tied her hair back. "You know his dad's a doctor, right?"

I didn't know if she meant that as a jab, but it put me on the defense anyway. "So what? Pills don't fix abusive."

She had to know I was right. Maybe that's why she changed the subject. "I get that you've been sick or whatever, but you never did explain why you ran away from me the other day. Or what's been going on with you." Her tone was kind.

She wrapped a pinky around mine, and that was all it took. My feelings for her came flooding back.

"Jess, I don't blame you for moving on. I just wish you'd rethink who you're moving on with. Dan is no good. He doesn't care about you."

"He told me that he's been out with lots of girls since we broke up, but it's different with me. He loves me."

"And you believe that?" I looked into her face. "He's manipulating you."

She sighed. "I know what I'm doing, Owen. He's cared about me for a long time."

"Didn't you tell me he yelled at you so bad one time you had your worst asthma attack ever? Ended up in the ER?"

She kept her eyes down. "At least he hasn't rejected me."

I couldn't believe it. I was the bad guy now, and Dan was the knight in shining armor.

She turned and walked the rest of the way down the bridge. I followed her. "Jess, I was never gonna dump you for that Cindy girl. And I'm sorry I ran from you the other day."

We made it to the end of the bridge, then she sat in the grass. I lowered myself beside her and tried to explain. "I'm going through something really, really serious."

She eased onto her back in the grass, looking up at the clouds. "Why won't you tell me about it?"

I lay next to her. Stared at the clouds too. "I have to figure things out on my own."

"Is there something I can do?"

I turned onto my side and leaned on my elbow, my face inches from hers. "You can stay away from Dan Bradford."

She grinned. "You're jealous."

"It's not funny. And I'm not jealous. I'm seriously worried about you."

"I can take care of myself."

There she was, shackled and surrounded by three chains and four cords, bragging about her independence.

I brushed the back of my fingers over her cheek a few times, and she let her eyes drift shut. She sank deeper into the grass, as if the weight of the world were pressing down on her. I reached up and stroked her hair, unable to resist sneaking glances at her cords.

unforgiving
self-hating
insecure
defiant

I felt like a stalker, like I'd just picked the lock on her diary. I had to admit, though, knowing Jess like I did, the descriptions were spot on. She tried to come off as confident—better than others, even—but it was all a mask. I was no psychologist, but I'd always known Jess had a hard time liking herself.

"Your shoes are coming untied." I moved toward her feet.

"No they're not." She grinned.

I pulled her laces loose, then tied them again, scanning the open cuffs at the ends of her chains.

bill edwin thompson

Her dad. Weird.

Her mother's name was on the next cuff. Weird again.

The third chain:

jeffrey joel thompson

Another relative, I figured, but who?

I went back to my spot next to her in the grass, our shoulders touching. I hesitated, then . . .

"Jess, has someone hurt you? A family member, maybe? Done something . . . unforgivable?"

She bolted up like I'd jabbed her with a cattle prod. "What do you mean?"

I sat up too. "Just wondering."

Her eyes glossed over, like she couldn't see anything but the thoughts inside her head. "Well," she practically whispered, "my dad has done some things. And . . ."

I got the feeling she wanted to tell me more, but she was scared.

"You can trust me, Jess." I meant it.

She looked almost catatonic for a moment, then snapped her head around at me. "Why would you ask me that? Slightly personal, isn't it?"

"Well, yeah, I just thought—"

"One minute you don't want anything to do with me, and the next, you want me to tell you my deepest, darkest secrets?"

She had a point.

I motioned for her to lie back down beside me, but she wouldn't.

I studied her face. "I have an idea." When she quit breathing so hard and relaxed her shoulders, I shared it: "What if you come clean with me, and I come clean with you?"

She thought about it, plucking up blades of grass and flicking them aside. "Fine, but you have to go first."

I wasn't thrilled about her counteroffer, but I was willing to go along with it, under one condition. "Promise me you'll *try* to believe me."

"Fine. Go."

Deep breath. "You know how I told you I drank some water in the woods, then started feeling weird and, uh, seeing things?"

"Yeah."

"Well, I'm still feeling weird and seeing things. Terrible things."

She turned toward me. "What did the doctor say?"

"I didn't—" Oh, yeah. My lie had caught up with me. "He wasn't any help. So I got the water tested, but the results came back clean. Nothing abnormal, Ms. Barnett told me."

"If you're seeing things, why haven't you, like, gone to a psychiatrist?"

I sat up. "Well, it's complicated, Jess. At first I assumed I was hallucinating, that I was totally delusional and needed psychological help. Serious help. But now, I'm not so sure. Some of the things I see actually seem to add up."

"What do you mean?"

Better to keep it vague. "I can see certain things about people—what they're struggling with. And who they're struggling with, I think."

She leaned away from me. "So that's why you asked if there's someone I can't forgive? You think that's my issue?"

"Well, yeah." I said it as nicely as I could. "It's *one* of your issues."

I obviously wasn't nice enough. She stood and slapped the grass off her legs. "What about *you*, Owen? What are your issues?"

"Mine?"

"Yeah. You're so aware of what everyone else needs. What about you?"

"Well, actually there are some of us who don't appear to have any issues." I knew it sounded arrogant, but it was true.

"How convenient. Looks like you're already a doctor, aren't you? You know everyone's problems and exactly how to fix them."

She stormed off, refusing to listen as I tried to explain that I actually had no idea how to help anyone. I called out to her, but she kept moving. She pounded out a text on her cell, hitting send as I came close to her.

I pleaded with her to come back—to at least let me drive her to my house to get her car, but within minutes, there was Dan, speeding up in his spotless red truck.

She hopped in, then rolled down her window. "You're psychotic, Owen."

Dan snickered, then gassed it, leaving me standing in the middle of the street.

My heart was stampeding like a herd of cattle. So much for trying to believe me.

I pounded the pavement back to my bike, then sped toward Ray Anne's neighborhood, my teeth clenched the whole way. I could have predicted that Jess had a *defiant* cord without ever reading it. I'd told her my personal stuff, but she'd shared nothing—and then insulted me.

I pulled out my cell to send Jess a text, but since I had nothing but hateful things to say, I didn't bother. The longer I drove, the more tense I got.

But by the time I finally spotted Ray Anne's house, I'd cooled off some. No doubt that the house was hers—there was a drill-team yard sign with her name on it.

It was a modest neighborhood. Mostly one-stories. I was ready to go straight for the kill—walk up to the door and knock. But something in the cul-de-sac caught my attention.

There were several small children chasing each other. Like the two boys I'd seen before, they didn't have shackles or anything abnormal, but when they faced me head-on, I could see a blinding, concentrated, colorful light near each child's heart, piercing through their clothing. It was like a blazing star, completely captivating.

It was similar to the illumination I'd seen on Ray Anne and the others at my school, only this was brighter and filled one tiny spot in their chests instead of shining around their feet. I stood there awhile, strangely comforted.

I snapped a picture with my cell, but everything extraordinary was missing from the image.

Eventually I faced Ray Anne's house again, walked up, and knocked on the door. Her mother answered—a short, plump lady with an apron on. She glowed too. Interesting.

"Hi. I'm Owen Edmonds." I reached out and shook her hand. I thought I'd feel some sort of sensation when making contact with a glowing person.

Nope.

"Is Ray Anne here?"

A minute later, she was on the front porch with me.

"Hey, Ray Anne."

She looked at me like I was wearing a dress or something.

"Owen." I pointed to myself like a preschooler, then slid both hands into my pockets.

"I remember your name. Are you okay?"

I was trying to act normal, but obviously failing. "Yeah. Absolutely. Look, I just want you to know that I'm sorry about what happened, with Jess, in the hall the other day."

She shrugged. "It's no big deal."

"So, what are you up to tonight?"

"Well, it's laundry night, so . . ."

"Awesome." We stared at the doormat and fidgeted. Crickets were chirping. Literally.

I took another stab at it. "Hey, you wanna go out tomorrow, you know, get to know each other?"

Her eyebrows pressed together. "You mean a date?"

"No. Just, like, me and you, going to dinner and talking."

Great. The textbook definition of *date*. I wouldn't have blamed her if she'd slammed the door in my face.

"Um . . . I can't tomorrow. But I can Friday night."

"Cool." I sighed, hugely relieved.

"But what about Jess? She's your girlfriend, right?"

"Oh, that's over. Completely."

"Sorry."

"No, it's . . . never mind. So, like six o'clock Friday? I'll pick you up. My treat."

"Sure. Um, tell me again why you want to go out?"

"Uh, I just want to get to know you. Like, yeah, get to know you better."

She blinked. And blinked. "Okay, yeah, sounds good." An eye roll, but followed by a playful smile. "Just so you know, my parents will want to meet you. You'll need to come in and talk to them before we go out, on our not-a-date." She chuckled.

"Yeah, of course." A bit old fashioned, but I could respect it.

We exchanged cell numbers, then talked a minute about how awful things had gotten at school.

She didn't know the half of it.

She was easy to talk with and even easier to look at, not only because she was cute but because her neck was shackle-free, and there was nothing but pretty blonde hair coming out of her head. I also noticed that her eyes were a striking light blue—not sure how that got past me before.

Funny how girls like Ray Anne could get so lost in the crowd at school. Pretty didn't cut it. Sexy got the job done.

I tried not to stare, but it was kind of hard, especially with someone who was glowing.

It was dark by the time I left. I hadn't planned to be out after sunset.

I nearly ran over a kid on a skateboard. He wore an "I survived a semester at Masonville High" T-shirt—my new life motto.

By the time I reached my street, the only light was in small patches under streetlamps. Wouldn't you know it, I picked up on a rancid stench. Then I saw it: a Creeper lurked in a driveway a few houses ahead.

I came to a stop and spied on the creature, observing its jerky movements. A man pulled his car up next to it. The guy was on his cell, fumbling with his keys as he meandered toward his house. The Creeper followed, then hunched down and selected a chain. By the time the man went inside, it was rummaging through his squirming cords.

I raced home.

As best I could tell, these hateful beings used a person's messed-up relationships and crappy attitudes to torment and manipulate them.

I couldn't figure out exactly how it worked, but I believed they tricked people into feeling so bad that they acted out. Like, the Creeper with **hopeless** on its forehead worked to make Riley feel hopeless, and the one sporting **accuser** threw accusations at my mom until she felt horrible and self-destructive. All without them knowing it.

Think about it. What better strategy is there to destroy an opponent than to go stealth? To do your most damaging work under the cloak of invisibility? And even if some cursed soul like me happens to discover what's really going on, the truth is so far fetched that no one will believe it. My stories sounded more like the plot of some crazy novel than real life.

And I was sure that was exactly the way the Creepers wanted it.

They despised the human race, but why? What had we ever done to them? Seemed to me they were attacking us without cause—like we were victims of their inability to do anything but hate.

At first I thought maybe they were out to take over Earth, to extinguish humanity and repopulate our planet with their debased species. But the more I observed them, the more it appeared like they were content to let us be here as long as they could abuse and assault us—but to what end?

I seldom gave much thought to God, but the Creepers seemed to be pretty concrete proof that he didn't exist. No loving, just deity would let these things run free.

The only "higher power" overseeing humanity was an army of invisible thugs.

The next morning, first period was miserable, not just because Dan was there, but because that nasty Lust monster was still tied to him. Like usual, Dan ran his mouth, rubbing it in my face that he was with Jess now.

Whatever. At least I didn't have a nine-foot ogre chanting spells into my soul.

Between first and second period, I noticed three Creepers huddled together in a dim corner. They paid no attention to me as long as I didn't say what was written on their faces. Interestingly, all three of these Creepers had the same name:

violence

They looked at each other as if communing—like soldiers in the same bloodthirsty troop, strategizing—but they verbalized nothing. They just nodded now and then.

One of them opened its massive hand and zigzagged a jagged fingernail across the surface of its palm. It shoved its palm in the other Creepers' faces. Then it flicked its wrist awkwardly, causing a thin layer of skin to fling off and float toward the floor.

I kept my eye on the grotesque thing.

The piece of skin sailed through the air, ushered across the hallway by the students' oblivious movements. I followed it all the way past the science wing and into the language arts pod, where it lodged on the floor against a locker. The bell rang. Finally, the hallways cleared.

I dropped to my knees and took as close a look as I could. It reminded me of elementary school, when my friends and I would paint our palms with Elmer's glue, then peel off a thin layer of what looked like dead skin. Only this really *was* skin. And it had an inscription:

52359M

I extended my finger, and the instant I made contact, the corner touching my skin deteriorated. I pulled my hand away.

A girl I didn't know turned down the hallway.

"Hey, will you come here, please?" I said it as politely as I could, then pointed. "Are you able to see that? It's not a piece of paper. It's something else."

"Yeah. What is it?"

"You see it? Are you sure? What does it say?" Could there finally be some proof of my sanity? I held my breath.

She crouched on the floor next to me. "I think it says five-two-three, then S-G-M."

"Yes! That's it!"

"Okay . . ." She got up. "So?"

My surge of excitement fizzled. What was I supposed to say? *"A Creeper wrote this note on its hand, then flung it to the floor"?*

Yeah, right.

"It—uh—someone dropped it."

She leaned over to pick it up. I freaked out. "No, don't touch it! It'll dissolve."

"Whatever." She walked off.

I felt almost euphoric. I didn't know how much that note could prove to anyone else, but it was crucial evidence for me. What I was seeing was real.

I took a picture of it, and there it was, in my photo stream, clear as day.

An assistant principal caught me on the floor. "I dropped something. I'm going to class now, Ms. . . . um . . ."

I left the note and ran to class.

This was a breakthrough discovery, for sure, but there was still a ton I needed to uncover about the Creepers. What was their mission? What were those numbers and letters about?

Most important, how could they be defeated?

I knew I should look for weaknesses, search for a vulnerability I could exploit, but I was afraid they had none. Creepers were clearly at the top of the food chain, the most vicious of hunters with no one brave enough or big enough to hunt them.

Or so I thought.

THIRTEEN

I WAS STILL MAD AT JESS, and my friendship with Lance was definitely strained, but I tossed my backpack on the sofa and texted each of them anyway: **Can you come over?**

I felt compelled to tell them about my latest finding. I knew they weren't likely to believe any of it, and I was probably making a huge mistake, but I wanted them to see the picture of the Creeper note. Maybe this time they'd at least give my claims some thought.

Lance replied: **Coming.**

I didn't hear from Jess, but fifteen minutes later, they both pulled up at my house.

They sat across from me, and I made my case like a trial lawyer pleading with a jury. "I told you both that I've been seeing some very strange and freaky things lately. Neither of you believed me, but I understand. I'd have a hard time believing me too. Jess, yesterday you called me psychotic." I acted like it didn't infuriate me. "I want to show you guys something—proof that I'm not crazy."

I pulled up the picture of the Creeper note. "See that?"

Jess took a look. "What is it?" She passed the phone to Lance.

"It's a note. But not just any note." I wiped my sweaty palms on my jeans

99

and exhaled. "Look, this is gonna sound like something out of a sci-fi movie, but it's not. It's real, and I need you to take me seriously this time. Okay?"

They nodded, but I doubted their sincerity. I was about to make a fool of myself again. I had to try, though.

"So there are these creepy, huge things that walk around our school—everywhere really, but there's tons at our school. They latch onto people and try to brainwash them or something. I don't know why I can see them and you can't, but I saw three Creepers—that's what I call them—grouped together today in the hallway, and one of them wrote this note, then tossed it to the floor." I left out that it used its fingernail to etch the message on its palm. No way I was going there.

"I chased the note down and took a picture of it, and I wanted to show you guys so you'd know I'm not making all this stuff up." I cut my eyes to Jess. "I'm not psychotic."

Lance stared at the phone again, then passed it back to Jess. She zoomed in, then gave it back to him. This back-and-forth went on for a while, like a stupid game of hot potato.

I forced myself to stay calm. "So?"

Lance cleared his throat. "Owen—" He paused for an eternity. "I'm really, really worried about you. This isn't funny. You need help, dude."

Jess nodded. "You do. This is scary."

"But what about the picture? That's proof that this isn't all in my mind. I wouldn't lie about this."

"You want us to believe that some invisible creature-thing wrote this?" Jess shook her head. "That's so crazy."

This was going nowhere. "Just forget it. Seriously. Don't worry about it." I stood and reached for my phone. "Thanks for stopping by. It's all good." Not really, but I wanted them and their metal appendages to leave.

I walked them to the door, hoping they would drive off and forget everything I'd just said. Unfortunately, Lance wasn't done. "Owen, promise me you'll go talk to someone, a doctor or counselor or something." I nodded, then shut the door and did the only thing I knew to do—flip on the TV and try to escape my distorted world for a while.

I fully believed by now that what I was seeing was real, but I had my moments—like this one—when I second-guessed everything.

Jess sent me a text: **I wish I could help you but I don't know what to think of your stories.**

I texted back: **I really don't either.**

My mother's new boyfriend dropped her off, and she barricaded herself in her bedroom with a bottle of wine. She'd been avoiding me ever since I'd tried to tell her about the Creeper two nights ago.

I did the best I could to finish some homework, but it was super hard to focus on anything other than the supernatural. I decided to type up a timeline of events, beginning with the day that I drank the water and developed a nonstop belly freeze. It was unbelievable how much had happened in just ten days.

On Thursday morning, I planned to stay home—but then Daisy stood outside my mother's bedroom door growling. I could handle seeing Creepers in public better than dealing with them in my house. I decided to go to school, and on the drive there, I analyzed how to play my cards right the next night with Ray Anne. I needed to get information from her without scaring her off.

I wasn't looking forward to Jess finding out that I was going out with someone—and she *would* find out. Ray Anne was on the drill team. Gossip among those girls spread around the school like mold on stale bread. It didn't matter that Jess was on the fast track with Dan. She was going to freak.

Odd—one minute I was worrying about endangered souls, and the next, about petty rumors.

Walking the hallways was extra challenging today. There were more of the vicious words scribbled all over the place this week than last, marking up lockers, bathroom stalls, ceiling tiles—you name it. Some appeared to be fading, while others looked fresh.

Finally, on my way to third period, I solved the mystery of the graffiti. I saw a Creeper raise its skin-and-bones arm and use its grimy finger to write the word hate above the entrance to the library.

For reasons beyond me, words were obviously significant to Creepers.

My moods were all over the place, but as I made my way to the cafeteria for lunch, I was boiling over with a sense of injustice. Everything about this was unfair. The way I saw it, humans were defenseless prey, sitting ducks with no camouflage or refuge.

Which was worse? Witnessing evil at work or being ignorant of it? Both felt like a death sentence.

I collapsed into a chair at my lunch table, a few seats down and across from Jess. Here came Dan, grinning, holding his new purchase up to his chest—one of those yellow "I survived Masonville High" shirts.

He lowered into a chair next to Jess. She rolled her eyes the second she saw him. "That's not funny, Dan."

She got up and started to walk away, but he grabbed her arm. "Sit down."

I thought for sure she was gonna deck him. Instead she swallowed hard, then sat. He didn't let go of her.

I'd had enough of this punk. I was already popping my knuckles when Dan clamped down harder on Jess's arm, and she winced. That was it. I shot out of my seat. "Let her go."

Dan looked me up and down, then huffed. "Or what?"

My fingers curled into tight fists. "Or I'll make you."

There was a collective gasp around us. I guess Principal Harding noticed. She came charging over to our table. "What's going on here?"

Dan had escaped to another table and was chatting with friends like he'd done nothing wrong. The principal looked at me. "Owen?"

Jess stared a hole through me, pleading with her eyes to let it go. I sat down. "Everything's fine."

Harding scanned the table, then finally left.

Jess dug through her purse and pulled out her inhaler, then took a hit.

I walked over to her and leaned down, speaking into her ear. "You have no business covering for that lowlife. And please, don't ask me to keep quiet like that ever again. You deserve way better, Jess." She took a second hit from her inhaler. "You all right?"

She nodded, her eyes pooling.

I rubbed a gentle hand over her arm where he'd grabbed ahold of her. There was no Creeper attached to Dan, provoking him. No excuse for what he'd just done.

As I went back to my seat, I seriously considered walking over and breaking Dan's nose, ruining his *GQ* face. But right then, Meagan approached Jess, dressed in her cheer uniform. A Creeper followed behind Meagan like an oppressive shadow. It motioned toward another Creeper.

I clenched my jaws. Two at once?

Not on your life.

I had no action plan, just charged over to Meagan. The accomplice's name stood out, a wound stretched across its forehead:

demise

I must have said it out loud. The snarly thing contorted its head and peered down at me for a heart-stopping moment, then went to work with its putrid partner. They shrank to the floor and shoved their wrists into two open cuffs. The sound of the cuffs snapping shut was like the slamming of massive metal doors.

I couldn't separate the visible from the invisible. "Stop it! Leave her alone!" A hush fell over the whole cafeteria, but I didn't stop. "You have no right to do this! Stop it!"

Meagan's eyelids went wide, and her cheeks flashed red. Jess stood up. "Owen, what are you doing?"

I heard Dan laughing, but it didn't matter. I grabbed a soda can off the lunch table and hurled it at the beasts. Sprite flew everywhere, but the can passed right through the Creepers. Meagan probably thought I was aiming for her—she started crying.

Words flew out of my mouth machine-gun style, aimed at thin air as far as everyone else was concerned.

The dark ritual continued as the Creepers moved in perfect sync. They thumbed through the cords drooping from Meagan's head and made their strategic selections.

But suddenly, the Creepers looked up, tilting their heads back, fear all over their mutilated faces. What could they possibly be afraid of?

I looked around . . .

And found my answer.

FOURTEEN

HE WAS ENORMOUS, at least five feet taller than the Creepers, and a blinding, crystal-white radiance penetrated the space around him. I was too astounded to cover my eyes, overwhelmed by a rush of euphoria—an extraordinary sensation of peace I never knew existed.

Although I could only stand to look at him for seconds at a time, I could see that his massive body was sculpted to perfection. He wore the most bad-looking platinum-silver armor I'd ever seen.

I don't know when I hit the ground, but at some point, it registered that I was on my stomach, straining to look up and steal glances at him.

And wow, the fragrance. He gave off a magnificent scent that overpowered the Creepers' putrid stench—like high-end men's cologne but better than anything I'd ever smelled. His movements were fluid and effortless, a supernatural being prepared for the fiercest of battles.

The human language cannot describe his flawless complexion or the passion and fury contained in his eyes. He didn't look much older than me, but there was nothing boyish about him. A thin gold crown encircled his glorious head, beaming over his wavy brown hair. I didn't need to be told that it signified authority far greater than any earthly power.

I felt a tight grip on my arm, but I paid no attention. I was witnessing another dimension, beholding a life-form that exceeded the most epic of fairy-tale heroes.

I was lifted upright, but my knees buckled, and I dropped to the floor again as another colossal being of equal stature and strength appeared on the opposite side of Meagan—this one dark skinned, with the most massive biceps.

The Creepers went ballistic, jerking and convulsing in their rush to pull away from Meagan's cords and cuffs.

I had the bizarre feeling that I was standing outside of time as the two immense allies closed in on the Creepers. I couldn't be the only one who felt the earth shudder! They had no weapons in their hands—they didn't need them.

Finally unbound from Meagan, the Creepers planted their faces to the floor and writhed but didn't hiss a sound. The mere presence of these glowing beings seemed to be unleashing suffering on the Creepers. At last, the tormentors were tormented.

The monsters slithered on their stomachs, inching away from the light until they were far enough to crawl, then they scrambled to their feet and ran.

I focused on the avengers, desperate to memorize every detail of their appearance. But I was interrupted by the sensation of pain in both arms. I was hoisted up, then felt my body spin, forcing me to face the opposite direction. Two male teachers had ahold of me. My feet dragged on the floor all the way to the nurse's office, then I tumbled onto the stiff plastic bed.

The nurse scrambled to take my temperature and blood pressure, then warned Principal Harding that my body was cold and my blood pressure soaring. That's what happens when you carry a blizzard in your belly and stand an arm's length away from supernatural rivals.

It was like a nightmare, only with a glorious finish.

I heard Lance ask the nurse if I was all right. I guess my secret was out. Everyone had seen me explode.

I wanted so bad to get up and find Meagan. I wanted her to know that she was at the center of an epic fight, the treasured prize of two fierce opposing forces. And I wanted to tell her that the good side won today. They won without ever having to raise a fist.

Principal Harding knelt down and spoke close to my face. Too close. "Owen, I just got off the phone with your mother. She's on her way."

I was relieved when she backed off, but then a school counselor got right back in my face. "Owen, how are you feeling?"

"I don't know."

"Are you aware of what just happened?"

I wanted to ask her the same thing.

"What were you doing, Owen?"

This was no time to crack and get thrown into a treatment center. I had to see those warriors again—appeal to them for help. "I let the stress get to me, that's all. I haven't been sleeping lately. I've been worried about college and my friends, with all this suicide stuff. I just lost it for a minute. I'll be okay."

She looked at me with big, adoring eyes. "Bless your heart. Why don't I issue you a homework pass so you can rest tonight, then come see me first thing in the morning?"

Whew. Dodged that bullet. I wasn't sure what to expect from my mother, though. As far as she was concerned, this was the second episode this week, and she was already leery of me. *Who knows? She might show up with a straitjacket.*

I stared at the ceiling tiles, trying to process what I'd just witnessed. It was larger than life. It was like watching life versus death.

I wiped my eyes. Why were they pooling? It wasn't because I'd completely humiliated myself, and it wasn't because I was afraid of what my mother would say. I wasn't sad, actually.

Clarity came over me like a soft breeze, but I tried to squelch it because it felt like something supernatural. No, it was more like something . . . spiritual. That was unfamiliar territory for me. But before I could stop the thought, it was echoing across my mind.

I've always believed we're alone, each of us left to fight life's trials on our own. But now I know better. Something—someone—cares.

That realization choked me up.

And it freaked me out.

Did God actually exist?

I dismissed the idea. I had to stick with what I could see and discount what I couldn't. Yes, I was aware of the irony. But the reality was, I hadn't seen God. I'd seen good forces triumph over evil today. That's it.

And where did the champions go? Why didn't they help more? Why not annihilate the Creepers entirely?

I closed my eyes and considered a new life equation: the war between good and evil is real, but evil doesn't stand a chance—so long as the good guys show up.

My mother spent a while in the counselor's office before I was released. I promised I was feeling good enough to drive my motorcycle home, and she didn't push back. I got the idea she'd rather *not* be confined in a tight space with me.

I went straight to my room, got my laptop out, and added to my timeline. What to call the avengers? I settled on *Watchmen*.

My phone lit up with texts. I figured it would help downplay the situation to reply and assure people I was fine.

If only that were true.

Ray Anne had texted. She must have been pretty horrified to hear that the guy she'd made plans with for tomorrow had completely flipped out in front of half the school. She asked if I was okay, and I replied with an apology and a promise: **I'm sorry I acted like an idiot today. I hope you still want to hang out. I won't cause a scene. I swear.**

She didn't break our plans—a huge relief. I still held out hope that I'd discover something revolutionary.

I just hoped I could keep my promise to not freak out and humiliate us both.

FIFTEEN

FRIDAY MORNING, I thought about skipping school, but I worried the Watchmen might show up again and I'd miss it. I really wanted to see them get physical with the Creepers. I had no doubt the Watchmen would put a major beat down on them.

I tried going straight to first period, but the counseling police summoned me to the office. That same big-eyed counselor lady explained that they'd arranged for me to have a mentor. "Given yesterday's cry for help, we believe you'll benefit greatly from the program."

"Do I have to?" Like I wanted some shackled stranger trying to fix me.

"We can't force you to participate, but we believe that meeting with your mentor twice a week will be highly rewarding for you *and* him. You've been assigned to one of Masonville's finest."

What I'd been assigned to was the official at-risk student list. Not my proudest moment.

In walked a tall man in a tailored suit. Polished shoes. Tarnished shackle.

"Owen, this is Dr. Bradford—a physician." The counselor turned to go, but not without repeating, "One of Masonville's finest."

Her cheesy attempt at flirting made things even more awkward.

Dr. Bradford shook my hand, firm and confident. His face was oddly familiar.

We lowered into chairs across from each other, and I mulled it over. *Bradford. A doctor . . .*

Then it clicked, so much irony I practically choked on it.

"You're . . . Dan Bradford's father?"

"Guilty as charged." He smiled—same dimples as Dan.

Even before our minute of small talk, I was ready to end this. But then . . .

"Owen, I know who you are. I was very close to your grandparents."

Wow. For the first time in my life, someone might actually tell me something about my relatives.

He leaned in toward me. "They were devastated when your mother ran away. I met them shortly after, as a teenager, and despite their grief, they graciously opened their home to me—at a trying time in my life. They treated me like I was their own son. Taught me countless invaluable principles about life. And spirituality."

There was no indication he was lying, and yet how could I believe him? My grandparents had been horrible, abusive people. That's the one thing my mother had told me.

"I made your grandparents a promise. If I ever had the pleasure of meeting you, I swore I'd tell you how much they longed to know you. If only your mother . . ."

It was too much to take in—the idea that my mom may have walked out on perfectly loving parents. Was she *that* messed up? That totally selfish?

I bolted out of my chair. "If you were so close to my grandparents, why'd they leave their estate to me and not you?"

He calmly stood, giving me a compassionate smile. "They wanted you in this town in the hope that you would someday carry on their family legacy here. Charitable works and religious activism." He stepped close. "Owen, I swore to your grandmother on her deathbed that if you came to Masonville, I'd teach you the principles and way of life they so diligently instilled in me."

He took a nostalgic glance at our surroundings. "And here we are. Matched in a mentoring program—can you believe it?"

I was still confused but found myself starting to believe him.

"I want you to know something." He spoke with the passion of a coach rallying an exhausted team. "I can teach you incredible things. Self-assurance. Keys to success and influence like you've never known."

I wasn't sure what to say to that.

"Do you have a father, Owen? A man who's investing in your future?"

I was willing to give an honest answer, but paralyzing shame came over me so that I could barely shake my head no.

"I understand," he said, placing a hand on my shoulder. "You know, you could be the son I never had."

I furrowed my brow. "You already have a son."

He dropped his chin and let out a long, exasperated sigh. "He's unteachable. Reckless." He looked me in the eyes. "Weak."

And that's when his whole vibe changed. The compassion was all gone from his face, but way worse than that, his eyes turned different. Dark and cloudy. Threatening as a Creeper's.

And the temperature in the room plummeted.

I took a big step back. "Um . . . I'd better get to class."

I darted out of there, swearing to myself that I was forever done with the mentoring program.

I admit that for a second there, I had liked the thought of having an accomplished man—a doctor, even—take an interest in my life. But Dr. Bradford was clearly *not* a good person.

What had I just witnessed?

I meandered to class and slid into my chair, even more curious and confused about my relatives. I glanced at Dan, in the back row as usual. It was hard to believe, but it was actually possible his home life was about as messed up as mine.

The Watchmen didn't bother coming back to Masonville High that day.

Jess texted me after school: **Miss you.** ☹ **You want to hang out tonight?**

I don't know which was more baffling—making sense of my paranormal world or trying to figure out why females do what they do. Why would she want to spend time with a crazy person? Her words, mind you.

Didn't matter. I had plans with Ray Anne. I was hoping to keep that on the down low though, so I took the easy way out: **Sorry, have to help my mom do stuff around the house.**

I always did most of the chores anyway, so it wasn't a total lie, just a mini-lie.

She replied right away: **Okay. Call me this weekend?**

I went ahead and said I would, then added: **Really hope you stay away from Dan.**

She replied with a thumbs-up. I could only hope that meant she would.

I jumped in the shower to get ready for my date—more like fact-finding mission. It was hard to tell if I was nervous because I was going out with a girl I barely knew or because I no longer trusted myself to act rationally. I didn't want to tell her too much, but I feared I would. And I hoped I could ignore the supernatural distractions, but I feared I couldn't.

I styled my hair to perfection and sprayed on some cologne. I talked my mom into letting me use her SUV for the night, then headed out the door, fighting back the nerves building in my gut. Adrenaline and a belly freeze didn't mix well.

Ray Anne welcomed me inside her house. Thankfully there was still nothing around her neck except a cross necklace.

I stood by the sofa and tried to figure out what to do with my hands. No matter where I put them, it felt unnatural. I was like a geek trying to look cool.

Her parents came into the living room together, both glowing— literally. They stood by their daughter for a moment, and a whiff of something wonderful hit me.

Weird, I know.

Mr. Greiner approached and gave me a super firm, confident handshake.

"It's great to see you again," Ray Anne's mom said, hugging me. Unexpected but nice, I guess.

They sat and motioned for me to sit across from them.

"So, tell us about yourself," Mr. Greiner said.

I'm a psycho who sees beings from another dimension. Mind if I take your daughter out?

I went with a different approach. "Well, I'm a senior. Moved here from Boston almost four months ago. I played on the basketball team at my old school; I run track here. And I always drive the speed limit." We all laughed, except Mr. Greiner.

The interrogation continued. "How did you meet Ray Anne?"

"She was the first person I met at Masonville High. I thought it would be good to connect again." A stupid answer, but it was the best I had.

"What are your plans for tonight?" Mr. Greiner crossed his arms and leaned back in his chair.

"I'm taking Ray Anne out for dinner. I mean, if that's okay with you."

Mr. Greiner stood and pulled me to the side. It was just as awkward as it sounds. "Owen, you look like a nice young man. You know that I'm entrusting you with one of the most precious people in my life. I have faith in you that you're going to act like a gentleman and treat my daughter with decency and respect tonight."

"Oh yes, sir, I will. Of course." I really did have good intentions toward her.

As Ray Anne and I headed out, Mr. Greiner gave her a hug and me a heavy pat on my shoulder. Really heavy.

I decided to take Ray Anne to the river walk in San Antonio. It was over an hour away, but I'd heard Lance say he and Meagan loved going there, and the long drive would give us more time to talk.

Our conversation on the way there was more comfortable than I'd thought it would be. We kept making each other laugh, which was cool.

I couldn't help noticing Ray Anne's beautiful, muscular legs, but I tried not to let my thoughts get away from me. Mr. Greiner's handprint still stung on my back.

By the time we got to the river walk and parked, the sun was setting. Ray Anne's glow looked even more spectacular in the dark. As unusual as it was, nothing about it felt weird. It seemed natural, like something everybody should have.

It was a good social scene—neon lights, live music, buzzing restaurants. But it made me jumpy. I hated crowds now. And of course there were Creepers in the mix.

The word *sick* was slopped on the side of a restaurant in huge lowercase letters. That didn't help my nerves.

I settled on an upscale seafood restaurant. Not cheap, but it had a great atmosphere.

It took almost an hour, but we were finally seated at a candlelit table next to a massive aquarium loaded with rainbow-colored fish and a few sharks. It was awesome. And, to be honest, slightly romantic.

In the dim restaurant, Ray Anne's illumination reflected upward, creating a soft shimmer on her face. It was so . . . intriguing. It was nearly a perfect moment—the only downer being that I kept catching whiffs of Creeper odor.

"So, what's your family like?" It was a reasonable question for her to ask—thoughtful even. But it threw me.

"It's just me and my mom."

"Oh." She cleared her throat. "Is she strict?"

"Not even a little."

"Lucky."

Ah . . . no. "It's not as awesome as you think. My mom is . . ." I took a sip of my sweet tea, as if I could swallow my discomfort.

"Come on. She can't be that bad."

"Trust me."

A cute smile crept across her face. "From what I can tell, she raised a good son."

I've never been one to blush, but she got me on that one.

"What about you?" I said. "Your parents seem like the perfect—"

"They're not." Her whole demeanor changed. I didn't feel comfortable pressing her for an explanation, and she quickly changed the subject, her tone upbeat again. "I heard you stood up to Dan at lunch yesterday, when he was being mean to Jess."

I was glad she'd brought that situation up instead of my soda-throwing meltdown.

I gave a nod, then leaned in toward her. "What's the deal with that guy?"

She had no problem making eye contact with me. "I know he's popular and all, but there's something dark about him. Sad, really."

If she only knew. She took a deep breath, then dropped her chin. "He made my brother's freshman year miserable. Picked on him . . ." She took a sudden interest in her menu.

"So you have a brother?"

She swallowed hard. Formed a polite smile as her eyes welled. "Had . . . He passed away."

Way to go, slick. I wanted to kick myself under the table. "Oh. I'm so sorry."

I wondered how he'd died, but it felt rude to ask.

"It's okay. Really." She smiled at me like we'd known each other forever. "I'm just glad you're willing to stand up for people. We need that at our school."

I'm not sure how she did it, but she made me feel like the most important guy in the room. I liked her already.

We scanned the menu and chatted about what foods we did and didn't like until our conversation was interrupted. I looked over my shoulder and saw a tall, well-dressed lady shouting at a man. Her husband? And there was that filthy Creeper I'd been smelling. Attached to her.

I turned back around. Ray Anne was engrossed in their heated conversation, mouth open.

"I don't know why I put up with you!" the lady said.

"What's wrong with you?" The man stood, and his chair fell over. More heads turned.

I looked back again, at the Creeper. *You just love destroying lives, don't you?*

The couple stormed away from their table, and the waitress chased them down.

"That's one way to get out of paying the check," Ray Anne said.

We both laughed, then went back to minding our own business.

I was stabbing ice cubes with my straw when Ray Anne said, "I can't imagine being attacked by one of those vicious things."

I nearly spilled my drink. "You see them too?"

She pointed to the aquarium. "The sharks?"

My excitement deflated. "Oh, yeah." I worked to regain my composure.

She inched her chair forward. "Are you all right?"

"Absolutely." I changed the subject. "So, everyone has theories about what's causing the suicides. How about you?"

She'd stuffed a fried shrimp in her mouth, but as soon as she was able, she said, "Honestly? I think it's the devil."

I gave her a blank, awkward stare. "That's a joke. Right?"

"No. I mean, I'm not like the protesters or anything."

"Good to know," I said, consuming a shrimp myself.

"Yeah." She giggled, but only for a second. "I do think it's a satanic attack, though." She dabbed her lips with her napkin. "Why our school? I have no idea."

"Let me get this straight. You believe in a literal Satan?"

She raised an eyebrow. "You don't?"

I sat up tall. "I do agree that our school is under attack—actually, I'm sure of it—but I can't say for sure what they are. Where they come from."

Now it was her turn to look at me with a confused, awkward stare. "What do you mean?"

You know that feeling when you're strapped into a megacoaster and it's about to change from clanking uphill to free-falling? That's how I felt. I'd promised myself I'd take it slow, but then again, I had no way of knowing our conversation would go in this direction, much less this quickly.

I let go of my fork, put both palms flat on the table, and lowered my voice. "Ray Anne, if I tell you something unbelievable, something frightening and absurd and—just totally bizarre, will you try to believe me?"

She thought a moment, tucking a strand of hair behind her ear and smearing what was left of her lip gloss in the process. "I will." She said it like she really meant it.

I was probably setting myself up for a major letdown, but I was actually tempted to believe her.

Our waitress came and dropped off the check.

I looked around. "Can we get out of here first?"

We spied a bench in a grassy area in the distance, away from the crowd and bright lights. Everything looked navy blue in the moonlight, except the sidewalk below Ray Anne's feet.

I gazed at the sky, but there wasn't a single star to fix my eyes on. Ray Anne stared at me like a kid at story time, anxious for me to get on with it. I was back at the top of the coaster. I took a deep breath, then went for it.

I started at the beginning, and by the time I'd told her how sick I'd gotten after drinking from the well, she'd slid to the edge of the bench and was hardly breathing. "Keep going," she said.

I explained how I'd seen the shackled jogger lady with chains and cords, and soon, I saw them on everyone.

She seemed to be tracking with me, making me believe it was safe to share more. So I told her everything—about the names on the chains and how they turned out to be real people, and the first Creeper I'd ever witnessed and how it had attached itself to Ashlyn. I eventually got to the note and how I wasn't the only one who saw it.

"I showed Lance and Jess, but they didn't believe my explanation."

By the time I described the amazing star-looking thing kids have, I felt lighter. It was liberating to get the entire horror story off my chest, out in the open air.

She asked why I'd gone berserk in the cafeteria yesterday, so I explained the whole thing. Then, as if I hadn't dumped enough on her . . .

"The reason I asked you out is because you're different. There are some people who don't have chains or anything. Instead there's this awesome glow-like deal around their feet. You have that, Ray Anne. Your parents, too. You're not a slave to the tormentors. And I want to know why."

I turned sideways to face her and moved closer. "I don't have a shackle, but I don't glow either. It's confusing. But I want to make sense of it all. I have to. People are hurting—hurting themselves and each other, and they don't even know why."

I eased back, expecting that any second, she'd dig her phone out of her purse and beg her dad to come get her. Or squirt pepper spray in my eyes.

"Show me the picture of the note."

Was she actually taking me seriously? I enlarged the image, then handed her my phone. She studied it, pulling the image close to her face, then holding it at arm's length, inspecting it like some expert detective. Finally, she handed it back.

"Owen?"

Here comes the hammer.

"It's really difficult to absorb everything you just said, and I honestly don't know what to think. But I don't think you're crazy, and I'm sorry no one has been willing to try and believe you."

It was like a cozy, warm blanket had just been wrapped around my insides.

"I'm willing to try, Owen. I'll try to believe you. And I want to be a good friend to you so you don't feel alone through all of this."

I wanted to give everyone on the river walk a high-five. Did I mention I really liked this girl?

"I'm sure once I think about things more," she said, "I'll have lots of questions, but if you'll be completely honest with me, I'll walk through this with you."

Finally, an ally.

We lingered in the silence a minute. I took a deep breath and managed a smile. "So . . . what's going on in your world?"

She laughed.

Wow.

Ray Anne wasn't kidding when she said she'd have lots of questions. On the drive back, she asked about everything from the water-test results, to the look and feel of the chains, to the size of the Creepers' hands. "Do they know you can see them?" On and on she went, all the way back to Masonville.

I loved every minute of it.

We were almost to her house when she mentioned she was thirsty, so I pulled into a convenience store. It was the least I could do. We were picking out drinks from the refrigerator at the back of the store when two Creepers passed through a wall, both named Terror. It fit them well.

By the time I noticed Ray Anne walking toward them, it was too late to grab her. I bit down hard on my bottom lip as she crossed smack-dab in front of them.

I couldn't believe it. They went out of their way to avoid her, leaning back, hands raised, careful not to cross into her aura or let her out of their sight. It was as if the light surrounding her was toxic to them.

"You coming?" She looked at me.

I tossed a few bucks on the counter, then walked off without my change.

"Did something just happen?" She studied my face.

"Yeah. I'll explain in the car."

I opened the passenger door for her. That's when a different kind of terror showed up.

SIXTEEN

"Looks like you had a change of plans tonight, huh?" Jess stood by her car, yelling loud enough for everyone in a one-mile radius to hear.

"Hey, I um . . ." Busted. Plain and simple.

"So I guess your mommy let you out of the house after all?"

Ray Anne frowned. Jess looked ready to pounce.

I tried to calm things down. "I'll give you a call later, okay?"

"No, it's not okay. You think you can just lie to me?" She shifted her glare to Ray Anne. "What are *you* looking at?"

Ray Anne lowered her chin.

It felt mean, but I didn't know what else to do—I ignored Jess, got in my car, and drove off with Ray Anne.

What were the odds? We were only there five minutes.

I'd had such a great night with Ray Anne. I hated for it to end like this. "I'm sorry about that."

"Did you lie to her about going out with me tonight?"

I reached up to loosen my collar, but it was barely touching my neck.

"I did stretch the truth a little, but only to keep from starting a lot of drama. That obviously blew up in my face. I should have been up front with her. I don't have anything to hide."

There wasn't time to say much else. We pulled into her driveway, and I walked her to the door. She stopped and looked up at me, and I thought maybe she was going to kiss me. No such luck.

"Owen, I need you to make me a promise. Right now."

"Okay." Where was this going?

"Don't ever lie to me. I can overlook a lot, and I know no one's perfect, but please, don't ever, *ever* lie to me. Got it?"

Like I said, I did lie on occasion. Maybe more than occasionally. But I could stick to the truth if I really wanted to.

"I won't lie to you, Ray Anne. I promise."

She hugged me—one of those annoying side hugs—then went inside. Before closing the door, she gave me an adorable smile.

I practically skipped to the car, unable to wipe the grin off my face. She had to be the sweetest girl I'd ever met.

I really meant what I said about not lying to her.

Too bad I'd soon have no choice but to break my promise.

SEVENTEEN

I TOOK THE EASY WAY OUT and apologized to Jess in a text message. She didn't reply.

I would have liked to hang out with Ray Anne again on Saturday, but I didn't want to come off as desperate. We texted back and forth that afternoon, then I called her to explain what had happened with the Creepers in the store. She fired questions at me, and I answered the best I could.

I asked her a lot of questions too, but her answers all struck me as unreliable. Sincere but misguided. If she was glowing, she said, it had to be because of Jesus Christ. He'd saved her.

Christ—a religious zealot who had been dead for twenty centuries.

I'd been an eyewitness to the paranormal for nearly two weeks at that point, and I had yet to see a guy in sandals pry a person out of a shackle. Or show up at all.

She said her beliefs, including her theories about Satan and his demons, were all based on the Bible, and she asked if I owned one. I told her my mom didn't want me bringing one in the house. Not that I'd ever tried.

"Promise me you'll keep an open mind."

"Always."

And we left it at that.

I hoped Sunday afternoon would be uneventful. I'd just washed my motorcycle—a chore I actually liked—when my buddy Walt and another track team guy named Marshall showed up at my house.

"Hey," Walt said from the passenger seat of Marshall's beat-up truck. "You wanna go shoot some hoops, white boy?"

I wasn't sure how I'd run up and down the court with my opponents lugging metal, but I really, really wanted to go. I threw on my favorite Nike shoes and jumped in the truck.

We went to Franklin Park. It was a hot, gorgeous day. It felt amazing to hold a basketball. I'd forgotten what a stress reliever it was.

We didn't keep score, but we knew who was winning. I barely came out on top, but I cut myself some slack. The word rebel was plastered on the basketball goal, and it distracted me, along with everything else.

We walked back to the truck, and Marshall pulled some sports drinks out of a cooler. I'd gulped mine down when Walt asked a loaded question.

"What's this we hear about you seeing freaky stuff?"

I crushed my plastic bottle with one hand. Lance and his big mouth. Some friend he was turning out to be.

"We heard you've been seeing chains and stuff on people," Walt said, "and big alien creatures." He and Marshall looked at each other and busted out laughing.

I leaned against the truck and crossed my arms tight, not amused. At all.

"Behind you!" Marshall pointed and ducked, cracking up.

It's not like I'd never been mocked before, but never about something so serious. I popped my knuckles. Concentrated on breathing in through my nose, out through my mouth.

"So, we're being hunted?" Walt put his hands up like he actually knew karate.

"Yes." I wasn't going to cower. "You are." I threw my crumpled plastic bottle in the bed of the truck, but it bounced out and landed in the grass.

"It was something you found in the woods, right?" Marshall said. "You drank it, and *bam!* Spidey powers. Can you leap over tall buildings?" He did an obnoxious, girly jump over a row of flower-bed rocks.

I rolled my eyes.

Walt made a sad face. "Is it true you're leaving our school?"

"What are you talking about?"

"To go to Sky High." They could hardly catch their breath.

"Laugh all you want. You girls don't have the guts to drink it."

"Are you for real?" Marshall wiped his watery eyes. "We're not scared. Give us some. We'll show you."

He and Walt did a chest bump.

I admit I wanted to punch them in the face—bad—but I'd have to have been heartless to serve them a cup of the living hell I'd been suffering. I told them both to shut up and that it was time to call it a day.

We piled into Marshall's truck. I wish I could say they drove me straight home and that was the end of it.

"These creatures," Walt said, refusing to drop it. "They've invaded our school?"

I nodded, thinking maybe I should walk the rest of the way.

"And they wrote you a note?"

"It's not like that."

"That's what Dan Bradford said."

Dan? How did he know . . .

Oh.

I felt my teeth grinding, the muscles in my neck straining. It was Jess who'd run her mouth, not Lance. She'd blabbed to her loser boyfriend, and now he was having a field day with it. I was livid, but I kept my cool. For a minute.

"Why won't you give us a sip?" Walt said. "Then we'll see too, right?" He and Marshall snickered like toddlers.

"Trust me, you don't want it." I should have stopped there. "So, what else did Dan tell you?"

Walt got a half grin on his face. "That Jess is glad to be back with him instead of you."

I seriously doubted she'd said that. I popped my knuckles again.

"And that you're making all this stuff up for attention."

I shook my head. "Why would I need attention?"

Walt cut his eyes at Marshall, hesitated, then . . .

"Dan says it's 'cause your mom's a sleazy drunk, and you don't know who your daddy is."

No. He. Didn't.

"Stop the truck!"

Marshall nearly swerved into a ditch.

"Dude." Walt reached out like he was about to touch my shoulder but stopped. "I'm sorry. I was just—"

"I said *stop!*"

Marshall slowed, then pulled over. I grabbed the door handle. I was panting, sweating harder now than when we were outside playing ball.

"Don't get out," Marshall said. "Please. Let me take you home. He shouldn't have said that."

I sat there. Fuming.

Thinking.

Plotting.

Walt tried to right the wrong. "I'm an idiot. Forget what I just said, okay?"

Impossible. You can't just unsay things.

I also knew two wrongs don't make a right, but that didn't stop me. I had to settle this. Now. "Make a U-turn."

"Okay." Marshall turned the wheel. "Where we going?"

Walt smiled. "I think I know."

There's a voice in your head that nags at you when you're about to do something wrong. I totally ignored it. All I could think about was sweet vindication. Walt and Marshall were about to regret every stupid thing they'd said—and so was everyone else who had doubted me.

My concern for these guys was bound in a headlock by my pride. I led them through the woods to the clearing, totally aware I was being 100 percent self-centered.

It was dusk when we got to the well. I hoisted the bucket. Neither of the guys paid attention to how it mysteriously filled. Had the old man shown up and caught me in the act, I'm sure I would have come to my senses. But he didn't.

Walt stared at his feet. "There's something moving under us."

"The dragon in his lair." Marshall smirked.

A fist bump this time.

I scooped water from the bucket into their drink bottles, then handed them over.

"Ready?"

"First, a toast." Walt held up his bottle and stared me down. "May this moment haunt you every day, for the rest of your life."

I swallowed hard.

"The time you made your friends get diarrhea," Walt finished.

He and Marshall smiled and bumped bottles.

"You go first," Marshall said.

"Go for it," Walt said.

They kept that up until I forced a solution. "How about you both drink on my count of three?" They were fine with that.

I stepped between them.

"One . . ."

Deep breaths.

"Two . . ."

Bottles up.

"Three."

Consumed.

A still, silent pause, then Walt erupted. "I see the light! I see the light!" His sarcasm was as thick as the shackle around his neck.

Marshall cracked up and threw his empty bottle at my head. "You're a liar, bro." He turned to Walt. "Told you I'd drink it."

Walt puffed up his chest. "You wouldn't have if I hadn't."

They kept it up the whole walk back to the truck—until Walt stopped midsentence and grabbed his gut. "My stomach hurts."

"Mine, too." Marshall grimaced. "And my head."

"That's just the beginning." The seriousness of what I'd done was only starting to sink in. Guilt mixed with elation. I was about to have not one but two people to back up my claims.

"What do you mean?" Marshall looked pale.

"You won't start seeing things right away. First comes the miserable stomach chill. The sightings follow later."

"Shut up." Walt hunched over. "That's not funny."

"I know. That block of ice in your gut, it never goes away completely. I can still feel the cold, even now."

"I thought the diarrhea thing was a joke." Marshall groaned.

Walt turned on me. "I can't believe this, Owen! You knew we were gonna get sick, but you let us drink anyway?"

I felt a tinge of remorse but mostly relief. Everyone was about to have to take me seriously. Including Dan.

"What have you done to us?" Walt stumbled to the truck behind Marshall, both clutching their stomachs.

Misery loves company, and I had two new houseguests. It was inexcusable. And irreversible.

"Look, you asked for this," I said. "It happened. Now we have to focus on what's next." I felt no need to coddle them. "You might as well learn what a Creeper is, before you see one in a few hours."

"A what?" Walt crouched low to the ground, wincing, massaging his head.

"Pretty soon you'll see the most horrific things you've ever laid eyes on, and you'll smell them too. But don't freak out. As long as you don't say whatever word is chiseled or burned into their face, they probably won't pay attention to you."

"What in the world are you talking about?" Marshall's bottom lip curled down.

"Hey, I went through this all by myself. At least you guys have me and each other."

Walt scowled. I deserved it.

"Okay, here's the plan," I said. "You guys come to my house and stay the night—"

"No," Marshall interrupted. "I'm going home."

"But you'll need me to—"

"We're going home, Owen!" Even Walt's dark skin looked pale now.

"Fine," I said. "But you have to come to my house first thing in the morning—like at six o'clock. You can't talk to anyone or even look at them. And don't try to go to your parents. You won't like what you see."

I was seriously starting to feel the weight of what I'd done now. "We'll figure this out, guys. I'll tell you everything tomorrow."

Walt bent over, hands on his knees, and breathed deeply, like he hoped to barf. "Tomorrow's Monday. I can't miss school. I have to get exempt from finals."

"Walt." I made him stand and look at me. "By tomorrow, you won't care about finals. Or school. Or anything except helping me figure out how to stop the Creepers."

They both looked pitiful, holding their stomachs, knees bent, trembling.

"I know how you feel right now, but it's gonna be okay." Another one of my mini-lies.

I offered to drive, but Marshall refused to give me the keys. We drove past a Creeper, and I cringed. *At least they won't be blind to it anymore. Maybe they'll thank me.*

Not likely.

Marshall got half of his truck into my driveway.

"Remember, guys." I got out, then spoke through the open window. "Get to my house at 6:00 a.m. Don't talk to anyone. Or look at anyone." I started to walk away, then turned back. "And whatever you do, do *not* look in the mirror."

I didn't have to deal with a metal reflection like they would. It might be enough to drive them insane.

By the time I got to my front door, regret covered me from head to toe, squeezing me like an extra layer of skin.

All I could do was wait.

At 6:04 a.m., I sent Walt and Marshall a text. **You coming? You okay?**

No response. I paced the living room. Had they gone to the emergency room? Called the police? Convinced an angry mob to march to my house, led by their outraged parents?

By 6:45 a.m., I was freaking out, contemplating whether to try and find Walt's house or stay put in case they showed up. I flipped on the

TV, a nervous habit. The news was on, the reporter broadcasting from my school parking lot. The sun was barely up, and already the protesters were there, acting moronic in the background.

"It appears that two more Masonville High School students have taken their lives," the reporter said.

"*What?*" I stood inches from the screen, hands cupped over my mouth. "Who?"

"Both of the students were discovered by their parents early this morning at their individual homes. Although the cause of death has yet to be determined, authorities fear it was a double suicide."

"For crying out loud, who?"

"According to their classmates, high school seniors Walt Davis and Marshall Roshkey were fellow athletes and close friends. Although many details are not being disclosed at this time, we do know that one of the boys was found deceased in his bed while the other is said to have been discovered on his bedroom floor."

"No!" I paced.

"No! No! No! No! *No!*" I collapsed to the floor. The room was spinning. Surely I'd heard wrong. Not Walt. Not Marshall.

I ripped my shirt off. Punched the floor. Knocked a vase off a table. What happened? Had they killed themselves? Or . . .

I curled up in a ball, withering in self-hatred. "Did that water . . . did I . . . ?" I grabbed my shirt off the floor and wiped my snot with it. "*I* did this! I can't believe I did this!"

My mother found me on the floor. "What happened, Son?"

I grabbed her ankles and sobbed. She bent down and rubbed my shoulders. "Tell me."

"Walt and this guy Marshall. They're dead, Mom."

She hugged me harder than she had in forever. "Oh, Owen, I'm so sorry. I'm so very sorry. Their poor parents."

She eventually let go. I didn't lift my head off the floor for a while—just lay there like a filthy clump of dog crap while my mother tried to coax me onto the sofa.

I heard my phone swoosh, an incoming text. Unreasonable as it was, I actually thought it might be Walt.

It was Ray Anne. **Did you hear? Two more.** ☹

There was no way either of those guys took their own lives. It had to have been the water. I felt like their blood was smeared across my face, dripping from my hands. I wanted to run away. Hide in a dark hole until I suffocated.

I had to leave. I picked myself up off the floor and searched frantically for my keys in illogical places.

"Where are you going, Owen?"

I didn't have a clue.

I finally spotted my keys on the coffee table and ran to the front door. I was shirtless but didn't care. I flung the door open.

Then froze.

"Owen Edmonds?"

Two police officers. On my doorstep.

EIGHTEEN

I WOULD HAVE DENIED my own name had my mother not spoken up.

"Yes, this is my son, Owen."

One of the officers looked to be in his midthirties. The other, an older man in street clothes, was holding a badge. "I'm Detective Benny," he said, "and this is Officer McFarland. We need to ask you a few questions. May we come in?"

My mother opened the door for them, then scurried around the living room, picking up empty wine glasses, like the police had come to arrest her for being an alcoholic parent.

Detective Benny motioned for me to sit on the sofa, then stared down at me, his protruding gut jostling over my head. "I take it you heard about Walter Davis and Marshall Roshkey."

Guess my bloodshot eyes gave it away.

"Yes. Just now, on the news. Really hard to believe." Most murderers have to pretend like they're grieving, but not me. The officers didn't seem concerned with how I was feeling, though.

"When did you last see Walt and Marshall?"

Think, Owen. Think.

"The three of us went to play ball yesterday."

"What time and where?" Detective Benny pulled a notepad and pen from his pocket.

"I guess it was about six-thirty when they picked me up. We went to Franklin Park." I stuffed my trembling hands under my legs, paranoid that my body language was all wrong.

"How long were you there?"

"An hour, I guess. I wasn't paying attention."

"Did either of them display any odd behavior or say anything to you about plans to harm themselves?"

"No, sir. They seemed fine."

My mind felt like it was in a blender set on high. I couldn't decide if it was in my best interest to fess up about the water-drinking incident or conceal it at all costs.

"Owen, Marshall's truck was seen headed into the woods behind Masonville High yesterday evening. Why is that?"

"Well, we went to the woods after we left the park."

"What for?"

"We wanted to jog. There's trails back there."

Detective Benny rubbed his chin. Nearly closed his eyes. "So after playing basketball for an hour, you wanted to go for a jog? In the woods?"

A ridiculous alibi, I realized now, but it was too late to change it.

"Yeah. Walt and Marshall wanted to race." Still weak, but it's what came to me.

Detective Benny responded to a call on his cell, then lowered to one knee in front of me. I felt hot splotches expanding on my neck.

"Wanna tell me why you sent both boys a text at 6:04 this morning asking if they were okay?"

"Well . . ."

Lying to my mom was easy. Lying to teachers, not so bad. Lying to the cops? Think tightrope walking between skyscrapers in Dubai.

Blindfolded.

Buck naked.

"Yesterday Marshall said he'd pick Walt and me up early so we could go grab breakfast before school. When they didn't show, I asked if everything was okay. I had no idea they were . . ."

Officer McFarland received a page on his radio, summoning him elsewhere. It seemed fate had dealt me a get-out-of-jail-free card. For now, anyway. But my heart still hammered like a nail gun.

Detective Benny assured me he'd be in touch. He looked at me the same way Ray Anne's father had.

Not good.

I quarantined myself in the bathroom and eventually showered, letting the steamy water clobber me in the face. The more I thought about it, the less doubt there was in my mind that neither Walt nor Marshall committed suicide. The cause of death was undetermined because there were no outward signs of injury. But the water had ravaged them from within. I was sure of it. The water I had scooped out and told them to drink.

I didn't mean to kill them, but that didn't make them any less dead. I was guilty of manslaughter. That was a tough one to swallow. I had no idea why the water hadn't killed me, but right now . . .

I wished it had.

It occurred to me to go to the police and confess everything, but how would I explain? If I hadn't lied to Ms. Barnett about where I'd gotten that water sample, she could have vouched for me, assuring the police I genuinely believed it was clean. But I had lied to her, and to go back now and try to explain the situation would only expose what a liar I was, making me a prime suspect.

To make things worse, I'd told Lance and Jess that the water in the woods had made me deathly ill. How would I defend my decision to serve it to Walt and Marshall? I'd clearly acted with malicious intent, and I was sure a prosecutor could spin that into a believable motive for murder.

I had no choice but to keep my mouth shut.

Call it a hunch, but I had a feeling prison would be crawling with Creepers. Getting locked up was not an option.

I turned off the shower water, then stood there, misery weighing so hard on me it seemed impossible to step up and out of the tub.

So this is what survivor's guilt feels like.

I was responsible for the deaths of two guys, two young people with their whole lives ahead of them. I tried to think of a way to make things right, as if life offers a miraculous Undo button when you really, really need it. But there was no undoing this. No last-minute hope or second chances. Just unbearable guilt and a skull-splitting headache.

I slid my towel off the shower rod and wrapped it around my aching head—face and all—pressing it against my ears in a useless attempt to silence the voice in my head:

"May this moment haunt you every day, for the rest of your life."

Walt's toast. A premonition of some sort? Or a well-deserved curse?

At some point, I talked myself into leaving the bathroom. I made it to my room, where I threw on some boxer shorts, then wrapped myself inside my sheets like a tortured mummy.

I basically stayed there for a week, eating just enough to keep my body functioning. Not that I believed I deserved to live—I just couldn't endure the pain of starvation.

My mom nagged me to go to school and ordered me to keep up with chores and acted appalled at my messy room, but I tuned her out. Maybe she'd realize now how much I'd always done for her.

I had no desire to speak to anyone during my self-imposed house arrest—well, except for Ray Anne. I made up an excuse for staying home all week, and she bought it. She talked about Walt and Marshall and at one point asked my opinion about the cause of death.

"There's a rumor," she said. "It may have been murder. Do you believe it?"

"No," I said, scrubbing the word guilty on my living room wall with a Mr. Clean Magic Eraser. "There's no way that's true."

The black letters weren't coming off.

Unfortunately, during my seclusion, I couldn't stop people from coming to see me. Detective Benny came by and asked a whole lot more questions. I did the best I could to give reasonable answers, but I was sure he picked up on the rotten stink of my deception.

That counselor lady from my school, who liked to talk obnoxiously close to my face, came to see me twice. She let me know that no matter how my grades tanked or my absences stacked up, any senior who stayed enrolled and alive at Masonville High until the end of May would graduate. That was good to hear, since I had no intention of doing schoolwork ever again.

She wanted me to talk about my feelings, my grief, and all my new-found phobias triggered by the suicides, so I just played along. I would have liked to confide in her, but those days were over. I couldn't tell a single soul what was really going on in my head, including Ray Anne. I kept up my charade with her, acting like I was grieving Walt and Marshall's deaths just like everyone else. Yeah, I broke my promise not to lie to her, but what choice did I have?

My seclusion brought zero comfort. Hard as I tried to get rid of the sickening thought, I couldn't stop imagining Walt and Marshall on autopsy tables. Scalpels probing their cold bodies inside and out.

On Sunday night, exactly one week after I'd led my buddies to guzzle down killer cocktails, I felt just as miserable as the moment I'd learned they were dead.

Walt's funeral was the next day, and Marshall's, the day after that. I killed them—the least I could do was pay my respects. Besides, skipping out on their funerals would make the police even more suspicious.

I had no idea how I'd keep it together while their parents and everyone sobbed, begging for an answer.

One minute I wanted to punch my own face, and the next, I was stressing over keeping my butt out of prison. If I'd thought my future was wrecked before, now it was totally annihilated. My dream of becoming a doctor went from majorly threatened to a definite no way. Saving lives is not an acceptable career for a murderer.

I didn't know what my future looked like, but words like *dark*, *lonely*, and *major depressive disorder* came to mind.

It seemed like our entire school was at Walt's funeral, along with half the city. Things almost got violent when protesters had the nerve to show up outside the funeral home, shouting their senseless accusations. Walt's dad nearly went to fists. I didn't blame him.

The press was there, of course, but I hadn't expected my mom to want to come. She smelled like alcohol, but oh well.

The front section of seats, behind family, was reserved for track-team members, so my mother and I had to sit there. So much for my plan to hide out in the back. A crowd spilled into the foyer and out the door onto the street. Detective Benny was there too.

I tried not to look at the shiny, gray elephant in the room: Walt's casket. It was open, and that really bothered me. I focused on the rolled-up program in my clammy hands, my mom's overstuffed purse on the floor, flowers lining the room—anything but his embalmed body.

While I watched the slide show of Walt's life, my chest felt like it was being severed in two with a dull knife. Baby pictures. Swimming lessons. Birthday parties. His senior cap-and-gown picture.

I squeezed my eyes shut.

If I felt this bad, how were his parents surviving? Walt's little sister looked just like him. She buried her face in her mother's lap and bawled. Walt's mom glanced over her shoulder and narrowed her eyes. At me? Did she know something?

I kept my head down for most of the funeral and made zero eye contact with Mrs. Davis, almost drowning in the mucus running down the back of my throat as I strained to hold in my emotions.

At one point, I felt a wave of chilled air hit my neck. Sure enough, a quick glance over my shoulder and I realized there was a Creeper looming in the back, too far away for me to read its name. It seemed like its dead eyes were fixed on me. I tried to put it out of my mind.

By the time Walt's uncle finished sharing some final words, I had slid to the very edge of my seat, ready to jump up and get out of there. But the usher signaled for our row to stand, then motioned for us to approach the casket in a single-file line, following the family.

I'd heard that when you hyperventilate, you're supposed to breathe into a paper sack, but I didn't have one. I cupped my hands over my mouth and heaved air into my palms. My mom looped her arm through mine, tugging me forward.

I stared at the dark-red carpet, dreading each step like a steer being led to the slaughter, only I was the executioner, forced to face my victim—a defenseless lamb.

Another step. The casket invaded my peripheral vision. I thought

I might faint and honestly wanted to. My heart ached. It burned as if someone had beaten and bruised it, then set my chest on fire.

The line moved forward again.

"I'm so sorry," I heard a lady say into the coffin.

And just like that, an epiphany.

I'd never get this opportunity again, to come face-to-face with Walt. I had to suck it up—be a man and say what needed to be said.

Another step.

I wasn't willing to look at him until the moment. I took in every detail of the flowers draped over the bottom half of the casket, mostly white blooms that struck me as pale and stark and cold.

One more step and it would be my turn. My mother's voice broke with emotion as she whispered something. How was I going to get through this?

She stepped away. The guy behind me bumped into me, expecting me to move. It took me a second. I closed my eyes and slid forward.

"Walt . . ." My voice was soft as a breeze but shaking like an earthquake. "I know I don't deserve your forgiveness, but—"

I opened my eyes.

And jolted backward, nearly falling.

NINETEEN

WALT'S BODY LOOKED atrocious—mutilated and horrible—but I couldn't take my eyes off of it. My arms reached and flailed, even though I wasn't falling and there was nothing to cling to.

Walt's chains and cords were coiled meticulously around his neck, encircling his shackle, but that wasn't the bad part. What took my breath away was his midsection. It was gone—I'm talking completely caved in, like a grenade had detonated in his gut, disintegrating his suit and stomach. And it left a filthy hole, not lined with blood or body parts, but with what looked like dirt.

Thick, grungy, dark powder.

I scanned the room. Why hadn't anyone warned me? Why was the casket even open?

"Son?" My mom reached up and gripped my arm, leading me through the sea of gawking, red-nosed faces toward the door.

"Mom, you should have told me that he . . . that he looks so . . ." I didn't know what to call it.

"I know it's hard." She started weeping again. "Seeing him lying there, like he's sleeping. So handsome."

"Mom, he looks terrible!" I pulled my arm away. "What *happened* to him? Why does he have that huge hole?"

The lines on her forehead deepened. "What are you talking about?" She gave polite smiles to all the eavesdroppers, then glared at me.

"Mom, he had that disgusting—" Oh. I finally got it. One more thing only I could see.

"Forget it." I shoved past the crowd and out the door, then wove through the masses until I made it to my mother's SUV. I looked back to see if she was coming, and she was—and so was *it*. That Creeper had tracked me all the way from the building. It was a few steps behind my mom.

"Hurry!"

She used her remote to unlock the vehicle for me, and I was inside with the door shut in seconds.

"Come on!" She couldn't hear me, but I yelled anyway. She got in just in time, and I locked the doors, then peered out the rear window. It was standing there, staring at me.

We pulled away, but not before I saw its name:

murder

A chill crept around my neck.

I went straight to my room and grabbed my laptop. I turned again and again and again to look behind me, officially suffering from OCD now. Once I pulled up my timeline, I made my strangest entry yet.

Monday, April 9—Walt's dead body has gross gaping hole.
Chains and cords appear to have been removed and spiraled
around his neck. Cuffs at the end of chains are gone.

I also documented how the Creeper had followed me. My guilt had probably led it to me, like bloody chum enticing a shark.

No way I was going to Marshall's funeral tomorrow. I hoped it didn't raise any red flags with the police, but I had to sit this one out. I couldn't face that a second time.

I was slumped over the desk in my room texting Ray Anne when my mom barged in and dropped a bomb on me. "Coach called. They need one more pallbearer tomorrow, and they thought of you. I told them you'd do it."

"By *pallbearer*, you mean one of the guys who carries the casket?"

"Yes. It's the least you can do." She turned to leave, dragging her chains along.

"No freaking way!"

She spun around, jaw dropped.

"Mom, you saw how I reacted today. It's too much. I can't do it!"

She crossed her arms, then proceeded to give a mouthful of clichéd advice. "Life isn't always easy, Son. You can't run from difficult situations."

I jumped up. "You're going to lecture me about not running? Not taking the easy way out? You, the woman who spends every day drowning her secret sorrows in alcohol and useless men?"

She jerked, like my words jabbed her. "I don't know who you think you are!" Her bottom lip quivered.

"Well, I don't have a clue who you are! You won't tell me anything. Your past, my grandparents. How do I know they were really the monsters you've made them out to be?"

"Excuse me!" Her eyes pooled now—an explosive mix of anger and pain.

"And what about my father?" I'd really marched into forbidden territory now. "You won't even talk to me about him."

She gasped. "How dare you! I've told you everything you need to know, Owen."

"Have you?"

Now I'd done it. She shouted so loudly and furiously that white foam gathered in the corners of her mouth. "How many times have I explained to you that I had a horrible upbringing and a terrible relationship with my parents? I never would have dreamed of introducing you to them. And I've told you over and over how your father walked out on us."

Because of me. I understood that.

"What more do you want to know, Owen? Come on!"

"For starters, how are you able to pay cash for things? Your Infiniti. Our house in Boston. You work, like, two hours a day—maybe."

I walked toward her, shoving my finger in her pouty face. "And why don't you have a single picture of my dad?"

"Like I said the last ten times you asked me that, it was too painful to hold on to that stuff. I got rid of it and started a new life." Her voice softened. "With you."

She put her hand on my shoulder, but I stepped back.

"You're hiding something, Mom. I know it."

"Well, you would know."

"What's that supposed to mean?"

"You don't think I've noticed the way you're acting lately? That you're hallucinating? Delusional? You're on drugs, though we both know you'd never admit it."

I felt my veins bulging in my neck. "So help me, if you accuse me of that one more time—"

"Quit denying it!" she shouted in my face, her arms stiff, fists tight.

I had to put some space between us, had to walk away from the urge to curse in her face. I leaned back against the wall. "I'm not gonna let you do this anymore, Mom."

"Do what?"

"Turn the microscope on me in order to take the focus off you."

"Just stop it! I'm leaving. I have plans with Frank." She stormed out of my room—the woman who'd just told me we can't run from difficult situations.

I heard the front door slam. Daisy was barking her head off. I looked out my window, and my mother was still crying. But she was no longer my concern.

Murder hovered at the end of my driveway. Peering up at me.

TWENTY

I SPENT MOST OF THAT evening staring out of my window. At sunset the monster—Murder—vanished. Still, I hardly slept that night. By morning, Daisy was sitting at the foot of my bed, panting like always, but with her eyes fixed on my window. I lifted a corner of the blinds.

Still no Creeper. For now.

My mom and I did the usual—acted like there was no conflict between us and mostly kept to ourselves. She'd spoken with my coach the night before and found out Marshall's casket would be closed. Given that fact, I decided I'd go ahead and attend the funeral and endure the pallbearer thing. I gave my mother one condition: Ray Anne and her mom would be there, and I wanted to sit by them.

Yes, I wanted Ray Anne near me because I really, really liked her, but also because I'd seen the way she repelled Creepers. And I needed some repellent right about then.

I kept looking outside while getting dressed.

"What is it, girl?"

Daisy remained facing the window, ears pinned back, eyes unflinching. I rubbed her head, but she wouldn't relax.

It was time to go.

I was headed down the driveway toward my mom's SUV when I noticed a black Escalade parked across the street. The dark-tinted driver's-side window lowered, and I immediately stopped. *What is* he *doing here?*

"Hello, Owen," Dr. Bradford called to me. "Hope you don't mind— I come here sometimes. The house brings such fond memories of your grandparents."

Of course I minded. It was weird.

He straightened his black tie. "Can I give you a ride to the funeral?"

"I'm going with my mom."

He nodded, smiling politely, but I could still see the disappointment on his face.

"You ever need anything, Owen, I'm here for you."

I could only bring myself to shrug. He smiled again, waved, and drove away. I watched him go, trying to shake off the uneasy feeling crawling up my spine.

Finally my mom exited the house. I lowered myself into the passenger seat of her vehicle and flipped on the air-conditioning while she talked in a flirty voice on the phone with Frank. Gross.

We were backing out of the driveway when I glanced up. The word that flew out of my mouth shocked even my mom.

"Owen!" She slammed the brakes and elbowed me. "What's the matter?"

"It's . . ." I took slow, controlled breaths. "Nothing. Never mind." She wouldn't believe me.

"Don't scare me like that. And watch your mouth."

"Just drive, Mom. Please?"

She drank like a sailor but never allowed me to talk like one. If she could have seen what I'd seen, though, she would have been more understanding. That Creeper, Murder, had climbed up our house and was clinging to the brick next to my second-story bedroom window like a venomous insect. The word *liar* was written above the glass.

Had it been crouched up there all night? My cold belly churned.

My mom and I didn't talk the entire drive. Just as well; it gave me time to think. Hopefully Ray Anne would come over later. Maybe she could run the Creeper off. If only I knew how to call on some Watchmen to exterminate the thing. Their neglect was troubling. Inexcusable, really.

Marshall's funeral was at a huge, plush church with more plasma screens than a sports bar. Masses of people were there, just like at Walt's ceremony. We met up with Ray Anne and Mrs. Greiner, then sat in the middle section together. It was calming to be around some glowing, chainless people. I saw more of them scattered here and there around the sanctuary.

Some preacher took the stage in a trendy dark-gray suit with a skinny black tie. He was baby faced, with blond highlights in his spiky hair, and truth be told, probably making a fortune off that enormous church. And he was glowing.

Maybe this whole thing is about being one of those churchgoin' types. Certainly Ray Anne's family fit that description. But how would that work? Follow the rules, endure mindless traditions and guilt trips, drop a few sizable checks in the offering plate, and suddenly your shackle falls off?

Not likely.

Two girls sang the saddest song I'd ever heard, then Marshall's relatives shared stories about him. All three females next to me were bawling. I struggled to hold it in. Marshall and I hadn't exactly been close, but he had been my friend. And his death felt personal.

One thing was certain—funerals are miserable, especially when the occasion is your fault.

The preacher stepped up to the podium again, but it was hard to pay attention. For one thing, Jess was there, sitting next to Dan, staring me down the entire time. We still hadn't cleared the air since the whole convenience-store debacle. And why was she still with him, after the way he had hurt her at lunch?

Second, I kept looking at Marshall's devastated parents. For a moment, I considered confessing my crime and begging their forgiveness. But the moment passed.

And third, the casket.

I wanted the preacher to hurry up so I could get my pallbearer duties over with.

What were the odds? Me, the guy who led Marshall to the fatal water, about to escort him again, toward burial.

I pulled one of the envelopes from a little box attached to the back of the chair in front of me and started aimlessly folding it into squares.

"Allow me to remind you," the preacher said, "of what the Bible says in Ephesians, the sixth chapter and twelfth verse. It says that in this life, our fight isn't with other people, but against the wicked spiritual forces in the heavenly, unseen world—the rulers, authorities, and cosmic powers of this dark age."

The hairs on the back of my neck rubbed against my shirt collar.

"That's why verse thirteen tells us to put on God's armor, so that when the evil day comes, we can resist and withstand the enemy's attacks."

"That's what I've been talking about," Ray Anne whispered.

It was the closest description yet of what I'd been witnessing.

The preacher asked us to bow our heads. I complied. My mom kept hers up. He prayed, then the other pallbearers and I came forward. We'd been instructed to carry the casket down the center aisle and out the front of the church.

I hoisted up my end of the coffin, and grief grabbed hold of me, compressing my insides, pressuring me to snap. I knew by now that heartbreak is more than figurative—sadness physically injures the body. And there's no quick way to medicate the wound. Well, unless you turn to mind-numbing addictions, but that was for lowlifes.

I had a choice: drown in despair or cling to determination. I sided with determination. And if I ever figured out how to dispel Creepers and free people, I'd never stop doing it. That was my vow, a kind of memorial in my soul to Walt and Marshall.

We made our descent down the aisle. It was twice as long as I'd thought and was lined with row after row of dejected, teary-eyed mourners. Under a sunny sky, we slid the coffin into the glistening black hearse, then I watched an elderly man with shaky hands shut the door. An old man. Something Marshall would never become.

I turned my back on the hearse and tried not to think about it—how

Marshall's body was about to be six feet under, beyond the reach of sunlight, oxygen, or human touch. Forever.

I hated myself all over again.

My mom turned onto our street, and I leaned forward, straining to look at our house. Murder was still there, towering, proud, on top of the roof now. And he wasn't alone. My mom pulled into the garage, and I hurried to the driveway, looking up. Accuser, my mom's assailant, was with Murder.

Some tag team.

Ray Anne had agreed to come over, but she wanted to change first. I drove my mom's SUV to her house and waited—no way her parents would let her ride on my motorcycle. I used the downtime to make a phone call. The receptionist answered, and I asked if I could talk to the man who'd just spoken at Marshall's funeral.

"Pastor Newcomb," she said. "I'll transfer you."

His assistant answered, and I repeated my request.

"Okay, what is this regarding?"

"Just some questions."

"Give me a second, please." She hummed a high-pitched melody. "I'm sorry, he doesn't have availability for at least five weeks. Are you a member here?"

"No. I was Marshall's friend."

"So you're in high school?"

"Yes." Never mind that I hardly went anymore.

"I tell you what. How about I have Scott call you? Our student director?"

I reluctantly agreed and gave her my number. For all I knew, Scott was shackled.

Waiting in the car, it didn't take long to relax into the headrest and let my eyes drift shut, drained inside and out from back-to-back funerals. Naturally, when Ray Anne's mother tapped on my window, I jumped. Then rolled it down.

"We'd love to have you and your mother over for dinner tonight. What do you say?"

My mom and I had never been anyone's dinner guests before. "Thanks, Mrs. Greiner. I'll check with her." I was pretty sure she'd pass.

Ray Anne eventually got in the car, still puffy eyed and sniffling. "I hate funerals."

"Not as much as I do."

She fastened her seat belt, then pulled a new pack of Mentos spearmint gum from her purse and handed it to me.

"My favorite. How'd you know?"

She smiled. "You had some the night we went out." I smiled back at her.

"How's your mom?" she said.

"My mom? Fine. Why?" I managed to peel my eyes away from Ray Anne's long legs and make the turn off her street.

"She seemed pretty uncomfortable today."

"Yeah. Church weirds her out."

"Why?" Ray Anne could never resist probing.

"Her parents. In public, they were devout, religious people. At home, really abusive. At least that's what she says."

"Oh. That's terrible."

"Yeah, I don't think . . ."

I would have let my statement go if she hadn't stared at me with those blue eyes, pulling it out of me. "I don't think I could ever become religious. I mean, I don't mind doing good things for people, and I could probably sit through church once in a while. But I could never see myself being a person who prays before meals and goes around talking about God all the time, like his existence is a reality. I doubt that's why you glow, but if it is, then there's not much hope for me. And seriously no hope for my mother."

"Well, maybe if you'd—"

"Religion is a farce, Ray Anne. A myth invented to give people hope. False hope. I'm the type of person who needs proof—reliable evidence, not wishful thinking."

"Funny, you of all people, needing more proof."

"Is it too much to ask that God would prove himself?"

She looked away but didn't mince words. "Sounds to me like what you really want from God is an apology."

"What?"

"For all the bad that's happened. Especially to your mom. And you."

The urge to get defensive shot up in me like a rocket, but I managed to diffuse it. "I suppose if God poked his head through the clouds and apologized to me, I'd accept that as proof of his existence."

She shook her head.

We turned into my neighborhood, and I caught her up on things—Walt's shocking appearance the day before and how Murder had been tracking me ever since.

"Why do you think it's after you?"

I never intended to keep feeding Ray Anne lies, but . . .

"I don't have a clue. All I know is he's on my roof right now, along with another one called Accuser. I thought maybe you could come over and . . ."

"What? You think I'm, like, Creeper kryptonite?"

I grinned. "Something like that."

"I'm here to help, but I am *not* climbing on your roof."

I loved that she was keeping a sense of humor. Mine had all but shriveled up and died.

I pulled up to my house. Ray Anne opened the pack of gum she'd gotten me and shoved a piece in her mouth before handing me one.

"That was interesting today," I said, "the pastor's comments. About forces of wickedness."

"I'm telling you, that's what's going on, Owen." She chomped down on her gum twice as fast as I did.

"What do you know about it?"

She sighed. "Well, it's not like I know everything. My church hardly talks about it. But I do know evil has been defeated."

"Really?" It took great restraint not to belly laugh. "Could've fooled me."

She quit chewing, stared me down, then pulled the fluorescent gum from her mouth. "Here."

"You—want me to hold your gum?" I wrapped it in a Kleenex.

She was out of the car already, charging up my driveway, mumbling something. Praying, I assumed.

I wondered how brave she would be if she could actually see what she was up against. I followed but not as fast. The two Creepers began to stir, bumping into each other.

I caught up and watched her, how her eyes scanned the rooftop. I could have stared at her all day.

"What's happening now?" she asked.

I glanced at the Creepers. "They look agitated."

"Good."

She took a big step forward, and they hissed. Another step, and they scurried to the edge of the roof, their heads facing the opposite direction from their decrepit bodies.

"Now?" She was amazing.

"They seem really bothered by you. I think they're leaving."

Murder and Accuser did an eerie maneuver, arching and contorting their backs, then fell backward and floated down. Their nasty feet made contact with the grass, but instead of running, they sank into the earth up to their waists, their torsos and heads still above ground. Then they defied more laws of nature by traveling backward in the opposite direction from how they were facing, until they were gone.

"Have they left?" Ray Anne was wide eyed, fully engrossed in what was happening.

"No." I couldn't resist. I stepped back, shielded my head. "They . . . they're coming! Right at you!"

I thought she'd run. Instead that girl stepped even closer to my house and planted her feet apart, shoving her arms straight out like a cop stopping traffic.

"No weapon formed against me will prosper!" She yelled it twice. "What are they doing now?"

I covered my mouth, exploding on the inside.

"They're trembling, aren't they?" She raised her fists in the air like a boxing-ring champion. "Aren't they?"

I was laughing too hard to talk.

"What's going on?" she huffed, dropping her hands onto her hips.

I finally came clean and told her she'd run them off minutes ago.

"Next time Creepers come crawling, don't call me." She turned away, only mildly mad as best as I could tell. I turned her around and hugged her.

Man, it felt good.

My mother actually agreed to go to Ray Anne's for dinner, but I'd asked her in front of Ray Anne, so she pretty much had to say yes. She even brought a loaf of freshly baked bread. Store bought, but still warm.

Mrs. Greiner ushered us into her home like the star of an HGTV show, proud to show off her small but well-decorated house. My mom did the half-smile thing, looking uncomfortable. She was allergic to kindhearted women. Don't ask me why.

There was quite a spread on the table. Place mats, cloth napkins, covered dishes. Ray Anne didn't seem to think much of it.

Mr. Greiner barged into the room like a cannonball, his voice loud and enthusiastic. "Well, hello! I'm glad you could join us." His smile was on par with Santa's. My mom glared at me like I'd forced her into this. Which I kind of had.

Ray Anne stood by her parents for a moment, and there it was again, a splash of that sweet scent I'd smelled the first time I'd come over.

We took our seats around the table, and when I finally got my napkin unwound, my set of silverware crashed to the floor. Nice.

About the time Mr. Greiner started raving about his wife's irresistible twice-baked potatoes, the unbelievable fragrance hit me again.

"What?" Ray Anne tapped me with her foot under the table.

"Nothing." I didn't feel comfortable announcing that, as best as I could tell, when a glowing family comes together, they give off a really spectacular scent.

Mr. Greiner offered to pray over the meal, then they all joined hands, reaching toward my mom and me. It was the third time in five minutes my mom made her uncomfortable face—the second was when I'd dropped my silverware.

The food was delicious. Pot roast and carrots cooked to perfection. Once we got past the heavyhearted discussion about our friends' funerals, there was lots of small talk. At one point, Mrs. Greiner mentioned her deceased son, Lucas, and Ray Anne narrowed and rolled her eyes at her mother. I didn't get it. Then the subject changed, and my mom contributed to the conversation better than I'd thought she would. Prom came up. "Owen, you already have a date, right?"

"Um, no, Mom. That fell through."

"You know, Ray Anne doesn't have a date either." Mrs. Greiner grinned like a kid who'd just found a chocolate bar. She clarified that several guys had asked Ray Anne, but she'd turned them all down for one reason or another.

It took all of about fifteen seconds for my unruly mom and Mrs. Manners to start giggling back and forth, making plans like Ray Anne and I couldn't think for ourselves.

"So how about it?" Mom looked back and forth between Ray Anne and me.

"It's only two weeks away," Ray Anne said. "I don't have a dress."

"What about that one at the mall you liked?" Mrs. Greiner was already reaching for her wallet. "You could buy that one."

I rarely saw my mom so happy, but I was still annoyed. It wasn't the idea of an evening with Ray Anne that bothered me. I was totally up for that. But a stiff tux, crowded dance floor, and Creeper-ridden prom scene? No thanks.

"What do you say, guys?" My mom practically mouthed the word *yes*.

"Sounds great," I said.

"Yeah," Ray Anne said.

Mrs. Greiner burst into applause, and my mom bounced in her chair. Whatever.

Seconds later, Ray Anne and I were out the door, on our way to the mall. Even if I had known what was about to happen, there would have been no way to prepare myself.

Not for this.

TWENTY-ONE

THE AUTOMATIC DOUBLE DOORS AT the food court slid open, and the smell of cinnamon rolls swarmed us, carrying traces of rotten Creeper funk. They were there, scattered and slithering around, some connected to people. There were plenty of them, but nothing like the mass numbers that stalked our school.

Thankfully Ray Anne had a specific store in mind. On the way, I told her about the awesome scent her family gave off. She shook her head and told me that was completely absurd.

I got a kick out of watching Creepers scatter—like cockroaches scurrying from a spotlight—to avoid crossing paths with my new prom date. Thin and fragile as she was in the material world, in the alternate dimension, Ray Anne was like a Jedi.

I followed her into a mirror-lined store with white marble floors and walls. Fancy dresses hung on long racks suspended by clear wire.

My mood hadn't recovered from attending two funerals in two days—neither had my guilty conscience—but I didn't want to sulk around Ray Anne. I spotted a seating area and dropped into a hot-pink chair that might as well have had a bowling ball for a cushion.

"This is the one I like." Ray Anne approached, holding up a sparkling red dress.

"Nice. I like the shiny things on there."

She laughed. "Sequins."

And that's how I became a guy who knows about sequins.

While Ray Anne waited for a dressing room, a freckle-faced boy jumped feetfirst into the chair across from me. Five or six years old, I'd say, with that starlike glow emanating from his chest. This close, it was even more brilliant—a multicolored flicker.

The boy's shackled mother told him to hold her shopping bags while she went into the dressing room. He shouted no and shoved her bags to the floor. A pair of shoes and some lacy undergarments spilled out.

She scolded him, picking it all up and warning him not to pull that again, then disappeared into a dressing room at the same time as Ray Anne.

I was watching the kid bounce like a monkey in his chair when something caught my attention. High above his head, glimmering specks floated and swirled. They began taking shape, flowing into formation like a marching band. A massive silhouette stretched from ceiling to floor.

The heaviness bearing down on my anguished mind just . . . gave way to an allover sense of relaxation, so freeing I thought I might lift out of my chair. Strange as it sounds, soothing heat somehow reached past my skin into my soul, like I was being hugged by someone gushing with acceptance for me. And as a huge bonus, it temporarily relieved the freeze I carried in my gut.

Fully visible now, a Watchman illuminated the store. He had a slender build, dark hair, and perfect facial features—the kind humans strive for. He wore minimal armor—a thick platinum belt over a loose-fitting, light-colored robe-type garment. The material looked white, but I couldn't say for sure with all the radiance.

As much as I'd complained about my visionary curse, in that moment, I wouldn't have traded it for anything. I already knew there was nothing more spectacular in the universe than a Watchman, and this only confirmed it.

I held on to my chair, hoping not to fall to my face this time.

Squinting, I observed the Watchman lower himself to one knee and place his jumbo-sized hand on the boy's head. I didn't understand that, or his expression. Serious. Grief stricken, even.

Despite the Watchman's majestic presence, everyday life continued.

"Son?" the kid's mom called out from behind the dressing room curtain.

"What, Mom?"

"Just checking."

"I don't need you to check on me. And I'm *sick* of holding your stuff." This time the boy hurled his mother's belongings in the air.

I expected her to come flying out of the dressing room and tear into her bratty son. What I totally didn't expect was two gnarled Creepers passing through the wall and closing in on the obnoxious kid.

My tranquil moment ended like a car crash on a Sunday drive. But I actually wanted to see this.

I tucked my legs into my chair and dug my fingers into the padded armrests. I was about to witness an epic beatdown, a Watchman defending a child against an evil no grown man could endure.

But the Watchman removed his hand from the boy. Just stood and stepped back. Gave the kid up like a dirty cop cowering to the mafia.

"Ray Anne!"

"Hold on," she said. "I almost have it zipped."

I couldn't just sit there. I jumped up and stood with my back to the boy, arms out, as if I could actually shield him from the double-team assault. I guess the kid didn't like me standing so close—he gave me a swift kick in the butt. I fell forward but caught my balance in time to turn around and watch the attack.

A Creeper named Thief plunged its atrocious hand into the boy's puny chest and literally ripped the shimmering light right out of him. He proceeded to crush it, smashing it in his hand until it turned to lifeless, ashen-looking dust—like the dirty stuff I'd seen on Walt's ravaged body. Thief opened its misshapen fingers and let the black, powdery substance trickle to the floor.

That's when the boy's mom came flying out of the dressing room. She got down on all fours in a white evening gown and demanded that her son help pick up her scattered belongings. A handful of shoppers stopped and stared.

Now the other Creeper made its move. Grotesque wounds stretched across its forehead, down its sullen cheek, and under its garments, but I could still make out condemnat—*condemnation*, I presumed. The creature hunched over and gathered the gritty grossness off the floor. Then it spit on the dirt, massaging the slimy concoction through its bony fingers.

What it did next was so off-the-charts freaky that I grabbed and squeezed a complete stranger's arm. As the boy stood and kept up his tantrum, the Creeper flung the muddy sludge off its hands onto the child's throat. And the stuff started moving, molding around the kid's neck like a fat, slimy leach. Within seconds . . .

It formed a shackle.

I couldn't hold it in. "No way!"

It turns out I was squeezing a store employee's arm, sending her into a panic.

"Let go of me!" She yanked away. There were even more onlookers now.

"I'm sorry, I . . ."

Thief walked behind the oblivious boy and grabbed hold of the back of his freshly fashioned shackle, then began a jerky pulling motion. Each time it tugged, it let out a bloodcurdling shrill—not because it was straining, but with what seemed to be a kind of sick delight—its lips drawn back in a fang-exposing, crooked smile.

I called for Ray Anne again. "Can you please get out here?"

"Coming. I'm getting dressed now."

My eyes were glued to the boy. Naturally, his mother glared at me. "You have a problem?" Apparently she was too leery of me to head back into the dressing room.

What would she have done if she'd seen the real threat to her kid?

Thief ran its calloused hands through the boy's gelled hair, then rubbed the back of the small guy's head in a circular motion. It uttered something, then out popped two cords, wiggling and contorting like disgusting worms, right out of the kid's scalp.

"Ray *Anne!*" I yelled so loud that everyone around me froze, including some people outside the store. That same rattled employee was on the phone now, probably calling security on me.

"One second," Ray Anne said. "Is everything okay?"

"Not. Even. A little."

I stared at the Watchman, but he didn't notice me. His gaze was fixed on the boy, the corners of his mouth turned down.

Condemnation wrapped its hand around its own wrist, then twisted back and forth, eventually pulling off a cuff that had somehow formed on demand. The disgusting creature crouched down and attached the metal cuff to the end of the boy's bulky chain, easy as twisting yarn into place. Then it used its index finger to carve an inscription on the cuff, while the other Creeper etched with its finger on both of the boy's freshly grown cords.

And finally, it was over.

The two terrorists melted into the wall, but the Watchman remained, hands clasped at his waist, still doing nothing. His head hung low. Then, gradually, he looked up, blinked in slow motion, and gazed into the ceiling. I was sure he was staring at something, something even I couldn't see.

The best way I know how to explain the atmosphere at that moment is to say it was like having the warmth of the sun on your face while an icy hailstorm pummels your skull. I stood there, plagued by an intense, troubling sense that good and evil were never meant to coexist, much less collide.

I was ready to bolt out of there, but first, a fast, up close look at the kid's cords.

self-absorbed
defiant

Like Jess.

His mother pointed in my face. "Get away from my son!"

"Hey, your son kicked him in the butt."

I have no idea why some soccer mom felt the need to stick up for me.

Ray Anne finally made it out of the dressing room, and I grabbed her arm. Too late now for her to run off the Creepers.

"We have to go." I tugged her toward the exit, and she accidentally flung the prom dress to the floor.

"Why are we—"

"Trust me."

Once we were locked inside Ray Anne's silver Hyundai, we sat in the mall parking lot, blasting the AC. I talked so fast my words ran together. She was having a hard time following me and, as usual, shot questions at me, one after another so that I hardly had time to respond.

I'd been desperate to know how people got their shackles. Now that I'd witnessed it firsthand, I seriously despised the answer. "Think about it, Ray Anne. It's only a matter of time before the light that children carry gets snatched, crushed by evil. Innocence gone."

I drummed my fingers hard on the armrest. How was this right? All a person had to do was live long enough and dare to defy authority, and they'd be attacked and fitted with a shackle?

Deep breaths weren't working. I popped my knuckles and nearly gnawed a hole in my lip. "Don't talk to me about good defeating evil, Ray Anne. Not after what I just saw. That Watchman did *nothing* to protect that child. And whether he couldn't or wouldn't, either way, humanity is doomed."

She put her delicate hand on my shoulder and waited for me to calm down. "I believe everyone does get shackled at some point," she said. "But there's obviously a way to get free. You know that, even if you aren't open to my explanations."

"I'm open, I'm just not willing to put my faith in failure."

"Humanity fails, Owen. Not God."

"How can you defend him?" I turned in my seat and yelled like she was much farther away. "What kind of cruel, pathetic, narcissistic being creates life, then sits back and watches his creation get pulverized by evil—enemies that *by design* outmatch us? Why weren't everyone's eyes created to see them? Why don't we have the physical strength to kick their—"

"So God *made* that child talk back to his mother? It's God's fault the kid acted out?" Ray Anne's passion matched mine.

"What kid *doesn't* talk back to his mother, Ray Anne? Haven't you done that?"

"Of course, but all that proves is that we're all rebellious. Our innocence isn't stolen, Owen. We give it up. We act selfish by our own choice, over and over without being sorry, and darkness rushes in. How can you blame that on God?"

Ridiculous argument. "If he exists at all, he made us this way. He set the rules."

Ray Anne got quiet, and about the time I was reveling in the idea that there was no way for her to counter, she jabbed back. "What if God gave us a choice, Owen? What if this whole thing is about what we choose—*who* we choose?"

"What choice do any of us have?" Sweet as she was, I was getting tired of her idealistic theories. Besides, they didn't really apply to me. I'd been spared a shackle—some sort of strength of heart I had that made me immune, I'd concluded. But as for masses of others . . .

Ray Anne's phone rang. Her mom, wanting to know how the shopping trip was going.

"Yeah, I didn't buy the dress," Ray Anne said. "The mall was crazy tonight. I'll come back and get it later. Tomorrow, probably." I could hear her mother's disappointment seeping through the phone.

By the time she hung up and we pulled out of the parking lot, I worried I'd been too harsh. I didn't want to run off the only friend I had—someone who was starting to feel like way more than a friend.

Who was I kidding? I wanted to kiss her so bad it hurt.

We stopped at a red light, and she took the lead in clearing the air. "Look, I know our conversation got a little heated, but if you can take it, so can I." She held out her hand, and I took in the way her tousled blonde hair framed her face. "No hard feelings?"

I smiled and shook on it. "No hard feelings."

Now I really wanted to kiss her.

She pulled up to my house, and I apologized for ruining her shopping trip.

"Yeah, well, that's what I get for going to prom with a guy who sees into the spirit world."

Adorable.

I tossed and clawed at my covers all night. For one, I kept replaying the awful scene from the mall. Then I'd think about what Ray Anne had said, how we all have a choice. That made me want to take my pillow and start whacking stuff. What good is free will if an invisible enemy is determined to use it against you?

I finally drifted off and had a horrible nightmare about being in the woods with Walt and Marshall. I held two loaded guns identical to the one my mom's ex back in Boston kept on the nightstand. Both barrels were aimed at their decaying heads.

Normally it would be a relief for a dream like that to end, but not when you wake in the middle of the night gagging on Creeper stench. I thrashed in my bed, twisting my neck in every direction. I didn't dare sleep anymore without my closet light on and the door wide open, so for the most part, I could see.

But in my world, seeing could be more terrifying than not.

There was a word plastered on my closet door, black lines still dripping.

fear

It hadn't been there when I went to sleep.

It's one thing to have the feeling you're not alone. It's another thing to be sure of it—and not know where the intruder is.

I pulled my knees to my chest and gathered my covers around me up to my nose. That's when I noticed that my dog was missing from my bed.

I whispered her name, scanning my room until finally I spotted her in the shadows, hunkered in the corner. Her reflective neon eyes were fixed on me.

"You okay, girl?"

She didn't budge.

TWENTY-TWO

EVER BEEN TOO SCARED TO stay still but too petrified to move? That was me, in my bed, shivering, barricaded under my thin sheets. I think my dog was paralyzed too.

"Come here, girl."

She gave a low-pitched growl. Adrenaline shot like fire through my veins.

Murder. Had to be. In my room.

I had a sickening idea of where it was likely hiding, but there was only one way to know. I leaned over the side of my mattress, slow and cautious. Grabbed a fistful of my blanket draped onto the floor, then dared myself to pull it back.

The longer I waited, the harder it got. I held my breath, then went for it.

A series of colorful words flew from my mouth, and I made it all the way out my bedroom door in two steps. I'd seen something poking out from under my bed. A grungy gray foot. Festering toenails.

Worst fears realized.

I basically slid down the stairs into the living room. There was my mom, sprawled on the sofa, wasted. I stood there, feet apart, knees bent, contemplating my next move. Then my heart stopped for the second time in less than a minute. A Creeper emerged from behind the sofa, stretching tall, in the process of connecting with my mother. I'd never seen this one before. *Ugly* doesn't cut it.

I might have tried to wake her had my attention not been hijacked. The stairs, popping and cracking. Murder, coming for me.

I grabbed my mom's keys and darted out of the house. I know only a deadbeat would leave his incoherent mother in a den of devils, but she was too drunk to run. And she wouldn't have believed me anyway.

I drove, fast and aimless. It was 5:00 a.m. I couldn't call Ray Anne at this time and couldn't stomach going back home. I wasn't even sure what a Creeper could do to me—I had no chains or cords. But I didn't want to find out the hard way. It wasn't like I repelled them.

I'm a creature of habit, I guess, because at some point I ended up driving by my school. I was taken aback by the sheer number of Creepers slithering outside—maybe since there were no humans inside to badger? They clung to the brick, scurried along the rooftop, huddled in groups, converged on the front steps. Like a hoard of insects, droves of them.

Why my school? I would have researched it if I'd had any idea where to start.

I pulled over and watched the spectacle—like a horror film, only the villains could leap off the big screen and come after you. Despair throbbed in my chest. These vermin had invaded my world and infested my life—had me on the run in my boxer shorts before sunup.

I banged my head on the steering wheel, feeling sorry for myself. And my species. The nauseating odor crept through my sealed windows.

What are they doing?

One by one, the Creepers scampered to a huddle, quickly forming a massive clump near the edge of the property, hunkering down. It was like a giant, shifting, slithering wall of black.

Across the street, twelve Watchmen were approaching, walking in sync in a triangular formation. I flew out of the car, climbing up the hood and onto the roof of my mom's Infiniti.

Wow. Colossal warrior bodies. Brilliant illumination. Full body armor light-years ahead of anything humanity has ever dreamed up.

Skin colors as varied as the human race. All looked to be in their early twenties, though I doubted they aged at all.

The Watchmen came to a halt, the brisk air ushering their one-of-a-kind fragrance my way—a mix of masculine body soap, a scented candle, and fabric softener. All power and cleanliness. I sucked it up my nose and held it.

The gleaming army stared at the shabby Creepers, eyes focused and stern. Surely this was it—the moment they would charge my school and destroy the evil army.

In sync, they lifted their crowned heads toward the sky, peering up at the first faint hues of sunrise.

And they stayed that way until the sun had dawned.

I climbed back into the SUV, not willing to expose my smiley-face boxers to morning traffic. Eventually I started the car and drove home, so dejected it was all I could do to turn the wheel. Those Watchmen were dressed for battle but did nothing more than pose. *What* was going on?

I opened my front door about an inch. The contaminated smell slapped me in the face. My mom was hunched over on the sofa watching *Good Morning America*.

"Owen?"

"Hey, Mom." I swung the door open and walked inside as if everything were fine and there was no horrid Creeper brooding behind her back. Not easy to do.

"Where were you?" Her speech was slow and muffled.

"I ran an errand."

"Please go do something with that obnoxious dog of yours. She won't shut up."

I dreaded going upstairs but told myself if Murder was going to brutalize me, I might as well get it over with. I made it to the top step unharmed. Daisy was there, nose pointed down at the living room. Maybe that meant my room was clear.

I locked my dog with me in the bathroom and showered with the shower curtain half open. Then I pulled Daisy by the collar and basically shoved her in my room and shut her inside. When I didn't hear her bark or growl, I went in. I could tell from the smell of things that the Creeper was gone. A courageous glance under my bed confirmed it.

Maybe I'd actually go to school today. That would get me away from my mom's monster, and it would put me in a prime seat in case the Watchmen decided to advance.

But by the time I got to school, they were gone.

I took a shortcut to first period and glanced at the depressing suicide memorial fence. I stopped.

I'd never taken a close look at the lineup of pictures, the desperate souls who'd taken their own lives, most of them before I came to Masonville. I eyed the first picture—suicide number one—and scanned the notes plastered around it, all addressed to Lucas.

Then it hit me. He looked just like her. A surge of emotion clumped in my throat.

Lucas Greiner.

Ray Anne's younger brother.

TWENTY-THREE

I STARTED TO TEXT Ray Anne but stopped. Better to tell her in person how sorry I was about Lucas.

As I dragged my feet to first period, the mysterious old man's words came back to me, what he'd said about my school: *"Tragedy ever since those doors opened. Untold loss."*

Ray Anne knew that as well as anyone.

Walking with my head down, I noticed there were Creeper notes all over the place, sailing a few inches off the floor and landing in random corners and in the gap underneath lockers. They all had the same number combination like before—**523**—but the three letters that followed were all different:

BTL, SMJ, RWF

What did they mean?

Ray Anne had noticed them too. She texted me some images and wrote, **So freaky.**

I got to first period, and there sat Dan with his two tons of cords and chains, grinning at me like a fat hyena. His eye was bruised, as though he'd been socked in the face. Too bad I couldn't take credit for it. "What?" I asked. I was in no mood for his antics.

"Jess is a sweet, sweet girl." He winked.

Tell me you didn't do anything stupid, Jess.

I studied his damaged face. "She do that to you?" Maybe she'd actually put him in his place.

He slumped and dropped his chin. "No."

I'd never seen Dan look so pitiful. So defeated. But I can't say that I minded.

After class, I searched the hallways for Jess but crossed paths with Ray Anne instead. Her head hung low, such a contrast from her usual cheerfulness. She exited into an outdoor atrium, and I followed her. She turned toward me but kept her eyes down.

"Today's my brother's birthday."

There was no way for me to know that, but I still felt like a loser that I hadn't. "Ray Anne." I put my hand on her shoulder. She kept her arms crossed. "I saw Lucas's picture. On the fence."

Her head sank even lower.

"How did—"

"How'd he do it? Don't you dare ask me that!" she exploded before I'd even had a chance to finish my question. She could hardly catch her breath.

I took a step back to give her some space. "I was just gonna ask how you guys celebrated his birthday before. In the past. But I shouldn't have asked anything."

She teared up. "Owen. I didn't mean to . . ."

"It's fine," I told her. "Completely fine."

She wiped her eyes, then exhaled long and heavy, like she was forcing herself to be strong.

"On the first day of school, Lucas was having a hard time finding one of his classes."

"Ray Anne, you don't have to do this."

"I want to." She swallowed hard. "He happened to ask Jess for help, and Dan saw them talking. Just *talking*. He came charging over and got in Lucas's face. Humiliated him in front of everyone.

"From that day on, Dan made my brother's life miserable. Called him out all the time. Cut him down.

"I knew Lucas was upset about it—sick over it, even—but I never, ever thought he'd . . ." Her fragile voice cracked. I hugged her, content to let her tears soak my sleeve.

Standing there, holding her in my arms, two things hit me.

Dan was even more messed up than I'd thought.

And Ray Anne meant even more to me than I'd realized.

At lunch, Jess finally got away from Dan long enough for me to talk to her, but she didn't seem to want to hear a word I had to say about anything—especially him. "Why do you put up with that lowlife? Cover for him when he lashes out at you?"

She grabbed my collar and pulled my face to hers, keeping her voice down.

"Look, I know Dan has issues, but you have no clue what his father is really like."

Actually I did. Mr. Wonderful on the outside, scary evil on the inside.

"Dan's trying to change," she said, "but it's kind of hard when something as stupid as not saying 'sir' gets you a black eye."

That's when it clicked.

All Dan's taunting, his harsh jabs about my missing father, and it turns out his was an abuser. Not that I could bring myself to feel sorry for him.

"I can't deal with this today." Jess stormed off before I had a chance to warn her that she'd never change him by letting him take his anger out on her—a concept my mom couldn't seem to grasp either.

I wish I could say that was as intense as my day got.

At dismissal, while walking down the hall with Ray Anne, I saw Lance and Meagan hugging at his locker. I was instantly queasy. That same Creeper that had stalked her before—Demise—stood close to Meagan, eyeing her. Worse, she had another Creeper attached. They were all gruesome, but this one . . .

A scorched word ran sideways over its face, starting at the bottom of its cheek and stretching across its shriveled nose, over its nonhuman eye, and onto its eroding temple. A word that struck the most terror in me yet.

I turned to Ray Anne. "See Meagan over there?"

She tried a casual glance but didn't pull it off. "Yeah?"

"She's linked up to a Creeper." I whispered it. "Suicide."

Her eyes went wide. "We've got to do something!"

Such a relief, the way I could count on her to believe me.

"Let's get over there," I said. "Your light will drive it away."

I walked up to Lance like the two of us were still good friends. He socked me in the shoulder, like old times.

"What's up?" I said.

"The mortality rate." Lance smirked. Meagan smiled but barely. Ray Anne and I froze.

"I'm Lance." He reached to shake Ray Anne's hand, then pointed to his girlfriend. "This is Meagan."

Ray Anne said hello and stepped closer to grip Meagan's hand. But . . .

It had no effect whatsoever on the Creeper.

Our small talk kept going, and Ray Anne inched over, nearly rubbing shoulders with Meagan. But Suicide used Meagan as a human shield, avoiding Ray Anne's light no matter what angle she came at it.

Then, as if Suicide exerted some sort of mind control, when it moved, Meagan would move, shadowing her tormentor like her subconscious was held hostage. Even the slightest gestures mimicked her captor. The Creeper looked down and licked its lips. Meagan did the same. I shuddered.

Ray Anne looked to me for some sign of what was going on. I rubbed circles on my forehead, exasperated. Ray Anne's potency was no match for the Creeper. Maybe it had to do with the fact that it was latched to a human host. The thing clearly wanted to avoid Ray Anne's light, but it wasn't willing to give up Meagan.

I looked up and around, wondering if Watchmen would come to Meagan's rescue again. But they didn't show.

I pulled Lance to the side. "Can I talk to you for a second?"

He followed me down the hall, beyond earshot of his girlfriend.

"It's Meagan."

His eyebrows pressed together. "What about her?"

"Lance, she's in serious danger."

He huffed. "What are you talking about?"

"I think she's going to hurt herself. On purpose."

He stepped back. Crossed his arms. Scowled. "I thought maybe you'd gotten some help, but you're still—"

"I know I've said some unbelievable things lately, but you have to take me seriously on this. Trust me. She's in big trouble."

A long exhale, then he clamped down hard on my shoulder, pulling me into a nearby restroom like he wanted to throw down or something. His face was an explosive red. "Look," he shouted, "it's a well-known fact that I think you've become psychotic, and it's also a well-known fact that you were the last person to hang out with Walt and Marshall."

"What are you saying?" I'd never seen him this angry.

"I don't know what you did to them, but maybe it's not a coincidence that they're both dead."

My gaze dropped. "You think I wanted to kill our friends?"

"That's what some people are saying. I'm getting tired of sticking up for you."

What? People suspected me? Since when? "Why don't you try listening to *me*?" I got in his face. "Hear me on this. Your girlfriend could die, Lance."

I flinched when he pointed in my face, his voice low, but so furious he was shaking. Creepers were flocking to the scene now. "You stay away from Meagan, and from me, you hear me?"

My back was pressed against a wall at this point, and a surge of anger kicked in. But I wasn't willing to go to fists with Lance.

Who knows what would have happened had some guys not walked into the restroom. It seemed to pain him to turn his back on me, and after a scorching glance over his shoulder, he walked out.

I lost that argument, but it was Meagan who stood to lose everything.

After school, I relied on my sense of smell and my dog's cues to determine if my home was safe or not. It seemed okay for now. The word *guilty* inscribed above my living room window was fading. The highlight of my day.

I sat on the sofa with a bag of Doritos, contemplating my next move. I refused to sit back and do nothing to help Meagan. I needed to talk to her, but without Lance around. And this wasn't something I could put off. The thought of her being number fifteen . . .

I couldn't let that happen.

Meanwhile, Ray Anne texted and asked if I wanted to go back to the mall with her. **My mom won't rest till I buy that dress.**

Not exactly as important as a mission to save a life, but of course I wanted to go. I'd have spent every second with her if she'd have let me.

A few minutes later, there was a knock at my door. Ray Anne, I assumed.

Wrong.

It was Jess, and by the time I answered, she was headed back to her car like she'd changed her mind. I went after her, and she turned to face me, trails of black makeup on her cheeks. She didn't look good.

"Did Dan do something? You need to dump him, Jess."

She shrugged, then leaned on me to keep her balance.

"Have you been drinking?"

She said no, but I knew better.

"Talk to me, Jess."

She plopped down on the cement, noisy chains and all. I sat next to her and waited for her to spill her guts.

"I'm so confused." Her voice quivered. "I think Dan cares about me, but I'm not sure. And after last night, it's too late anyway."

I wanted to strangle him with my bare hands. I also wanted to shout, "I told you so!"

"It wasn't what I thought." She crumpled a tissue. "I wanted it to be special, to feel close. Loved. But instead I feel . . ." She choked. "It made the memories worse." She buried her face in her hands, then leaned on my shoulder.

"Memories of what?"

"No, I can't tell anyone. I promised."

"Jess, who did you promise?" I cupped her chin and lifted her face. "You can tell me."

She swallowed tears, then started talking, describing how her dad's brother, her uncle Jeff, came to live at their house for a while a few years back, when he was going through a divorce. Her parents let him stay in their guesthouse—a posh two-level living area at the back of their property.

It took her a while to say it. "He didn't stay in his room at night." Her palms pressed over her eyes. "He came into my room. I was twelve."

She became hysterical, gasping while explaining how she'd confided in her mother. Together they'd told her father, but he'd accused her of exaggerating. He'd made her promise never to talk about it, to put it out of her mind and move on.

"My mom told me to let it go too. She's chosen country clubs and luxury cars over me. And my dad still hangs out with my uncle like nothing happened."

She fell into my arms, and I hugged her as tight as I could, with her entrapments and all. My heart broke for her. I wanted to find her uncle and put an end to his manhood.

Then, it was like a light went on.

The name on one of Jess's chains was Jeffrey Thompson. Uncle Jeff. And her parents' names were on the other two. It made sense now. But Jess had a fourth chain today. I guessed it before I looked.

daniel quinton bradford

Dan. That sorry excuse for a man was now baggage around Jess's neck, a worthless weight she'd carry around for the rest of her life. Unless I found a way to free her.

I had to pull back and let go of her. The chill was too much. Still, I tried to comfort her. "Jess, I'm so sorry that you—"

A Creeper passed through my neighbor's fence across the street, striding in our direction. I cleared my throat and stood.

"Get up."

"What?"

"We have to go, right now."

"I'm not going anywhere." Her defiant cord was in full swing.

At first I thought Murder was coming for me. But I could see now it was a different one. "Get up. *Now!*" I reached down and grabbed her arm, but she slapped my hand away.

"We're in danger, Jess. Please trust me. Stand up!"

"Oh, I get it. This is another one of your delusions."

It was closing in. Regret, a few feet away. Its comatose eyes feasting on Jess. It circled us, hissing, fangs exposed. I flung myself on top of her.

"What are you *doing*?"

I was smothering her, sheltering her from the breeze and pine trees as far as she was concerned.

Regret stopped and lowered to the ground behind Jess.

"Leave her alone!" Why did I bother?

"Stop it, Owen. You're freaking me out." She elbowed me in the chest. "Get off me."

"You don't understand." All I could do was hold her and watch the rancid thing extend its wrist into her newest cuff.

But it suddenly pulled back. Then ran.

What the—?

I turned my head. "Ray Anne."

She stood at the edge of my driveway, mouth open, keys in hand. "I . . . I thought I'd come by since . . ."

"Since we're going to the mall."

I peeled my arms off Jess, who stood and made a puckered-lipped face. "He's with me right now, so . . ."

"Right." Ray Anne backed away, then hurried to her car.

"Wait. Don't go."

But she started her car and pulled away.

"What did *she* want?" Jess said. More like whined.

"Don't be rude. She just helped you."

That went over her head, like I knew it would. She grabbed my hands and pulled, wanting me to hug her. But I stood stiff.

I'd just hurt Ray Anne.

I had to make things right.

TWENTY-FOUR

I DROVE TO RAY ANNE'S HOUSE, but her mom politely told me she was taking a break from company. We both knew that meant me.

"Can you please give her this?" I handed Mrs. Greiner a garment bag with the red-sequined dress inside. "I think it's the right size."

"Let me reimburse you."

"No, I want to do this." I'd dipped into the savings account my mom said was for emergencies. It felt like an emergency to me.

Meagan's house was in the back of Ray Anne's neighborhood. I drove up as the sun was setting and knocked on her door. A stubby ceramic gnome stared up at me from the overgrown flower bed, all chubby cheeks and a sneaky grin. I tipped it over with my foot.

Meagan answered but barely opened the door.

"Hey. You have a minute?"

A nod.

"I don't know what Lance has told you about me lately, or what anyone else has said, but I just want to talk to you. Will you come outside?"

She peeked over my shoulder.

"It's just me."

She stepped onto the porch barefoot, her toenails painted fluorescent purple. Her suicide-obsessed companion followed. It seemed taller than the others, and the smell reminded me of the time a rat had died behind the refrigerator in my garage. I stepped back and tried to ignore it—the dip in temperature, too.

"I'm not dressed." She had on baggy shorts and a faded T-shirt, her hair pulled back in a sloppy knot.

"I don't care. I'm here to tell you something."

Her eyes grew wide. "What?"

I didn't know her all that well, but I swear, I would have done anything to help her, to get that Creeper off her back. "I have no idea what's going on in your life, Meagan. But I want you to know that you matter."

She pressed her lips together and blinked fast, fanning the moisture building in her eyes. "What makes you say that?"

"It's true. You're important, Meagan. The universe knows your name and needs you."

You would have thought I'd addressed the Creeper by name. It snarled, pressing its head down at a steep, impossible angle toward me. Did that thing even have a spine? I worked hard to keep my eyes on Meagan.

"You may not understand this," I said, "but you have incredible, indescribable value."

Suicide moaned, a low, monotone shriek that rattled my eardrums. A tear fell from Meagan's cheek to her shoulder.

"I'm sorry." She shook her head. "I don't know why I'm crying."

"I do. You're being attacked."

And with that, Suicide drew its hands to its chin, gurgling and hacking until it puked up a slimy, brownish-green mucus, mouth stretched wide so that it oozed onto its palms. It was as disgusting as it sounds.

I grabbed my gut. Covered my nose.

It rubbed its vomit-covered hands together, and I heard something, a chorus of cursing and wailing. Whispering howls that made my skin crawl. It was getting louder.

"Owen, what do you mean?"

"Meagan, don't believe the voices." I grabbed her shoulders. "The lies in your head. You are meant to live. You have a destiny. Do you believe me?"

She nodded. "Yes." Another tear.

Suicide opened its palms, fingers spread, and the ghoulish groans became so loud I doubted I'd be able to hear my own voice. There was a deep gash in each of its hands, a horizontal slice that began to stretch and tear open. Then a tongue jutted out of each palm, black and long and twisting.

Suicide lowered its hands, the newly formed mouths slurping inches from Meagan's head. I couldn't help but let go of her, but I didn't stop pleading.

"Don't let anyone—anything—talk you into giving up."

"I won't," I heard her say.

"Promise me!"

"I . . ."

The Creeper slammed its grimy, licking hands over Meagan's ears, fingers interlocked on top of her head. Instant quiet for me, but who knows what was echoing in Meagan's mind now. The hands were sucking, tongues plunged into her ear canals even though they were way too big. Dark drool spilled down either side of her neck like tainted syrup.

"Can you hear me?"

"Yeah." She smirked like I was a moron.

"You were about to make me a promise."

"Huh?" A blank stare, all emotion stripped away.

"That you won't give up, no matter what."

She shrugged. Total disconnect. "Are you going to Stella Murphy's party?"

"What? No, I—Meagan, there's something blocking . . . You have this . . ."

She pulled out her cell and started scrolling, tapping the screen fast.

"Meagan, you have to be strong. Fight for your life."

She held her phone up to my face. "Look." A blurry picture of Lance walking into a jewelry store. "Do you know if he's been looking at engagement rings?"

I moved the phone away and focused on her face. "I know he cares about you." There had to be a way to get through to her.

"Um, I need to go, okay?"

It wasn't okay.

I asked her not to, but she went inside anyway. Suicide's hands still squeezed her head, spewing some kind of white noise that drowned out my voice.

Probably *any* voice of hope.

I drove home, my gut churning. In my room, I sank into bed and worried myself sick. Would the press be at my school in the morning? I'd tried to stop number fifteen, but had I?

TWENTY-FIVE

I CAUGHT UP WITH Ray Anne before first period. No camera crews outside. Major relief.

"Thanks for the dress." She looked up at me. No smile. "Very thoughtful. But I'm not sure that we should go to prom together."

"Yesterday was a stupid misunderstanding." I stepped close. She arched a brow. I explained the situation—how what looked like a big hug was really me trying to shield Jess from an attack. Even though I couldn't.

"We're not a couple, Owen. I know that. This isn't about me being jealous."

Oh. Well . . . that was too bad. I mean, I wouldn't want to see her wrapped around some guy.

"It's that you broke your promise. You didn't outright lie to me, but you kept something from me. The fact that you're seeing Jess again."

"But I'm not seeing her. I swear. And I wasn't trying to keep anything from you." Not that, anyway. My promise to Ray Anne had actually died with Walt and Marshall.

"If you're going to prom, Ray Anne, I want to be your date."

"Oh, I'm going." She gave a playful huff. "My mom is determined."

She stopped her overloaded backpack from sliding off her shoulder. "Let me think about it, okay?"

What choice did I have?

"Call you later. Hope you have a good day." She turned to go, but I stopped her.

"Can I ask you something? Why do you let Jess intimidate you so much? You're an incredible, brave person. A lot more secure than she is, really."

She stared down at her turquoise Converse. Shrugged. Then finally: "Maybe 'cause girls like her never listen to girls like me."

All I could do was nod. Jess didn't exactly listen to me, either.

She turned again, and I watched her walk the entire way down the hall, lighting our school.

When I got home, Frank's blue extended-cab truck was taking up nearly my entire driveway. Great.

As expected, there they were—on the sofa, giggling like middle schoolers, my mom sitting on his lap. Disgusting.

She didn't seem to notice I was home three hours early.

"Hey, Owen!" As if we had a thriving mother-son relationship. "Do me a favor, sweetie. Run to Walmart and pick up the cake I ordered. It's Frank's birthday."

Yeah. That's what I wanted to do, celebrate her shackled boyfriend's birth.

I looked him over. Snakeskin boots, skintight jeans, a button-down shirt that needed to be buttoned higher. I mean, who needed to see his chest hair?

One tacky cowboy.

"And grab some candles."

She and Frank started laughing again. Whatever. At least an errand would get me out of the house.

I blared my music and drove fast. How long would it take for Ray Anne to call me?

I also worried about Jess. I held out hope that she'd dump Dan. For good this time.

Then there was Meagan . . .

My mind was on overload.

I stopped at a light and glanced to my left. There were two shackled homeless people under the overpass, but that's not what got under my skin. It was the horde of Creepers—about eight of them—swarming the hoboes.

The man and woman covered their heads while the invisible bullies jabbed and slapped them, striking high and low with swift blows. The man reared back and threw a weary punch in the direction of one of his attackers, but his fist passed right through its dingy garments. The woman shouted nonsense. At least, I assumed it was nonsense.

A honk. I hadn't noticed the light change. I drove forward, still looking to the side.

Deranged and strung out or not, those people were under attack. And they knew it. They could see the Creepers—or at the very least, feel their presence. It made sense, I guess. Homeless people walking around swatting and mumbling into thin air. Maybe the Creepers had actually driven them out of their functional lives into panhandling and street-corner babbling.

I'll probably end up under a bridge with them someday, suffering and swinging away.

I wasn't surprised Walmart was crowded, but I didn't expect that many Creepers. Who knew?

On my way to the bakery, I strolled through the book section, just in case there was something that might shed some light on my nightmarish life. I spied a hardcover book about demonology that, according to the back cover, was written by some well-known theologian. I thumbed through it, stopping in the glossary.

demon: A wicked spirit sent from the devil. Sometimes demons lived in people, but Christ could force them to come out.

I'd never seen a Creeper press completely inside a person's body. Man, I hoped that wasn't possible. Attached was bad enough.

I scanned down, landing on

devil: Satan; formerly Lucifer; a spirit being; ruler of demons; the enemy of God and human beings

Ruler of demons. A month ago, I would have laughed.

I dropped the book in my cart, then headed to the bakery. The cake turned out to be ginormous—enough for twenty-five people. Go figure.

I kept my head down and covered my nose as best I could on the way to grab some candles. I turned down an aisle, and a lady slammed her shopping cart into mine, distracted by a menacing mob—a baby slobbering in the child seat and two more little people bouncing around her.

"I'm sorry," she said.

"It's fine."

Her tiny daughter in a polka-dot dress started crying, stomping her four-inch foot. "I want a toy!"

"I told you no," the mom said while we both worked to realign our carts. Then her son took off running. She called his name, then followed after him. Little Miss Polka-Dot stared up at me, still sniffling.

"You better do what your mother says," I told her.

"I don't have to."

I bent down and spoke into her pouty mini face. "Oh yes, you do. 'Cause if you don't, an evil monster will charge at you and rip the light right out of your little chest and crush it into a million disgusting pieces, then plaster it around your peewee neck, where it will stay. Forever."

She dropped her head back and wailed like a police siren. Hey, I never claimed to be great with kids, and at least I told her the truth.

Her mom returned, and I grabbed a pack of candles and pushed my cart like nothing had happened.

I got into the shortest checkout line I could find and scanned the gum selection, still waiting on Ray Anne's call. It was almost my turn to check out when a heavyset lady stepped in front of me, grabbing the hand of the large man who must have been holding her place in line. Lucky me, she was linked to a Creeper.

Never fails. The cashier called for a manager, bringing our line to a standstill. I stood there, gagging, looking for a shorter line. There wasn't one.

"Man, it stinks." I thought I'd spoken under my breath.

"Excuse me?" The woman in front of me spun around like a tornado and faced off with me. "Did you jus' say that I stank?"

Oh, boy. "No, I was talking about—" Like an idiot, I pointed to the Creeper, but to everyone else it looked like I pointed at her boyfriend.

"Oh no you didn't!" Her lower jaw jutted out.

For the first time in my life, I thought a woman was going to kick my butt. She turned to her man, whose swollen bicep boasted a tattoo of a fractured skull. "Did you hear what that fool jus' said 'bout you?"

He nodded, looking me over from head to toe, straightening the gold nugget ring on his middle finger. The cashier stared at me too. Along with the other people in line.

"That's not what I meant." I shook my head. "You guys don't stink at all."

"Yes, they do." The little boy behind me seemed to think that was funny.

Tattoo-man pointed his finger a centimeter from my nose. "You better shut your son up!"

Really? "He's not my son."

"Hey!" The boy's mother was offended. "Who are you telling to shut up?"

"Okay, this needs to *stop*!" I raised my voice. "This is crazy."

That's when the turban-clad cashier intervened, his accent so thick I had to focus to understand him. "Sir, please refrain from calling our customers crazy. No one is crazy here."

"I *didn't*."

"Yes, you did." The little instigator was at it again.

"Son," his mother said. "Leave the young man alone."

"But he's a meanie."

184 || LAURA GALLIER

"Hey, I'm not mean." Never mind that I had a demonology book in my cart.

"Yes, you kind of are, sir," the cashier said.

"Okay, you know what?" I threw cash on the counter. "I'm out of here." I pushed my squeaky shopping cart out the door.

Errands were no longer the mindless break from life that they used to be.

That night, my phone finally rang. But it wasn't Ray Anne.

"Can you come see me? I need to talk."

"I'm not your therapist, Jess. And you never take my advice anyway."

"Please. I don't want to be alone right now."

I wasn't any good at rescuing people. I already knew that. "Where are you?"

"Franklin Park."

Where I'd played ball with Walt and Marshall. On *that* afternoon.

"Please, Owen?"

By now, I should have known better.

TWENTY-SIX

I PULLED INTO THE parking spot next to Jess's convertible, but she wasn't in her car. The only lit area was the basketball courts, and she wasn't there, either. She called to me, and I followed her voice, moving in the faint moonlight past a merry-go-round and slides until I came to a swing set.

It stank.

"Thanks for coming." Jess rocked herself back and forth in a swing, sniffling.

"You okay?"

No answer.

My eyes adjusted better to the dark, well enough to see a hulking black silhouette behind her. I shined my cell. Jess's makeup was smeared again. The Creeper was familiar too. Regret. So it had gotten its disgusting hands on her after all.

"Get that light out of my face." Never mind that light was the one thing she needed. "I'm sorry, but I didn't know who else to call."

"Are you and Dan still together?"

"I guess. I don't know how committed he is."

"Why don't you end it?"

"Because. I'm scared I'll have more . . ."

"Regret?"

I wasn't surprised when the Creeper bent down and snarled at me. Then it stayed hunched over, mouthing something in Jess's ear, a garbled whisper.

She slumped, no longer rocking. "I mess everything up."

"No you don't, Jess."

Regret whispered in her ear again.

"My life is one big mistake."

"That's not true."

"It is true, Owen. The ugly, miserable truth."

I couldn't hug her, not while she was tethered to a Creeper, so I fought for her from an arm's length away.

"Jess, it's like you talked about in the woods, those feelings that follow you. I know what you mean now. They're real, and they're attacking you, tricking you into thinking you're worthless and—"

That was all the time I had. Regret was reaching down, hands moving toward Jess's ears. I shut up and stepped back, hoping to spare her the added brainwashing.

The Creeper froze. Finally, it put its arms down.

She took a deep breath, a long exhale. "Ashlyn. She's the one to worry about."

I knew Ashlyn was in danger—I saw my first-ever Creeper swoop in on the girl—but I wasn't sure what Jess's angle was. "What's going on with her?"

"She's popping antidepressants. Way too many. And . . . hurting herself."

"Hurting herself how?"

Jess sighed but said nothing, protecting her friend's privacy, I guess. I thought about the Creeper that had closed in on Ashlyn. The slices all over its face and skin . . .

"Is she cutting?"

Jess looked up fast. "How'd you know?"

"I . . . saw it."

She dropped her chin again, blinking hard. "She tries to hide it, but yeah, I've seen her scabs too. She's been talking to a counselor, but she's still struggling. I don't know what to do. I want to help her."

"I understand." I really did.

"It's not fair to put this on you." She turned her weepy eyes on me. "You can't fix this."

"You have no idea how much I wish I could."

We sat there awhile, then she stood and pulled out her keys, leaned forward, and kissed me on the cheek.

We went our separate ways.

Another failed mission.

I stayed up all night researching demons. I flipped through my new book, then pulled up online interviews, articles, and video documentaries—trying to learn about everything, from accounts of subtle demonic activity to full-blown possessions.

Even with as much wickedness as I'd already seen, this stuff was scary on a different level. People completely overtaken by evil, their bodies ransacked like flimsy tents—growling in inhuman voices, foaming at the mouth, contorting in backbreaking fits.

I'd have dismissed it as theatrics if it weren't for the eyes. After coming face-to-face with Creepers, I recognized that people in demonic spells have the same dark, dead eyes—something some people without visionary powers claimed they could see. An unmistakable depravity. Venomous aggression.

You can't fake that.

What also blew my mind was the possibility that the same invisible beings preying on humans today had been doing this for thousands of years—maybe since the beginning of time. Our lives on earth come and go, but from what I was seeing, Creepers never stopped hunting people, one generation to the next.

Did they have an end goal beyond wrecking us? I stewed over that one.

Some people at school made a big deal out of it being Friday the thirteenth, but trust me, that date is a cultural superstition with zero significance among dark forces. Creepers did the usual—littered the place with their confusing notes and used people's faults against them. Sometimes Creepers examined every squirmy cord lagging from a person's head, then let go and moved on to inspect someone else.

Made me glad I had none.

Good news for me, people pretty much steered clear of me—Lance and Meagan included. Neither Demise nor Suicide was attached to her today. That felt like a victory.

It was a good thing I decided to stop off at the upstairs water fountain after school, otherwise I would have missed him. An enormous Watchman stood in front of the big window at the end of the hallway. His waist was higher than most students' heads.

He had glistening, caramel-brown skin and wore a thick, titanium-looking breastplate that probably weighed more than my mom's SUV. His eyes focused upward, as if gazing into an alternate cosmos.

He was so bright my eyes watered. I stepped toward him, the hallway steadily clearing as students poured into the parking lot. By the time I reached him, I felt like I'd been pumped full of morphine, all warm and happy.

His shin guards were nearly as tall as my legs.

He and I were alone in the hallway now. This was my chance.

"Sir?" I'd never felt so inferior in my life. But I had to try. "I need your help."

Nothing.

"Can you hear me?" I waited. "Please, my school is in trouble. People I care about. I know you can stop the attacks. I've seen it."

A slight nod of his flawless head, but not at me. At whatever stratosphere he was caught up in.

I lowered to one knee, my hands clasped and raised. "If you help me, I'll do anything you ask."

He didn't budge.

Desperation took over. I got lower, stretched out on my stomach at his feet. "I'll serve you."

Imagine an atomic bomb, an explosion so loud and hot and bright that your teeth rattle and you can't see, or hear, or feel your limbs.

I don't know exactly what he did to me, only that when I came to, he was gone and I was on my back, a good ten yards from where I'd been lying. I didn't hurt, but the exhilarating high was gone. It took me a while to stand and a few more minutes to steady myself and walk out of the building.

On my way home, I gave up on waiting for Ray Anne to contact me and called her instead. "I learned something about Watchmen today."

"You did?"

"They really, really don't like it when humans bow to them."

Saturday morning, I convinced my mom to let me borrow her car and talked Ray Anne into letting me take her out for breakfast. "So," I said on the way to The Broken Egg, "have you made a decision about prom?" It was a week away.

"Yes." She cleared her throat. "I think we should still go together."

I tried to keep it cool and not smile too big. Not because I was getting to go to prom, but because I'd be with her when she wore that red dress.

"I need you to do something, though." She turned down the music.

"Okay?"

"Look me in the face and tell me you'll never keep anything from me. Like, purposely hide something."

Ugh.

I stopped at a light and let go of the steering wheel to face her. "I don't want to keep anything from you, Ray Anne." My way of being honest. Without being honest.

She didn't nod or acknowledge my statement at all. Maybe she was on to me, women's intuition or something. But she left it at that.

Breakfast was good, and everything was going fine—better than fine—until we left.

"You have any errands you need to run today?" I wasn't ready for our time together to be up. "I can drive you."

"How about we head toward our school?"

That threw me.

"To the woods, where that clearing is."

"What for?"

"I want to see the water well."

My heart went from beating to banging. The thought of her ever drinking from it . . .

"You said the bucket miraculously fills, right?"

I opened my mouth, but nothing came out at first. "I don't think that's a good idea."

"Why not?"

Slow exhale. "The fewer people who know where to find it, the better."

"I won't tell."

On the off chance that she would drop it, I didn't say anything. A minute later . . .

"You don't trust me?" Her eyes weren't straying from my face.

I had to put an end to this. I pulled over and shoved the car into park. "I need you to trust *me* on this, Ray Anne. You can't go near there. No one can. Ever."

"But I only want to—"

"Please. Don't ask me again. Okay? It's serious."

Most people would have copped an attitude at that point. Ray Anne just got quiet.

I pulled back onto the road. I didn't like being the cause of Ray Anne's heavy-eyed look of disappointment, but I'd rather see that than risk seeing her in a casket with her eyes glued shut.

TWENTY-SEVEN

WHEN I WOKE on Sunday morning, I found a bright-yellow package on my nightstand, a milk chocolate bunny inside. My mom gave me one every Easter.

I got dressed and headed to church.

Yes, church.

I parked my motorcycle in a shady spot under an oak tree, across the street from the big sanctuary where Marshall's funeral had been held. The church that was supposed to have someone call me but never did.

I watched the people, mostly coming, some going, all dressed in their Sunday best. I wished I could capture people's shackles on camera so I could show Ray Anne how wrong she was—not to rub her face in it, but to get her to stop pushing her faith on me. I didn't resent that she believed; I just wanted her to accept that I didn't. And this stakeout helped prove my case.

Yes, there were glowing people at the church, admittedly a higher number than usual. But there were lots of shackled people too, carrying Bibles, shaking hands with the smiling ladies at the doors, making an effort to sit through church just like the Lights.

I'd started referring to shackle-free people as Lights, by the way. Just made things easier.

I also noticed that within families, some members were shackled and others weren't. There were shackled husbands whose wives were Lights and the other way around. Also shackled young people whose parents weren't, and occasionally shackled parents whose kids were Lights.

Clearly being a Light was not inherited.

I sat there spying, thinking about how, to everyone else, there was no difference from one person to the next. But through my eyes, it was night and day.

Freedom and slavery.

Then there was me. No shackle. No light. An exception to a rule I still couldn't figure out.

The church marquee read: "Prayer Changes Everything."

But how? Speak a request into the universe, and the universe processes it and actually rearranges itself for you? Hey, I'd try just about anything if it meant gaining an advantage over evil. So there, alone in the shade, I gave the prayer thing a whirl. Even bowed my head.

"Whatever or whoever is listening right now, if anyone is listening, I ask that you keep the Creepers off my mom, Jess, Meagan, Ashlyn—the people I care about." I felt like a moron, like I was baring my soul to my handlebars. "And please stop the suicides. The end."

The next day, the vibe at my school was different, like a heightened intensity was stirring among the Creepers. There were more of them around, if you can imagine that, and they were all spastic and restless and linking up to twice as many people as usual.

I saw Jess in the hallway, still bound to Regret.

So much for prayer changing things.

My mom came home around six o'clock in a great mood and asked me to go to dinner. I wasn't expecting that. We sat at a booth at a Mexican place and couldn't stop laughing about a guy who was singing in the mariachi band. He kept shaking his hips . . .

Guess you had to be there.

Anyway, I was trying to enjoy myself but battling the urge to warn my mom yet again. Such a helpless feeling, knowing someone important to you is being terrorized by evil on a regular basis—and is completely clueless about it.

After finishing our meal by plowing through a batch of sopaipillas, she pushed her plate to the side and leaned on the table. No more laughter. "Are you doing okay, Owen? I need you to be honest with me."

I put my fork down. "Sure."

She gave a dejected nod, the same kind I gave her when I knew she was lying. "You've made some outlandish statements lately, and you seem on edge. And I've noticed Lance and the guys aren't coming around. What's going on? I know Walt and Marshall's deaths were difficult for you, but what else is it?"

I wanted to tell her everything, to collapse into her arms like boys do with their mothers when they're little, but I couldn't. Telling the truth would only make things worse.

"Is this about your father?" Her tone was high and soft.

I stared at her. Was she kidding? This was the only time in my entire life that she'd ever brought him up. I wasn't about to miss this opportunity. "I want to know about him, Mom. Anything."

She looked away and tipped her wineglass at our server.

"There's not much to tell you. I thought Robert was a good man, that he loved me and we'd be together for life, but . . ." That's all it took for her eyes to well up.

I waited for the server to refill her glass. "I don't understand, Mom. Why would he leave just 'cause you got pregnant?"

She chewed the inside of her cheek. "Owen, do you know what I want from you? *For* you?"

I shook my head.

"I want you to get back what was taken from your childhood. A happy family. A marriage that lasts. Children who look up to you, grow up under the same roof as you." She dabbed a napkin under her eyes.

I sipped my tea, then took a turn. "You know what I want from you, Mom?" She put her glass down after having lifted it halfway to her mouth. "Quit giving in to negative thoughts that pile up until you cave." I purposely avoided looking at her glass. "And quit drinking. It's a worthless addiction."

Her chin sank into her chest, and she got way too emotional for a public setting. "Don't you think I've tried?"

That's when I decided I'd go for it after all. "You'll never get better until you realize that your struggles aren't just with yourself. You're being oppressed, intentionally made to fall down and fail."

"You think Frank is holding me back?"

"No, Mom." I moved my plate out of the way and leaned forward. "This has nothing to do with Frank. It's something else. Even worse . . ."

"What?"

"I told you before. I call them Creepers." She squirmed in her seat. "I think they might be demons."

That's when I lost her.

"Don't you dare bring that stuff up with me!" She asked the waiter for a to-go cup, her way of letting me know the conversation was over.

I drove us home, hoping we wouldn't get busted for having open alcohol in the car. By the time we turned onto our street, she'd put the whole experience behind her and was quizzing me to see if I knew the meaning of the Latin root word *acidus*.

Duh. It's where we get the English word *acid*.

When we pulled up to the house, Ray Anne's mom was knocking on our door. My mom stuffed her Styrofoam cup into my hand, then approached her.

"Hey, Susan." Mrs. Greiner smiled, then after some small talk she said, "I'm hosting a prayer meeting at my house at ten o'clock tomorrow morning. Some moms are getting together to pray for the Masonville High students and our community. I realize your workload may conflict, but I want you to know you're invited."

Really? Hadn't Ray Anne told her mom not to bother inviting my mother?

My mom pulled off a polite smile. "Thanks for the invitation. I'll be there if I can."

Yeah, right.

More small talk, then Mrs. Greiner left, and my mom and I went inside our graffiti-stained house. I flipped on the TV but kept the volume down so she could hear me now that she'd gone into the kitchen.

"Mom, I know you'd never go to that in the morning, but just in case you feel obligated, let me assure you, it's a total waste of your time. I know for a fact that prayer doesn't work."

My mouth hadn't closed yet when my dog started barking like I'd unleashed a herd of cats into our living room. Then I understood.

And jumped up.

A Creeper charged at me through the wall, stopping so close to my face that I had to lean back to read its infected scar:

faithless

The putrid thing began to circle me. I froze, hands up, determined not to freak out. What was it trying to do? Even though I didn't have cords or chains, around and around it went, eyeing me like a wolf sniffing a slab of meat, frothing at its filthy mouth.

I didn't move—until it let out an ear-shattering growl. I couldn't help it—instinct kicked in, and I sprinted out the door to my motorcycle.

I don't think I touched the brake one time on the way to Ray Anne's. I ran to her porch and pressed the doorbell twice, straining to catch my breath. But I gasped again when I saw Faithless charging up the driveway, coming for me.

I called Ray Anne's name and pounded the door with both fists. It opened, and I practically jumped into her arms. Faithless got to the doorway, then stopped suddenly like it had slammed into a concrete wall. It wouldn't—or couldn't—trespass into Ray Anne's light.

She shut the door, and I clung to her the whole time that I explained things. Had her parents overheard me, I think they probably would have called 911. Or the guys in white coats.

"What were you doing when the Creeper showed up?" Ray Anne acted like she was an investigator tasked with solving a crime.

"I was talking to my mom."

"What did you say right before it appeared?"

I had to think about it. "I told her I know for a fact that prayer doesn't work."

She gave me that stare I was getting to know too well. "Way to go, Owen."

"What?"

"Don't you get it?" She dropped her hands onto her appealing hips.

It took me a second. "You think I summoned the thing?"

"Your comment led it right to you."

It was possible, I guessed.

But the next day, the impossible happened.

TWENTY-EIGHT

I KNEW IT WAS ONLY A matter of time before Faithless came back—maybe even teamed up with Murder—which didn't help my insomnia one bit. And for the record, I determined to be way more careful about what I let come out of my mouth.

I realized that if being faithless was evil, it had to mean faith was good, but I couldn't help that I didn't have anything to put my faith in. The Watchmen hadn't exactly proven dependable. And God? Even less so.

When I got to school on Tuesday morning, I learned there'd been another suicide. A freshman kid who was in the marching band. Thankfully I hadn't known him, but I still took the news hard. Another casualty of an invisible war.

I felt like I'd failed him somehow.

As an eerie twist, "number fifteen" was ranked fifteenth in his class.

There was talk about yet another suicide, but it turned out to be a false alarm. A girl was really sick, but rumor somehow had it that she'd hung herself. How the facts can become that twisted is beyond me, but then again, we're talking about high school.

I saw Meagan in the hallway, and Lance was a distance away with his back to her, talking to someone. I seized the moment.

"Hey, Meagan, how have you been?"

She was Creeper-free, and on top of that, had a cheerful grin on her face. I hadn't expected that.

"You look . . . better," I told her.

She grinned bigger.

"Thanks for coming by the other day and talking to me."

"I just wanted to help."

She put her hand on my shoulder. "You did, Owen."

I couldn't remember the last time I'd felt that relieved. Had I actually managed to ward off Suicide?

Sure enough, Demise came creeping along the ceiling above our heads, alerted to our conversation through that maddening eavesdropping ability Creepers had. And as if one wasn't bad enough, there were now two Creepers spying down on us, *both* named Demise.

Still, Meagan seemed much happier today. Her old self.

I stepped closer to her. "You know if you ever need anything—"

"What's this?" I hadn't noticed Lance approaching. "I thought I told you to stay away from us."

"I was just saying hi." I cleared my throat. "And reminding her that she's an awesome person with an amazing future. Lots to look forward to in life."

Lance looked me over like I had a skin disease, then grinned at Meagan. "I know who's got my vote for most likely to succeed—at being weird."

I don't know if Meagan stood up for me or not—I walked away at that point.

Ray Anne was ecstatic when I told her about Meagan's improvement.

After that, the day carried on like a sad song. Creepers wrote on everything like psychopaths. There wasn't a wall, a row of lockers, or a window left untainted by their vicious black words.

I was on my way to fourth period when a refreshing scent blasted through the hallway. I looked but didn't see anything. I ran up two flights of stairs, stopping halfway to type out a text to Ray Anne: **Watchmen are here.** I was sure of it.

I stepped onto the second floor by the library, and a blinding light hit the left side of my face. I shielded my eyes, infused with a sense of calm but also giddy with adrenaline the instant I saw them. Five breathtaking, armor-clad Watchmen in a V formation at the end of the hallway. This time they peered out, not up, staring intently at the oblivious students.

I took refuge beside a section of lockers and sneaked peeks at the celestial giants, anticipating that at any second they would charge. Not that I was scared of them. I just didn't want to get in their way. Neither did the Creepers, apparently—there wasn't a single fiend in sight.

Minutes later, the bell rang, and the last few students rushed to class. I came out of hiding one slow step at a time, until I stood facing them across the hall, their radiance so powerful I was actually tempted to bow down again, even if it meant triggering a colossal blast.

Suddenly, it happened. In perfect sync, they strode, covering a massive amount of ground with each step. And they opened their mouths, creating what felt to me like a massive wind tunnel as they blew on the lockers, walls, floors—everything in their path. The rotten graffiti shriveled to dust and disintegrated, disappearing into the whirlwind.

As if that wasn't astonishing enough, the Watchmen plunged their humongous hands into the walls, pulling hissing Creepers out of hiding by their necks, arms—whatever. I hightailed it back to my post beside the lockers as they passed by me, all of them clutching at least three Creepers in each fist, dragging them along. The Creepers thrashed like they feared for their immortal lives. Whined like they were begging for mercy.

The Watchmen made a sharp turn and stormed down the steps, clearing nearly an entire flight of stairs in one stride. My knees were weak, but I managed to follow, watching as they traveled the length of the main downstairs hallway, blasting graffiti into oblivion and snatching more Creepers out of hiding. They stopped at the end of the hall and hurled the life-sucking vipers through a locked set of double doors, out of our school.

One of the Watchmen turned and faced a stairwell down the hall from me. Just stood there, staring down at . . . what?

I took careful steps that way, then spotted her. Ashlyn, slouched over on the bottom step, an anguished expression on her face as she tore through her purse, searching for something.

There was a Creeper behind her, crouched low, as if it could actually hide from the Watchman. *"Do it,"* I heard the Creeper hiss at her, in perfect English.

Ashlyn pulled a pill bottle out of her purse and eyed it.

"Do it!" The Creeper was more forceful this time. Ashlyn popped the lid off the bottle. I approached her at the same time that the Watchman closed in on the Creeper, pinning it against the stairs by its crooked neck.

Ashlyn looked up at me, and I extended my open hand toward the pill bottle. Her gaze went right back to the pills, longing in her eyes.

"Those are hurting you," I said. "Not helping."

The Watchman took a big step back, ripping the Creeper off of Ashlyn's chain as if the links were made of tissue paper. The thing flailed its arms and legs like a dying cockroach as the Watchman chucked him out of the school.

Ashlyn stood, peering into my face, thinking it was just the two of us in that hallway. I still held my hand out.

She swallowed hard. "Throw these away for me?" Her eyes pooled. Finally she set the bottle in my hand.

"I will."

I'd suspected it before, but now I was sure: my life's purpose was to help people. Not just the ones in physical pain but the tons of people hurting on the inside, battling enemies of the soul. Yeah, I had a lot to figure out and learn in order to pull it off, but I was hopeful that if I didn't give up I'd eventually find answers.

I had to. Nothing else seemed to matter now.

I was so jittery that it was hard to sit, but I managed to slide into my fourth-period chair. Ray Anne had replied to my text: **I'm not surprised Watchmen are here. Look at the time.**

10:17 a.m.

So?

Then I remembered. Mrs. Greiner's prayer group. Did that somehow commission the Watchmen? I didn't know, but I didn't see any more of the warriors that day, or that week.

I can't tell you how discouraging it was to watch the Creepers steadily reemerge, staining my school all over again, desecrating the place with their hatred and degrading words.

I needed something to take my mind off things, and I found it. It was finally time to see Ray Anne in that little red dress.

TWENTY-NINE

My mom said I looked like a million bucks in my tuxedo. I had to agree.

For just a moment, I felt like a normal eighteen-year-old. Yeah, my mother's chains scraped the pavement as she hurried up Ray Anne's driveway beside me, handing me the corsage box. But still, I was about to experience a time-honored American tradition. I would knock on the door and check out my prom date. Nothing paranormal about that.

I have to say, the sight of Ray Anne in that red sequined dress did not disappoint. I forced my eyes away several times, unable to shake the paranoia that her father could see right through me. Man, she looked amazing. And her perfume was working its magic on me.

All the parents took a million pictures. My mom got teary eyed—a little awkward—but so did Ray Anne's parents. Mrs. Greiner's tears spilled over.

Finally the camera flashes stopped, and my date and I could go be alone.

My mom had agreed to let me rent a brand-new Camaro for the night, especially after I rubbed it in that it was *her* idea that I go to prom with Ray Anne. I'd placed a long-stemmed red rose on the passenger seat. I opened the door for Ray Anne, and she blushed.

"Red's my favorite color." She inhaled the scent of the petals.

I studied the curves of her body in that fitted dress and eyed her matching high heels. "Mine too." I drove to the end of the street, then stared at her again. "You look stunning, Ray."

She gasped. "You just called me Ray."

"Yeah?"

Her smile grew at the same time that her eyes became glossy. "That's what Lucas used to call me."

"Oh. Well, if you don't want—"

"I love it." She rested her hand over mine and smiled bigger. Seemed to me she was having just as hard a time taking her eyes off me as I was her.

We met up with some other couples for dinner—a few of Ray Anne's friends—and that went fine. I'd learned how to enjoy a meal even with Creeper funk wafting in my direction.

By the time I paid our bill and we left, the sun was setting, making the sky a breathtaking collage of oranges and yellows and pinks. It's not like me to notice that sort of thing, but I've heard that the mundane becomes exquisite when you're falling in love.

As we drove toward the swank hotel for prom, I really wanted to skip out on the high school scene and do something else entirely, just Ray Anne and me. I figured she'd hate the idea, but I probed just in case.

"So, you're really looking forward to this, right?"

"Um, yeah. I guess so."

"You want to go, don't you?"

She sighed. "Well, honestly, I've never cared much about prom."

Looked like things just might go my way.

"My friends have dreamed about it their whole lives," she said, "but not me. This night actually means a lot more to my mom than me."

Just the open door I needed. "So what if we ditch the plan, Ray Anne? Do something else?"

"Like what?"

We were both smiling now, energized by spontaneity.

"I have an idea," I said. "I just need to stop off at a store for a second, okay?"

"Um, sure . . ." She got her cell out. "But what are we doing? My parents will kill me if I don't tell them where I am."

"Well . . . I was hoping to surprise you."

Ray Anne eyed her cell but didn't press any buttons. She bit her bottom lip. "You'll still have me home by 1:00 a.m.?"

"Of course."

After a minute, she sighed and put her cell away. I got the feeling this was the most rebellious thing she'd ever done in her entire life. "Okay, surprise me." Now she was grinning just as big as I was.

A lot of girls would've nagged and tried to wear me down so I'd give up the surprise, but not Ray Anne. She wasn't the type that had to be in control all the time—one of many things I loved about her.

I parked at a hole-in-the-wall grocery store. "You want to stay in the car? We're slightly overdressed."

"Who cares? I'm coming."

I managed to push our grocery cart even though it had a wheel that wouldn't spin and kept pulling to the right. Someone snapped a picture of us. "Say cheese," the lady said. Ray Anne held up a block of mozzarella.

She stopped off at the makeup aisle, and I grabbed a few things without her seeing—a package of strawberries, some Hershey's chocolate bars, cold drinks. I found a big, rolled-up blanket and threw it in the basket.

Ray Anne met up with me as I was finishing checking out. She put a plastic sack over her shoulder and walked around like it was her purse. She cracked me up.

I drove awhile—traveled two towns over—and it was around nine o'clock when we finally parked at our destination. I hadn't been there in years, but lucky me, it was still there—a colorful, vintage-looking carnival next to a big lake. Lights hung overhead, strung from one ride to the next. A handful of people enjoyed the nightlife and lake view.

A really cool atmosphere, if you ask me.

Ray Anne's face lit up like a child at Christmas. "This is beautiful! How'd you know about this place?"

"When I was a kid, my mother used to make road trips to Texas to see a friend of hers. She'd bring me here. I have some good memories."

I helped Ray Anne onto the mermaid-themed merry-go-round, and she sat with both feet on one side of a giant seahorse. I stood and held on to her waist—you know, in case she started to fall or something. Cool air blew off the water, fanning the wisps of hair framing Ray Anne's face. I gave up on trying not to stare.

I was more leery of getting on the rusty Ferris wheel than she was, but I sucked it up. I didn't want to ruin the moment by saying how freaky it was to look down from way up there and see Creepers scattered among the people, so I kept it to myself. I also didn't mention that the toothless man operating the ride was linked to a Creeper named Insanity.

We survived the ride, and after a few more, made our way back to the car, talking the whole time. I drove us farther down the lakeside road until there were no more lights or people, then found a place to park and spread my new blanket near the water. It took Ray Anne a few minutes to relax, but she finally slipped off her high heels and sat by me.

This wasn't exactly a tropical paradise, but the lake looked spectacular at night, moonlight rippling across the surface. Ray Anne cast a soft, golden glow onto our blanket—and I let out a belly laugh. I hadn't realized the blanket had the Run-N-Go grocery store logo imprinted across the front—a smiling shopping cart with huge pink tennis shoes.

We munched on strawberries and chocolate and laughed about all kinds of things, but after a while, the conversation got deeper. She asked me questions about my childhood.

"My mom has issues."

She shrugged. "Whose doesn't?"

I crumpled an empty wrapper, and then surprised myself by opening up way more than I ever had. With anyone. "My mom drinks all the time. Every day. For as long as I can remember."

Ray Anne got really still. "I'm sorry. I had no idea."

"Yeah." I exhaled, hoping to seem relaxed. "She does the double-life thing pretty well."

Ray Anne cleared her throat. Looked up at the moon. "My parents do too."

"No way." Of all people.

"Their marriage has been falling apart ever since my brother died, but they refuse to get help. It's like they dread admitting we're not perfect."

I'd somehow come to believe they were. "I guess Lights struggle too sometimes."

"Of course," she said.

I think she meant to bring up something positive next, but . . .

"So, why did you move to Texas?"

This one was under lock and key. Way too personal.

She obviously sensed my reluctance. "Is it hard to talk about?"

I nodded, trying to think of a way to change the subject. But she was too fast.

"Something with your mom?"

I nodded again, my defenses steadily giving way to a growing sense of vulnerability that I fully intended to squash.

"You can tell me."

Don't ask me how, but she had a way of begging with her eyes. I tried to avoid them, but in the silence, the situation grew more intense until I found myself giving in. For months, I'd refused to think about the night my mom and I left Boston, so it took a while for me to get going. I spoke slowly.

"It was Christmas Eve, and no surprise, my mom's boyfriend was wasted. The whole time Tim lived with us, I'd hardly ever seen him sober. I overheard him arguing upstairs with my mom—nothing new either. But then there was this loud . . . thump, like something had slammed the wall. I ran upstairs—"

I had to pause my story. Force my emotions into submission.

"I opened the door, and Tim was . . . he was choking my mother. Her face was blue. She was dying on the floor, right in front of me."

Ray Anne covered her mouth.

"I saw Tim's gun on the nightstand. And I—I grabbed it. Then aimed it at him."

I felt myself breathing hard, fury rising up in me just talking about it.

"If he hadn't let her go, I would have had no choice but to shoot him." I looked her in the face. "And I know I would have, Ray Anne." She was speechless. I didn't blame her.

"Tim took off, and we threw our stuff in the car, fast. Emptied the mailbox, then sped away. We spent Christmas Day in a musty hotel. I was sitting there, looking through about a week's worth of mail, when I came across a big envelope—inside it was a set of keys. To a house. My grandparents' estate, left to me."

Ray Anne wiped her cheek, brushing away a tear, I think. She leaned in. "Owen, you have so much courage."

I shrugged, then took a long, deep breath. Out came another majorly personal admission: "Sometimes I wonder what it would be like. If my dad had never left."

She searched my face while I stared out at the water. "I feel sorry for him," she said.

"Him?" I glared at her. "He's the one who left us."

"And he's the one who's missing out on knowing his son. He totally blew it."

It's not that it had never occurred to me to think of it that way—I'd just never been able to convince myself it was true. But it was a nice thing for her to say.

"Wow." I swatted grass off our blanket, eager to lighten things up. "I didn't mean to ruin our night."

"Are you kidding me? It's been unforgettable."

Time for a change of pace. I took out my phone and selected a play-list. Yes, I had a collection of slow music—I can admit that.

Once I had my bow tie off and collar unbuttoned, I stood and reached out to her. "Dance with me."

She put her petite hand in mine. I pulled her body close, and my cold stomach did a flip. She rested her head on my chest, and I inhaled the sweet vanilla of her hair. Just like that, my sad stories faded away, back into the recesses of my mind.

She smiled up at me. "Did you purposely play this song?"

"I didn't."

A 1980s classic, "Lady in Red," had come up first on my playlist. It really was a coincidence.

We swayed back and forth next to the glistening water, my hands resting on her lower back, her warm arms wrapped around my neck. It was like the moon was shining just for us. Like the stars aligned so that we'd be there, at that very moment.

I didn't think it could happen like this—not this fast. But I'd totally fallen for her. My heart belonged to her, whether she'd intended to capture it or not.

I looked down at her, and she tucked her head like she was feeling shy. She started to say something, then stopped, then started to say something else, but stopped again.

"What is it?"

"I'm sorry." She loosened her embrace. "It's . . . I can't find the words."

"You?" I leaned back and gazed into her face. "It's okay, Ray Anne." We were barely moving now. I ran my fingers over the back of her neck, then lifted her chin. "Just tell me."

She exhaled slowly, like she was nervous. "I guess I didn't realize when we blew off prom that we'd end up alone in such a . . . well, a place this romantic."

"So?" I stared at her glossy red lips.

"I just want to be careful. I love that we've become such good friends, but I guess I'm afraid of taking things further."

I heard what she said, and I really did care, but I couldn't resist. I leaned in, desperate to kiss her. But she turned her face and pressed her head to my chest again.

Crushing rejection.

It took me a second to regroup. "I'm sorry, Ray. I didn't mean to—"

"No, it's not your fault." She let go and stepped back. "You didn't know."

"Know what?"

She crossed her arms. "Look, you can make fun of me all you want. I don't care."

"What? Why would I do that?"

"'Cause that's what people do."

"Who?"

"People I've told."

I pulled her close again. "What are you talking about?"

She pulled down on my neck, speaking directly in my face. "I'm saving my first kiss for my wedding day, okay? I've never kissed anyone." She let go and tapped her foot. "Go ahead. Start teasing me. I can take it."

I hugged her and laughed. "I'm not gonna tease you."

"But you think it's stupid, right? Well, it's not stupid to me. I've made up my mind."

"Hey, I didn't say it was stupid."

She sat down on our blanket and motioned for me to sit too. "So what *do* you think?"

Honestly, not kissing until marriage seemed really over the top, but at the same time, I couldn't help but respect her for it. "You really wanna know?"

"Yeah, I do."

I sighed. "I think it's awful."

"What?" Okay, so Ray Anne could cop an attitude.

"Wait." I smiled. "Let me finish. I think it's awful except . . ."

"Yeah?"

"For the incredibly lucky man who gets that kiss."

Her pout rose to a grin. "Thanks. Seriously, it means a lot."

I nearly tried to kiss her again but remembered that was a no-no.

"Owen?" I had a bad feeling about what was coming next. "I want us to stay good friends, and I'm worried that if I open up my heart to something more, it won't end well."

I didn't get it. "Well, since we can't even kiss, isn't 'friends' the only choice we have?"

"That's what I'm talking about. You don't even know how to be more than friends without fooling around. I want something more meaningful than that. And I want someone who loves the Lord like I do."

She might as well have clobbered me in the face with a fistful of dirt. "Are you saying I'm not good enough?" I probably sounded hurt. 'Cause I was.

"No. I'm saying *I'm* not good enough—not strong enough—to date you. I think it would make it difficult for me to keep my priorities straight. And saving things for marriage—that would be really hard since you don't believe in that."

I guess that was her attempt at putting a humble spin on things, but to me, she was still saying I flat out didn't measure up.

"Look, we both know I'm not a church boy and faith doesn't come naturally to me, but I really am trying—more now than ever. And if you're asking me to keep my hands off you because you've set your heart on saving yourself for marriage, I'll do it. I'll respect your wishes because . . ."

I almost took the coward's way out and said something about how much I admired her.

"Because I care about you, Ray. A lot."

THIRTY

"SOMEONE HAS SOME pep in his step today."

I rolled my eyes. My mom could be so dorky. But I really was feeling the best I had since my world had imploded. I'd actually slept so well the night before that I'd pressed snooze on my phone, like, five times.

I lowered myself onto my motorcycle and made a mental note. *Only six more Mondays before graduation.*

I couldn't imagine what the next phase of my life would be like, but I was 100 percent sure who I wanted with me.

I'd just started my bike when my cell rang. I hoped it was her.

Nope.

"Did you hear?" Jess was sobbing so hard it didn't sound like her. "About Meagan?"

All my happiness hit the pavement.

"What happened?"

"She overdosed. She didn't die, but they're saying it doesn't look good. She's in intensive care."

"What?" It was like my throat had clamped shut, but I still managed to talk. "She was better! Much better!"

"Sometimes it just seems that way."

"No!" I couldn't accept that. "I'm telling you—Suicide was gone!"

"Huh?"

"What hospital is she at?"

"I don't know yet." She cried even harder. "I'll call you back."

I hung up and drove around in a daze, my blood pressure rising like the Texas heat in July.

I'd tried to stop her. But she gave in, surrendered to the hate-filled lies of an enemy whose only motive is destruction.

Why couldn't Lance listen to me?

Why didn't the Watchmen intervene?

I'd known she was in trouble, but it hadn't mattered. I saw her, clear as day, charging toward a steep, unforgiving cliff called suicide, but no one would help me hold her back. I had thrown her a rope, but she'd let it slip through her fingers.

I swerved onto the grass alongside a desolate road and parked my bike, breathing so hard I thought my lungs might explode. The pain of injustice burned inside my chest like I'd been impaled with a steel-tipped arrow.

I stumbled onto the grass. Pounded my fists into the earth.

"What's the matter with you?" I lifted my head and raged at the universe and its supposed Maker. "How could you let this happen?" I picked up a good-sized rock and hurled it into the street, watching it splinter into a thousand rolling pieces. "If the Watchmen work for you, you suck at commanding your army!"

I kicked a hard mound of dried mud and glared up at the blue expanse. I didn't care if I became fitted with a shackle. I wasn't done talking.

I cupped my hands around my mouth and shouted as hard as my throat would let me.

"GOD! I HATE YOU!"

I collapsed in the grass beside my bike, then slammed my elbow against my front tire over and over and over. I finally pulled my knees into my chest and rocked back and forth. It was quiet on that backstreet, no sound but an easy breeze. But my declaration rang in my ears, echoing across a realm where words travel faster and farther than light, and superhuman beings are always listening.

I wanted them to hear me. I'd meant what I'd said.

My phone rang. I scrambled to yank it out of my pocket.

"Owen?"

It was Lance. No hostility. Just sorrow. "Can you come to Central Hospital? Meagan—"

"I know. I'll be there."

I started my motorcycle and adjusted the rearview mirror. No shock to me, Faithless was watching me a short distance away with two more Creepers at its side. I gassed it.

Of course the press was there, reporting outside the hospital. If they were at all grieved by Meagan's tragedy, I couldn't tell.

I refused an interview.

Lingering outside the entrance was another nuisance: the crazed redhead—the most insane of all the protesters. He had countless chains—even more than my mom. He glared at me, and I scowled right back, way too on edge to put up with one of his outbursts. Good thing he kept his mouth shut.

Inside the hospital lobby, that dusty, soot-looking stuff was everywhere, blanketing the floors and smeared on the walls and chairs and couches. My classmates were there too, tons of them huddled together, and the powdered residue was stuck to them, on their shoes and clothes. A nurse walked by, and she was really covered—clumps of the ashy dust on her face and lips and all in her hair.

I looked down, and it was already stuck to my shoes. And I was so cold, my ears and nose and fingers were numb.

Out of the corner of my eye, the walls appeared to breathe. I looked closer and realized they were teeming with Creepers, crammed full, all shoving and shifting like worms slithering in a Mason jar filled to the top. No doubt feeding off an atmosphere of human suffering and death.

And despite the sunlit windows and lighting fixtures, the hospital was dim, like the air was soiled with smog. I was tempted to go back outside, but then I saw Ray Anne, her light so bright and cleansing that the space around her was clean. She walked to me, and everywhere she set her feet, she left clean footprints.

She hugged me, and I could take a breath.

"Have you seen Lance?" I asked her.

She pointed. He was exiting some double doors. People swarmed him, but he came straight to me, eyes bloodshot and puffy. Guess I'd underestimated how much our friendship meant to him after all. I didn't know what to say, just put a hand on his shoulder. The dust from his shirt stuck to my hand.

He bit his lip, working to keep his emotions in check. "You can't go into her room, but they said I could have someone back there with me."

I didn't want to go near her or anyone else spiraling toward death, but I followed Lance anyway. Even if things between us weren't like they used to be, I wasn't willing to turn my back on him. Not now.

The ICU was darker than the lobby, the walls just as possessed. We passed numerous rooms on the way to Meagan's, and at first I mostly kept my head down—until I noticed something horrid. A sickly old man appeared bound to his hospital bed by thick, spiderweb-looking strands woven over his bony body. The grayish threads stretched out and clung to the walls. A Creeper hovered overhead, watching.

I forced myself to keep walking. The patients in the following rooms had webs too.

"Wait here. I'll be back." Lance went to Meagan's bedside, and I peered in from the hallway. More webs. She was on life support. Had already been resuscitated once, I heard her parents say.

Meagan's mom, normally an attractive woman, looked half-dead herself. And Meagan's dad—well, let's just say he was doing good to be standing.

Meagan was hooked up to all kinds of machines and monitors that beeped and blinked, and tubes stretched in every direction through the spidery threads. Her shackle was still in place, chains draping to the floor, and her jagged cords sprawled across her pillowcase.

Lance came back into the hallway. "The doctors say that we should . . . that we have to consider letting her . . ."

He closed his eyes and broke, sobbing on my shoulder. I had no clue how to console him, but I was willing to stick it out until the very end. Which probably wouldn't be long now.

When Meagan's brother showed up, having sped all the way from College Station, the environment became so intense and emotional that I had to take a break and walk away for a minute. Meagan's family was falling to pieces, wailing. I couldn't take it.

I wandered down the dingy hallway, my mouth completely dry, but I was reluctant to drink from the water fountain. The place felt contaminated. A few more steps, and something bright caught my eye. An elderly lady, propped up in her bed. A Light.

Nothing sinister on her body, over her bed, or in her room.

She looked a century old, but her radiance was extraordinary. It lit the bottom half of her bed with a shimmering aura.

Her neck was layered with wrinkles and covered in brown age spots, but it was visible—which was more than I could say for most people. I stood by the door, watching her sleep. I inched closer, intrigued.

Her room was peaceful and way cleaner than the hallway. I stepped in farther, my face and fingers thawing the closer I came to her.

"Is that you, John?"

I nearly had a heart attack when her eyes sprang open and she spoke. I looked over my shoulder. No one there. "Um, no, ma'am. I'm Owen."

"Come here, son." Her eyes drifted closed again, but she was smiling. Not a tooth in her gums. I stopped a foot from her bed. She reached with her wobbly hand, motioning for me. I stepped forward, and she gripped my fingers the best she could. Her knuckles were enormous.

"You remind me of my son." She grinned again and squeezed my hand. "He died in the war. Twenty-three years old."

"Oh."

Her eyeballs were so deep set, it was like they'd fallen back into her brain. She fell asleep again. The light around her feet was bright enough to penetrate through the bedsheets.

"It's so nice of you to come see me." A sudden burst of consciousness.

"Sure."

She tried to focus her cloudy eyes on me. Given the circumstances, it seemed okay to ask. "You have this incredible glow. Do you know why?"

She let out a raspy laugh that shook her whole body. "I'm going home soon." Then she was out again.

Poor lady. From the looks of things, she was never going home again. But she had a lifetime behind her. Meagan's life was just getting started.

I draped the nice old lady's arm over her bony chest and slipped my fingers away. I stepped into the hallway, and an announcement blared through the intercom. I knew enough about hospital protocols to recognize that the term *code blue* wasn't good.

Medical personnel raced by. Into Meagan's room.

I had to get down there, for Lance. I raced down the hall.

What I saw next will never, ever leave me.

THIRTY-ONE

I STOPPED OUTSIDE the doorway of Meagan's room. It was a hurricane of activity. A doctor hovered over her, clutching an electric paddle in each hand. The only thing louder than the monotone alarm of Meagan's cardiac flatlining was the high-pitched squeal of the defibrillator charging.

"Clear!" the doctor yelled. She plunged the paddles against Meagan's chest, jolting her body. Meagan's mom fainted. Her brother was frantic, yelling at the doctors to keep trying.

They hit her a second time. Still no pulse.

Lance fell back into a chair and covered his face. I was a statue—frozen, numb with disbelief.

They shocked Meagan a third time. The doctor stepped back. No response.

But then everything changed.

Suicide sat straight up in the bed, extending out of Meagan's torso. I rubbed my eyes, trying to comprehend it. But the realization was unbearable.

It had never left her, never truly detached. Instead Suicide had somehow pried its way through her skin and stuffed itself inside her body, sabotaging her night and day from within. The ultimate act of trespass.

Now that Meagan's heart had stopped, Suicide used its long arms to hoist up and out of her, cackling in the face of her family's anguish. It passed through the third-story window at the same time that two other Creepers oozed out of the webbed wall above Meagan's bed. One pounced on her chest and tore her cords out of her head while the other ripped her chains off with one hand. They wrapped them around her shackle, winding and squeezing against her neck like they wanted to suffocate her even though she'd already stopped breathing.

One Creeper, Damnation, charged through the side of Meagan's bed and stood on her—*inside* of her—at her waist, grinding its teeth, drooling on her. The other one, Thief, peered down from the opposite side, arched over her head.

Like calculated serial killers, they plunged their hands into her stomach, then pulled, ripping a shadowy figure out of Meagan, leaving a dusty, gaping hole.

My knees buckled and I hit the floor.

The shadow was Meagan.

Her soul. Kicking. Screaming. Flailing. Begging for mercy.

They dragged her off the bed, away from her body, and clawed at her with repeated blows. She fought back, twisting and straining to grab onto something. Anything.

"Daddy!" Her bloodcurdling cries sent tremors through my body. "Help me!"

Her pleas fell on deaf ears.

I couldn't breathe. Couldn't comprehend it. Couldn't stop the abduction being carried out ten feet away from me.

They struck her in the mouth, silencing her, then pushed her down to the dust-covered floor, whipping their heads back and forth now so fast that they became a dark blur.

Out of the ashen ground cover, a being emerged. He had the bodily frame of a Creeper but was considerably bigger. A face as pale as a corpse. No infected markings or letters.

He was draped in long, shredded garments that may have been light colored at one time but were now a filthy gray—completely saturated with that nasty dust and stained with what appeared to be splatters of dried blood.

A black crown of spiky thorns was pressed into his head, and he had wispy, long hair—even whiter than his colorless face.

Damnation and Thief released Meagan's soul to this superior presence, then ran back into the wall like spooked rats.

All went silent.

I thought I was going to pass out. I struggled, disoriented, like I was outside of my body too. The pale Creeper's presence was disrupting my equilibrium, throwing my senses out of whack.

He bent to the ground and lifted Meagan's chin, gazing down on her with the most nightmarish eyes I'd ever seen—white pupils floating in a pool of black.

"Please, have mercy," Meagan sobbed, shaking, laboring to speak. "Don't hurt me. Send me back. I beg you!"

I waited, hoping against all odds. But her captor narrowed his ghostly eyes and snarled, answering her pleas with heartless contempt. The floor suddenly crumbled beneath them, and they sank down, swallowed by the ground.

"No!" I reached to her.

Out of the black crater, Meagan grasped with both arms, battling to cling to the hospital floor, her legs dangling into darkness.

"Meagan!" My body was so heavy I could barely move, but I managed to get into her room and pull myself toward her, stretching my arm as far as it would go.

She lifted her upper body out of the hole, and I grabbed for her, but my hand passed through hers. Hard as I tried, I couldn't make contact. Her soul was in another dimension now, far beyond my grasp.

That instant, a white hand reached up from behind Meagan, spreading its clawed fingers across her forehead.

My eyes met Meagan's, a final word on her shivering lips. "Owen!"

Her head jerked backward, and her arms gave way. I saw her drop, disappear into darkness. Banished from the land of the living.

"NO!"

I rolled onto my back and convulsed, unable to cope. Terrorized from limb to limb.

I saw Lance hovering over me, then all went black.

I don't remember waking up or how I got into a chair, but I do know I was wrapped in a blanket, and a lady in scrubs had handed me a cup of water. I was seated by the nurses' station, not far from Meagan's room. Her empty body still lay in the bed, a hollow shell, her midsection ravaged just like Walt's. No more monitors or lights or sounds.

Lance stroked her hand.

I heard a nurse say that someone from the morgue was on the way.

Lance bent down and kissed the back of his girlfriend's hand, tears dripping down his cheeks. Then he backed away, into the hall. I shrugged the blanket off my shoulders and pushed down on the arms of my chair. It wasn't easy to stand. Or to make sense of reality.

"Lance." I meant to call his name but instead barely whispered it. I stepped toward him, working to keep my balance, struggling not to break down. He saw me and came the rest of the way.

Then snapped.

"You said this would happen—did you talk her into it? Put dark thoughts in her head?"

"What? I . . . no!"

"Did you want her dead?"

Several nurses stopped. Meagan's distraught brother looked over his shoulder.

"People around you keep dying, Owen!"

"I cared about her." I backed up.

He closed the gap between us and shouted in my face. "Get out of here! Now!"

"I came because you—"

"I said *leave*!"

A police officer looked our way. I turned my back on Lance and made my way down the hall, the effects of trauma so severe that I honestly couldn't tell if I was dreaming or not.

I was nearing some exit doors when a nurse called to me.

"Excuse me, sir?" It shouldn't have scared me, but it did. "Are you a relative or friend of Ms. Ida Knowles?"

Who? I couldn't think. I didn't need this.

"I saw you talking to Ms. Ida earlier. Did you hear?"

"Hear what?" I grabbed the collar of my T-shirt and twisted it, breathing heavy through my mouth.

"She passed, a few minutes ago."

I couldn't stand still. "And?"

"I thought you might want to pay your respects."

I bent over, hands on my thighs, beads of sweat trickling down my face despite how cold I was. "I didn't know her."

"You're the only visitor she's had."

"That's not my problem!" I yelled so loud, the police officer started down the hall.

I stood upright, hands cupped over my mouth, trying to come to grips. Lance was walking in my direction now with Meagan's brother. I couldn't take another confrontation. I ducked into the deceased old lady's room.

Another soulless body, yet this was nothing like what I'd just seen. Her glow was gone, but her flesh was untouched—no bindings, no hideous, dust-covered wound. The room seemed serene and quiet. And a lingering, vitalizing scent let me know a Watchman had been there. Maybe several.

"Good-bye, Ms. Ida."

It was the best I could do.

I stepped out of the haunted hospital into the afternoon sun, so shaken that I actually tried to outrun my own shadow. Once home, I hid under a pile of blankets in the corner of my closet, curled in a fetal position, suffering from cold sweats and night terrors even though the sun lit up my room. It didn't matter whether my eyes were open or squeezed closed, I saw Meagan's face. The horror in her eyes.

I never wanted anyone to say my name ever again.

THIRTY-TWO

POST-TRAUMATIC STRESS DISORDER WAS more than a psychiatric term in a textbook for me now.

    I quit going to school.

    Quit eating.

    Quit living, really . . .

    For fifteen days.

IT FELT LIKE I'D DROPPED OUT OF life for fifteen years. My only connection to the outside world was Ray Anne. I told her what had happened to Meagan, and for several nights after that, the only way she could sleep was if her mom was lying next to her. She missed some school too, exhausted and sick with sorrow.

My mom nagged me to get out of bed, but I was determined to isolate myself until my mind quit rehearsing Meagan's demise.

And I refused to go to the funeral. I was done with burying the dead. Meagan wasn't in a better place and couldn't possibly be resting in peace, and hearing someone say that she was would have pushed me over the edge.

I didn't know where that captor had taken her soul, but I was sure it was unbearable.

It took a while, but I finally came to understand that I'd never get over her death, not even slightly—because she wasn't truly dead. Her body was, but not *her*.

It was a Thursday afternoon when I pulled the covers back, tired of nursing a wound that couldn't heal. I wanted to strike back, take some

228 || LAURA GALLIER

revenge. I was so desperate to put the Creepers on the defensive that I was willing to try just about anything. My frustration gave birth to a plan that I knew had almost no chance of working.

My dog was fixated on my mother's closed bedroom door, barking her head off. Perfect conditions. "Stay there, girl. I'll be right back."

I went to Home Depot and bought the biggest, highest-powered flashlight on the shelf, then hurried home, ready to shove my mom's bedroom door open and shine the light directly into the Creeper's eyes. They have an aversion to people's light, right? So maybe this was worth a try.

As I neared my house, it was clear my experiment would have to wait. A patrol car was in my driveway, and Detective Benny was pacing next to it. He saw me before I could make a U-turn.

I parked my bike and sipped a bottle of sweet tea as I approached him, like his presence created no anxiety in me whatsoever.

"Hello, Owen." He was one of those guys who nearly fractures bones when he shakes your hand. "I need you to follow me to the station, right now. We've got some more questions to ask you."

I dragged my feet back to my motorcycle, then texted Ray Anne and my mom. I told Ray Anne I'd be off the grid for a while, unplugging to clear my mind. I told my mom the truth.

I was escorted to a gray-walled interrogation room, where Detective Benny lowered into a chair across the table from me, then tapped his pen over and over on a yellow notepad like some sort of mental torture technique. My mind was fragile enough.

"Can I get you something to drink, Owen?"

"I'm fine, thanks."

He glanced at a clock on the wall, and I counted four cords spewing from the back of his thick head.

"Please recount the events that took place the day before Walt and Marshall's deaths. Start with what you did that morning and early afternoon, then explain, in as much detail as possible, what happened once you met up with the two boys. Leave nothing out, please."

He wouldn't have brought me here if he didn't have increased suspicions and probably some new evidence on me. But there was no time to think up a new cover story, and besides, I'd watched enough episodes of

Dateline to know that was a big mistake. He'd be listening for inconsistencies. So I told the same story I'd already told him twice before.

Believe me, I was tempted to crack and come clean about the water, but how would I explain my decision to hide it until now? Let's face it—guys like me get killed in prison, and death was to be avoided at all costs. I'd seen the grim reaper in the flesh and knew now that his kingdom of eternal darkness was real.

I spoke for about twenty minutes, concentrating so hard I got a headache. Or maybe my soaring blood pressure caused it. I worried the detective could feel my pulse reverberating across the table. I tried to act normal even though normal was a distant memory.

I didn't kill them on purpose.

I said it over and over in my head, trying to convince myself that I wasn't a real murderer and certainly didn't deserve to share bunk beds with men who were.

But I didn't believe me.

I'd committed an incredibly selfish act that had resulted in the loss of two lives—two young souls I now imagined had been sucked into the same black pit as Meagan. Justice demanded some sort of penance on my part.

But I couldn't bring myself to confess. Human nature at its worst, I guess.

"Owen, some of your classmates have expressed concerns about your mental and emotional stability."

"Let me guess—Dan Bradford? He'd say anything to get me in trouble."

Lance might have squealed too.

"Well, for starters, your girlfriend, Jess, says you've been acting delusional and even claiming to see scary creatures. She said you recently jumped on top of her and nearly smothered her, supposedly because you believed you were protecting her from something unseen that was out to get her?"

I made a fist, barely resisting the urge to punch the table.

"She's my *ex*-girlfriend, and with all due respect, sir, what does that ridiculous accusation have to do with Marshall and Walt's deaths?"

"According to their autopsies, the cause of death appears to be the result of having ingested a hazardous substance of some kind. The problem is these two young men don't fit the profile of kids who wanted to kill themselves, and we have to do our due diligence to investigate all other possibilities, including homicide."

That's all it took for Murder to poke its grisly head through the wall.

"I've already told you everything I know." I strained to keep my eyes on the detective, not the predator staring me down.

"But I haven't told *you* everything *I* know, Owen."

I gripped the sides of my chair, bracing myself for physical evidence that I couldn't explain away.

"Walt's mother said her son came home that evening complaining that you made him drink something that made him very sick. Are you starting to connect the dots, son? He likely died of poisoning and said *you* were the one who coerced him into drinking the 'weird water,' as he called it. And your classmates are saying you're not in your right mind. That doesn't look so good, does it?"

I had no choice but to pull the rip cord. "I'd like to speak with my lawyer."

I didn't have one, but it was time I found one, fast.

Detective Benny let me go.

My mom was in the parking lot, rushing toward me.

"Owen! What did they want?"

"It's a big misunderstanding, Mom. People are making up accusations about me, like I had something to do with Walt and Marshall's deaths." I could hardly tell the difference between the truth and my lies anymore.

Her face turned as white as a bleached sheet. "I'll get a lawyer."

Ray Anne invited me over that evening, and I jumped at the chance. I told her I'd help her get her math homework done even faster, but yeah, that didn't happen. I was too distracted—by the astronomical stressors in my life, of course, but also by her. On the sofa next to me.

All I could think about was how badly I wanted to pull her on top of me, escape for a little while under the weight and touch of her body. Her megablue eyes were getting to me, making me wish I'd never committed to her to hold back. I actually felt a tinge of resentment that she'd asked that of me.

I guess she sensed my longing—she scooted away and tucked a throw pillow between us. I could have ripped that pillow apart with my bare hands.

I wanted to respect her commitment to purity, as she called it, but at the same time, it presented a provoking challenge. Could I persuade her to give in to me?

I leaned toward her, my elbow crushing the ugly pillow, mouthing soft words close to her ear. Giving it my all.

"You want something to drink?" She stood, basically dumping a bucket of ice water on my head.

"Sure."

She went into the kitchen, and I stayed on the sofa. Alone. Just me and my frustrated ego.

But not for long. A Creeper poked its head through the front door, its lethal eyes targeting me. Its name was easy to read:

lust

So Creepers can smell pheromones, I guess.

It didn't stay there long and didn't dare come in—not inside a home full of Lights. But I was still disgusted with my behavior. I'd never thought of myself as a Dan Bradford, the type that uses girls. And the thought of Ray Anne being used filled me with rage. Yet I wanted to.

We drank some purple Kool-Aid, then I went home, wrestling with my motives while also trying to get the image of Meagan's face out of my mind. I couldn't go very long without seeing it.

I sat down at the desk in my bedroom and couldn't resist texting Jess: **Thanks for trying to get me arrested.**

A minute later, my phone rang. She spoke without taking a breath. "I know you're probably furious, but the police came to my house and questioned me, and at first I didn't say much, but the more they asked me about you, the more I just told the truth about stuff.

"After they left, I felt really bad, like I'd betrayed you or something, and I thought about telling you, but I just didn't know how. I don't think you did anything bad whatsoever to Marshall and Walt, Owen."

I was prepared to really sock it to her, but I lost all momentum after she groveled. *I'm sorry* was not in Jess's vocabulary, but I knew that's what she meant.

And honestly, I kind of understood where she was coming from. I knew from personal experience how distressing it is to lie to the police.

What was eating at me now, though, was that she had refused to believe me in the first place.

"Jess, are you even slightly willing to consider that my warnings to you are true?"

For all I knew, her ears were being blocked.

"Owen, what do you expect? I can't possibly believe what you're saying. No one could. Besides, your claims are really terrifying."

I was well aware how terrifying they were. That's why I wanted her to take them seriously.

Oh well. There was no sense in trying to convince a shackled person to believe me.

On Sunday night, there was a candlelight vigil being planned in Meagan's honor and in memorial of the other suicide victims, at Franklin Park of all places. My mom tried to guilt me into going, but eventually we made a truce. She'd leave me alone about it if I started going to school again.

Done.

Masonville High was a mess. The graffiti was out of control—every solid surface had more black than blank space. The halls were lined with Creeper notes, but people paid no attention, trampling them without a thought. I tried pointing them out, even showed one guy how they dissolved when you touched them. All he said was, "Dude, get off the floor."

I spotted a hulking Creeper in an empty bathroom and took the opportunity to put my megaflashlight to the test. I pulled it from my backpack and aimed it at the Creeper's hazy eyes. I might as well have thrown baby powder at its cheeks. No effect whatsoever.

I shook it off and kept brainstorming.

By now, I could look at a certain classmate or teacher and recall which Creeper tended to torment that person. I would see someone, like my friend Sammy, for example, and think, *Hey, Sam. Where's Aggression today?*

My goal of helping people seemed like a pipe dream now. I'd lost all confidence in my ability to encourage people out of their bondage. I'd seen where that got me with Meagan. With Jess and my mom, too.

At least Ashlyn seemed to be doing better. She'd agreed to help Ray Anne start a Fellowship of Christian Athletes chapter. I told Ray I'd be glad to hang their FCA posters. But that's about it.

I was on my way to fifth period, navigating around people's chains, when the Creepers began charging in the same direction, scurrying like the Watchmen were back. Naturally I followed.

One by one, they threw themselves to the floor, lying prostrate in single-file lines that stretched all the way across the cafeteria, which was clear of tables this time of day. I ran up a nearby stairwell to watch, stopping on the landing between the first and second floors, overlooking the open space.

The Creepers were falling into a pattern, every other one facing the direction opposite its neighbor so that their heads were beside one another's feet. They clung to each other's ankles, creating tight Xs with their lanky bodies, blanketing the floor like a mildewed, mutilated carpet.

The bell rang, but I stood there, enthralled.

Like the pounding of a thousand bass drums, I felt it in my chest when, all at once, they began chanting in unison. It was loud, much louder than I'd ever heard them before, but I couldn't understand them at first. Then . . .

"Ave rex! Molek! Dominus Mortuorum!"

They rolled their toxic tongues in one accord.

Latin. I knew exactly what it meant. Then came the proclamation in English.

"Hail the king! Molek! Lord of the Dead!"

Over and over they chanted with raspy, booming voices, in one earthly language after another.

That's when my body was seized by a mind-altering sensation that threw my balance off and gave me a nauseating high. My freezing, clammy palms slid down the metal banisters, and I caved to the floor.

I felt sweat fall from my forehead, only it appeared to travel up from the ground back onto my face at a delayed speed. I wanted off the ride.

Then I saw him, emerging from the suicide memorial fence outside and passing through the wall, into the cafeteria, looking like an elaborate Halloween costume—only this monstrosity was alive. Two Creepers crawled on their hands and knees, trampling on top of their prostrate coconspirators, straining under his weight. He dominated his slave escorts using reins attached to sadistic face harnesses, a foot crammed into each of their swayed backs. Every twist of his wrist elicited agonizing shrieks, to which he lifted his chin all the more.

It was him again, the same monster who had plunged Meagan's soul into the depths of the dead.

He closed his eyes and slowly swept his head back and forth, like the Creepers' praise infused life into his soulless existence. Once he trod over his submissive subjects, they rose to their hands and knees and crawled behind him, forming a massive entourage, never lifting their brainwashed heads.

I couldn't turn away. Despite my hostility toward him, his presence had a seductive power that mesmerized me.

Could this be God?

I shoved my face between two banisters to steady my wobbly, swollen head and watched as the Lord of the Dead—Molek—finally came to a halt in the center of the cafeteria.

The Creepers huddled on their knees at his feet, hands lifted high, yet wincing, visibly troubled by his presence. They didn't dare look him in the face.

The king lifted one gigantic hand, and all activity instantly ceased. He paused, then shoved his other hand out, clawlike fingernails so long and thick they were visible from where I was. The Creepers moved back at once.

I remained doubled over on the stairwell, bewitched by fascination mixed with despair. It only got worse when the dictator belted out a command—an inhuman word that called forth an inhumane world.

THIRTY-FOUR

THE GROUND SPLIT OPEN.

The cafeteria floor tiles disintegrated before my eyes, unveiling a place of unimaginable anguish. The walls looked like human body tissue and stretched down so far that I couldn't see the bottom. A fire appeared to simmer below. Out of the tissue hung the dusty remains of countless arms, legs, heads—all kinds of scorched human appendages reaching and flailing to a sound track of agonizing crying, cursing, and wailing.

I didn't know how much more my body could take. I thought my heart might give out—too despondent to contract.

I pressed my eyes closed as hard as I could, but not before seeing Creepers crawling over the pulsating walls of the pit, jabbing any shadowy soul that dared to try and claw out.

It was a hate-filled place of torment that smoldered with heat but somehow worsened the chill in my stomach. All I could think about was how badly I didn't want to go there, how no human belonged there.

I opened my eyes, hoping it was over, but instead I saw the Creepers outside the pit leaning away, pushing against one another like they dreaded falling into the fiery chasm.

Their crowned cult leader motioned for a certain Creeper to come forward: Traitor. He approached and stood by Molek's side, then leaned and whispered into the king's ear.

A sinister grin crept across Molek's face.

One by one, he summoned Creepers forward. They were shoved to the ground, made to kneel before him, battered heads hung low. Sixteen in all, tattled on by Traitor. I could only assume they'd blundered their assignments—somehow failed to live up to the scars on their faces.

Then came the king's swift judgment: a ferocious kick to the chest, sending each of them hurtling backward into the sweltering hole. Immediately they went to work, patrolling and punishing captive souls—the dead, I presumed.

Molek nodded at Traitor, releasing it to rejoin the ranks, but as soon as it turned, he shoved it from behind, plummeting the snitch into the pit with the others.

I knew by now this king couldn't possibly be God. If a Master of the universe existed, surely he didn't need an informant to tell him anything. Even I knew that.

Molek resumed his exalted position up front, mounted on the crooked backs of the same two Creepers. Then, like the ocean tide rushing up the shore, the ground closed over the pit, concealing the suffering dead.

That's when Molek's demeanor changed. Narrowed eyes. Spastic movements. Intense, sharp gestures. Like old footage of Adolf Hitler. I couldn't decipher his speech—his dialect was not of this earth—but his body language spoke volumes. He was mobilizing his troops, rallying them around a mission.

He pointed outward and also to the ground as if referring to my classmates and my school. And he motioned toward certain groups of Creepers, giving them specific instructions.

The energy in the room changed. The Creepers quit cowering and began to stir like fight dogs nearing an arena, frothing at the mouth.

And with that, their leader tugged hard on the reins, commanding his slaves to carry him away. His back was to me.

"I see you . . . Molek."

I only whispered it, but that's all it took.

His head snapped, rotating 180 degrees, his paralyzing eyes missile-locked on me. The reins fell from his hands, and he charged at me so fast I had no time to brace myself. No time to react at all.

He lifted off the ground like he was racing up an invisible staircase, and in seconds, his face was inches from mine. His eyes were much more horrendous than I'd thought, black as the abyss he'd thrown Meagan into, pupils empty, not white like they'd appeared before. He hovered in midair, wrapping his long fingers around the banisters, the only barrier between us.

He despised me. It was more than the callous look on his face—I could physically feel his hatred for me, like every cell in my body was being crushed under his heel of absolute loathing.

He proceeded to open his mouth wide enough to swallow me whole, dislocating his jaws, his ghastly face now shockingly stretched. He let out a growl that felt like it might snap my bones.

I officially began to hyperventilate.

His fury didn't last long—his skin began to crumble like ashes, and he faded into a smoky pollution, vanishing into thin air.

The Creepers dispersed, but I stayed slumped on the stairwell, hands pressed around my throat, trying to breathe. The thought that my friends might be in that place, trapped in that hopeless hellhole . . .

No matter how hard I tried, I couldn't catch my breath.

Finally I was able to pull myself up, then stand as the bell rang. People poured onto the stairwell.

"Owen?" Ray Anne found me.

I threw my arms around her and wouldn't let go.

"You're trembling. What happened?"

"I saw him, Ray Anne. The one who took Meagan. But he doesn't just capture dead souls. He's the one plotting against us."

"The suicides?"

"All of it!" I gripped her arms and pulled her to me. "Molek, he's leading the charge, commanding the Creepers. And there's something else coming. I don't know what or where, but they're planning it. A mass attack. Something terrible!"

She pressed a hand to my chest, over my lungs, her way of trying to calm me.

"Come to my house after school," she said, "and we'll figure this out." She hugged me tight. "It will be okay, Owen. You'll see."

I didn't believe her, but I was grateful beyond words for her.

I skipped my last two class periods, parking my bike on a back road while I waited for school to get out. Sitting there with no noise, alone, just my thoughts, the sick irony of it hit me. Creepers want to be on the earth, attached to our lives, dwelling inside us if given half a chance, I'd imagine—far away from that pit of eternal torment. Yet they work tirelessly to see us end up there, tossed into the fire like bags of garbage while they go look for more victims.

By now, I genuinely believed in heaven—a glorious place where people like Ray Anne and Ms. Ida are welcome, where Watchmen go to relax and hang their armor for a while and interact and maybe even laugh with human souls. I believed it because I felt it every time I laid eyes on the Watchmen—the undeniable sense that they hail from a kingdom all its own, a universe of peace far beyond the turmoil of this world and the evil that stalks it.

But me? Would I be welcome there?

My cell phone swooshed, and I jumped, still so jittery it was a challenge to unlock my screen.

It was Jess. **Are you going to Stella's party tonight?**

Speaking of another universe.

After school, Ray Anne welcomed me inside, and we sat in her dad's cramped home office—the most private place in her house, which wasn't saying much. Her parents liked to dive-bomb in on us every few minutes.

"So what happened?" Ray Anne was anxious to know.

"I get that every day or two I have some ridiculous story to tell you about things you can't see or hear or anything, and you always seem to believe me, which is so awesome. But I have to warn you, Ray Anne. This is heavy."

She nodded.

I told her everything I'd seen, and she buried her face in her hands. "I can't think about that pit. It's too terrible."

I wrapped my arm around her.

When she eventually removed her hands, I could see that she'd teared up. "Molek . . . You think he's Satan?"

"Whoever he is," I said, "we have to stop him—figure out what he's planning and put an end to it." Not that I'd been even remotely successful at stopping Creepers up to that point, but it wasn't in my nature to wave the white flag.

I was prepared for Ray Anne to start preaching at me about how we needed to ask for God's help. Instead she leaned close, so close I thought she might kiss me after all.

"Think how much more helpful I could be if I could see, like you do."

"No!" I yelled so loud that Mrs. Greiner came running around the corner. It took Ray Anne a few minutes to convince her that we were fine.

"I've already told you," I said when we were finally by ourselves again. "Going to the well is never an option, much less drinking from it."

"But we could be a strong team, and—"

"Ray Anne, listen to me." I lowered to my knee in front of her chair, my hands on her shoulders. "That water will make you really, really sick. Like, deathly ill. You can never drink it. Ever. Okay?"

A blank stare.

"Promise me you'll never try to find it."

More staring.

"Ray Anne?"

"Okay. Yes. I understand." I sat in the chair beside her. "But I'm not afraid," she said.

I grabbed her hand. "I know. You're a very brave person."

"Which is why I think you need me to be able to see."

"I need you to keep your promise."

We left it at that.

My mom eventually texted and asked me to come home. I wasn't sure what that was about. Ray Anne walked me to my motorcycle, and we noticed a train of cars lining the curb at the end of her street.

"Stella Murphy's party," she said.

I saw Dan go inside Stella's house, some girl clinging to the back of his polo shirt. What did Jess see in him?

I gave Ray Anne a hug and thanked her for being the best friend anyone could ever ask for. But I wanted to say more.

"Ray Anne?" She looked up at me through her long eyelashes. "You're the only thing that's right in my world. The best thing that's happened to me." She blushed. "Look, I get it if you're not ready to commit to me, but I can't help it—I'm committed to you, Ray."

Another hug. The one place I felt at home.

When I got to my house, my mom was waiting for me, a home-cooked meal on the table. Something was definitely up.

"Everything okay?" I eyed her.

"I hope so."

"What do you mean?" I sat across from her, trying to push the image out of my mind of her trapped in that pit someday.

She took a bite of her chicken. Washed it down with her wine, then sat back in her chair. Some silence. "I've arranged a meeting for you with a good defense lawyer."

"Thank you."

Another silent pause. "Son, you know I'll stand by you through thick and thin, no matter what."

I nodded.

"But I need the truth. I'm not accusing you of harming those boys, but whatever happened, I need you to tell me. Right now."

This wasn't like her, insisting on getting to the bottom of a situation. But then again, I'd never been a murder suspect before.

I wanted to come clean—I seriously did. I was sick of deception, tired of having to spin my web of careful lies. But she refused to be open and honest with me. As long as I could remember, she dodged me every time I pressed her, changed the subject or shut me down completely.

This wasn't fair of her, demanding honesty of me.

"All we did was play basketball, Mom, then chill in the woods awhile. That's it. I swear."

I know—like mother, like son.

I tried to watch TV, to take a load off my mind, but it didn't stop the images of suffering. The memory of Meagan's terrified face.

Stella's party crossed my mind. I started thinking maybe that's where the Creeper plot against my classmates was set to go down.

I texted Jess: **You at the party?**

She replied: **Almost there.**

No sense in warning her to stay home.

I had a choice—to sit there and keep mulling things over, or to get up and try to make myself useful.

I threw on my black Converse and texted Ray Anne: **Stopping by Stella's to check on things. I'll tell you if I need you, okay?**

I knocked on Stella's door. Would they let me in? My reputation wasn't great these days. Some girl opened the door, and the smell of beer, weed, and Creepers assaulted me. The typical party scene—plus chains and cords and evil beings.

The lights were dim, but I could see well enough to spy Dan in the corner with a girl on his lap. No sign of Jess yet.

A guy from my third-period class struck up a conversation about college over the loud music, and I maintained that I was going premed. He was quick to say he was headed to A&M in the fall to be an engineer. It seemed like forever since I'd thought about career plans.

I didn't see any Creeper activity beyond the usual, but things got interesting when I stopped by a group gathered around a coffee table, playing with a Ouija board. My mom had always warned me to stay away from those things. I could see now that she was right.

Two girls were touching the pointer, giggling and gasping as it slid across the board, spelling out one girl's middle name. People looked on, debating whether it was the girls or ghosts moving it.

"Neither," I said. "It's demons."

Gazing into hell's terrors has a way of making you want to cut through the fluff and tell it like it is.

"Shut up," one of the girls said, the bigger airhead of the two.

I leaned over and spoke in her ear. "It's yanking a new, squirming cord out of your head right now, to abuse you with whenever it wants." A fifth cord added to the four she already had.

"You're sick!"

"These are enlightened spirits who've crossed over," the other girl said. "They don't want to hurt us."

"Really?" I almost laughed. "The one pushing the pointer is named Pain. And it's staring straight at you."

Of course it gnashed its teeth at me.

"How would you know?" a guy said to me. A dozen people were watching the conversation go down.

I didn't bother with an explanation. They were all shaking their heads at me anyway.

I walked away and scooped a few M&M's out of a snack bowl, then spotted Jess coming my way through the crowd, being careful not to spill her drink. When Jess finally made it to me, Dan walked up behind her and put his arm around her neck like he hadn't just been all over another girl.

"What's this psycho doing here?" he said, eyes on me, his typical arrogant smirk on his face. "Looking for his next victim?"

Jess averted her eyes to the floor.

Dan opened his big mouth again, talking loudly. "Everyone, I'd stay on alert if I were you. We've got a murderer among us."

He was in my face. I stepped within a centimeter of his. "Watch it, Dan. You could be next."

I get that I'd technically just threatened his life and, in a sense, admitted I was responsible for Walt and Marshall's deaths. But I'd gone from disliking this guy to despising him so bad that I could actually envision myself making him suffer.

He pressed his finger in my chest, then made a gunshot sound under his breath, motioning like he'd just pulled a trigger.

"Stop it, Dan," Jess said.

He pulled her away from me, into the crowd.

I waited for the right moment—and found it when Dan stepped outside with some guys.

"Jess, let's leave. Don't stay here with him."

"I'm sorry about earlier—he can be really mean sometimes." Her speech was a slurred mess.

"You can't drive like this. I'll take you home."

She took another sip of her drink, her dark hair plastered to her clammy neck, trailing down to her low-cut blouse. "Dan's taking me."

I was ready to walk away at that point. I'd done my best. But something caught my attention when Jess's midriff peeked out between the bottom of her shirt and her low-waisted jeans. It was strange and brilliant and alarming—and coming from her. I bent down and pulled her shirt up an inch, then stared at her midsection.

"What are you doing?" She laughed.

I grabbed her hand and led the way through the noisy, overcrowded hallway into a bedroom, closing the door behind us. "Jess, you have to leave with me. We're going. Now. And put that drink down."

"Why?" She took another big swig, and I grabbed the bottle and set it on top of a tall bookshelf.

"Give me that!" She did a pathetic jump-and-reach. "You're always protecting me from *nothing*."

"This isn't about evil beings. It's nothing like that. Don't you know?"

"Know what?" Her smile was flirtatious, intoxicated.

I blurted it out. "You're pregnant, Jess."

She stood there stunned, mouth open—then burst into laughter. "I am not." She walked over to the bed like the ground was tilted toward it, then turned and fell backward onto the comforter. "And how would you know, anyway?"

There was a tiny, laser-strong light emanating from her body—her uterus, I guess. It wasn't much bigger than the tip of a fountain pen, but it was as bright as my megawatt flashlight.

I sat beside her and hoisted her to an upright position. "It doesn't matter how I know, Jess. I know. You're pregnant. I promise."

She got weepy. I wasn't sure if it was the hormones, the alcohol, or that she actually believed me. She put her head on my shoulder. "I've done so many things lately that you would be unhappy about." A tear came streaming down her cheek. "Why are you even talking to me? I sold you out to the police."

She looked up, her eyes pitiful and longing.

"We can talk about that later. Right now we've got to leave."

She slid her hand across my cheek, then behind my neck, pulling my face close, her lips nearly touching mine. The smell of alcohol on her breath made me want to puke.

The door flew open. Given my luck, I figured it was Dan.

I turned.

Ray Anne.

THIRTY-FIVE

"RAY ANNE!"

I called to her, but she had already shoved her way out the front door. "Wait!" I rushed to catch up.

She bolted on foot toward her house. I sprinted until I was close enough to reach out and touch her.

"Ray Anne, stop!"

She finally did, and we both stood there, sucking air under the night sky.

"Ray, that wasn't what you think."

"Let me guess. You were saving her from a brutal attack."

I'd never seen her cheeks that red, that kind of anger in her eyes.

"No, it was something else. I'll tell you if you'll just calm down."

"No, Owen! I won't! You promised not to hide things from me, but you keep sneaking around with Jess." She pushed against my chest. "Just say it. You want to be with her. I don't care!"

She turned and kept stomping down the street.

I followed. "If you don't care, why don't you stop and let me explain?"

She spun around and raged at me. "Because I can't *stand* liars! And that's what you are, Owen Edmonds! Don't deny it!" She went back to stomping. "I'm such an idiot. To think I believed your stories." Her voice cracked, the pain seeping through her tantrum. "Creepers? Shackles?"

"Ray Anne, please, there's an explanation."

She ranted in my face again, her eyes narrow and disgusted. "You aren't *committed* to me. You aren't even a loyal friend! I can't believe I took you seriously."

That's when the kingdom of hate showed up—three Creepers, headed right for me. A really bad time to ask Ray Anne for help.

"Hey," I said. "Let's talk this out, at your house."

"I'm not ready to go home, and I wouldn't let you in, anyway."

She stopped her angry march and shouted toward the black sky. "How could you let someone deceive me again? Are you even there, God? Do you care at all?"

The Creeper trio was closing in fast.

"I know you don't want to hear this right now," I said, "but there's three—"

"Oh, shut up!" She stopped under a streetlamp, arms crossed. "I'm done listening to you. Leave."

I recognized Faithless, but its accomplices were new: Betrayal and Distrust. They fanned out.

But not around me.

"Ray Anne." I went to her. "I get that you're angry, but you have to listen to me. Something's happening—not to me. To you."

She stuffed her index fingers inside her ears.

Distrust plunged its hand underneath the neckline of its grimy garment and pulled out some sort of burlap sack, dark and dilapidated. Without taking its eyes off Ray Anne, it rummaged through the bag, pulling out two chains. It stepped closer, careful not to cross into her light.

"I said leave."

"There's three of them, and one has chains."

"That's enough, Owen!"

Distrust tossed a chain to each of the Creepers on either side of Ray Anne. Betrayal went first, locking its wrist inside the menacing cuff, then hoisting the chain in the air, whipping it toward Ray Anne. It fell and slammed the pavement.

"They're after you!"

She put her flexed hand in my face. "Not. Another. Word."

Faithless tossed its chain at her too, and finally, after a few attempts, they both managed to whip the links around her throat.

"The Creepers are attacking you! We have to run!" Surely her parents' combined light would make a difference.

"Creepers are afraid of me, remember? Try to keep your stories straight."

Distrust pulled four cords from the bag, much longer than the ones that hung from people's heads—at least fifteen feet long. Then it discarded the shabby sack, tossing it not far from me, and began the sickening process of burrowing the cords, two in each palm. Once the cords were nestled deeply, Distrust swung its bony arms in the air, sending the grisly cords soaring behind Ray Anne. They pounded her in the back of the head and stuck, latching on to her scalp like bloodthirsty leeches.

I watched as Ray Anne's fractured heart crumbled.

"Everyone lies to me." She sank to the ground, her hands buried in her hair. "I can't trust anyone."

Her tearful confession flipped a switch in the alternate world. The three assailants began to moan, a monotone hum that covered me in chills, and more Creepers emerged—dozens of them, spilling out of the shadows between houses, crawling from the street gutters, dropping like bats from the dark sky.

I crouched down. "I know you're upset, but you have to stop this. Stop talking and let me walk you home. Please!"

"Don't lecture me, Owen!" I thought she might hit me. "I can make my own rules!"

The evil forces were really stirred now. They pressed in close, making a tight circle around us, just beyond her aura, all moaning a morbid, one-note chorus with no need to pause for a breath.

I couldn't sit there and watch them batter her soul. I rushed to Faithless and read the inscription on the cuff around its wrist, eye level with me.

"Who is Tori Deanne Lansing?"

"What?"

"Tori Lansing! Do you know her?"

"She was a bully in elementary school. She used to make my life miserable. Why?"

I charged over to Betrayal and read that cuff too. Mrs. Greiner's name. *Okay?*

"Your mom's middle name is Ruth."

"How'd you know that?"

I slammed on my knees in front of her. "Ray Anne, those names are on the cuffs, on the chains being used to torment you right now." I squeezed her hands. "They're around your neck. And there are cords attached to your head—and tons of Creepers in a wall around us right now, watching you."

"I—I don't know."

I pushed back and pounded a fist on the concrete. "I'm not lying to you!"

I was out of options.

Then hope shined down on us.

I stood, straining to see over the Creepers. Sure enough, help was coming, lighting the atmosphere. Seven Watchmen, dressed for battle, were charging toward us.

"Watchmen! They're here to rescue you, Ray!"

I counted down the seconds, grinning, ecstatic at what I knew was coming—Creepers squealing, pleading, fleeing the wrath of Ray Anne's avengers. Any second now.

The three oppressors linked to Ray Anne kept up their assault, but the others turned outward, hissing like venomous snakes, assembling tighter around their prey.

This was it. Time for the Watchmen to rain down judgment. I held my breath.

But they slowed their pace. Then stopped completely, glaring down at the mob.

"Something's wrong," I said. "The Watchmen, they're standing still. They look frustrated." I lifted my arms. "Hey! Help!"

No movement.

"Please, stop," Ray Anne said.

I looked down and saw she was shivering. I turned to her.

"I feel awful," she said. "I'm so confused. And scared."

I grabbed her hands and held them to my chest. "Ray Anne, listen to me. You're playing right into their trap. You've got to stop. Come back to your senses. Remember who you are. What you believe. What you stand for. Can you do that? For me?"

She closed her eyes and released her head back, a runaway tear traveling down her cheek. Deep breaths. Deeper still. Then a nod.

"Lord, please forgive me for—"

Instant chaos, so loud and intense that I hunkered down and covered my head. But not for long. I wanted to watch, take it all in. I saw Watchmen hurling Creepers so hard that some flew a hundred feet away. Creepers ran and hid in obvious places, trembling. One tried to float up, but a Watchman grabbed its foot right out of the air and slammed the Creeper to the cement. It sank into the earth like the pavement was water.

It didn't take long for every last one of them to be driven away. I looked back at Ray Anne, and the chains and cords were gone.

"I wish you could have seen that!" My arms were raised like an MMA champion. But then I noticed her. Sitting still, face to the sky, eyes closed. Tearful.

The Watchmen were still poised for action, looking for stragglers, but one of them stopped and gazed down at Ray Anne. He was magnificent, arms and legs like a bronze statue, calf muscles bigger than my head.

He crouched and put his hand across his chest. Then he used his other humongous hand to wipe a tear from Ray Anne's minuscule cheek with the tip of his finger.

I felt it—compassion filling the atmosphere like the warmth of a morning sunrise. I threw myself to the ground beside him, attempting to look into his radiant face. "Thank you! Thank you so much!"

He didn't even glance my way.

He and his companions peered into the sky, then charged off in the opposite direction they'd come from.

"It's over now." I sat next to Ray Anne, welcoming the new calm. A quiet, victorious moment.

There was no denying that I'd just seen Ray Anne's prayer ignite a drastic change in the unseen realm, but was the difference maker the actual prayer or her personal resolve to resist the Creepers' manipulation?

I also wondered, if Lights could be refitted with chains and cords, why hadn't I seen glowing people dragging stuff around? It was worth thinking through; now just wasn't the time.

I told Ray Anne about the Watchman's affection toward her. And after a while, I told her what really had happened with Jess—pregnancy and all.

"That's serious." She wiped her cheeks. "I'm sorry I freaked out on you. I have a huge fear of being lied to, and sometimes I overreact."

I put my arm around her. "What happened? To make you so afraid?"

She stared at the cement. "Lucas told my mom he was having suicidal thoughts, but she didn't want to burden me with the news. My dad thought it was best to tell me, but my mom talked him out of it. I knew Lucas was depressed and seeing a counselor, but I had no idea . . ."

She covered her face. I waited.

"There's so much I would have said and done if I'd have known. Maybe things would have even turned out differently." I pulled her closer. "I've forgiven my mom, but it still hurts sometimes. Especially if I think someone is holding out on me again."

I'd buried my friends but never a brother. I ached for her.

We sat awhile in the silence, my arm tight around her the whole time.

"What do you think happened tonight?" she eventually said, twisting her hair into a knot. "With the Creepers coming after me?"

My sweet, trusting Ray Anne was back.

"Creepers look for any opportunity to get in our heads. I think tonight, they threw your past in your face, so to speak—used your old chains and cords against you. Took advantage of you in a low moment. And as long as you stayed down, they had you."

"Where'd they get my chains and cords from?"

"There was a sack." Speaking of which . . . it was still lying there, in the street. I pointed. "You can't see that, right?"

"See what?"

I walked over to it and took a close look. "They pulled stuff out of this bag."

"I wish I could see it."

I reached and touched it, and felt what had to be cords and chains, back in the sack now. The instant I my fingers made contact, a crushing, overwhelming sense of guilt hit me—a crippling feeling of defeat. It was so agonizing, I jerked my hand back. The oppression instantly lifted.

And then I saw something, messy stitches in the fabric. I read them out loud: "RBG."

"My initials?" Ray Anne stared at me.

"They're on the bag." That was weird, but not as weird as what happened next. A shriveled hand reached up through the pavement and snatched the sack, pulling it beneath the earth's surface.

"Um, Ray Anne. About that bag . . ."

"Wait!" She jumped up so fast it scared me. "Three letters, like the Creeper notes." I pulled up the images on my phone. "They're initials, Owen!"

It was all clicking now. And actually about as unsophisticated a code as you can get.

"All targets of a mass attack," I said.

"How do you know?" She paced in front of me.

I showed her another Creeper note image, zooming in on the numbers. "523." She could hardly talk fast enough. "Same numbers on all of them."

"What if it's a date, Ray Anne?"

She sank to the curb, eyes wide. "May 23 . . . a month away."

THIRTY-SIX

I BOUGHT RAY ANNE a cup of Starbucks and brought it to her house for our "mass attack" brainstorming session. We weren't positive we were right about our theory, but it was the best intel we had. She had note cards, highlighters, two spiral notebooks, a white board, and dry erase markers set out on the kitchen table next to a schematic of the school that she'd found online and printed.

"Really?"

"One more thing." She set a leather journal on top of the office supply explosion.

"What's that?"

It took her a moment to answer. "I wrote things in here for my brother, then gave it to him as a gift. I'd like to read some of it to you now."

I didn't know what she'd put in the journal, but I figured it had to be important.

She motioned for me to sit down. "All I ask is that for the next few minutes, you listen."

I agreed and lowered into the chair beside her. She proceeded to explain what she called the plan of salvation, flipping through the journal and reading Bible passages she'd copied by hand. It was like she was the teacher and I was a kindergartner on a story-time rug. Not that what she said was childish—just the way she pointed to the text and moved her finger under each word.

In short, she said I needed a Savior, and if I prayed to receive Christ into my heart, God would forgive everything I'd ever done wrong, and I would glow, like her family.

"It can't be that simple. Everyone would glow."

"You would think," she said, "but not everyone is willing to accept God's invitation."

I wasn't suddenly blown over with faith, and it didn't add up to me that one prayer could erase every wrong I'd ever done. But out of the two of us, she glowed, not me. So maybe there was something to this. And I was willing to try anything at this point if there was a chance it could save me from afterlife torture.

Problem was, the last time I'd talked to God, I'd shouted that I hated him. If there was a Creator who bothered listening to people's prayers, I doubted he'd be willing to hear mine. But like I said, I'd try anything.

"Do I need to take my hat off?"

Ray Anne reached for my hands. "You can, but I don't think a Browning ball cap is going to mess up your prayer." She was so giddy I thought she might break out into one of her drill-team dances.

"Do you get some sort of award at your church for making a convert?"

"Of course not." She bowed her head, then looked up again. "Well, I technically get my name in a drawing for a Subway gift card for sharing the plan of salvation, but that's not why I'm doing this."

"I know. I'm just giving you a hard time."

We faced one another, and I clutched her fingers in mine, our knees and bowed heads nearly touching. She led me in a prayer that I repeated after her, admitting I had sinned and committing to give up my old self-centered life for a new one where God would save me and lead me and help me discover his plans for me. It was nice enough, as far as prayers go.

We said amen, then I sat there, staring at my feet, waiting for a burst of light—at the very least, an energizing feeling—to wash over me.

It never did.

"Well, you're my witness. I tried."

For me, the issue was settled once and for all. Religion was not the answer.

Our brainstorming session turned out to be about as productive as that prayer.

The following week, I went to the meeting my mom had arranged with the defense lawyer—"scumbags," I'd always called them, but not anymore. I told the same story I'd already told the police but added that Walt and Marshall must have ingested something they regretted, then blamed me as their scapegoat. There was the essence of truth in it.

The lawyer agreed to represent me. He said he thought investigators would probably leave me alone for the next month until after I graduated, to avoid a surge in negative publicity. "Your senior class has been through enough, but after graduation, I imagine they'll come after you. But don't worry, we'll be ready."

I made a fat payment and left.

Over the next few weeks, I spent every second with Ray Anne that she'd let me, and we kept racking our brains about May 23. Her plan for stopping Molek and the Creepers between now and then was to pray every day. Not the most reliable action plan. Not that mine was any better.

I tried convincing people to skip school that day. They just looked at me like I was weird. As usual.

In the middle of May, Ray Anne's parents went out of town, and I fantasized about her inviting me over and us taking advantage of the privacy. But I knew better. Ray Anne would kick me out of her life before she'd go back on her convictions—something I admired about her but had a hard time liking on occasion. I tried to behave—didn't want to draw any Lust monsters.

That Saturday, my mom handed me the keys to her SUV and a long list of errands to run. While driving, I got to thinking about how no one would be there to see me at my high school graduation except her. Why should I go? I had new priorities in life now, and long school assemblies weren't one of them, even if it was the last one.

Along the way, I found a ceramic crucifix in the parking lot of our dry cleaner's and held it up to a Creeper attached to the guy behind the counter as he handed me my mom's clothes. The guy stared me down like I was a weirdo, but other than that, nothing happened. Shocker.

On my way home, I turned onto the street with the railroad bridge—the place where Jess had brought me, then taken off with Dan. After I begged her to stay away from him.

Sure enough, I spotted her Mustang parked beside the bridge now, but it was the *way* she was parked that bugged me. Her car was angled toward the curb like she'd flung it there blindfolded. I had no desire to get in some long conversation with her, but I found myself parking.

At first I didn't see her, but I took a few more steps along the bridge, and my heart skipped a beat. She'd climbed over the railing and was facing the rushing water some fifty feet below, holding on but leaning over like she might let go at any second.

"Jess!" I hurried to her. "What you are doing?"

Even before I made it to her I could see how hard she was crying, her chest expanding and collapsing with every gasp. Her asthma working against her.

I reached out to her. "Take my hand!" We both knew she couldn't swim.

Her cheeks were flushed, and she gazed out at the turbulent water like it was her best friend now. "Leave me alone."

"What happened?" I started to climb over the railing, but she raged at me.

"Don't! I'll jump!"

I'd never seen her like this. So volatile. So shattered.

I stopped climbing but pleaded with her to tell me what was wrong.

"You were right, Owen. I'm pregnant."

"Jess . . ." I slid my hand down the rail toward hers, but she loosened her trembling grip. "Please!" I yelled. "Don't do this. We'll figure things out."

She shook her head, still fixated on the river. I noticed her clothing was torn, her skirt ripped up her thigh. I got a sick feeling.

"Dan . . . Did he hurt you?"

She winced, and another downpour of tears fell from her chin into the current. "I told him no this time, but . . ."

I'd felt anger countless times before. Fury, even. But this was something else entirely. Like hatred and vengeance igniting in a blazing furnace lodged inside my rib cage. I'd been willing to kill in self-defense, in order to save a life. But I'd never *wanted* someone dead.

Until now.

"I want out." Jess closed her eyes. "Life's too hard."

She had no way of knowing what her words had just done, who she'd instantly summoned across paranormal airwaves.

Suicide came crawling out from the nearby trees, but before it could pounce on Jess, the Lord of the Dead arrived, stopping Suicide in its tracks. Molek rose up out of the water without a drop on him and hovered midair, his spiteful face looming in hers. His lips formed a gruesome, reeking smile.

I knew what was coming—I'd been through this with Meagan and lost to a less powerful Creeper than this one. But I wasn't going to abandon Jess to him.

He tilted his head and pressed his decaying lips to her ear.

I made an effort to drown out his voice with my own. "Whatever thought goes through your head, Jess, don't listen!"

"You're so stupid," he said to her.

"You tried to warn me about Dan," she said. "I'm so stupid."

"No." I reached out again. "Give me your hand."

Molek injected more poison into her mind. *"You're a used-up piece of—"*

Before he could even finish, she bought into it. "I'm a used-up piece of trash."

"It's all lies, Jess. From someone who despises you." Molek bolted toward me at warp speed and growled in my face; surely there's no worse stink on earth than what came out of his festering mouth. No eyes more petrifying than his. But I stood my ground. "I'm here, Jess. Take my hand."

Molek flew back to Jess. *"You can't,"* he hissed into her ear.

"I can't," she recited.

"Yes, you can." I swung with the only weapon I had—my words. "The truth is, you *can.*"

"You're better off dead." He lowered his gaze to her abdomen, then dragged his hand over it, smearing that familiar grungy dust over the tiny light. *"So is* that.*"

I spoke before she could quote him. "You're meant to live, Jess." I swallowed hard. "You both are."

Molek placed his contaminated hands on her shoulders.

"Jess!" I cried out.

Too late. She let go. The same instant, he pulled her from the rail and plunged her down into the water.

Without hesitation, I was over the rail and in the river. But where was she?

I called Jess's name again and again while being carried downstream by the unyielding current, rocks slamming and puncturing my legs through my jeans. I searched underwater, but there was no sign of her.

I came up for air, and water clobbered me in the face, making me choke. It had to have been over a minute now since Jess had jumped. How long could she hold her breath? Would she even bother?

I managed to keep my chin above the tide even though my feet barely touched the bottom, and I called out to her as loud as I could.

A growing sense of defeat was exhausting my hope at the same time that my arms and legs started burning from exertion. I used what strength I had to turn myself against the tide and look back toward the bridge.

There she was, flailing on top of the water—floating, but it wasn't the water holding her up.

An armored Watchman cradled her, so tall the river only came to his waist. So bright he rivaled the sun.

He waded through the river toward me. Jess thrashed her arms and legs, whimpering and fighting to stay afloat. She didn't know it was impossible for her to sink.

Within seconds, he brought her to me. It was the first time a

Watchman had looked me in the face—the first time I'd gotten an up-close glimpse at the gleam in a Watchman's eyes.

He extended his arms, and when Jess saw me, she cried out and latched on to me so tight, I knew she no longer wanted to die.

"It's okay, Jess. I've got you."

That fast, and he was gone. Vanished like a rainbow behind the clouds.

It was hard to get us both onto the riverbank, but I did it. Once on the grass, she clung to me and sobbed. "As soon as I let go, I knew it was a mistake."

She hugged me even tighter, both of us waterlogged and shaking. "Thank you, Owen." She kept saying it as if I'd saved her life. But I knew the truth.

This time, I didn't wonder why the Watchmen don't intervene more. I wondered how many times they do, and it goes completely unnoticed.

THIRTY-SEVEN

I FOLLOWED BEHIND Jess as she drove her car home and watched her until she was safe inside. She promised me she'd report Dan to the police.

When I got home, still shaken up, I was surprised to see Lance's Jeep in my driveway.

"Hey," he said, with no hint of anger. "Can we talk?"

I hated to admit it, but I missed having him around—the good ol' days when we'd make jokes and I was blind to evil's existence. I worried about him now, especially after Meagan's death. In a way, it felt like he had died too. Like I'd lost a good friend overnight.

As I went to slide into Lance's Jeep, someone ran up behind me and shoved a black bag over my head. I couldn't see anything, but it didn't matter at that point. I'd already taken the bait and impaled myself on Lance's camouflaged hook of betrayal.

Lance instructed the guy to bind my hands; I could tell they were using duct tape. After blaring earphones were crammed onto my ears, I was pushed into Lance's backseat, then shoved onto the floorboard.

Minutes later, I was yanked from the vehicle, my head still bagged, music pounding. I was pulled by the arm, forced to stumble over uneven terrain. It was hard to judge how long or far we traveled, but finally we stopped. The sack and earphones were ripped from my head.

The woods behind the school. My property.

Lance eyed me like a hunter checking a trap. Then I saw his accomplice.

Dan.

What I would have done to him had my arms not been restrained . . .

A group of seven or eight guys made their way over to us—bulky seniors, several on the wrestling team, I think. All there to beat my face in, I imagined. I admit I was nervous, but my plan was to be a man and take the blows as they came.

Dark figures darted through the surrounding trees, Creepers drawn to human hostility like rubberneckers at a fatal car crash.

"Guys . . ." I tried to keep my cool even though I knew I was in for it. They closed in around me, Dan posting himself directly in my face. I narrowed my eyes at him. "I know what you did to Jess. How can you stand yourself?"

"It's time," Dan said, showing no hint of remorse.

Lance got in my face but just stood there, fists ready but not swinging. Breathing hard.

"You said you'd do it," Dan shouted at him.

Lance inflated his chest. But still no blows.

"Are you just gonna—"

"Shut up, Dan!" Lance turned back to me. "I don't know if the cops are on to you or not, but we are. You did something to Walt and Marshall, and it's time to pay."

"And this is justice? Tricking me into an ambush?" I didn't deny that I deserved to be punished; I just seriously resented the deceptive way they were going about it.

"Go ahead." Dan worked like a pressure cooker on Lance. "Get us started." He reminded me of a Creeper, encircling us, enticing violence.

Then a real Creeper dropped down over us, hovering above our heads.

"It's me, Lance." Hard as I tried, I couldn't pry my hands loose. "Don't do this."

"Hit him, Lance!" Dan said. "Or I'll do this my way." He tugged on a thick leather strap across his chest, and I saw it—a rifle strapped to his back. Was he about to shoot me?

"Do it!" Dan kept prodding. "For Meagan."

Lance's fists remained tight and ready for action. But he couldn't bring himself to punch me.

Finally, Dan stepped in front of him, teeth clenched, literally shaking with anger.

And that's when the Creeper made its move, swooping down and prying its way through Dan's back, taking residence inside of him. Its shape shifted so that its huge frame was crammed inside its smaller host.

The mutations began immediately. Dan's eyes rolled back in his head, replaced by devilish pupils. Then his skin turned gray like the Creeper's, and his face contorted, his features twisting into something beastly and petrifying.

I fell backward into the guys behind me, but they shoved me forward, right back in Dan's rearranged face.

He opened his mouth to curse me, and a low, threatening voice came out. I looked around—was I the only one witnessing this? His words were cruel and violent—even for Dan. But his mouth wasn't his own. His tongue had been hijacked.

The veins in his neck were bulging. Then I saw it, beneath the surface of his skin, a scar across the indwelling Creeper's forehead:

rage

Of course.

Dan reared back and shoved me so hard it felt like a train hit me. He stood me up again, and that's when I felt a burst of pain in the back of my head, like someone had bashed me with a baseball-sized rock. I caved to my knees, and the guys kicked me in my ribs, punched me in the face, even pulled my hair. All I could do was hunker down while they struck me in the mouth repeatedly, calling me a murderer, among other things.

The distinct, disgusting taste of blood flooded my tongue, and a black haze settled over my vision. Were they going to beat the very last breath out of me? Leave my body in the woods to rot after my soul was ripped out through my gut?

As the light-headedness got worse—I felt like life was draining out of my veins—all I could think about was her. Sweet Ray Anne. That kiss I'd never get. The jerk who would.

I was outnumbered and a bloody mess, but I fought back with all I had, scoring a few good kicks to shins and ankles. But then Dan dealt a serious blow to the side of my head . . .

Ears ringing.

Earth spinning.

Consciousness leaving.

And that's when I saw him, lying across from me, his pose mirroring mine exactly.

Molek.

His mouth moved in slow motion, and I heard his voice, but not in my ears—in my mind. The sound of a thousand disturbing whispers, all out to get me at once.

"Come . . ." He caressed my face. *"I've prepared a place for you."*

With every nudge of his clawed fingers on my skin, fear shot through me, paralyzing and cold.

I was no match for the pack of wolves devouring me, no threat to the Lord of the Dead who'd come for me. But I refused to surrender, mustering every shred of strength to keep my eyes open.

Hard as I tried, though, I couldn't survive this.

I'd lost. Everything. Right down to my soul.

That's when I heard a familiar voice demanding that I be left alone. Finally, the old man had returned. Don't ask me how, but he ran the guys off—they left me there in the mud.

When I pried my eyes open, Molek had disappeared too.

The brown-skinned, gray-haired man in overalls hovered over me, casting a dazzling glow onto the earth around his work boots. "You okay, son?"

He used a pocketknife to get the tape off me, then helped me sit upright, patiently holding on to me as my spinning head threw off all sense of balance.

Horrible as I felt, I had to make the most of having him there.

"Who are you?" It hurt to move my mouth. "What have you done to me? Besides ruin my life."

"*Done* to you? You're an eyewitness to a war few believe exists. I'd say that's a privilege."

Seriously? I groaned. He pulled a rag from his pocket and used it to wipe blood from my face.

"I don't get it—why me?"

"This is your land now, ain't it?"

"So?"

"He thinks it's his. Staked his claim over a century ago, and has no intention of leaving."

"You're talking about—"

"The Spirit of Death." He lowered down, eye level with me. "Molek."

Just the mention of his name made me cringe. "He was here," I said. "Just now."

"I know." The old man nodded. "He's a dominant wicked power that patrols this land, and he's working hard to expand his territory."

I looked around. "Why *this* land?"

He stared out into the woods, deep in thought. "More than a hundred years ago, this was a plantation, run by the cruelest of masters. Molek was at home here with him, the soil soaked with innocent blood."

That was disturbing. I leaned forward in an effort to stand but collapsed back. "He still wants people to suffer tragic deaths," I said.

Another nod. "He and his satanic forces."

Satanic forces.

There it was, out in the open, affirmed by a man who obviously had major insight into the supernatural.

He helped me onto my feet. Slowly. "The more people give in to his deadly plans," he said, "the more powerful he becomes."

"It's not fair." I struggled to lock my knees. "The Creepers have good people in shackles. People I care about."

He gripped my shoulders, steadying me as I swayed too far to one side. "People are enslaved by their own evil attitudes and impulses—their hard hearts. Dark forces exploit that. Prey on people's brokenness. Thrive in a culture of unbelief."

"What do they want from us?"

He searched my face. "Surely you know by now."

When he put it that way, the answer was as clear as the water that had gotten me into this catastrophe. "Our souls," I said.

He nodded. "Cut off from the light. For eternity."

I was stirring inside, experiencing a resurgence of determination, fueled by frustration. "They never should have built a school here. We have to warn people—convince them to stay off this property. Shut down Masonville High!"

He raised an eyebrow. "You watch the world news? Evil isn't confined here. Wicked overlords stretch across land and sea—until someone drives them out."

"By *someone*, you mean the Watchmen?"

He gave me a half smile. "Suppose you can call 'em that. But no. They watch over humanity, but the responsibility to drive out wickedness, that belongs to mankind." He looked toward my school. "You guys all run in fear, evil will stay—lie in wait to strike the next souls who come along."

It was a lot to take in. Then he dumped more on me. The realization of a lifetime.

"Last people who owned this land only fed into the evil. Held rituals here."

"Rituals?" I tried to take a step, and man, it hurt.

"Occult gatherings," he said. "Blood sacrifices that Molek received as worship unto himself. His army grew in strength and numbers."

"Wait." Dazed as I was from the beating, that sobered me up. "My grandparents owned this property."

He didn't flinch. Nothing he didn't already know.

"But . . . they were religious," I said. "Made my mother go to church every week."

"For appearances' sake, son. And to look for vulnerable recruits."

Shocking as it was, it solved a mystery that had plagued me my entire life. "My mom . . . she was raised in the occult. That's why she ran away—why she's so messed up."

"Few people make it out alive." He extended a hand to help me walk. "You're blessed to have her."

I never thought I'd feel grateful for my mom, much less admire her. But somewhere inside that shell of a woman was a girl who'd fought hard to survive. Harder than I could probably imagine.

The old man let me lean on him the whole time we journeyed through the woods. I ached all over, but that didn't stop me from firing questions at him Ray Anne–style: nonstop and direct. Frustratingly, he gave mostly life principles instead of the straight-up answers I needed. And he offered no explanation about why he glowed, how he knew so much, or why the water was way more than just water.

When I asked his name, he said, "I'm not here to make a name for myself," and left it at that. But then he warned me: "That old water well can open eyes or shut 'em for good. Best that you tell no one about it."

I stopped walking, stinging with shame over what I'd already done. "How's that?"

He waited for me to look into his face. "People know how to conceal their motives, but there's no fooling that water."

I was still trying to make sense of what he'd just said when we arrived at the street that ran alongside my school. He told me to wait there, then turned like he was about to leave.

"Wait! There's so much I need to understand. People I have to help."

He lifted his face to the blue sky. "I'm just a messenger."

I heard a car horn and turned to look. Ray Anne was slowing and pulling over. I turned back to the old man. But he was gone.

Ray Anne drove me home, explaining how she'd made a last-minute decision to turn onto that street; otherwise she never would have spotted me. She was horrified by my bloodied appearance, but I was just grateful to be alive.

She pulled into my driveway and said she'd be back soon to check on me. I insisted on walking to the front door by myself—my way of proving that I really wasn't a weakling, even if I did just get my tail handed to me.

I hobbled into the house, and my mom took one look at me and went nuts. I felt different around her now. I was actually glad she was home. And sober.

It would have been difficult to bring up what I'd just learned about her, even on a normal day, but now definitely wasn't the time. She pulled out a first aid kit I never knew we had and demanded to know who hurt me.

I didn't tell her. She knew where Lance lived, and she was acting like one of *those* moms—you know, the kind that would take on a Navy SEAL if she found out he'd messed with her boy. I told her it was some guys I didn't know.

She wanted to drive me to the ER, but I refused. So she bandaged me the best she could and tanked me full of pain meds.

My head was so sore it hurt to rest it on my pillow, and I was sure I had some broken ribs. No matter how I turned, I couldn't get comfortable on my mattress, my body throbbing and my mind racing.

There was no doubt now—I'd witnessed Dan in a full-blown possession. I tried telling myself it was Rage, not Dan, who'd attempted to beat me to death today, but I couldn't stop blaming Dan.

Lance, too.

I finally fell asleep but woke around midnight to answer my cell. Mrs. Greiner, of all people, calling from out of town.

"Have you heard from Ray Anne? She's not returning our calls, and we're worried sick."

Come to think of it, she never came back to check on me. That wasn't like her at all.

Her mom's voice shook with distress. "Our neighbor saw her late this afternoon, and she said she was headed to the woods, of all places. You have any idea why?"

"Uh, no, I . . ."

I dropped my phone.

Please tell me she didn't.

THIRTY-EIGHT

IT WAS PAINFUL TO get dressed. I hobbled out the door and drove my motorcycle like a madman to the dirt path in the woods that leads to the water well—where eyes could be opened or sealed forever.

I still didn't understand the old man's explanation about motives. But I knew the outcome of drinking that water was severe, no matter the motive.

When I saw Ray Anne's car parked by the dirt trail, I nearly went into cardiac arrest. I grabbed my big flashlight and charged as fast as I could through the maze of towering pines, dodging fallen branches and scrawny shrubs and slippery rocks. Ray Anne didn't know where the clearing was, but she did know what to look for and what it would sound like—thanks to me.

I made it there and shined my light in every direction. No sign of her. I shouted her name, bracing my aching rib cage, unwilling to consider that I might be too late.

As I approached the well, I stepped on something. A yellow cup, the same kind the Greiners kept in their kitchen cabinet.

"Ray Anne!"

I ran around the perimeter, shining my light in sweeping arcs, desperate to find her yet terrified that I'd see her body.

Finding nothing, I walked back in the direction of her car, taking a close look along the path. Minutes later, my world flatlined. There she was. In the brush, lying on her side, her back to me.

Totally still.

I dropped to my knees behind her and gently pulled her over, onto her back. Eyes closed. No signs of life. Then . . .

"Owen?"

It was so faint it was almost like I'd imagined it. But her eyelids parted. I let out the biggest sigh of relief of my lifetime, then bent down and pressed my cheek against hers. She was freezing.

There was no time. I scooped her into my arms. She winced and grabbed her stomach. "It hurts."

"I know. Just hold on, Ray. I'm getting you out of here."

I hoisted her off the ground, then walked the best I could in the dark, my injuries screaming at me. The walk was bumpy and exhausting, and she moaned the whole time, eventually mumbling, "Are you mad at me?"

"No. I'm mad at myself."

I pulled her keys from her pocket and lowered her into the passenger seat of her car. I worried she'd be dead by the time I walked around to the driver's side. When I slid into the seat, she was pale, shivering, and hardly able to keep her eyes open. But alive.

I pulled onto the road and floored it.

She couldn't quit rubbing her gut and forehead, just like I'd done. Just like I'd seen Walt and Marshall do.

"I didn't know it would hurt this bad." She faced away from me, knees bent into her chest.

"I'm taking you to the hospital."

"What?" She managed to angle toward me. "I just need to sleep it off, like you did."

"No, Ray Anne. You can't."

I felt like I was going to throw up, only something much worse than vomit was about to come out—a heinous confession. I waited until we passed through a brightly lit intersection and faded back into the cloak of night. She reached and dug her nails into my arm, groaning.

"Ray, you're going to hate me once and for all for this, but there's something I haven't told you. I haven't told a single soul. But I have to tell you now. It's a matter of life and death."

I swallowed the lump in my throat and smothered an avalanche of emotion. "This is really hard to say, but you deserve to know the truth. Ray Anne, there's a very strong chance that . . . that you may not survive this."

She pulled her cupped hand from her mouth. "What do you—"

"It's my fault. Walt and Marshall—they're dead because of me!" I couldn't help but yell. "They wouldn't quit insulting me, so I took them to the water. Dared them to drink it. And it killed them. And it's probably doing the same thing to you." I gassed it through a stop sign, jaws clenched. I could actually feel the blood vessels in my eyes throbbing.

She let go of my arm and sank back into a ball in the seat, shaking with sobs. My confession had destroyed her, just like I thought it would.

"I would ask your forgiveness, but there's no forgiving this, Ray Anne. I know that. You begged me to be honest with you, and if I would've just had the guts to own up to what I did, you wouldn't be in danger right now."

The pain of my selfish choices was sharp and deep, like a knife in my chest. I wiped my face, then reached for her hand, stroking and squeezing her fingers. She didn't squeeze back.

"You didn't deserve this." I said it over and over.

Then finally, the ER. I waited in the lobby, slouched over in my chair, shoes buried in death dust—might as well call it what it was.

A nurse got in touch with Ray Anne's parents, and they were trying to get a flight home. They'd already lost one child. Surely fate wouldn't make them bury two. I hoped.

A doctor approached and questioned me—not Dan's dad, to my relief. "She keeps saying it was just water, but that doesn't make sense."

"It is water, but it can be harmful." I wanted him to understand so they didn't chalk it up to something as basic as the flu and release her.

"How do you know?"

I struggled to maintain eye contact. "I just know."

He looked me over, furrowing his brow at the sight of my busted-up face. "What happened to you?"

"Some guys . . ."

He turned my chin, taking a closer look. "You were attacked?"

I nodded. "But it's her I'm worried about."

He instructed me to follow him, then led me through some double doors into the ER. He motioned for me to sit on a stiff chair in a small room that smelled like Band-Aids and alcohol, and he made it clear I was to stay there. Finally, he left me alone.

I couldn't sit. I paced the room, agonizing. It hurt to walk, but I deserved it.

From day one, all Ray Anne had wanted was to help me. And now that desire was destroying her.

I heard the doctor say my name, and when I peeked out the door, he was pointing in my direction. I scrambled back, trying to gather my runaway thoughts. There was no way out—of the room or my circumstances.

I faced the door and squared my shoulders, waiting. Seconds passed. Then Detective Benny found me.

I'd never been inside a squad car before. From the backseat, I could see Detective Benny and Officer McFarland through squares formed by metal bars—a barrier to keep deviants and thugs and liars like me away from law enforcement.

We were parked outside the hospital, engine running, both officers waiting for an explanation as to how yet another person connected to me was suffering.

This whole ordeal had gone way too far, and I'd do anything if it could somehow help Ray Anne survive. But would they even believe me if I told the truth?

Benny turned and scowled from the passenger seat. "Why don't you tell us what's really going on, son? So we can help you?"

I had to give up my old story, even without my lawyer there. I took a deep breath. Held it awhile, then . . .

"I've been living a lie, and I'm sick of it."

Detective Benny pulled out a digital recorder and motioned for me to keep going.

I told him about the well—how I drank from it and felt like my body was shutting down. "But the next day," I explained, "I woke up, completely fine. Still sick to my stomach but fine. I can't say why for sure, but it bothered me. I'd expected to die—you know, have everyone grieve my death—but instead, I had to face another ordinary, depressing day. That's when I started making things up."

"What kind of things?" Benny said.

I worked to look him in the eye.

"I pretended to see people wearing shackles, like they were enslaved by aliens or demons or something, and I was the only one who could see it. That, and also chains and gross cords draping from people's heads. At first it was cool, like a thrilling thing in my mind. But then . . ."

"Then *what*?"

"I got carried away and started telling people, like it was real. I even said I saw evil beings attacking them."

Officer McFarland glared over his shoulder.

"I know it's weird, but it's not like I'm crazy. I just liked the attention. The excitement, I guess."

Detective Benny shook his head. "Did you tell Walt and Marshall these stories?"

"Not exactly. They heard it from someone else, then they brought it up the day we went to the park. They came down on me so hard about it, I wanted to make them pay—but not with their lives. I swear! I thought if I took them to the woods and gave them a sip of the water, they'd get sick, like I did. I never meant for anything worse than that to happen."

Benny huffed. "Why'd you keep this from us?"

I tried to swallow, but it felt like I had a wad of cotton in my mouth. "I got scared. Even though I had no idea that the water could be deadly, I was afraid that if it somehow now turned out to be, it would look like I meant to kill them."

I shifted in my seat, weighing what I was about to say next. "And I was ashamed—really embarrassed about how out of control my fantasies had become. I couldn't bring myself to come clean."

Benny wanted to know why Ray Anne had drunk the water, and I explained that she'd wanted to see the supernatural stuff like me, even though I'd warned her over and over not to do it. "She actually believed my stories. She believed them so much that she searched for the water and drank it, knowing it would make her sick."

Officer McFarland put the car into drive, and the detective made a phone call, arranging for some forensics people to meet us. I sat back in the worn seat, looking out at familiar street signs and intersections, mostly empty this time of night.

How had my life come to this? My small world—so intense and complicated. And Ray Anne's life hanging in the balance.

We parked in the woods, and when Benny's team arrived, I led them to the infamous spot.

A lady in gloves retrieved the yellow cup and put it in a plastic bag. They found a sports drink bottle in the brush and bagged it, too. Had to be Marshall's or Walt's.

They hovered over the well, raising and lowering the bucket, collecting numerous samples of the water that had destroyed my life and annihilated others'. About the only good that had come from drinking it was that it had led me to Ray Anne, but even that was a train wreck now.

A forensics guy shined his flashlight down into the well, then back at the bucket several times. He finally spoke up. "This well looks dry."

The woman next to him smirked. "Clearly it's not." She tucked the water samples into a bag.

The guy shined his light back and forth a few more times but kept his mouth shut.

If there was any trace of toxins on anything, I'd be faced with proving it wasn't my doing—that I wasn't some kind of serial killer. If it was clean, I'd likely walk away. But if Ray Anne didn't survive, it wouldn't matter if they labeled me a sociopath and locked me up forever.

They let me leave on my motorcycle—still parked near the clearing—and it was almost four in the morning when I got back to the hospital. The walk to the front desk was unnerving, like I was shuffling down a narrow plank, about to be shoved into the deep ocean or allowed to stay on board depending on the answer to my question.

"Excuse me, how is Ray Anne Greiner?"

The lady scanned her computer monitor. The longest thirty seconds of my life. "All I can tell you is that she's been transferred to a recovery room."

My upper body collapsed onto the countertop like a wet noodle, my forehead pressed against the chilled granite. "Thank you, God."

It rolled off my tongue without any thought. A cliché, really.

"Visiting hours aren't until 9:00 a.m.," the lady said.

I went home and took a long, very hot shower. Death dust doesn't wash off, by the way. It has to erode off of both clothing and skin. I tried not to think about where it came from.

At exactly 9:00 a.m., I sat in a chair next to Ray Anne's bed, scooting close enough to touch her hand, but careful not to wake her. The color had returned to her face. It made me smile. I watched her breathe, the soft, rhythmic sound like a melody in my ears. I'd never had feelings for someone like this—not this much or this strong. Sitting there watching her, an unfamiliar certainty took hold of my will and emotions: I'd spend the rest of my life with this girl if she'd let me.

If she'd let me.

I'd really blown it this time.

I leaned in and stroked her cheek with the back of my hand, taking in every curve and detail of her face. Her lips—easy for the taking. But I'd stolen enough from her.

It was May 21, two days before the suspected mass attack. But I couldn't worry about that right now. I eased back into my chair and waited for Ray Anne's blue eyes to open. Unfortunately, I couldn't stop my own eyelids from drifting shut.

The next thing I knew, Ray Anne was cowering in the corner of the room, glaring at me.

I stood. "Ray, I'm so glad you're okay." I stepped toward her, reaching out, but she wedged herself deeper into the corner.

"What is it?" I took two more steps, and she sank to the floor.

"Don't! Stay away!"

"What's the matter?"

I took another step, and she shielded her head. "I see it."

"See what?"

Slowly, she lowered her arms, then pointed at me. "You . . . you have a shackle, Owen. Around your neck."

THIRTY-NINE

I RACED OUT OF the hospital like I was on fire. In a way, I was. Once I learned that I was shackled like masses of other doomed human beings, my last few shreds of hope went up in flames.

What a sick joke. I was on a mission to figure out how to free others, and all along, my soul was caught in the same unrelenting trap.

Once home, I rushed upstairs and stared at my pathetic reflection in the bathroom mirror. I was cut and bruised from yesterday's beating, but other than that, everything looked normal. I could see others' bondage with such clarity, but my own eluded me.

I stumbled into my bedroom feeling like I weighed a ton—like gravity had a heightened hold on me. And the one person I would normally run to at a time like this now considered me a monster. Ray Anne would want to stay as far away from me as she could. Probably seek out other glowing people and pity the rest of us from a distance.

The thought came to me to take my life, but I shoved it out of my mind. Molek would come claim my soul someday, but I wasn't going to serve it to him on a silver platter. In my condition, death was a worst-case scenario. Of epic proportions.

I sank to the floor and wrapped my arms around my frostbitten gut, imagining another form of escape. I had to leave—leave Masonville behind and go somewhere. Anywhere but here. I'd start a new life, but this time, I'd keep my stories of terror all to myself.

No friends. No attachments. No dreams of happiness. Just survival.

I knew full well that my new plan would likely land me under a highway overpass, filthy and stinky and swatting at Creepers, but if that was my fate, so be it. I wasn't willing to stick around and keep exhausting myself trying to take on Creepers and rescue people.

Who was I kidding? If Molek and his underlings were planning to rain down a holocaust tomorrow, there was nothing I could do. Maybe if I glowed, I'd discover a way to fight back, eventually even expel him from Masonville for good. But no. I was just another shackled freak.

I got to my feet and started throwing clothes into the biggest duffel bag I owned. I decided I'd drive east and see where I ended up. Maybe I'd leave the country at some point. Settle down in a different hemisphere.

I had access to the funds in the savings account my mom had built up for me. I figured I could withdraw some cash and live off that for a while until I got a job doing . . .

Whatever lonely, uneducated, tormented people do.

I knew better than to think I could outrun the Creepers or my sadistic sightings, but at least I could remove myself from the constant torture of seeing people I cared about be abused. And I could stay away from everyone who hated my guts and, quite honestly, never wanted to see me again anyway.

There was just one thing I had to do before I started my nonlife.

I learned Ray Anne had been released from the hospital, so I went to her house. Just showed up unannounced and rang the doorbell. She flung the door open.

"Ray Anne, you'll never have to look at me again if you'll just do one—"

She hugged me so tight I almost fell forward. Then she jerked away fast. "They're freezing."

My chains. I felt hideous, like a metal-clad Cyclops.

"Owen, I'm so sorry for the way I reacted to you this morning, but don't worry. We'll get you out of that shackle. You'll see. And oh my goodness, the Creepers are terrifying! You told me they were awful, but I never dreamed they would be this horrific. But you're right. They do avoid me and my family, thank God!

"And I can see the glow, Owen! It's all around my feet!" She lifted one foot, then the other, reveling in her new superhuman senses.

She didn't seem to be holding a grudge against me. Still, I kept my head down. "I need you to do one last thing for me."

"Last thing?"

"Please. Tell me the names on the cuffs of my chains. And the words on my cords. I've got to know."

She crossed her arms, then pressed a balled fist to her mouth, as nervous as I had been weeks ago to examine my mom's.

"I know it's disgusting." I turned my back to her. "But I need you to do this." I waited, as tense as a convicted felon facing sentencing.

"You have four chains."

The mere thought made me weak in the knees. "What do they say?"

She dropped to the ground. "The first one says *Susan Lynn Edmonds*."

My mother.

"Next?"

"It's Lance. *Lance Gregory Wilson*."

No surprise there. I had no way to prove it, but that chain was probably less than twenty-four hours old. Attached during the few hours I'd slept.

"Keep going."

"*Daniel Quinton Bradford*."

Dan. Of course. I popped my knuckles. "And the last one?"

"*Stephen James Grayson*."

I drew a blank. That name meant absolutely nothing to me, except the middle name was the same as mine. I kept my back to her. "My cords now."

She stood, and I felt her step closer, studying my head.

"Don't touch them," I said. "Just read."

Then came the character assassination.

Deceptive.
Unrepentant.
Proud.

Cynical.
Lustful.
Judgmental.

Six cords? That was practically twice the average. I balled my fists, anger boiling so hot it was all I could do not to walk over and bash Ray Anne's garage door.

Everything in me wanted to defend myself—launch into lengthy justifications about how those labels were all wrong and I was seriously misunderstood. Misjudged. But I recognized that for what it was. I knew from living with my mother that human nature despises admitting guilt.

I was no different. If the powers that be pronounced those as my transgressions, what could I do?

I turned to leave.

"Wait!" Ray Anne called out after me. "Where are you going?"

I climbed onto my motorcycle and began walking my bike back, out of the driveway.

She tried to grab the handlebars but missed. "Stop! We need to talk. I need your help with all this!"

I wasn't trying to abandon her—I was doing her a favor. Ridding her of my inferior presence. And I had to get home and settle something with my mother. Right now.

I didn't allow myself to look in the rearview mirror. Just sped off.

Look at you, so full of selfish pride. My own thoughts turned against me, allying with the dark side.

"Shut up!" As I argued back and forth with myself, I was aware I'd plummeted to an all-time low, into the hostile mental territory where psychopaths and schizophrenics live. More confirmation that I needed to leave town and live an isolated existence.

I burst through the front door of my house like a SWAT team officer and walked straight over to my mother. She'd been working on her computer with her back to me but turned, startled. I dropped to the floor, inspecting each of her numerous cuffs among the mess of chains.

"What are you doing?"

Sure enough, on the eighth cuff, I found it.

FORTY

"WHO IS STEPHEN JAMES GRAYSON?"

She stood, leaning so far away from me that she was practically on top of her desk, eyes wide.

"Who is Stephen James Grayson? Tell me, Mom!" My newfound admiration for her took a sudden backseat to my frustration over her never-ending secrecy.

She started crying.

"Where did you—?"

"It doesn't matter, Mom. Just tell me who he is and what his connection is to us."

She walked away. "It's complicated."

I followed her. "Try me."

She suddenly started sobbing uncontrollably, turning and collapsing into my arms. But I pulled away, not willing to let her use me as a crutch.

"I'm so ashamed. I have so much regret. If I could go back, I swear to you, I would do things differently, Son—I swear!"

I knew now what was going on here. Exactly who that man was.

I stepped within an inch of her. "Are you going to tell me who Stephen Grayson is, or do I have to say it?"

She caught her breath but still didn't have the guts to speak.

"He's my father. Isn't he?"

She sank backward onto the sofa. I bent down and vented in her face. "You told me his name was Robert—why? I don't understand!"

"Because I promised his parents."

"What are you *talking* about?" My body was shivering even though I felt like I was burning with rage.

She asked me to give her a moment while she grabbed some tissues from a box across the room. I paced in circles, hands digging through my hair. She motioned for me to sit, then lowered herself onto the floor by my feet.

"I loved your father very much. We were young and in love and anxious to get married. Neither of us cared about having some big, elaborate wedding, so we eloped, just the two of us. I never intended to get pregnant right away, but I did."

"And he left, Mom—I already know this."

"No." Her face crumpled with grief. "I was afraid, nervous about how he'd take the news. He was attending an Ivy League university, and we barely had two pennies to rub together. He had high hopes of becoming a successful doctor someday, like his father.

"I knew his mother wasn't very fond of me, but I decided to confide in her about the pregnancy, thinking perhaps his parents would be supportive and offer to help us through what was sure to be a challenging time. But instead, she was cruel to me. She told me I was not an acceptable match for her son. Even accused me of getting pregnant just to trap Stephen so he'd have to stay married to me. Oh, that infuriated me!

"I spent the next few days agonizing and started thinking perhaps they were right—he deserved someone more refined and intelligent than me, someone from a stable, wealthy family, someone who wouldn't hold him back. And I convinced myself he would resent me for the pregnancy.

"That week, while Stephen was at school, his parents came over. Drove across three states to come talk to me. They said they had the perfect solution and made me an offer that would benefit everyone."

"What kind of offer?"

She turned her face away. "They agreed to pay me a sum of money every year for eighteen years, ensuring you had a good childhood and received a quality college education. It was enough for me to get my education too."

"Under what condition, Mom?"

She slouched over, still avoiding my face. "Providing that I left town, legally terminated the marriage, and never said another word to their son. Ever."

"So—you're saying my dad didn't . . ." I couldn't bring myself to accept it.

"He never knew about you, Owen. I'm so sorry. Your dad never knew he had a son." She shook with each violent sob while I sat there, doubled over now, piecing together a few of the countless loose ends that had troubled me since childhood.

I stood and released nearly two decades of pent-up anger and confusion. "Now I understand why you cried for three days when I told you I wanted to become a doctor. I was following in the footsteps of my father and his father and I didn't even know it! And now I get how we've always had plenty of money! And why there aren't any pictures of my dad. You didn't want me to know what he looks like. You didn't want to run the risk that I might go looking for him and tell him what you'd done! That's why you kept his real name from me!"

"Please forgive me." Her voice quaked as she begged, on her knees. "I did what I thought was best at the time. I know now that his parents were wrong, and I should have told the truth and trusted Stephen to love me and accept me—to accept us. I just couldn't at the time, and then it was too late to go back. He eventually remarried."

She wiped her soaked face with her sleeve, then made the most wretched confession I'd ever heard in my entire life. "We needed the money, Owen."

I dropped to the floor and grabbed her shoulders. "How *dare* you! What I've needed is a *father*!"

She wailed, then pleaded with me again. "I told myself that when you grew up, I would help you find him, and you could know each other. I had no idea he wouldn't make it."

"What did you say?" I let go of her, more bruised inside now than out. "What happened to my father?"

She struggled to talk through involuntary gasps. "About a year ago, he traveled to a dangerous part of the world, in Africa, and he was never heard from again. He's presumed—well, they think he's likely . . ."

She was too weak of a person to say it.

"Dead."

"I'm so, so sorry, honey." She reached out to hug me, but I twisted away. "Can you please forgive me?"

Just hours ago, I'd made a shamed confession to Ray Anne, but my dishonesty spanned a matter of weeks. My mom had been lying to me my entire life. "You expect me to just let this go?"

I grabbed the last of my things and strapped them to my bike. She chased after me.

"Where are you going?"

"I'm taking off for a few hours." By the time she realized I was gone for good, there'd be no finding me.

She stood in the driveway bawling, begging me not to go. I drove away, content to never speak to her again.

Just like she'd done to my father.

FORTY-ONE

My RESOLVE TO LEAVE forever didn't waver as I drove beyond Masonville city limits on a one-way trip to isolation. It felt like the gray storm clouds brewing above my head were escorting me, eager for me to leave. Now that I'd heard my mom's confession, even the scenic Texas hills along the winding highway looked hideous to me—like splotchy lumps lining a crooked spine.

I drove for miles, lost in thought, trying to reprogram my brain to the idea that it was my mother who had abandoned my father, not the other way around. All this time, I'd believed he resented me—thought so little of me that he didn't care to know even one thing about me. And now that I knew the truth, it was too late to see what he would really think of me.

By late afternoon—after a few unsuccessful stops to clear my mind— I reached San Antonio and took a random exit heading north. I noticed there were just as many shackled people in this part of the state as there were back in Masonville. And there were Creepers scattered around—not all concentrated like they were at my school, but still haunting this region.

After about seventy more country miles, I ended up at a mediocre motel in Kerrville, Texas—a hick town where people weren't likely to look for me. Assuming anyone would come looking.

I dropped my bag on the dilapidated bed and stood silent awhile. I was supposed to start college in the fall, begin my journey toward medical school. Instead I'd fallen out of life.

The ambitious young guy with no end to his potential was spent at eighteen. Limited at every turn.

I bought my dinner from a vending machine and yanked my motel curtains shut. Why watch the sunset? Nothing was majestic anymore.

My antique room actually had Wi-Fi, but I wasn't ready to research my father. My worst fear was that we'd look alike—that I'd see myself in him with no chance to show myself to him.

I checked my phone. A flood of voice messages: some from my mom, others from Ray Anne, then one from Detective Benny.

"The lab results are in," he said.

I dropped onto the stiff mattress and listened so hard that my eyes pressed shut.

"We found no trace of contaminants or toxins on any of the specimens collected at the site." His tone was flat. Zero enthusiasm. "And the well water is pure enough to drink. Pure enough to bottle and sell. Imagine that."

He paused so long I thought maybe that was it.

"So Owen, we have no evidence to prosecute you." He cleared his throat. "At this time."

I let out a really long sigh. The jacked-up water had pulled it off again—managed to conceal its toxic, transcendent nature from analytical minds.

Guess I was a runaway now, not a fugitive.

Jess texted me that night to let me know she'd followed through and reported Dan to the police. **Good**, I texted back. **You did the right thing.**

I had a miserable night's sleep, thinking nonstop about all the brutal ways my father could have possibly been killed in Africa. Adding to the torment, I kept rehearsing the accusations etched on my six cords, handwritten by Creepers. I couldn't stop rubbing the back of my scalp. And wincing.

The next morning, my ringing cell woke me—a number I didn't recognize. Another voice mail. I played it and was surprised to hear his voice. "Masonville's finest." Dan's abusive father, Dr. Bradford.

He obviously didn't know yet that his son was being charged with a crime. Or maybe he did, and he'd disowned him completely. Or figured he could get some big-name attorney to make it all go away.

Dr. Bradford practically begged me to reconsider allowing him to mentor me. "It's what your grandparents wanted," his voice mail said. "I'm prepared to teach you things you'll never learn from someone else. Powerful things."

It made sense to me now, why my mom's parents had willed their estate to me. Even though they were dead, they were still recruiting me—luring me to Masonville so Dr. Bradford could single me out and entice me into their sinister world.

I wasn't exactly a God-fearing person, but I knew better than to get caught up in that occult stuff, even before I could see hell's creatures. And how stupid would I be to let someone who raised a son like Dan be any kind of father figure to me?

I deleted his message, then showered and left the motel.

It was a long day of driving unfamiliar roads, aimlessly mulling over where and how to begin my secluded life. Before moving to Masonville, I had felt so in control of my decisions. Now I was like the ball in a pinball machine.

At nightfall, I sat in the corner of a Starbucks, clutching my laptop and a grande vanilla latte—extra hot, with no foam. I marveled that the dreaded date was nearly here: 523. Mass attack day.

I remained content to leave the situation in the hands of fate. I'd watch from the sidelines, which in my case meant I'd tune in to the news tomorrow to see if anything really even happened.

I sipped my drink, plagued by curiosity about my father. How tall was he? What kind of doctor? What kind of man?

I tapped my fingers on my closed laptop. *Should I . . . ?*

Eventually I opened my Mac. It felt weird typing his name.

Waiting for the search engine to populate, I could feel my heart pounding in my neck—erratic uncomfortable thumps. Like a bass drum was lodged in my throat.

Then, just like that, I saw him. Images of my father's face.

It took my breath away. My eyes pooled before I even had a chance to register the emotion.

Had I run into him in person, I swear I would have known he was my father. The resemblance was undeniable. I looked a lot more like him than I did my mother—a realization that hurt just as much as I'd feared it would.

The sense of loss was crushing. We'd probably have been the most important persons in each other's lives, if only . . .

I had to look away. Take some deep breaths. More sips of my drink.

I spent hours there, reading all about him—articles about his humanitarian efforts, his bio on multiple physicians' websites, the reports that he'd gone missing.

He was a cardiologist with a thriving practice, and he frequently traveled to Third World countries to perform surgeries for impoverished people. He was married and—

I nearly choked on my second cup of coffee.

He had two daughters.

I wasn't an only child after all. That was hard to comprehend.

What I read about his disappearance matched what my mother had told me. He'd traveled to Uganda fourteen months ago and hadn't been seen or heard from since. Some of his belongings had been found strewn in the brush outside a village ransacked by a militant regime. Among his items, a blood-soaked shirt.

I had to take a break, walk around and pretend I actually wanted to look at a display of coffee mugs. I asked for an ice water and didn't sit until I'd downed the whole thing and chewed every piece of ice.

His wife was an attractive lady, a blonde with a pretty smile. I imagined she was devastated. Their daughters, too.

For the life of me, I couldn't envision him ever having been in love with my mother. He looked nothing like the type she brought home.

Even though it pained me, I liked reading about him—his accomplishments, all the ways he helped people. I clicked on an article written by a reporter in his hometown of Tulsa, Oklahoma, published less than a week before he vanished. My father acknowledged that he was going into dangerous territory, and when asked why he would go to such great lengths to help small, remote tribal groups, his answer surprised me: "I'm going to serve and meet their medical needs the best I can because I want to show them God's love—something I believe every person on earth deserves."

My dad was a man of faith? It had never crossed my mind that he might be religious. Still, I admired his willingness to go above and beyond for others. Way beyond.

The more I read, reciting the words he'd once spoken, the more I wished so bad that I could have met him. Looked him in the face and told him I exist. There's nothing I wouldn't have given to have even one minute with him.

A few seconds.

My father had been brave and selfless and lived every day with purpose and passion. Although the pictures didn't allow me to see it, I was sure he had been a Light. If I could have called him up and made plans to go see him—if he were still alive and well—all of this would have felt too good to be true. But the fact that I'd come this far only to still be worlds away from him was like torture.

There wasn't a single statement of his I read that didn't move me somehow, but it was the final quote I came across that completely rocked my world. I typed it into my cell notes app, word for word, then tucked my phone in my pocket. I threw my backpack over my shoulder . . .

Then walked away.

Away from Starbucks.

Away from my motorcycle.

Away from my pointless life.

I traipsed deep into a nearby field of tall grass and buzzing insects with just the moon to light the way. I don't recall the specifics of all that ran through my mind, only that something was stirring in me— something new and strong.

I eventually spied a lonely boulder and made my way to it. I climbed up, gripping the cool stone, hoisting myself on top, then stood and looked up at the massive canvas of stars. I was about as far removed from civilization as I'd ever been.

I pulled out my cell, opened the notes app, then read the words out loud—my father's response when asked why he was willing to make such extreme sacrifices and risk his life for others, especially knowing there was no way he could help them all . . .

"'The fact that I've seen and empathize with their suffering tells me I'm called to intervene and help. I refuse to sit back or run in fear and leave it up to someone else to try and save them.'"

How was it possible? That his words, spoken over a year ago, applied directly to me, like they were meant for me at that very moment?

It hit me all at once—what a coward I'd been, running off and leaving Ray Anne and my classmates when I knew full well that an evil army, led by a demented commander, was likely preparing for their destruction tomorrow.

I knew what I had to do. More than that, I finally realized how to do it. Of all the tactics I'd tried against the Creepers, I'd overlooked one of the most powerful, obvious weapons. And it was time to use it.

There was no guarantee I'd survive, much less rescue anyone, but my father's example had changed everything.

I understood now . . .

Lots of men fight to defend themselves. A real man fights for those who can't defend themselves.

Even if it costs him everything.

FORTY-TWO

I'D CLIMBED DOWN OFF the rock and was jogging back to my bike when I saw something that stopped me in my tracks. Towering in the distance on top of an enormous hill was a massive illuminated cross, tall as a high-rise building. It stood firm as a soldier against the dark backdrop of the night sky.

I wasn't one to believe in signs, but that didn't seem like a coincidence.

I rushed to my motel room and threw everything in my bag. It was nearly five in the morning, but I texted Ray Anne anyway: **So sorry I left you. I'm coming home. Whatever happens tomorrow, I'll be there with you. I won't let you down this time.**

It was around seven in the morning when I finally turned onto my street, too full of adrenaline to feel the effects of no sleep. There stood Ray Anne, in my driveway, shielding her eyes from the sun. She waved like a spaz the instant she saw me. I parked, then hurried toward her, grabbing her and hugging her tight. I let go fast, though, and stepped back. I still felt hideous. "I know I look horrible to you."

"Don't say that." She moved close to me again. "I'm so glad you're home."

I wasn't expecting that kind of welcome, not after the way I'd left her.

"I'm sorry I walked out on you, Ray. Especially now, when you need me the most. That was wrong. *I* was wrong."

Her response was like a splash of cool water across my thirsty soul: "All is forgiven, Owen."

I stood there, gazing down into her adorable face, blown away by her mercy. I reached over and slid my fingers between hers. "You're my favorite person in the whole world, Ray."

That's when my mom came flying out of the house.

"Owen James Edmonds, where have you *been*?" She pointed in my face.

"Mom, I—"

"I just got off the phone with the police. I was begging them to start looking for you!"

I was still furious with her—couldn't even bring myself to look at her—but to get her off my back, I swore I'd never disappear like that again.

Minutes later, Ray Anne and I were in her car, headed toward our school. She reached from the driver's seat and touched a gentle finger to a bruise on my cheek. The swelling in my lip had gone down, but the cuts were still stinging, and my left eye had dark purple under it.

"Why'd they want to hurt you?"

I instinctively lowered my head. "They blame me for Walt and Marshall." It was awkward bringing up their names with her. "You know I never meant for them to . . ."

She rested her hand on the middle console over mine. "Of course."

I exhaled, hoping to never bring it up again. That lasted about a second.

"I've been thinking about the well, Owen. How drinking from it affects people. And I think it comes down to motive."

Interesting. In all the craziness, I hadn't had time to fill her in on what the old man had told me, yet here she was, piecing things together on her own.

"Think about it," she said. "Why'd you drink the water in the first place?"

I really did have to think about it. "The old man said I'd get answers. I wanted to know the truth."

"A pure motive, right?"

I nodded.

"So, why do you think Walt and Marshall drank it?"

The horrid memory was as fresh as the wounds on my face, but even more painful. The insults they'd thrown at me. The fatal water I'd handed them in return. "It was about showing me up, I guess. And proving how brave they were." I angled toward her. "What about you? Why'd you drink it?"

She looked at me. "So I could help you. Because I care about you."

My stomach dropped like I'd leaped out of an airplane.

"Get it?"

"Get what?" Her sweet comment had derailed my concentration.

"You and I drank the water for selfless reasons, but Walt and Marshall's motive was self-centered. I'm not saying they deserved to die—not at all—but the motive makes all the difference, I think."

"But how could motive affect a person's bodily response to a substance?"

"You still don't understand?"

I really didn't.

"Whatever's in that water isn't physical, Owen. It's spiritual— different from natural laws."

She acted like there was nothing even slightly strange about what she'd just said and I was dense for not picking up on it too.

"It's like this." It was all she could do to keep her hands on the steering wheel. "Drink the water with a pure heart? You're exposed to the truth. Drink it with the wrong heart? The truth exposes you."

I was impressed, but before I could say it—

"I know what I'm talking about." She lifted her chin in total confidence—a Ray Anne trademark I found irresistibly attractive.

"By the way," she said, "I spoke with several Lights at school, and I told them to be on alert today, in case I need them."

"Didn't they want to know why?"

"Of course. I told them I could sense evil forces and I might need their help warding them off."

"And they believed you?"

"Well, yeah. They're Lights. It's the shackled ones who don't believe."

Her comment socked me in the gut, but I knew it was true.

Ray Anne made the final turn on the way to our school.

"How's your stomach?" I asked.

"It quit hurting yesterday."

I was happy for her. My stomach had never shed the queasy chill.

The closer we got to Masonville High, the more my nerves kicked in. Ray Anne started taking long, drawn-out breaths.

I suddenly second-guessed bringing her here. I understood that out of the two of us, she was much more equipped to stand up to the enemy, but if things went tragically wrong today—if she got hurt because of me, *again*—I'd never recover.

"Ray Anne, maybe you should let me do this. Alone."

She pressed down harder on the gas pedal. "You need me today, Owen."

We were nearly to the school when I asked her to pull over. She stopped and looked up at me. "I need you tomorrow, too, Ray." I cupped her face. "And every day after that. So be careful, all right?"

She nodded, then cut back fast into the flow of traffic.

It occurred to me that maybe we'd read too much into the Creeper notes—misinterpreted them completely, and there was no attack at all planned for today. But one glance at our school, and there was no doubt. Something was definitely going down here.

Something catastrophic.

FORTY-THREE

Our school was surrounded by eerie, unnaturally straight rows of Creepers stretching from one end of the campus to the other—lurking behind the school, lining both sides, and spewing all the way from the entrance doors into the parking lot.

Hundreds of them standing inches apart, peering down each other's reeking necks.

Their hands were crossed at the wrists and pressed against their sunken chests. It reminded me of how dead people in horror movies are positioned in graves.

More Creepers were pouring in from every direction like rats, then filing into place like they'd rehearsed their formation before. They stood so still they looked like corpses, their tattered garments hanging limp despite gusts of wind.

"I . . . I . . ." Ray Anne was at a loss.

"This is it." The sheer *number* of them . . . I drew a deep breath, determined not to panic. *"I refuse to sit back or run in fear and leave it up to someone else to try and save these people."*

We parked in the back of the lot, then stood by Ray Anne's car like it was some sort of protective home base. Surely an army of Watchmen would arrive any minute. Shoot, I'd settle for a handful. Even one. But all we saw were more Creepers flocking to the scene like demented zombies ready to feed.

"How long do you think they're going to stand there like that?" I'd never seen Ray Anne so nervous. Not that I blamed her.

"Until each nasty one of them is accounted for, I imagine."

Students were arriving in droves now. I heard a familiar voice and looked back. Sure enough, Lance was headed toward the school with a group—guys who used to be my friends. He passed by me like I didn't exist.

Just as well. There'd be no convincing him he was walking into a malicious mob. And did he deserve a warning? After what he'd done to me?

But there was Riley—the shy freshman I'd talked to in the cafeteria who'd been linked to Hopeless. She was Creeper-free today, but some senior guy had his arm around her.

"Riley!" I motioned for her to come talk to me. She walked over, a big smile on her face. She'd gotten her braces off.

"Hi, Owen."

"Riley, listen. I know this sounds crazy, but don't go to school today."

"Why?" She crinkled her nose.

"It's not safe," Ray Anne said.

Riley looked over her shoulder, right at the horde of Creepers, but her spiritual blindness deceived her. "What do you mean?"

I was sick to death of arriving at this same impasse over and over. Trying to help people understand the serious threats around them only to sound like a lunatic. "We can't really explain. But trust me, you don't want to go inside."

Her boyfriend was getting impatient.

"Um . . ." She looked back at him and his loudmouthed friends. "Everything looks fine to me."

Of course it did.

Off she went, like a gerbil wandering into a lion's den.

By the time I spotted Jess, she and Ashlyn were headed through the entrance doors. I sent her a text: **Please come outside!!!** Who knew how long it would take her to see it, much less do it.

"You stay here," I said to Ray Anne, "and I'll check out things inside the building."

"No." She pressed her hand flat against my chest. "I'm going. I'll have an easier time getting through the Creepers. You keep watch out here." She sucked in a breath. "I'm ready." Then she clamped her nose shut.

"Wait!" I turned her toward me and wiped a strand of hair away from her eyes. "Don't try to be a hero today. If something doesn't look or feel right, promise me you'll back off. Let me handle it." I pulled her closer. "I have a new weapon now. Something I've never come at them with."

"Tell me you didn't buy a bigger flashlight."

I smiled. "No."

I turned her around so that we both looked out across the ranks of Creepers. "Think about it. If you're right, and faith is part of the formula that activates forces of light, surely fear must empower the kingdom of darkness."

She faced me again.

"Fearlessness, Ray. I refuse to cower to Creepers anymore. If I come face-to-face with Molek today—Death himself—I will not give in to his demented need to see me sweat."

She looked down, a disappointed frown.

"What?"

"Fearlessness is good, Owen . . ." She stared into my eyes. "But it's not enough."

"You were there when I tried, Ray Anne. When I prayed."

"It's not a *try* thing. It's a *surrender* thing."

I pulled her to me. "Trust me. I've got this."

She wrapped her arms around me. "Lord, protect him. Help him understand."

And with that, she let go and popped her knuckles, the first time I'd ever seen her do that. Then she held her nose again and began her descent toward the school, walking right up to the ranks of Creepers. Sure enough, they leaned away, allowing her to pass, then quickly resumed their positions.

I lost sight of her in the maze of black, and I hardly moved until I saw her again, passing through the entrance doors. Talk about fearlessness. Ray Anne was turning out to be the most daring person I knew.

A strange movement in my peripheral vision caused me to turn my head. In the untouched acreage next to the school, grass and soil shot up into the air like a giant snake was charging underground toward Masonville High. Bizarre as it was, I couldn't tell if it was a paranormal sighting or something anyone could see.

It stopped at the front line of Creepers, then a being emerged, rising up from the earth with a thorn-crowned head and outstretched arms.

Molek had arrived.

He stayed frozen like the rest of them for several seconds, then threw his robed arms back in a dramatic, sporadic motion. At once, the Creepers sprang into action, some scattering, while others rushed to form what appeared to be predetermined groups. Assigned posts or something.

Their movement blasted a suffocating stench my way, and I nearly gagged.

Despite my determination to rid myself of every ounce of fear, I couldn't force it away entirely. But I chose to act in spite of it. That was my understanding of true courage anyway.

I texted Ray Anne: **Creepers on the move!**

I eyed the building, watching them slither in droves along the rooftop and scurry up and down the brick exterior like tarantulas. I'd lost sight of Molek.

Had he gone inside?

I called Ray Anne, but she said everything was fine—not a single Creeper in the building. Weird.

Across the campus, Creepers clumped together, communing through their mystical telepathy. That's when I saw the redheaded protester glaring at me. The depraved one-eyed freak had trespassed onto school property and was standing outside the gym.

He was surrounded by Creepers, but worse than that, he bore the ghastly appearance of evil—a demented state I recognized as full-blown possession.

I was mad at myself for not connecting the dots a month ago. I had no clue what he was plotting, but he was today's human culprit—I was sure of it. A homegrown terrorist about to strike. An arsonist, maybe? For all I knew, he had explosives under his baggy shirt, ticking down to detonation.

I narrowed my eyes at him, and he took off running, sprinting fast around the side of the building. I had to get inside now and warn Principal Harding, but a horde of Creepers clumped together like an impenetrable wall on the front steps of the school.

There's a first time for everything, right? I ran at them, then forced myself to plunge forward, fighting through their soggy garments, stepping over their raunchy feet, working my way to the entrance doors. The experience was brain twisting—the disgusting feel of damp, rough fabric against my skin, yet my body passing through them like they were mere shadows. Like they existed in the air. Present but without matter.

It was so cold and dark and rank and just flat-out evil that everything in me wanted to turn back.

But I didn't.

I kept pushing, weaving between them like an earthworm among anacondas.

Finally I broke through. I charged into the school on a straight path to Harding's office.

But wait.

Why were the Creepers flooding the building now, filling the foyer like frenzied maniacs?

I turned, and in walked Dan. He stopped in the middle of the crowded foyer, then slipped his arms out of a camo-print hunting jacket, releasing it to the floor. No cocky grin. No words or expression on his face at all.

Just hate in his eyes.

And two rifles strapped to his back.

FORTY-FOUR

THERE WAS NO TIME TO REACT. No way to warn people or tackle him in time.

Dan reached over his shoulder and clutched one of the weapons, then aimed it at the mass of students. It happened in an instant, but I somehow still managed to think about it . . .

The unsuspecting parents, devastated for life. The siblings left behind, forever regretting not saying good-bye this morning. Flags lowered to half-mast from coast to coast.

I'd witnessed untold terror for weeks now. But this . . .

I literally could not breathe.

It seemed like slow motion.

Dan racking the rifle.

A few wide-eyed students attempting to run.

Then the ear-shattering blasts. The screams.

The collapsing bodies.

It was like a dream—a far-removed experience. Stella Murphy got struck in the back and hit the cold floor.

Dan stormed deeper into the school. I knew there would be more casualties with every passing second.

I scrambled for a plan, a way to stop the massacre, but the shock of it all was working against me. Once again I was helpless, standing there while Molek's merciless assault unfolded.

Some students rushed past me, managing to run outside, while others tried to hide, crouching under tables, behind wall columns—whatever they could find. But I hadn't come here to save myself.

"Owen!" Ray Anne charged toward me from a side hallway, but she stopped short, dropping to the floor next to a crumpled form. I saw that it was Ashlyn, in anguish, clinging to life.

Ray Anne grabbed her hand, weeping. "It's okay. I'm here—I won't leave you!"

Principal Harding's voice trembled over the intercom: "Lockdown, lockdown, shooter in the building—this is not a drill, I repeat, *not* a drill!"

Classroom doors were slamming all over the building.

I could still hear Dan firing off shots, in the main hallway now. There were Creepers everywhere, but a horde had left the foyer with him, a massive entourage of evil that had pressed in around him the second he'd aimed his weapon.

Finally the rapid gunfire ceased, and I heard Dan yell, "Jess! Where are you?"

Ray Anne looked up at me and gasped.

I had to find Jess. I wasn't afraid to search for her through the body-strewn hallways. What scared me was the thought of getting to Jess but still having no way to protect her.

"No," I scolded myself. "No fear."

I took off running up a nearby stairwell. I was sure Dan would look for her in our first-period class, and even though the odds were way against me, I set out to beat him there. Hopefully she was locked inside the class-room, but I had no way of knowing what he was capable of—what deadly forces had been set into motion before this day ever dawned.

As I hurried down the second-story hall, there was no sign of Dan, but he'd definitely been here—his victims were scattered on the floor. Yet there were Watchmen present—some were standing guard in front of closed classroom doors. Others were on bent knee next to injured students.

I kept running, trying not to let the horror of it all steal my focus.

As I passed the library, someone said my name. I turned fast, and there was Lance, slumped against the wall, with a blood-soaked shoulder and a leg so shattered, the bone was exposed. All the color had drained from his face.

I ran to him and dropped to my knees. "Lance . . ." I could hear sirens closing in. "Help's coming—hang on!" My grudge against him seemed so petty now. So cold blooded.

As if he hadn't been brutalized enough, several Creepers scurried around him, whispering cruelties to his traumatized soul. But I stayed close.

His eyes started to roll back in his head like he was losing consciousness. "Help me, God," he muttered. Then barely mouthed it again. I'd never known Lance to be the praying type, but . . .

A radiant Watchman came charging toward us, sending Lance's tormentors into hiding. He wore a platinum breastplate on top of flowing white garments, but no armor beyond that. I gladly moved out of his way and watched through squinted eyes as he knelt down, then placed one giant hand on Lance's wounded shoulder, the other on his mangled leg.

I had no doubt this Watchman was far stronger than any Creeper, but it didn't look like he was here to fight. My own aching body found instant relief in his presence, convincing me he'd brought some of heaven's healing to earth.

To Lance.

I didn't want to move, but then a scream jerked me to my feet. Dan emerged from a restroom at the end of the hall, dragging Jess out with him, a rifle pressed into her side. A crowd of Creepers led the way as he pulled her into a stairwell.

As I ran that way I noticed Jess's spilled purse caught in the restroom door, her inhaler visible among the clutter. I grabbed it and started down the stairs, holding out hope that a battalion of armored Watchmen or a team of police—ideally both—would storm our school any second and confront Dan.

Dan stepped off the bottom step onto the lower floor and yanked

Jess behind the first door he came to—a backstage entrance to the auditorium.

I hurried to the door, took a deep breath, then opened it fast and stepped inside. I looked left and caught a glimpse of Dan and Jess nearing the end of a long, narrow hallway infested with Creepers. The door automatically closed behind me.

It was pitch black now.

I reached for my cell, but it was gone from my pocket. I couldn't see a thing.

I thought I heard Jess crying, but it was hard to tell. The Creepers were in an uproar, shrieking and hissing. But Dan couldn't hear all that, so I had to step lightly.

I put one foot in front of the other, moving through the dark hallway—as black as the pit I'd seen Meagan fall into. I felt movement all around me and loathed the thought that I couldn't see the Creepers but they could see me.

Then again, that had been my reality before I'd drunk from the well. Humanity's predicament.

It was like I was inching my way through a haunted tunnel, blindfolded and alone.

I ran the tips of my fingers along the walls to guide me. It was so chilly in here my teeth started chattering. But I kept going—until my hand grazed something ice cold and slimy. I muzzled my mouth with my other hand, determined not to make a sound.

There was no telling what I'd just touched, but I couldn't stop now. I was sure I could hear Jess gasping.

I moved forward again but kept my hands wrapped around my gut. Suddenly I was surrounded by dim red light. I could see now that I'd made it backstage, and an overhead set of stage lights had been flipped on. I could hear Jess crying hard, and she seemed close now.

Rows of black curtains hung along the side of the stage. I took careful steps between them—and there she was. Center stage. Dan's terrified hostage.

I spotted Dan. Unfortunately, he'd seen me, too. "I knew you'd come for her," he said. He stood stiffly behind Jess, one arm wrapped around her neck, the other clutching a rifle. She was panting, looking like she was about to pass out.

I held up the inhaler and stepped forward, straining to keep my voice calm. "Dan, her asthma . . . She has to have this."

"She's meant to die today. With me."

I took another slow step. "No one is meant to die here today."

Creepers closed in around us, and I could see now that Dan's eyes weren't right. Pupils off center and corrupted. It was Rage again, looking at me from inside Dan.

"Let her go." I lifted both hands now. "Take me instead."

"She stays with me!" He was sweaty, his voice erratic. "I'm in control here!"

"No." I swallowed hard. "You're *being* controlled."

Dan narrowed his eyes, then shoved Jess to the ground, freeing up his hands to aim the gun at my head. He racked the rifle, and I saw the moment for what it was—the final second of my life. A signal to Molek to come confiscate my soul.

But when Dan noticed Jess starting to crawl away, he pointed the gun at her. "You think you can leave me, Jess?"

She froze, laboring even harder to suck in air.

This was it. Time to make my move.

I tossed the inhaler toward Jess and rushed forward, knocking Dan to the ground so hard that the back of his head slammed onto the stage. The gun fell from his hands, and I reached for it, but he grabbed the other rifle and bashed me in the temple with it. I fell onto my back and he rolled on top of me, shoving the rifle barrel under my chin, his snake-like eyes inches from mine. I thought for sure a bullet was about to rip through me, but I threw a fast punch and busted his nose, sending him to the floor, a bleeding mess.

Both of us reached for weapons and scrambled to our feet.

We stood at the same time, facing one another, out of breath, clutching rifles.

Aimed at each other.

Blood poured from my forehead where Dan had struck me, dripping into my eyes and down my cheek, but I didn't dare take a hand off the gun. "This is between you and me." My finger stayed on the trigger. "It doesn't involve her."

I could hear Jess taking hits from her inhaler and hoped she'd have the strength soon to run.

"Ready to die, Owen?" Dan asked. That instant, the spectating Creepers all hit the floor, faces down, while one of the shadows behind Dan charged toward him, taking shape behind his back.

Molek.

I wasn't sure I could pull the trigger before Dan pulled his, and I knew bullets were no match for the real assassin in the room. But I kept my rifle pointed at Dan, poised to shoot.

The Lord of the Dead extended an arm, and one of Dan's chains lifted into the air—raised up by itself—until the cuff hit Molek's wrist, then snapped shut like the slamming of freight train doors.

"Shoot him!" he hissed in Dan's ear, looking at me. *"He deserves to die."*

Then Molek moved toward me, gliding behind my back. It took everything I had to keep my eyes forward.

Another clash of metal, then Molek's voice echoed in my ears and inside my head. *"Shoot him! He deserves to die."*

Same vengeance. Different target.

The tempter moved out from behind me, and I could finally see it— a sickening glimpse of my captivity. Chain links stretched from behind me, attached to Molek's wrist. Same as Dan's.

There Dan and I stood. Two weapons, ready to fire. One dark lord, bound to us both, enticing us to destroy one another.

Believe me, I wanted to pull the trigger. But that's what Molek wanted too.

And I couldn't stomach letting him get his way.

There was the sudden muffled sound of men's voices, then a door flung open—the same door I'd entered through. Footsteps now stormed our way.

"The cops are here." I lowered my weapon an inch. "We have to put our weapons down."

I didn't survive this standoff with Dan just to get shot by police. How would they know which of us was the shooter?

Dan was cracking under the pressure, shaking so bad now that he struggled to aim his rifle.

Molek moved in on his weakened prey—he jerked away from my chain and rushed at Dan, cursing and demanding that he not surrender. When Dan started to tear up, Molek snapped. He ran at Dan and slammed into him.

Inside of him.

That second, Dan kicked my legs out from under me with superhuman speed and strength, then aimed his rifle once again. My weapon fell from my hands and slid across the floor, out of reach.

I'd thought for sure that whoever I'd heard approaching would have intervened by now. But no. I'd been outplayed, outmaneuvered by an immortal mass murderer and a fanatical human being who'd rather kill than not get his way.

I closed my eyes tight, unwilling to look at Dan's possessed face while he blasted my soul into eternal death.

"You're mine," he said.

The shot was so loud. So fast I felt nothing.

I didn't move. Just waited for my heart to stop.

Another shot.

But then came something else—multiple sets of doors slammed open at the back of the auditorium. I looked over and saw police rushing toward the stage, the blinding glare of flashlights coming at me.

Jess wailed now, somewhere behind me.

I gazed down at myself—I couldn't see a wound. And then it registered: I hadn't been struck by a bullet.

I stood and spotted him—Dan, backed into the side-stage curtains, on his knees. He aimed his rifle again . . .

At himself.

There was trauma in his eyes, but they were his own again. Molek had left him to die by himself, Suicide looming over him.

I held my breath, hoping Jess wouldn't see this. But before Dan could pull the trigger, armed men overtook him and pinned him to the ground.

I lifted my hands fast in surrender, then turned, hoping to get a glimpse of Jess before the authorities restrained me. Jess was behind me, cradling a limp body in her lap. A girl with blonde hair . . .

Ray Anne.

Not moving.

Her blouse soaked with blood.

"She jumped on top of me!" Jess cried to the police. "When Dan started shooting!"

I was already collapsing when officers rushed me. Already crushed before my face ever hit the floor.

FORTY-FIVE

It DIDN'T TAKE LONG FOR the cops to realize I was innocent. They let me up just in time to run to Ray Anne. She was on a gurney, being whisked out a back door by EMTs into the parking lot.

I followed them outside into the chaos—a blur of first responders, the campus perimeter lined with news crews and distraught onlookers.

I made it over to her. "I'm so sorry, Ray!" The words tore from the depths of my soul. "It should have been me."

Her hand moved like she wanted to reach out to me, but she was too weak.

An EMT warned me to get my hands off her and to make it quick. The Life Flight helicopter was closing in overhead.

"Please hold on, Ray Anne."

I fought against the light-headedness and shock attempting to over-take me.

She managed to whisper, "Is Jess . . . ?"

"She's safe. Because of you."

She couldn't open her eyes, but her lips moved. "Pray."

I'd have done anything for her. *Anything.* But . . .

"I . . . I don't know how." My heart was exploding with raw emotion.

I put my ear above her lips, hanging on her every breath. "Don't leave me." I cried it again and again. But there was no response.

I gazed into the sweetest face I'd ever known, fearing the worst. She was so pale now, drifting away in front of me.

I wouldn't let her leave this world without it—without a first and final kiss. From me. I leaned in, but a heavy hand gripped my shoulder. Another paramedic. "We have to take her now." He turned to the EMT beside him. "We're losing her."

There was only one thing I could do.

One thing left I knew to say . . .

"I love you, Ray."

And then they took her away from me.

A police officer grabbed me and escorted me to an ambulance. Under the bright lights, a paramedic examined the gash on my forehead. I kept asking what city hospital they were taking Ray Anne to, but no one would answer me.

A sheriff approached. "I'm told you stood up to the perpetrator. Cornered him until our men arrived."

I couldn't bring myself to nod.

"You should be proud, young man." He patted me on the shoulder.

I'd never been less proud in my life.

They wanted to take me to the local ER and stitch up my face, but I said no. I staggered out of the ambulance into the pandemonium, nauseated and weak. The press was swarming. It seemed like all of Masonville was there, watching. There were ambulances everywhere, filling with students. Lance was among them.

There were a few Creepers scouting the area, but most of them had moved on, their master plan carried out. The crazed redhead stood among the crowd—nothing more than a bait and switch that the wicked forces had used today to throw me off.

Jess called to me from inside an ambulance. "Owen! Here." Still trembling and crying, she held Ray Anne's leather journal out to me. "I found this on the floor. I think she dropped it."

I took it and clutched it to my chest. Jess tried to thank me, but I was desperate to be alone. I removed myself from the crowd and sirens and flashing lights, taking one laborious step after another away from Masonville High. I saw my mom in the distance, peering at the school with the other hysterical parents. But I kept going, wandering into the tall grass, then the woods.

This was my property, my land to protect, and I'd failed. Failed every student at my school—dead or alive.

I walked deep into the woods, allowing myself the freedom to cry, to give in to the bitter pain.

I'd been played.

From day one, those Creepers that had been tracking me—Murder, Faithless, Lust—they'd had an agenda bigger than me. Of course they had; I was no threat to them. The one they really wanted was Ray Anne.

They'd been banking on my bad influence to weaken her so they could get a foothold into her life. But they'd underestimated her. Her faith.

Sure, evil forces were out to harm everyone they possibly could today, Jess included. But Ray Anne had to have been their prized victim. The bull's-eye Molek had been determined to hit all along. He saw the power and purity in her, and he hated her for it. And like a blind fool, I fell into his trap. Led her right to him.

I continued through the dense woods, crying so hard I was shaking, my injured face leaking blood all the way down my shirt. I felt myself breaking on the inside in a way that I never had before. Never even thought possible.

I got so light headed, so exhausted, that I literally couldn't take another step. My knees buckled, and I hit the ground, one palm pressing down on pine needles and mud and pebbles, the other clutching Ray Anne's journal. Both hands stained with her blood.

I was done. My self-reliance incinerated by absolute defeat.

And for the first time in my life, I let go.

Completely.

"God. I know you're there. Please . . . don't turn away from me.

"I see it now. My stubborn pride. My hard heart.

"I know that you are merciful, that you shine love on humanity. But we push you aside. I have . . . all my life. I never took the time to know you. Didn't want to. Just blamed you for every bad thing. But I've seen the way your Watchmen look at evil—the contempt in their faces. And how they look at us . . . with such compassion . . .

"I have questions—lots of them. But I want to tell you something right now . . .

"I'm sorry—sorry for trying to control everything. And for thinking I somehow didn't deserve a shackle.

"I've failed miserably at trying to rescue people—I admit it. I'm the one who needs saving."

I took a deep, shuddering breath.

"I'm asking you, God—if your Son really died . . . died for *me*— please help me. Save me. If you'll have me, I'm giving my life to you. I mean it this time.

"And please—*please*, God—save Ray Anne. Spare her life."

It occurred to me that my request might be too late.

"No matter what happens . . ." I curled up on my side. "I surrender."

FORTY-SIX

When I opened my eyes, my face was lying in a pool of blood. I just lay there beneath the towering trees, having no desire or strength to hold myself up. I felt like at any second my eyes might close again and I'd fade out of this life forever.

The sunlight had been replaced by overcast hues of gray. All was calm and still. Gusts of wind skimmed the side of my face, and it took me back to that lakeside carnival. I'd had an unforgettable time there with Ray Anne, but while lying here now, all alone, slipping in and out of consciousness, I dreamed of the evenings I'd spent there as a child, with my mother.

I recalled the sound of her laughter and the feel of her hands lifting me onto the rides when I was too small to climb up on my own. How I'd begged her to stay a little while longer, over and over again, and she had. Over and over again.

How was it that I'd spent all these years despising her every day for her shortcomings, rehearsing her failures—while overlooking the ways she'd cared for me? No denying she'd made some serious, costly mistakes. And had lied to cover her shame.

But so had I.

I decided right then that if I survived this day, I would show my mom the same mercy Ray Anne had shown me. Forgiveness without conditions.

If I survived . . .

I was trembling uncontrollably now, battling the sensation that there wasn't enough oxygen in the air.

I wanted to hate Dan for what he'd done, but somehow I couldn't. I was still angry at him, but my rage was mixed with an unshakable awareness. Dan's soul had been victimized long before he opened fire at our school—beaten and bruised over and over by the one man who was supposed to love him. Dr. Bradford had made gaping wounds in his son's soul, and evil had rushed in.

A shrill whisper echoed through the woods, and my body tensed. The trees rustled, then gave way to a flurry of movement. Creepers moved among the branches like ravenous shadows. And here came my relentless adversary, staring down at me, lips drawn back and fangs exposed.

Death had come for me, once and for all.

I didn't want to go out like this, a weakling lying limp in the dirt. Twice I tried to stand, but twice my strength failed. Molek paced circles around me like a prowling lion. I was on my back, but I shouted up at him, "I'm not afraid of you!"

For once, I truly wasn't.

I closed my eyes and waited for his next move—the ripping away of my soul as my body bled out.

It never came.

Instead, I felt someone pick me up. I was lifted high off the ground. My stomach dropped, and my equilibrium spun. I swayed with each step taken by whoever—whatever—had hold of me.

I strained to see, but I was disoriented. Just soil and ground cover below, mixed with flashes of blinding light.

I made a final effort to lift my chin, and there, where I'd been lying, was Molek, fuming and eyeing me with revulsion.

He dropped to the ground and slammed his fist into the earth, raging like a caged bear.

He wouldn't rest until he tasted retribution. But for now, I felt safe—a sensation that made me drowsy. I tried to stay awake but couldn't.

Darkness overtook me.

I was too weak to open my eyes, but I sensed warmth on my face. Sunrise? I felt the grit of dirt under my elbows and fingertips. Desperate to see where I was, I blinked and balled my hands into fists, fighting to gain strength. And finally, little by little, I could see my surroundings—the wooded clearing, only now it was radiant with light. The water well stood there, as scenic as a postcard picture.

Energy surged through my veins, rousing my body. I drew in a long breath, inhaling the most invigorating scent.

I knew it well.

I managed to lean onto my side. There, sitting beside me, was an enormous Watchman, with glistening skin and gleaming eyes.

Peering down at me.

When he spoke, it felt like a massive waterfall reverberating against my chest. *"Don't worry. You're safe."* He was smiling at me. Actually smiling!

He stood, and I marveled at his commanding presence. No armor, but enough majesty and light to dispel the darkest of beings.

He turned to go.

"Wait!" I just wanted to understand. "Where were you yesterday? Why did you let evil win?"

He turned back to me, his gaze unwavering but kind. So kind. "They didn't win. They fell into a carefully planned trap. You'll see, in time."

"But all those students . . . And Ray Anne . . ."

"She interrupted evil's plan. Chose to offer herself to protect other lives."

It hadn't occurred to me that Jess could have been Molek's intended target all along. Not just Jess, but the tiny light she carried. And Ray Anne had taken Molek by surprise.

"Is Ray Anne alive?"

He lifted his eyes to the sky. "Trust, Owen."

Peace poured over me like a soothing summer rain.

I didn't want him to leave, but he wasn't subject to my orders. He disappeared into the forest.

I was willing to trust—to have faith that Ray Anne would survive and we would be together, and that somehow, some way, yesterday's tragedies would result in something good.

I stood, and that's when it hit me.

There was no sunrise pouring into the clearing like I'd assumed, no Watchman here now to infuse the space with light. It was still night, yet it wasn't dark.

The light I was seeing—

Was emanating from *me*.

It glowed on the ground all around me. And that miserable chill in my stomach . . . was gone. Finally, completely gone.

I felt warm and wonderful all over, like I'd come to life. More than that, I felt free—free to live and love and light the way for others by telling my crazy, incredible story. Like I'm doing with you now. But this is just the beginning.

There's more.

Much more.

You do believe me, don't you?

CAN'T WAIT
TO FIND OUT
WHAT
HAPPENS
NEXT?
Visit www.DELUSIONSERIES.com
to sign up for information on the
next book in the series!
CP1323

ACKNOWLEDGMENTS

As I consider all the incredible people who have helped to bring the vision of this book to pass, I am humbled and overwhelmed with gratitude.

I'd like to thank my literary agent, Don Jacobson, for being among the first to believe in this project, even when others doubted, and for encouraging me with God's promises when I myself battled doubts. Throughout this winding journey, you have proven to be a person abounding in wisdom, integrity, and faithfulness.

I'm so very grateful for the talented team at Tyndale House! Linda Howard, I thank God for the day we met and am so appreciative of how you've championed this project. Sarah Rubio, your editorial expertise did wonders for this book, for which I will always be thankful. (You truly are the bomb dot com!)

I'll never forget the support shown by Kim Andrus, Linda McClendon, Griff and Mindi Jones, and Adam and Jennifer Cole. You have blessed me more than you'll ever know!

I'd like to thank Corey and Dana Grindal and Jon and Kay Nicholson for going above and beyond to see this message travel far and wide. You've stepped out in faith with me in big ways!

It's impossible to express how truly thankful I am for the *"Delusion* Dream Team"—an extraordinary group of ladies who've offered endless prayers, support, advice, and encouraging hugs. I have learned so much from each of you. We're in this together, and I wouldn't have it any other way!

Rachael Donohoe, you have made a lasting mark on this project. I treasure the fountain of inspiring words you so often share and am honored to travel this road with you.

Kelley Allison, your enthusiasm and passion for this project are second to none, and I'm sure I could write a book thicker than this one if I were to list all the ways you've blessed my life. You've taught me invaluable lessons about faith and friendship and have brought ongoing joy as you've walked beside me every step of the way.

Patrick, you've made countless sacrifices—small and big—to allow me to pursue the call of God on my life. There's no one I love and admire more than you.

Madison, Avery, and Levi, my love for you inspires everything I do, and I couldn't be more proud of the spiritual champions that you are.

ABOUT THE AUTHOR

In a culture intrigued by the paranormal yet often skeptical of biblical claims, **Laura Gallier** seeks to bring awareness and understanding to issues surrounding the supernatural. Having battled her own enemies of the soul throughout her teen and young adult years, she is on a mission to expose deception with the light of truth, bringing hope and healing to a generation in need. Laura lives in the greater Houston area with her husband, Patrick, and their three children. Get to know Laura better at www.lauragallier.com.

- ## Has this book made an impact on you?

  Share your story with author Laura Gallier by emailing mystory@delusionseries.com.

- ## Want to go deeper?

  Get your copy of *4 Freedom*, a Bible study based on *The Delusion*, ideal for individual reflection or group studies. Available at www.DelusionSeries.com.

- ## Want to stay connected?

  Sign up for free email updates regarding the novel series and movie-making journey at www.DelusionSeries.com. Find @DelusionSeries on social media and join the online community.

- ## Curious about the author?

  Learn more about Laura and her speaking events at LauraGallier.com. To inquire about booking Laura to speak, email info@lauragallier.com.

- ## In need of help?

  If you or someone you know is struggling with thoughts of suicide, talk to a parent, teacher, pastor, or youth leader, or contact a suicide hotline. Remember, God loves you and there is hope, even in seemingly hopeless situations.

  THE HOPE LINE
  www.thehopeline.com
  1-800-273-8255

  NATIONAL SUICIDE PREVENTION LIFELINE
  suicidepreventionlifeline.org
  1-800-273-8255